MAD NOMAD

Eric Jay Sonnenschein

Mad Nomad

© 2015 by Eric Jay Sonnenschein

ISBN #978-0-9861-159-0-5

For Marilyn

Based on a true story

Nothing ever becomes real until it is experienced–even a proverb is no proverb until your life has illustrated it.

–John Keats

Contents

BOOK 1
PEACE CORPSE

1

BAGGAGE CHECK

I won't pretend it was well thought out, planned from A to Z. I was 21 with a lot of future on my hands and I didn't know what I was getting into. But that doesn't mean it was a cynical act. Helping people, teaching English, learning a different culture, adapting to a new environment—it all sounded great.

It was senior year and the country was in recession. After four years of working extremely hard in the liberal arts, I had nothing more to anticipate than a summer job on a maintenance crew, mowing lawns, trimming bushes and polishing doorknobs for the minimum wage. I could hear my mother's summertime lament, "Is this what I sent you to college for?"

People were shocked at the carefree manner in which I joined the Peace Corps. They were convinced it was a CIA front. Friends asked gravely if I knew what I was doing.

"No," I replied. "If I did, I probably wouldn't go."

I was after intrigue, not information. Since Tunisia was probably the last place on earth I would go for any reason, stating a coherent motive for going there was senseless. Tourists make plans; adventure has no itinerary.

But exploration and escape did not draw me to the Peace Corps. In my view, these were fringe benefits. Even a slave of impulse like me needed a more compelling reason to act, and I had one—Cerise.

Cerise was the French teaching assistant my sophomore year, one of 20 women on a campus of 1,200 men. Strutting through the dining hall, shoulders straight, round buttocks shifting in velvet pants, black hair twisted in a *chignon,* a shoulder bag tight against her side, she transformed the stuffy cafeteria into an international bistro with the drift of her perfume. Laughing uproariously and rolling her eyes at the next table, as she puffed athletically on pungent French cigarettes, Cerise had a knack for turning pompous people to pumpkins and their inane talk to drivel with a wink of her sparkling eyes.

Like many others in the room, I fell in love with Cerise over a series of brief exposures. But unlike my rivals, I could not enjoy from afar the perplexing, agitating inspiration Cerise stirred in me or nurse secret crushes before submerging them, as I had done when I was 15.

Indulging a great passion was one of my non-academic goals and I would not be denied. The first time I had lunch with Cerise I marveled at how smoothly she ate, drank coffee and smoked in sequence. Cerise conversed with the elegance and skill that great soccer players demonstrate in passing the ball. She was subtle, quick and had an unerring instinct for those around her. With a timely smile or infectious laugh she kept the fun going and made you feel appreciated.

When Cerise rose from the table, I noticed her velvet pants were worn at the thighs and I knew inexplicably that I wanted her.

Our first date was a walk through the bird sanctuary. We came to the bank of a creek and sank in deeper than her black boots, spattering her pressed, white jeans with mud.

"That's the last time I follow you through the woods," she declared with exaggerated ire to make light of how angry she was.

Cerise. Her sophisticated ways and tight pants made her the older woman of my dreams; all I wanted her to do was to teach me how to love her. I would do my best; she would laugh indulgently, peck me on the cheek and send me back to my studies guilt-free.

Four years later she had not sent me back.

4

•

Fargus and I were in Phan Tuan's Vietnamese Restaurant in Philadelphia, Tuesday, 2 PM, an hour before boarding the bus to JFK, our first leg en route to Rome and Tunisia, when the frog legs arrived in a Busby Berkeley formation around the platter. Fargus, my hotel roommate during the two-day staging session, leaned over the table and asked, "So why are you *really* here?"

To such a blunt question what could I respond without giving myself away as a total fraud? Beyond the particular values and circumstances related above, I had not verbalized my motives for joining the Peace Corps, fearing that they would sound ridiculous. But Fargus, whose red curls and round face might have qualified him as a cherub if his blue eyes were not ablaze with mischief, had confided intimate details of his life: how his girlfriend of five years had recently eloped with his best friend, how the VISTA center he helped build with his own hands in a rundown small town business district was torched by the people it served and then the *coup de grace*—a letter from the state of New Jersey, threatening to impound his old car for unpaid parking tickets. I had to come up with something, yet remained mute long enough for him to resume.

"You want to know my biggest mistake?" he asked to gain my confidence with one more story of frailty. "I had my chance with a married woman and—I blew it."

"Blew it!" I gasped.

"Yeah." He exhaled before swallowing a pair of frog legs.

Tales of masculine ineptitude never failed to win my sympathy and interest. Prowess was heroic, predictable and incredible, whereas weakness, uncertainty and confusion were more believable. I leaned forward to hear more.

"This woman I knew, well it was obvious she wanted me,"

5

Fargus began. "So one evening she invited me over to her house. Her husband was out—*bowling.* We were on the couch and she told me to relax. Then she got up and left the room. When she came back, she sat closer. She had taken off her bra. She was almost in my lap. But I couldn't go through with it."

"Couldn't do it? Why not?" I asked, slack-jawed and stupefied. There were enough bad dates, clumsy moves and blown chances in my short résumé to grieve over, but I hated failure so much that even other people's botches bothered me. The way I saw it, this was our time. If we missed it, we would have nothing left.

"I couldn't stop thinking about her poor husband. What if I were bowling and it was my wife seducing some guy? That killed the moment."

Fargus chewed his frog legs with serene satisfaction, as if this were the reward for his moral act. He ruminated on his food and his anecdote at the same time, and when he swallowed he passed judgment. "Dumb, huh?"

"No," I said to redeem his loss with a kind interpretation. "With so many women in the world, why commit adultery?"

Fargus studied me with amusement as if I had missed the point. He snapped off the feet of more frog legs with his teeth and expectorated them on his plate. "So, Rick, why'd you sign up?"

"Promise you won't tell anyone?" I asked, with the confidence of one spy extracting a promise from another.

"Who wants to know?" he grinned. "You're sort of paranoid, aren't you?"

The Mongolian volcano beef arrived. Its blue flame waved across the brown, slick mound, making it resemble a chemical log.

"I'm on a mission of love," I said.

A strip of volcano beef slithered from Fargus's chopsticks as if alive. "Love?" he asked. "You mean you love helping people in developing countries learn English?"

"No," I whispered. "My girlfriend lives in France."

"So you're going to North Africa because your girlfriend lives in France?" He stared at me like a perplexed psychologist.

"It's as close as I could get," I admitted.

He chewed thoughtfully, as if his molars were trying to make sense of my psyche.

"You couldn't just go live with her?" he asked.

"We already did that—it's complicated," I replied, privately embarrassed by what I knew but could not say about Cerise and me in outline form. I *had* proposed to Cerise that we live together in letters ranging from passionate to pleading. Some phrases of her response remained tattooed in my memory.

Dear Rick,

For days I have debated whether to send this letter. I thought that during those months of silence you would forget me. I still can't understand why you love me and I am sorry that you're depressed.

I understand you're worried about your future and the hard choices you must make.

Your coming to Bidonville next year would not be suitable at all. Truly, such ridiculous ideas, if repeated, could easily make me lose faith in you. You are an American and should find work in America—not in Europe.

You suggest that I would adapt well to a condition that I've endured (your staying with me) and you're probably right. Even suffering can become a habit...

To be honest, Rick, I was bitter about our six months together. It was the most traumatic period of my life, whose most vivid memories are of sleepless nights spent crying by your side, of feeling tortured by your knack for disturbing my work and studies.

There were holidays ruined by your incessant demands and intestinal excesses. There was the time you locked yourself in the bathroom when I invited two male colleagues without warning. And how could I forget that afternoon you invited two schoolgirls without telling them about me? You ingeniously tormented me and criticized all I did, said or was.

Would you be hurt to learn that I did not miss you when I returned for the fall and you were gone? Would it be cruel to relate how relieved I was? Please let me know your plans—and make sure they are different ones.

To the love of a less determined person, those words would have dealt a lethal blow. But here I was, scheming to overpower her resistance.

Fargus rubbed the corners of his eyes and stared at me with fraternal sympathy.

"You haven't studied military history," he said. "England is the best approach to France. Your conquest may be doomed."

"Maybe. Nothing good comes easily."

I swallowed these brave words with more difficulty than the volcano beef. Fargus was right. I had not considered military history, though I should have, since Cerise and I staged our own war of attrition when we shared a place in Bidonville during my junior year. But since my English advisor averred that war was a cheap metaphor for love, I forswore the analogy. I *hoped* Cerise would be moved by my going 4,350 miles to be a mere 900 miles away from her and that occupying the same hemisphere would bring us closer.

After a long silence punctuated by our pensive mastication, I

said, "I don't want to have happen to me what happened to you.
No offense."

"What was that?" Fargus searched my eyes with alarm.

"Losing the only woman I ever loved for lack of trying."

Fargus nodded wistfully at the memory of his girlfriend, who
asked him to marry her and, when he hesitated, married his friend
a week later. He wiped his mouth and glanced at his watch. "How
do the Tunisians say it? It was in the guidebook. *In sh'Allah!*"

●

In a hotel conference room in Philadelphia, ten minutes
before boarding buses to the airport, Irving P. Irving, the Peace
Corps director from Tunis, delivered a soul-searching message.

"You can leave Tunisia when you want," he said. Even across
the inscrutable darkness of his *Ray Ban* lenses, I could feel his
eyes scrutinize me, "But if you have even the slightest doubt about
staying the full two years, I want you to walk out that door. Go on!"

Irving nudged his aviator shades up his broad nose and
scanned the volunteers' eyes for doubt. After his searchlight had
passed over 120 eyes, he stroked his rough and ruddy jowls,
apparent burn victims of his after-shave, and nodded, reassured
that no ambivalence was in sight. After giving our group a gut
check, Irving grabbed his abdomen and bolted from the conference
room.

Later at the airport, Irving removed his sunglasses to check
one last time for the contraband of equivocation in our eyes.

"When you board this plane, be damned sure of why you're
going and what you're doing," he growled. "This is no pleasure
cruise or summer vacation. You are not tourists on a package deal,
but professionals on a complex and demanding mission."

9

No one asked Irving to define our mission. That might have indicated doubt—or a failure to read the materials.

Irving's pep talk was effective in suppressing doubts, but did not remove them. The more I hid my concerns, the stronger they became. Only when we were finally airborne did I feel any relief, because it was too late for Irving P. Irving to stop my adventure. The man who boasted that he could read a man from cover to cover in ten minutes or less failed to decode me or uncover my scheme.

"I'm really going," I thought. "My future is starting."

As we flew over the ocean, my mind drifted over recent events. For the first time since graduation, I looked back on my commencement address, only a month ago. It was the biggest moment of my life and I did what I had always dreamed of—I told a large group of people how I really felt.

Rain pounded the roof of the dirt-floored field house. I strode to the podium, knees shaking, throat parched and tight. Five thousand people were listening, including a secretary of state, captains of industry, professors, noted scientists and thousands of proud parents.

"Friends, faculty, fellow students," the mic thundered. I couldn't recognize my voice. I thought it would crack. I had not rehearsed, fearing that if they knew what I was going to say, they would not let me speak.

"Graduation should be a time of great joy and satisfaction, a moment that shines for a lifetime, a time of optimism, when one looks forward to a life of infinite possibilities. So why am I weighed down with pessimism and doubt?"

Five thousand people waited silently under the relentless slapping of the rain for me to tell them.

"After four years of hard work, of sacrifice, of going into debt, of working summers in menial jobs, I cannot look my mother in the eye and tell her what difference this education made. I face a dismal future and a lack of prospects. I am on the edge of a dark abyss...

"Most of you don't agree. You came to this place of privilege with privilege of your own. You will return to privilege, just as I will return to poverty.

"Transcendence, we are taught, can be achieved through the life of the mind. Will a vibrant inner life enhance the job of mopping floors, which I have done to help pay for college? Will I ever be able to transcend the random fate and banality to which I am assigned? Good luck and watch where you step. City sidewalks won't be as clean as those at Brockwurst College."

The silent field house erupted in mechanical applause. As we recessed from the field house, many students scowled at me. Others cursed. One voice cut through. It was my professor of existential philosophy. "Rick, there are only a few Buddhas in every generation."

Why did I dwell on this now? Since the greatest moment of my life was also my biggest blunder, I clung to it like a broken trophy. Like many disasters, at the time it seemed like a good idea. Instead of delivering a typical commencement speech, full of optimism, I proclaimed my pain to a captive crowd of thousands and testified that four years of the finest liberal arts education had been a waste of time. I never considered that my jeremiad might undermine the college's most important event, although this was probably my tacit objective. At my zenith I foresaw my oblivion, which was now occurring over the Atlantic, and I did not care whose pomp and circumstance were ruined on my way down.

It also never occurred to me that if just one of the distinguished guests had approved my message, a door might have opened and the future I dreamed of might have been assured; I never viewed this speech as an introduction, but as a farewell. Now, three weeks after sharing my torment with 5,000 people, it was alone with me again.

I dozed off over Newfoundland. In my dream I was in a foreign port. After many years I saved enough to sail home, when suddenly my teeth fell out like petals of a spent flower. Then my money was stolen. I worked for years for new teeth. Finally I sailed home, where Lina waited for me. Lina was the voluptuous, blond model from Amsterdam who blew a gigantic bubble on the cover of the *Stud Magazine* my friends gave me before I left.

"You'll need this," they said.

Lina would be my companion between visits with Cerise. Lina had a beauty mark on one round breast. In my dream, Lina would not remove her blouse until I guessed which one.

Suddenly I awoke in a sweat. *Lina! Oh my God!* The *Stud Magazine* was still in my suitcase and we would be passing through customs in a Muslim country. Irving had warned us not to carry inappropriate material. A volunteer in his 30s had already been *pre*-terminated in Philadelphia for "attitude problems," when Irving noticed him perusing porn magazines at a newsstand. As soon as we arrived in Tunisia, my adult material would be discovered in my valise and I would be terminated on the spot.

I considered the humiliation in store for me if the magazine were confiscated. Being discharged for possession of smut was dishonorable, no matter how extenuating the need. Worse, everyone would know why I brought it.

Panic precluded sleep. I slumped in my window seat and stared at the blackness of the porthole. We were somewhere over the dark Atlantic when for the first time since I left home three days before, I was assaulted by the question Fargus asked and I avoided—what was I doing here?

I craved daylight. If I could gaze out the dense, round window at blue skies and cirrus clouds, the answer would come. But the dense porthole cast a vague, distorted reflection. Antibodies were coursing through me. My body ached with mild vaccine symptoms from the many injections I had received. Sleep was impossible and there was no one to talk to. The other volunteers were dozing, curled up under blankets, impervious to doubt.

Until now I had floated on the elation of escape. I had dodged a hot summer, beat the odds of unemployment and avoided living at home. But the thrill of taking my first step of adult life was wearing off. For 72 hours I had held my nose, closed my eyes and endured needles of all sizes. An interminable series of briefings, seminars, cross-cultural exercises and a dry cocktail party had left me with a hangover. It occurred to me that I would not be with Cerise in France, but in Tunisia with 60 volunteers. Who were these strangers? What was happening to me? I stifled my panic. Turning back was impossible. There was no returning to the past.

I stared at the distorted reflection in the porthole window and knew I had eluded nothing. Fate had its way. The only step I had taken was into its hands.

2

TOILET TRAINING

We were sprawled out at the end of the terminal at Leonardo da Vinci Airport, Fiumicino, Italy, surrounded by a marshy field infested with tall weeds—nowhere, Italian-style. Rome was close on the map but far out of sight. I tried vainly to sleep as the sun pouring through the grime-smeared windows kept me painfully red-eyed. We were stuck on pink, plastic Barcelona chairs, like refugees waiting for a way out.

Irving stood on a chair and waved his arms for quiet, though we were too stupefied to do more than groan occasionally or snore. "There will be a delay," he said. "The baggage workers may go on strike. We're working on it so keep calm."

"Will we be here overnight?" asked a woman in a Cub Scout uniform. "I can stay with my mother. She lives in Rome."

"We could be here for days or for another hour but don't go anywhere. Ha!" Irving forced a laugh and did air-push-ups with his palms in the international "Calm down!" salute.

Two hours passed. I had finally dozed off when there was a loud squeal like a thousand hungry birds released from a cage. Italian paratroopers zigzagged among us in their camouflage suits and helmets, waving automatic weapons as their combat boots skidded on the rubber floor covering.

"What are they doing?" I asked Fargus.

"They're terrorists, or they think we are," he deduced, rubbing his nostrils as he lifted the glasses off the bridge of his nose, then replaced them gently. "Either way, I'm too wiped to care."

Irving remounted his chairs to report the latest information.

"The airport is trying to get the union to make an exception for our flight. It looks 50-50 we'll leave today."

The Cub Scout woman spoke again, as if on cue, "Can I see my mother if we have to stay overnight?"

"Sure, sure," Irving conceded. "You can all see her mother if we have to stay." Irving laughed faintly and slumped in the scoop chair. The paratroopers hovered over us like animals waiting to be fed. Whatever enthusiasm we had about the trip had been wizened in the bright, throbbing heat. The glass walls and ceiling made the terminal look and feel like a casserole dish.

Yet even this hellish terminal had beauty, if you ignored that it was 120 degrees, that the décor was sterile *and* dirty and that you were going on two hours sleep. If you stared out the windows long enough you might believe you were in a chapel. The sun illuminated the mud swirls on the soaring windows of Fiumicino, transforming them into frescoes of dry drips, embedded insects and bird droppings impastoed in black dust. This was nature's revenge on modern art. Sacred music in this chapel was provided by the traction of policemen's boots on the floor mats, squealing like mice.

I stared at the windows with all their drips and spatters until I must have hallucinated—because it *all made sense.* I realized for once that Jackson Pollock wasn't painting an abstraction, but a detailed representation of what he saw—nature's random design.

Since Fargus's eyelids were twitching, I accosted him with my theory.

"Life is funny. Here I am halfway around the world, 20 miles outside the Eternal City, hot and tired, with no food, water or *lire* to buy them with."

"It's not funny. It's a depressing fact," he muttered.

"I know. But even in this squalid predicament, beauty shines through."

"No way. Where?"

I pointed emphatically at the glass wall of Fiumiccino.

"Even that filthy glass window has a strange beauty."

"Strange," he whispered. "I'm not getting the beauty. How'd you get weed on the plane?"

"I'm high on insight. Don't you see? Nature is the supreme artist. Its masterpieces are even here in this hellhole. Check out that glass canvas. You see bird droppings, water drips, mud and dead insect carcasses, right?"

"I don't see a thing." Fargus groaned, as he squinted into the sun glare.

"Open your eyes."

Fargus blinked and shaded his face with his arm.

"It takes no imagination to be disgusted, Fargus. Of course, it's vile! But look closer—or stand back. Take in the whole picture. It's dynamic and has its own logic. It's better than Abstract Expressionism. Nature's a natural. I'm taking a closer look."

"Go ahead, man. I'll watch."

"I bet you your first ten *dinars* that in ten minutes you'll be looking, too."

I was so sick with dread that I was indifferent to consequences; fear overwhelmed restraint. I stood up and staggered on cramped legs to the great window of Fiumiccino to observe closely nature's infallible brushstrokes. Soldiers were watching me because they were as bored as I was.

I pointed out brushstrokes, lines and textures of mud, dust, guano and images suggested by the squalid mayhem. I was talking to myself, but Livia, the dark haired volunteer in the Cub Scout cap and shirt, joined me at the window. She had been in New York long enough to recognize culture when she saw it and even when she didn't. Others came to the window. I assumed an erect posture, elevated my discourse and tried to sound like a docent.

"So Pollock was a realist, imitating nature. And this environmental mural is how nature expresses itself. You can feel the rhythm. The glass is the canvas, the dust, rain and bird dung are the media. It's the final chapter of modern art. The only question is, where is the signature?"

A group of soldiers surrounded us and indicated with crude gestures that we should stop what we were doing. They took exception to our staring and pointing at their dirty windows. Yet, a few were intrigued by our study of found art. They asked me to explain myself.

I kissed my fingers and stretched my arms wide, to indicate the vast masterpiece before us, then pointed emphatically at the curves and lines. These were Italian soldiers. They had a deep-seated feeling for art and took pride in their people's contribution to world culture. Curious and attentive, they viewed the window as a potential discovery. Some may have been art students before their mandatory military service. They studied the window and turned to each other to discuss it, until their sergeant dispersed them with sharp reprimands and ordered me to sit down.

Deprived again of art and audience, I relapsed into my prior despondency. One question now wracked my aching brain: why had I come halfway around the world, to languish 20 miles outside the Eternal City and bake under a scorching sun without food or water or *lire* with which to buy them? I needed a dark, quiet place to be alone, think and relax. Only one location came to mind—the john.

The guards asked in Italian where I was going.

I understood well enough to answer in English, "To the toilet." I didn't believe they understood or care if they did. "Am I under surveillance?"

The policemen laughed and said, "*Bene!*"

I passed a newsstand and gave the mass-market paperback tower a spin. A slim English volume on "decoding body language" seemed useful, but at 20,000 lire, it was way out of my price range. I stared at an Italian tabloid and was able to translate the headline "Newlyweds Raped and Beaten at the Colosseum." It was just what the moment called for. I had not studied Italian, so reading the paper would be like solving a puzzle. But I didn't even have the 4,000 *lire* for that. However, the canny vendor, noting I was American, asked if I had dollars, and agreed to sell the paper for a buck. "Great," I thought, tucking the paper under my arm. "This news will cheer me up."

After the wheel, the toilet must stand as the greatest achievement of our species. Where else can simple relief and solitude be found? Dimly lit lavatories were always my special place to reflect, study, meditate and pray. Even when I was four I toddled to the potty to construct my own images of the world.

I took the stall at the end, per usual, so that no more than one person could sit near me, and dipped into the Italian paper. As I deciphered a story titled "Phantom Doorbell Ringer Kills Two," the restroom suddenly blazed with light. Men barked and boots crunched. Then came a violent rapping at my stall door. I tried to remain quiet and still, and even lifted my feet to avoid detection, hoping the soldiers would go away. But the barrel of a machine gun probed under stall door like a cold, rigid snake and tapped my foot.

Public restroom privacy is nowhere in the Bill of Rights, but it is a mainstay of American civility. This violation of my stall-space was a shocking cross-cultural experience, yet I was too scared by the shouting, door banging and gun wagging at my feet to protest.

"Okay, okay!" I yelled. As I stood up, tugged on my pants and reached for the flush-wand in one spasmodic motion, hands clasped my ankles. "I'm coming, damn it!" I yelled as the hands pulled me down and out of the stall.

I lay on the floor with my pants hiked around my thighs. Soldiers prodded me with their guns as if hunting for ticklish spots and taunted me with sounds like, "Eh, eh!" I pulled up my pants and two soldiers hoisted me by the armpits to my feet. Frustrated and angry, I drove my elbows into their chests just as the door swung open. It was another restroom patron. The soldiers turned and I broke free. As the new restroom visitor came between the soldiers and me, I bolted into the hallway.

They were shouting and their boots squealed behind me.

"You jerk!" I shouted at myself. "They'll shoot! Go down! Go down!"

I closed my eyes and dove for the deck, anticipating the end. The soldier closest in pursuit tripped over me and landed on his gun. A portly man with shaggy eyebrows and a rumpled suit broke into the circle of soldiers who now jeered at me. I tried to appeal to his civilian instincts.

"I'm an American!" I cried.

The man with the caterpillar eyebrows conferred with a soldier, then told me in rolling English syllables to get up and follow him. We walked a flight down and entered a dark, airless room that was smaller and dirtier than the john.

"You were using drugs in the men's room," the rotund man mumbled matter-of-factly, as casually as if he had seen me do it.

"That's a lie."

"Then what were you doing in there?"

"I was relieving myself. You know, *doo-doo, poo-poo, ca-ca?*"

He looked at me skeptically.

"You were in there a long time."

"I was reading the paper."

"Where is the newspaper, please?"

I looked at my hands, before nervously checking my pockets. My reading material was gone.

"It must be in the men's room," I said. Noting his incredulity, I explained. "They pulled me out of the stall so fast I didn't have a chance to pull up my pants!"

The detective spoke to the soldiers in Italian. After a short discussion, a paramilitary extracted my newspaper from his pocket.

"Is this yours?" The man in the rumpled suit tossed the paper on my lap.

"Yes. This is the one."

He narrowed one eye, widened the other and smiled furtively.

"This is an Italian paper. You read Italian?"

I saw the trap he set now that it was clamped around my neck. The evidence that might have freed me could now seal my guilt.

"I studied French. Italian isn't hard to read. *Phantom Doorbell Ringer Kills Two!*"

The police cohort chortled. Even the detective smiled. He spoke to a blue uniformed *carabinière*, before turning to me.

"Speta!" he said. "You know what that means? Wait!"

He left the room and returned with Irving in tow.

"I'm sorry," the detective told the Peace Corps director. "We have problems with terrorists—as the world knows."

"Do I look like a terrorist?" I pleaded.

The portly detective man ignored me and continued to address his apology to Irving. "Men's rooms are their favorite workshops. They make their bombs and before we know it—boom. And it's too late."

"I was relieving myself," I reiterated to let Irving know how innocent I was, since he seemed to believe that I incited this fiasco.

"Yes. And you left proof," the detective replied with exaggerated gravity. Exhaling with offended dignity, he turned to Irving, like one omniscient authority commiserating with another. "Our young friend neglected to flush."

"Forgot to what?" Irving's jaw seized and his eyes flashed as though confronted with an unspeakable atrocity. Had I violated a Peace Corps rule? He shot me a look no doubt reserved for vermin. "What happened to your manners?"

"They dragged me out."

"Would you shut up?"

He turned to the portly detective and said, "I'm sorry for any inconvenience."

"Quite all right. I'm used to it," the rumpled detective replied with absurd magnanimity, grasping the upper hand Irving extended to him, when the phone rang. His face blanched and his eyebrows quivered. He hung up, grunted instructions to his *carabinièri* and moved with unforeseen speed to gather his personal effects.

"An explosion near the *Quirinale*. The Red Force again. *Permisso*, gentlemen..."

Irving lambasted me all the way back to the Peace Corps encampment.

"What on earth were you doing in the men's room? You weren't authorized to be there. Don't I have enough to worry about? I could have you terminated on the spot and sent straight back to the States for inciting a public disturbance."

"I was in the men's room, trying to relieve myself in peace, when I was scared shitless by a platoon of storm-troopers, yanked from my stall, poked, prodded and chased by soldiers with automatic weapons, accused of being a drug user and a terrorist, and mocked for not flushing after being pulled off the seat by my ankles. And you're telling me it's all my fault?"

Irving stared at me with clinical contempt as if I had made it all up.

"Why are you so defensive?"

3

DOWN TO EARTH

As we passed over Sicily into African airspace, I experienced a new wave of fear more intense than I'd ever felt. Europe was similar enough to the United States to seem safe and familiar, but Africa was entirely different. The anticipated escape, so appealing days before, was now a terrifying bondage to the unknown.

We touched down in a field surrounded by high palms. Stewardesses tossed jasmine garlands around our necks. A breeze conveyed the odor of rotten eggs toward the landing party. The sun was still strong at seven. I was trembling; my throat was clawed by thirst. I staggered down the ramp, one hand on the railing, while the other stuffed jasmine petals against my nose to deodorize the environment.

"Nosebleed?" A tall, strapping man with a pencil mustache smirked down at me and offered his strong hand.

"Bill Dozier," he said. "I'm the assistant director."

Dozier applied four times the required grip to convey warmth and twice what it would have taken to break a normal hand. His handshake was less welcoming than challenging, but it distracted me from my thirst, the bad smell and my malaise and fatigue. As I pumped the blood back into my hand, Dozier pulled a linty tissue from his pocket and dangled it in front of my eyes. "Kleenex? Nosebleeds can be serious. People die from them."

"No thanks," I said through the filter of the jasmine nosegay.

"Are you sure? You don't want your nose to bleed in your jasmine necklace. They only give you one."

Dozier's pomposity came so naturally to him that it was clearly his gift.

"My nose isn't bleeding. What smells?"

Dozier furrowed his eyebrows like a stern kindergarten teacher.

"Oh that. It's *le Lac de Tunis*, the world's largest ground level sewer. It's one of the unnatural wonders of the world, which is why we don't discuss it." He coughed artificially into his fist, wished me luck and advised me to avoid the belly-dancing joints in town—they were bogus. Then Dozier offered his hand to the next unsuspecting volunteer.

The landing field looked like a movie set. We were the only ones on the tarmac. An impish man with a scruffy beard offered his hand. It looked like a strange flower with only three fingers and the thumb sprouting from the palm. When my eyes widened and I flinched, he advanced the other hand with a wry smile. "I'm Rodney. I know it's not much of an ice-breaker, but I was taught as a kid to introduce my birth defect when I introduce myself."

"That's cool," I said. "I'm just relieved I wasn't hallucinating."

He laughed. "I'm the procurement officer. So if the food's bad, you know who to bitch to."

"That's comforting, thanks."

A woman in aviator shades approached. She was pretty, wholesome with a golden tan and a mole on her cheek.

"Welcome aboard. I'm Tasha Theodore, the camp director."

I was tired and disoriented, and her confidence, energy and beauty overwhelmed me. I looked at her mutely like a doofus.

Tasha tilted her head and half of her long brown hair from the center part came loose and hung like a tapestry down to her bare shoulder.

"Rick Murkey?" A warm smile crossed her face as her white teeth gleamed under sheltered eyes.

"That's me," I replied, perking up at the familiar sound of my name. "Are we...Where is—customs? I mean...do we—you know?"

"We go straight through," she said. "This is for you."

Tasha handed me a letter in a square rag envelope. On the upper left hand corner was the ambassador's seal. Across the envelope my name was written in calligraphy. The message inside was brief and tantalizing.

Rick: Please call me as soon as you arrive.
Lauren A.

4

DIPLOMATIC IMMUNITY

The next morning, giraffes munched on breakfast leaves and chimpanzees screamed in the trees, as I crossed the Belvédère zoo to the American Embassy to receive my first rabies vaccine. I tapped the envelope in my pocket to make sure Lauren's note was still there. It was my ticket to experiencing something better than the 100-bed dormitory where I had spent my first night in Tunisia. A charge went through me when I touched the envelope. Each spark transmitted a memory of sensual moments, expectations and letdowns, new stirrings and a confirmation of my special destiny.

By coincidence, Lauren's father was the Ambassador to Tunisia, but how did she know I was here? The Ambassador must have told her. But why would he know? Were new Peace Corps volunteers of diplomatic concern? Despite going for 48 hours without sleep, I had lain awake for much of the previous night, perplexed by the invitation. Moving my hand over the exquisitely textured paper connected me with a sublime reality across the mundane void I occupied as a passive herd animal, stripped of privacy and identity.

I had barely seen Lauren in two years, which made the direct appeal of her note more intriguing. I filled the time waiting for the notorious rabies needle by putting her together in my mind as a puzzle of attributes: tall and tan, long-limbed and voluptuous, freckled nose and full lips, blonde hair down to her shoulder blades. Lauren's shy smile and the lowering of her brilliant blue eyes seemed inconsistent with her bold stride and reckless essence. Yet this expression, which I remembered best, revealed a simplicity that contrasted with her sophistication and privilege.

A four-inch-long needle injected the rabies vaccine into my hip. The syringe contained so much amber serum that the injection drained its burning contents for several minutes and left a massive bump on my side.

I phoned Lauren. She was bright and elusive as ever, at moments direct, at others teasing me with oblique remarks that ended like private roads, promising more stories to be told and feelings to be expressed.

Lauren went to an all women's college down the road and we took a few classes together at Brockwurst. Before Cerise, Lauren and I had spent enough time together to know we wanted more. Our intimacy was a series of exciting oases surrounded by loneliness. She didn't need to tell me but I knew it was true—she lived in a different world. She was a socialite. Her life went around and above and through mine like a Klein bottle that made a mockery of three dimensions. I occupied a small place in her vast world, while she hovered over mine with sporadic personal appearances that made me feel smaller.

I spent half our relationship feeling lucky and the other half hurt and dissatisfied. At times, I was not even sure we had a relationship. During long stretches when she slipped away, I vowed not to see her again—until she came back and I forgot my pride in the pleasure of being with her. Finally I kept my vow. Cerise came along and Lauren penciled me out of her schedule.

That was long ago. Now the touch of the letter transmitted a new message. I seemed to gain prestige and weight as I approached my date at the Ambassador's Residence. Over lunch, I would discuss diplomacy, offer a grand design of the balance of power and take my first step into world history.

A black Lincoln limousine pulled into the circular driveway of the embassy. The driver got out and opened the back door for me while my peer volunteers watched in bafflement. Never again would I have to boast about what I had done or seen. A guest at the Ambassador's Residence would be perceived as someone of consequence—if not a figure of taboo—and not just another unemployed college grad escaping a recession. *Somebody*—that's all I wanted to be.

The Ambassador's Residence was a hybrid of the White House and a Tunisian villa. It was a sleek rectangle of white concrete and dark glass, with classical Arabic arches bending the cool, clean lines of a newly minted art museum. A soaring, vaulted doorway opened to a skylight atrium, where two tall palms stood like house guards in the center of mosaic tile floors. Richly dyed tapestries from Kairouan and Gabes hung from white stucco walls, while a glass panel in back revealed an inner courtyard enclosed by an arcade.

Lauren's sister, nine-year-old Chloe, skipped into the atrium to say that Lauren was on an overseas call from New York and she'd be right down, *really*. It was classic Lauren: breathlessly beckoning, then making me wait. Chloe was evidently well coached in delivering Lauren's messages. She had every intonation down so precisely that I laughed, rather than indulging my old grievances with her sister. At any rate, the residence was sumptuous enough to entertain me.

"Have you been here long?" Chloe asked.

"Less than a day. How about you?" I asked.

She smiled shyly and shifted uneasily. Her social expertise seemed limited to conveying Lauren's communiqués. An extended conversation with a strange adult was apparently something new.

"I go to the American School. I've been here a year. But I think I'm going to school back in the States. I don't know!" Chloe exhaled in response to the strenuous effort of explaining herself, as well as the uncertainty in her life.

"What did you do before you came here?" she asked.

"I had a big shot. A vaccine for rabies."

"You did a good thing," she said. "Rabies can kill you, you know. It makes your eyes bulge and water and you drool and—it's a good thing you got the shot."

"Then I guess it's worth the pain," I replied.

"Rick! You're here!" Lauren cried. She raced toward me across the atrium, tall and elegant in a royal blue *jellaba*, her arms wide apart. She looked like a priestess of a blue cult, her body translated into the color of the sky. She threw her arms around me in a hug, but her lips on my cheek were the only place our bodies touched.

"You knew I was coming," I said.

"But now you're *here*. And that's much better. I hope you're hungry."

I told her I had consumed nothing but *lait orgeat* in expectation of an ambassador's lunch. She crinkled her nose.

"We're having typical 4th of July barbecue food, you know, burgers and hotdogs, but with couscous on the side instead of fries. Cross-cultural. Totally."

We strolled through the courtyard. A fountain sent watery crescents high above the clay shingles. Lauren played tour guide, pointing out the floor mosaics depicting the three or four important events in Tunisian-American relations over 200 years— the Barbary Pirates and the Battle of Kasserine among them.

"Were you surprised to hear from me?" she asked.

"Shocked," I said. "How did you know I was here?"

She laughed.

"My father has a list of Americans in Tunisia. There aren't many, and there are even fewer Brockwurst grads. He was on campus for his reunion and must have recognized your name. Didn't you speak at commencement?"

"Yes," I said guardedly. Most of the distinguished guests had objected to my remarks. Could Ambassador Ardsley have been among these detractors?

She smiled at me in her wry, prescient way.

"What is it?" I asked.

"How could you be shocked to hear from me? Like you didn't know my dad's the Ambassador?"

"I knew he was *an* ambassador. I didn't know where."

"So, you didn't come to Tunisia to be with me?" she asked. "How disappointing!"

Lauren guided me out through glass doors to the biggest blue sky I ever saw and a lawn with a patio and a full-length pool overlooking a steep cliff. The Mediterranean Sea 300 feet below extended for hundreds of miles and met the sky at the horizon line in a seamless sheet of blue. We sat down to a meal as hybrid as the house—deviled eggs made with *zit zitouna;* a spicy tomato soup with orzos; burgers; *salade Tunisienne*—tomatoes, onions, cucumbers and peppers chopped fine; and ripe, assorted fruits— succulent plums, plump figs and melons of white, pink and orange flesh.

Chloe joined us and insisted on leaving the table after every course to wash her hands.

"It's so I won't get cholera."

"She did a school project on diseases," Lauren explained. "She still hasn't recovered."

"It's horrible," Chloe said. "People used to get it all the time, especially on ships. And going west in covered wagons. They didn't have clean water. You'd better watch out for it. It's disgusting."

This conversation was making me acutely aware of the recent rabies vaccine burning at my hip. Once Chloe had exhausted her knowledge of cholera, she went on to dysentery, salmonella and giardiasis. She was also fascinated by ascariasis, in which an infected person's leg swelled to four times its size and resembled a soft, bloated trunk.

"I saw a picture once," Chloe said, "where they showed the insides of a person's intestines. The worms were as big as telephone cords!"

"Chloe, can we change the subject?" Lauren asked.

Lauren took her cue from the color of my face. I was having side effects from the rabies injection, a low-grade simulation of the disease: lethargy, weakness, irritability and nausea. Chloe's vivid description of her science project exacerbated these symptoms.

"It's all right," I said. "I used to love talking about diseases at the dinner table. I'm still fascinated with them. I remember how disappointed I was when my parents told me to be quiet."

"You look *terrible*," Chloe said, staring into one of my bloodshot eyes. "Do you think it's cholera?"

I reassured her it wasn't, so she changed the subject from the physical to the spiritual.

"Did you ever see something happen and you knew you'd seen it before, but like in a daydream?" she asked. "That happens to me all the time. It's like I see things when I'm daydreaming and then when they happen I don't know if it's real or I'm daydreaming it. It's weird."

"Actually that could be useful," I said, "Usually I have no idea what's happening to me."

"You must be so confused," Chloe said.

"Tell me about it."

We all laughed.

When Chloe went into the house to practice piano, Lauren and I were finally alone.

Lauren sipped her iced tea and observed me with an appraising smile. "I'm sorry we haven't had time to talk."

"Chloe is remarkable. I felt I was talking to an adult."

"She's too young for you, Rick. Don't you prefer older women?"

I fidgeted under Lauren's sibylline smile. She stood with her legs together. Her arms reached high with clasping hands, then lowered like a widening fan, so that the sun seemed to emerge between them. Sensing my discomfort, she walked around the table and cuffed my head playfully.

"Come, let's walk and talk."

She crocheted my arm in hers and we strolled around the courtyard. In the shade of the loggia the sun poured through the arches like spotlights.

"So, Rick, what have you gotten yourself into?"

"The Peace Corps."

"You know what I mean."

Lauren always knew how I was feeling. She claimed it was because she was a Pisces, an emotionally perceptive sign, but I attributed her insight to her experience of people and her penchant for psychology. I had met her in "Intro to Psych" freshman year. After class we often walked to the cafeteria for lunch and discussed the latest chapter—consciousness, learning and human development. Social psych was her favorite. She said her life was a human behavior lab and when it came to love and social influence, what tricks, lines, or acts had she not encountered or devised? When we crammed for exams she always cited better examples for the many theories and effects than were in the text.

Suddenly, coming here seemed wrong for my fragile state of my mind.

"You came to Tunisia because I was here," she said. "Even if you didn't consciously know it. Accidents like this don't just happen. You must have known *subconsciously*."

She believed so keenly in the destiny of my coming to Tunisia that I started to believe it, too.

"Will you be around this summer?" I asked.

"No. I'll be in New York in two weeks. I'm starting my TV job."

"So if I came to Tunisia to be with you, my subconscious really blew it," I replied.

We sat in wicker chairs under the spray of a fountain. The statues were from a familiar myth of a semi-clad woman reaching for a shepherd.

Lauren closed her eyes in the sun, said it was hot, unbuttoned her caftan and let it fall from her body to the cool tile. She adjusted the straps of her black bikini, smoothed her shoulders and sat with crossed legs to focus on me.

"Is your true love in the vicinity?"

"No. Why do you ask?"

"Isn't she why you came?"

"Sort of."

"What happened?"

She stared at me with a sympathetic fixation. Her eyes seemed to roam inside my head, as she tried to evaluate and solve my problem at once.

Why did I hold back? Lauren knew me long enough to see through me, but if I told her about Cerise and Bidonville, her refusal to live with me and our plan to meet in Tunisia that summer, she would conclude that I was a victim of romantic illusions, as she suspected, and that Cerise and I were on love-support. I couldn't bear her pity, yet she dispensed it freely.

"How did this happen? I care about you."

I shivered from the fountain's mist, the burning serum draining from the bump at my hip and the sensation of Lauren's mind slipping through areas of my life that I needed to keep private and secure. Her questions were chisels, her insights were hammers and I knew my shack of a life could not withstand her rough inspection.

"Why are you doing this?"

"What?"

"Analyzing me."

"Because we're friends."

"My being in Tunisia has nothing to do with you."

"If you keep saying it, you may convince yourself. There's a Tunisian saying. *Tout dépend de tout.* Everything depends on everything. I know what you're going through."

"I'm not going through anything!" I groaned.

"—What you're *not* going through then. I can't help but think that we had good times and that things might have been different."

This discussion was depressing me. How presumptuous Lauren was! I had enough trouble with the present and future and now she was loosening my grip on the past.

"We had good times but I hated it when you weren't there."

I hoped this summary would put the past in its place.

"So now Cerise isn't there."

Lauren's legs unfolded and extended, her toes wiggled in the fountain mist. Her arms stretched high, yet not triumphantly. She only seemed satisfied that she had delivered the prophetic message for which she summoned me. I was deflated. To avoid the humiliation of being so dissected, I lashed out at her.

"With Cerise, I'm the only man in her life. You can't understand that."

Lauren stood abruptly and placed her palms on her hips, indignant but unsurprised. She sighed, stroked my shoulder and said, "Let's swim. You did bring a swimsuit."

"*Bien sur*. I expected my first swim in the Mediterranean."

"Sorry. You'll have to settle for a pool."

She dove in the deep end and I followed. We splashed each other and swam in circles. Then I headed toward the other end and swam laps, hoping to shed my anxiety and relax. With each smack of the water and submersion of the head, I tried to shut off thought and relieve uncertainty. But the serenity swimming often provided did not come. Rather than glide through the water, I thrashed in it to scare off my fears. Finally, I stopped thinking, swept back the water and slipped through it, lifting and dropping my head, until a sudden shiver ran through me and I shook uncontrollably.

I lay by the pool like a reptile in the sun. Lauren mummified me in towels stamped with the Ambassador's seal. She wrapped herself in a white robe and straddled a chair. With her chin and arms along the back she studied me from behind black-rimmed shades.

"Would you do me a favor?"

"Sure."

"I'm starting as a TV interviewer next month. Can I practice on you?"

Immediately I felt my ego surge. How could I resist? Lauren leaned forward and regarded me with professional gravity.

"Long-distance love seems impossible today. How do you do it?" she began.

"I don't do anything. I just love," I replied.

"Aren't there too many temptations and complications to

make it work?" she asked.

"It's hard. But it's worth it," I answered.

"Is long-distance love a cop-out?"

"No, it's a total commitment."

"Are you really committed if you don't live with someone every day? If you never argue and fight and get on each other's nerves and have to work things out?"

"We're always fighting in letters. She misunderstands what I write and I misinterpret her. She thinks I'm holding back or lying. Our fights take weeks to clear up. We overcome slow mail and postal strikes. That's commitment."

"Do you cling to this relationship to avoid living, because it's easier than being alone and dating other people?"

"No. I love my girlfriend because she makes me feel special."

Lauren regarded me as if she knew I were lying.

"So your relationship is perfect. Is being far away the best thing for a relationship?"

"I don't want to paint a false picture. She also makes me feel like crap. But that's how love is, isn't it?"

Lauren looked at me with the steady eyes of a seasoned interviewer, who answers with questions.

"Is it? We'll have to find out. Thank you, Rick."

Lauren broke the spell with a wink. "Well done. Thanks."

After the interview I got dressed. Lauren and I stood in the atrium and said our good-byes.

"Just one thing before you go," she said. "Being exclusive doesn't make you special, but it can make you exclude a lot of special things."

I reflected on Cerise's letters, how she rebuffed my request to live with her. Were we special or marking time? It was all that Lauren, the mind reader, needed.

"I hope you get what you want," she said.

As we waited for the car to come, Lauren closed my hand over something cold.

"Take this," she said. "Hold on to it and think of me."

Her long fingers uncoiled my fist. In my palm she placed a pool of antique silver. It was a braided chain with an oval pendant. The medallion, which held the meaning of the gift, lay under the cool, slinky links that were like the diamond markings of a snake. I lifted the chain carefully as if it were alive and dangerous. The chain uncoiled until the oval pendant alone lay against my palm.

I expected a universal icon—the sword and serpents of Asclepius, the Hand of Fatima, a peace sign, even the long face of a Yoruba deity, or a scrawled inscription from a profound scripture. What was delicately etched on the oval plate was nothing I had seen before. It was neither abstract nor concrete.

"They're tea leaves," Lauren said. "People read the future in them."

The Embassy car pulled up. Lauren lowered the chain around my neck and slipped it under my shirt, pressing it against my heart. She brushed against me and kissed me on each cheek.

"You're special to me. Just remember today when you're in a dry God-forsaken place. When I see you again, you'd better have this chain."

I forced a smile through my sadness. She read my mind again and knew how hard it was for me to leave all I knew, loved and aspired to. I lowered myself into the car. The door closed with a heavy click.

Lauren whispered through the open window, "*Bislema. In sh'Allah.*"

The car pulled away and I turned to look at Lauren one last time, but she was already gone.

5

THE LONG AND WINDING ROAD

The next day was the 4th of July. Instead of fireworks there were sore buttocks and exhaustion. We piled into tour buses for the long trip to training camp. Our destination, Ayn Draham, was in the mountain forests of the north near Algeria. The region was famous for cork, mineral water, mud spas and wild boars.

I was in turmoil and the rabies vaccine was not to blame. Lauren's enchantment lay over me like the traces of a lovely dream in blinding daylight. I tried to reconcile the intensity of yesterday with the banality of the bus engine's groan, the transport of dishevelled strangers, reminiscent of summer camp. Which was real—the pool in the sky or this trek across a tract of kaleidoscopic splotches, vaguely green through the tinted windows?

It might have been beautiful country we crossed, but the bus reduced eruptions of boulder, jagged rock and hillocks bristling with thyme to blurs. Every bump and bounce on the hard road recalled listless trips down the Jersey Turnpike to face summers of menial labor living with my mother.

Even sleep failed to arrested these gloomy reflections.

Blistered feet, walking home six miles in the haze of hot, monoxide highways. Cinderblock office, three-story garden apartments with laundry rooms of lint, halls reeking of melon rinds, drums of lemon cleaner, me staring through a patch of clear glass in the painted door, looking out for the boss's blue Corvette. Reaching in the fridge with the green light that makes everything, hand included, look rotten, to grab a soda. A female black widow and her suitor are in the butter box rubbing their spiky, jointed legs. Everything in the world is getting some but me. I slam the fridge door. No spider porn!

My eyelids snapped open. Tasha was shaking my shoulders. My shirt was soaked with sweat.

"Are you okay?"

"What happened?"

"You must have had a bad dream."

I had the sickening sensation that my pocket had been picked, my passport stolen, and that my overstuffed brain had burst open, strewing my personal information across the bus for my new colleagues to evaluate. I couldn't betray myself, my past, the nothingness from which I came. If they knew, they'd ostracize me. As my mother warned, "If you talk about yourself, people will use it against you."

"Did I say anything?"

Tasha smiled at me curiously.

"No, you mainly flailed your arms, pounded your head into the headrest and mumbled incoherently."

"Oh, that's good," I replied with palpable relief.

"Is it? It didn't sound good. Oh, you did keep repeating something. I think it was, 'spiders born.' Does that mean anything to you?"

"Oh, that's nothing," I reassured her. "Spiders being born is one of my usual nightmares."

She looked at me doubtfully and tended to another volunteer who looked nauseous nearby. How reassuring it was that I had not exposed myself!

"Béja on the left!" Tasha belted like a tour guide. A blue and white honeycomb of box buildings and strands of wandering walls sprawled along an undulating hill, surrounded by golden fields of fine shaggy wheat. Béja, home of *hobze,* maker of bread, glowed in the middle of its corona of grain. For that moment, it was the most beautiful place in existence. In this dry, rugged land, where so many kilometers lay vacant, a town's presence was mysterious and wonderful.

The road narrowed and ascended. Without warning we found ourselves in a caravan of phlegmatic wrecks, old canvas lorries, reconditioned ox-carts, mules and people riding one another piggyback. We came to a stop. A truck had broken down a mile up-mountain. We were stuck between a rock-face and a precipice. All we could do was get off the bus and hike up to the breakdown to investigate and heave the wreck over the cliff if necessary. Arab farmers wearing white baggy-assed short pants observed us with disgust as if we were responsible for the tie up.

The air was acrid as we approached the smoking vehicle. Four aged men emerged from the fertilizer truck in their white airy knickers and pointy-toe slippers, with rolled prayer mats under their arms. They placed the straw mats carefully by the side of the road and prostrated themselves in prayer.

"People praying up ahead!" Tasha announced. At prayer times, driving took a back seat. A stalled truck, a ten-mile backup and a column of hostile motorists were nothing, compared with an almighty deity. Our bus driver, a secular man from Tunis, waved his arms and muttered a tirade that sounded poetic to my foreign ear, though his delivery conveyed pure exasperation.

"Believe me, I am sorry for this. I want to take you to your new home before dusk to be back in Tunis before dawn," he told Tasha and anyone else within earshot. "But there is nothing I can do. I am not religious and I will probably go to hell. *Alors,* someone must go, so why not me? *Quand même,* I must respect those who pray, regardless of the inconvenience. Tunisia is a paradox, *vous savez?* We have those who are modern like the French and the

Americans. We also have traditional people, like our friends with the truck. Tunisia is a beautiful mosaic, a complicated puzzle, or a mess—you choose!"

We were lucky to have such a lucid guide put this extraordinary scene in context. Meanwhile, the fertilizer truckers genuflected with their heads to the stone ground, as their feculent cargo formed an invisible wall around them.

When they completed their prayers, our driver looked under the hood of their fertilizer truck and found the problem—a broken fan belt. He removed one of his nylon socks, tied and knotted it in a band and installed it. Within ten minutes the truck was rolling.

At sundown, we barreled under the pink arch of Ayn Draham, like a slow missile through a flickering wicket. Arrayed with toy cherubs and Christmas lights, the arch was a town marker and talisman to protect its denizens from evil.

That first night was damp and chilly. Draped in striped blankets, the volunteer cohort walked up the steps of Ayn Draham, searching for a meal. A cloud had settled on the small town, obscuring the cliff. Under the steps, an open sewer in a shallow trench emitted a shrill, hollow sound and a putrid stench.

Dogs howled on the ridge. We couldn't see them in the fog, but we heard their wailing clearly on that cool July night. Wrapped in a blanket, I felt at home in the clouds.

6

A DAY AND NIGHT IN TUNISIA MULTIPLIED BY 20

Training camp was a passive place. All my senses were aflame with pure air, strange, exciting vistas and an unfamiliar way of life manifest in so many unique and unusual details.

Avenue Bourguiba, Ayn Draham's main street, skirted the

ridge, offering a variety of groceries and household necessities. There were barrels of grain and exotic powders, bakeries, pastry shops, a butcher's shop with sheep tripe glistening from a hook in a paneless window, like a large gob of fly-infested spit; and stores selling miscellaneous cloths, candies and plastic sundries. From one end of the street to the other, beggar children with clear skin and shining smiles darted about, murmuring *"Otini flous!"*

My eyes took over. They were the only instruments I could use unseen. Impressions bombarded me, impeded only by the boredom of the routine, a restraint imposed by others' eyes and my intention not to fall out of step.

We had classes seven hours a day, six days a week. Our main objective was to learn the host languages. But training camp was also an exercise in behavior modification. We were being taught to fit into a new system. Supervisors were everywhere prying into our minds. If a volunteer stared into space, felt poorly, or complained about the long lines to use the john after breakfast, a supervisor appeared suddenly to wrap the negative attitude in cocoons of questions and grind down our antagonism into weary acceptance. One day when I commented that the couscous was dry, Donna, a six-foot tall woman with a craggy face, looked at me as if I were a six-year-old and said, "We must provide our own moisture."

"Obviously she never heard of *KY*," Fargus muttered.

We came here to escape conformity, but our minds were being probed, analyzed, judged, reconfigured or repressed so we could give and take orders in a highly structured high school environment. A penchant for free expression, we were told, would work against us in a society where divergence from the norm could spell disaster. Our only hope for survival, the veterans warned, was to suppress our personalities and mimic Tunisian teachers. If we submitted to this basic truth, we would win our students' respect and the acceptance of colleagues and supervisors who might otherwise resent our presence. It appeared that our handlers aimed to crush our individuality and spirit, but they claimed that they only wanted us to succeed.

Tasha was the queen of the camp. The lovely, golden skinned woman with the mole on her cheek made a point of being one of us—eating, talking and hanging out with the new recruits—but she was every bit the boss and managed the camp like a machine, cost-efficient and scheduled down to the second. We were fed two small meals a day, just enough to keep us alive.

I tried to be independent and hold onto who I thought I was, but living in a barrack with seven other men, being constantly observed or herded to a planned activity, I became a peace corpse.

•

Each morning, bright sunlight peeled open my eyelids. Lattice shutters, lazily askew like a summer dress, framed a scene of cactus, fences, dust and an outhouse, the walls of a stadium and the high yellow stone ridge from which the wild dogs howled their nocturnal serenades.

Now the dog crooners were asleep and a lovely woman ruled the morning airwaves, singing, chanting, moaning, humming and clucking the Tunisian top 40. Her voice was fragile and appealingly unsure. Hearing her vocalize was like eavesdropping on a woman's intimate emotions. Saida, the tall, young maid, swept near my bed.

"*S'balkhir, labess?*" she inquired in her musical voice, perhaps to give me needed practice in Arabic, Lesson 1.

I stretched in a twist of sheet and blanket. "*Aslema. Labess. Hamdulleh!*" I replied with just the right inflection.

"Hamdulleh!" Saida gasped as a warm smile brightened her pretty face. Moving gracefully, efficiently on sleek, brown legs and wearing a faded, flower-patterned dress, Saida radiated a simple joy in being. She sang softly.

"A feeling like this is a treasure/to fulfill it would be a dream."

This was the lyric I imagined as she moved briskly by my bed, her smooth leg grazing my arm. This lovely woman who greeted me each day would always live mainly in my imagination. Her strong, lithe body, which came close enough in her light cotton dress to always remind me of a woman's vitality and warmth, must always be for inspiration only.

•

"Otini flous! Otini flous!"

On our way to class along Avenue Bourguiba, a barelegged child in white jockey shorts and a baseball cap placed himself in our path, whispering the beggar's refrain. *"Otini flous! Otini flous! Donne moi d'argent."* ("Give me money!")

Even beggar children were bilingual for better business. The boy's mother, squatting in her white *safsari*, surrounded by her children, moaned softly, *"Otini flous, Monsieur, otini flous."* Nearby, her husband stood impassively selling ices, his weather-leathered face bespeaking patience and suffering elevated to high art.

Along the swerving main street, sunken out faces watched silently. Eyes appeared to be the last living organs in the people's bodies. They lived through them.

"Watching is a major pastime here," Tasha explained, "People who are restrained from doing, watch. And they are extremely observant. They miss nothing."

It was appropriate that I was in the middle of a passive, watchful society. I had not received a letter from Cerise since leaving the States but could not even be hurt or angry since it was unclear that this silence was her doing or due to poor mail delivery. Like my Tunisian hosts, I could only watch and wait.

●

At five o'clock, the sun no longer beat against us through the windows as a diffuse, blinding light. It had drifted far enough away in the evening sky that we saw its distinctive yellow circumference and felt its golden beams cross the doorway and the blue railing, like the hand wave of an old friend saying a last goodbye.

Salah, a teacher with velvet nerves, stood before us, his thin, febrile body arched like a cat's, eyes bulging, voice rasping as he tried to drive Arabic 101 into our skulls.

Afternoon classes were a torture after siesta. Just when your brain started to clear and your head ached less from a truncated sleep, you reverted to a zombie—repeating, repeating and repeating.

Salah was a law student whose resonant voice was fortified by a habitual intake of harsh, black *tabac*. This was his summer job and it was easy to imagine what he thought when he accepted it— seven weeks in the mountains, free room and board and a generous stipend to teach his native tongues—French and Arabic.

Now he had to wonder how such a great deal turned to dung.

Salah strained as he craved his nicotine. His methodology was reduced to rolling eyeballs when students repeated the wrong answers with the wrong sounds. He had a reputation as a tyrant, unfairly so, since he was a bright, earnest man who knew how easy a language could be if you already knew it and how simple it would be to teach students if they were only awake. The distinction nobody made for him, not wishing to insult his brilliant legal mind, was that law does not need to be interesting, but education does.

If only Cerise were teaching this class, I thought. Cerise knew how to keep students interested. It wasn't only about her voice and charisma and her flair for the dramatic. She needed to connect with people, to understand and be understood. She was totally involved with her students when they were in a room with her.

Salah bellowed at wrong answers to breathe oxygen into the dying class, but two women in the back felt demeaned and they devised a brutal revenge. Since Salah made them feel dense, they would give him back more stupidity than any teacher could tolerate. The women repeated the phrases of the textbook with raucous monotony.

"*M'nin jet?*" (Where do you come from?)

"*M'NEEEEEN. J-E-E-E-E-E-E-T!*"

"*N'hib noshrub cawah cahaley.*" (I want to drink black coffee.)

"*NHEEEEEEB NOOOOOOOSHRUB CAAAAAAAWAAAAA CAAHAAALEEEYYY.*"

Their exaggerated responses were funny once, but soon became as unbearable as Salah's hand-slapping exhortations. We were sitting in the middle of a verbal demolition site. Language crumbled and nerves were shattered by jackhammer voices.

Cerise was a beautiful teacher with her smiling face and sparkling eyes. She clapped her hands and rolled them before her as if spinning an idea into existence. She never failed to point her forefinger upward to acknowledge a right answer or an intelligent remark and she burst into musical laughter when a student made a funny comment. It wasn't a matter of methodology; she just loved teaching.

The "revolutionary approach to teaching Tunisian Arabic" inscribed on our textbook cover was becoming a plain revolution. Salah knew the two women in the back reduced his language to ugly noise to spite him. His velvet nerves were frayed, his sensibilities offended. His head twitched on his shoulders. His nostrils flared rapidly as if timed to his accelerating heartbeat. A vertical vein that cut his forehead into left and right banks knotted and quivered. The poor dude only wanted to teach for a few ducats but he found himself in a struggle he could only lose. With desperate eyes, he banged his head against our resolute indifference.

Could there be any doubt why our Tunisian language teachers stayed to themselves during off-hours? Even after volunteers complained of their aloofness, the Tunisians stayed apart, not due to snobbery or anti-imperialistic resentment, but self-preservation.

"B'kadesh bernous kbir behi yessir?" ("How much is the large, very nice cape?") Salah bellowed and cringed, bracing himself for the imminent, thudding response, devoid of intonation, cadence or any quality resembling spoken language. His eyes squinted as perspiration trickled along his bulging forehead vein.

"OTINI FLOUS, OTINI FLOUS, OTINI FLOUS..."

The familiar beggar's line began with the women in the back and soon engulfed the class. It was the only phrase in Tunisian Arabic we heard often enough to pronounce perfectly.

Salah's face hung limp, his mouth flapped open. A gust of hoarse laughter roared out of his belly, cracked and squealed, flicked the tip of his spine and wracked his fragile physique. It was a mirth that had been compressing and expanding for weeks, threatening to explode in our faces at each fractured phrase and mistaken word we spoke while we tried to enunciate the right one.

This was the laughter at the end of a journey across dry-mouthed deserts of wasted labor.

The class was over. Salah would soon be gone. The teacher had left him. As a student, you saw it happen. The instructor was stripped of control, his knowledge devalued like rags at a flea market. We students had bludgeoned him into the pre-verbal, emotional state that often ruled us and prevented us from learning. The mystique of education gave way to giggling boredom.

●

That evening I kept thinking about Cerise and what a great teacher she was. I knew this first hand. I started auditing her class after we were together for a while, when I felt secure enough to do it. At first I was proud of her. I indulged the adolescent boy fantasy of visualizing the hot teacher without her clothes. Except with me it wasn't a fantasy. I spent one class with a hard-on, imagining what we would do afterwards.

But my teenage regression wore off. I started getting involved in the class and looked at Cerise and what she was doing from a strictly student perspective. This made me jealous. I saw her impact on my peers; how they responded to her and all that she gave to them. I felt like a voyeur, watching my girlfriend make love to 15 people. At times I wanted to stand up and shout, "She's mine! We made love last night!" Instead, I stopped attending the class.

I could not jeopardize her job or ask her to change her profession. I needed to think this through and overcome my jealousy. We were having sex; wasn't that the most intense pleasure and most significant act two people could share? For Cerise, in particular, sex was a huge commitment, yet she gave her students in class what she could not give me in bed.

Teaching was more than Cerise's job or vocation—it was her power. Students tugged at it like playful kittens, but they gave it back to her; they wanted her to have it. They watched her, anticipating what she would do next. Teacher, student—in Cerise's class, they were one.

I read once in a book by Victor Frankl, a psychiatrist who survived Nazi death camps, that starving prisoners had detailed food fantasies. Freud called it "primary process thinking." Cerise was having this effect on me. Now apparently out of my life, she pervaded my thoughts. The more I mused about her, the better I understood why I lurched into this Peace Corps situation, which was all the more depressing since she never wrote. It was obvious that I came here for the wrong reason. I was angry at Cerise for forsaking me and at myself for being naïve.

•

After school, Tasha and a group of us stopped at the *restaurant populaire,* which should have been renamed the *restaurant celibataire,* to honor the multitude of young bachelors who dined there. For a dollar we ordered *chakchouka,* a stew of potatoes, tomatoes, peppers and an egg; or a *brique a l'oeuf,* a fried *crêpe* stuffed with an egg; or a *poulet rôti en sauce,* roasted chicken in a piquant tomato ragout. Tasha was the only woman in the room, not counting the poster of Sylvie Vartan, a French sex siren, taped to the wall. The Tunisian men stared at her so intently that they misfired with their forks and got food on themselves. We ate quickly and headed to Slim's.

Slim's was our "after hours" hangout, the only hotel or western style café in town and the first establishment as you entered Ayn Draham from the south. Madame Slim, plump and chic in her Parisian dress, smart coiffure and high-heeled *hauteur,* served up globes of ice cream and tall glasses of fresh *citron presse,* as she bore with weary dignity her solitary mission to lend class to the town.

Mr. Slim was less the genial host than a feckless male relative, paunchy and sullen, who sauntered on the patio in his tunic and beaded slippers, looking befuddled. He blinked at customers as if to say, "Who are these people?" Yet, his listless, aristocratic bearing continued the lackadaisical tradition of the Turkish pashas, whom the French imperialists displaced at the turn of the 20th century.

At a table near the black wrought iron fence dividing Slim's flagstone terrace from the dirt sidewalk, Tasha and I enjoyed the cool eight o'clock breeze and watched the sun lower on the horizon like a red egg melting in butter. Tasha worked on her pistachio ice cream in quiet rapture. She had taken charge of me like a big sister and often reminded me how fearful I looked when we landed in Tunis. "You were positively green!" she laughed. She teased me to keep me humble and I smiled along. Her friendship was crucial to my plan. I would have to ask Tasha to see Cerise.

When it was dark and Christmas lights strung along the wrought iron, stonewalls and bougainvillea cast the only light, Tasha expounded on bargains at *les puces,* her beloved flea markets, while I obsessed on Cerise. The camp director was offended at my inattention. I immediately apologized and offered *chakchouka* indigestion as an excuse for my abstraction.

"You always focus on your stomach," she reproved me. "The problem is in your mind. Listen. I'm trying to tell you how to survive in Tunisia!"

"How to buy cheap dresses in flea markets?"

Tasha often admonished me when I came late to class. It was

part of her job to be a disciplinarian. This was different. She wasn't telling me anything I had to know. She was talking about herself. Her tone and manner suggested that she expected more from me, like personal attention.

We were close enough to the street to hobnob with every beggar, eccentric and conspirator in town, and beggars, in particular, often straggled by Slim's on the way home to their caves. Begging was an acceptable practice; holding out the hand a form of manual labor. A regular panhandler approached our table. He was so hunchbacked that his head looked like a chest extension. Bedecked in bedclothes, a woman's dress and long johns, all coated with dust and sweat, this beggar set himself apart from his competitors with an unusual accessory—sunglasses.

Slim's was the only chic café in town, so the proprietors took special care to exclude anyone but attractive people. Though good looks may have been in short supply on a given night, there was still a tacit cut-off line for ugliness and our sunglassed visitor failed to meet the minimum standard.

Mr. Slim shuffled to our table and exhorted the beggar to be gone. The hunchback cowered near us for protection. Hairs like bent antenna wires sprouted from a growth on his cheek. I handed him a *dinar,* which he did not accept as charity but as a fee for the floorshow he was eager to perform. He removed his sunglasses to reveal eye sockets that were pink, leathery hollows. Tasha shrieked.

"I see too well and I know too much," the beggar said in French. "Don't stay. Get out before it's too late."

Slim arrived brandishing his weapon of choice, a broom, but the sunglassed, hunchbacked interloper had already scuttled off.

"I thought I'd die," Tasha said, her palm pressed against the embroidery on her peasant blouse. "I've been in this country two years and that's a first."

Slim apologized for the horror. He brought Tasha a complimentary pistachio *glace* and stood by our table while she ate it approvingly.

"*Il est fou, celui là,*" Slim said. "He is crazy. They say he lives in the woods with wild dogs. That he howls at the full moon. But I think the dogs run away when he comes."

"He didn't smell great," I acknowledged, "but I wish I knew if he was talking to me, you know giving me a message."

"Rick, he didn't see you," Tasha replied. "He has no eyes."

"Still, I wish I knew what he meant," I insisted while I replayed the eyeless beggar's warning in my head. "Having no eyes might give him a more profound vision. Did he mean we should leave Slim's or Ayn Draham or the Peace Corps?"

Tasha stared at me incredulously. "I wouldn't waste my time wondering what he meant."

"People like him don't often say much so when they do, we should pay attention," I said. "Besides, he was a showman. He reminded me of Elton John."

•

A few minutes later, we were walking down the stairs of Ayn Draham toward our compound, when I heard stones smacking the concrete. One nicked the back of my neck. I turned and caught a rock in the face. Under attack, we ran down the stairs as sewer water sluiced below us, and rocks and concrete nuggets showered us from above. From the ridge a choir of children's voices echoed. "*Franceowi! Franceowi!*"

"I thought they liked us," I said, once we reached the safety of our valley camp. Tasha had been hit on the shoulder. Her blouse was flecked with blood.

"I exaggerated," she admitted. "It's more like love-hate."

•

When I returned to my house at night, sleep eluded me. The supervisor in the top bunk, who had just separated from his wife, played *I Ching* with coins, a book and a flashlight. Other roommates snored or had nervous legs that bicycled and flailed, tossing covers and shaking the bedframes. But these summer camp phenomena did not prevent me from sleeping.

I felt like a blindfolded passenger. Days passed, events happened, I moved through my experience without understanding or enjoying it.

My colleagues unnerved me. I did not object to their habits, odors and idiosyncrasies so much as to the manner in which they viewed their lives. They seemed perplexed but were in no hurry to solve their enigmas. Most of them were a few years older. They had worked full-time, signed leases, paid bills and owned things, yet they were as unsettled and marginal as I was. They had renounced what I never had and now were satisfied to start again with nothing.

Their flight from America made my decision to join the Peace Corps seem like a shrewd move, yet it also disturbed me. It suggested that my commencement speech was on the mark—there really was no hope for me at home. At the same time, our collective escape was undirected—*from*, not *toward*. It did not solve problems or clarify confusion.

Carl, on the lower bunk across the room, had a goatee and the cool air of a beatnik, with a subtle smirk that hinted at a gentle wildness. In all respects Carl was a good volunteer—early rising, uncomplaining and studious. This was his second stint in the Peace Corps. After a tour in Mali, he floundered in the States, so he re-applied to the Peace Corps and came to Tunisia. Carl did not need hope or ambition; he was on his own private mission. He never renounced his citizenship, but he seemed quietly resolved to renounce American culture. Although he never said it, he intimated that he meant to make his life in Tunisia and would never return to the States. Like most of the volunteers, Carl was never worried or in a hurry. He was in *the flow*. The possibility that I could become like Carl scared me.

Only Cerise could save me from this floating ambiguity, which was why her silence made it worse. Wondering what she would do or if we were still *together* kept me awake. She alone connected me to who I had been. Our history was one certainty I had in this free-falling, language learning, rule following, role-playing limbo. The emotional vicissitudes she put me through made me more than a green kid with a BA. They gave me depth.

As I tried to sleep, the dogs howled on the ridge beyond the stadium. I went out to observe them. Their long torsos were gray, arching silhouettes in the moonlight. With heads rocking on distended necks, in turns and in unison, they barked cacophonous serenades of an inconsolable yearning they could not expel. This was no mating cry. They screamed to the sleeping world that they were alive.

The canine cantata roused me to a nervous excitement. I went to the narrow restroom in back, where a toilet, shower-pipe and sink were aligned. I had a choice—to masturbate and risk someone pounding on the door in the midst of autoerotic bliss, or to take a cold shower. Since I wished to avoid being known as a late night shower masturbator, a reputation that could easily enter my personal file and follow me through life, I showered coldly and obsessed on the letters Cerise failed to send. Would she ever love me as I was? If not, would she set me free? I doubted the former and dreaded the latter. Duly numbed by the cold water, I dried off and went to bed.

While my bunkmate flipped coins, arranged toothpicks and consulted a book of *I Ching* to decide his future, I lay in bed trying to reconstruct the past to explain my present.

•

It was just three years before.

Cerise and I walked to the top of Memorial Hill, stood on the sundial of the war monument and kissed. Her skin was damp and soft and exuded a sweet, sultry scent. Her lips were warm and full. We held each other close. She pulled away.

"What is it?"

"Oh, nothing."

"Are you with someone else?"

"There was someone. Now it's over."

I laughed joyfully. There was no one else and therefore it would be me. We kissed and walked to her dormitory.

"Good night," she said with an intimate growl, "I'm sure I'll be seeing you around."

I held her against the inner door and kissed her repeatedly in the dark vestibule. She pulled free, chuckled and eluded me through a second door, then turned and flashed a mischievous smile. "If you'll excuse me, my panties are wet."

I gaped at her with my mouth unhinged while the idea of her vaginal lubrication overwhelmed my orgasmic mind.

Just before she left my view one flight up the stairs, Cerise turned and winked in the same obvious way that charmed me in the dining hall. Was she putting me on? As the clicking of her boot heels grew fainter, I could not stop thinking about her damp panties. No other woman ever revealed herself to me in such detail.

The next day was Friday. I expected to spend the weekend exploring her moisture, but Cerise was not in her room or anywhere on campus. She had left for the weekend—*comme ça!*— after telling me how much I turned her on. What a tease! I left a note on her door with a cryptic message: "The game is almost over." It made no sense, I left no name on it and she would have no idea who left it, yet somehow it felt like the perfect face-saving *lettre de rupture.*

If she could take off so casually and leave me hanging like a wet jock, I swore I'd forget her just as fast. That Sunday afternoon I was in my room, having sex with a girl, when Cerise stopped by my suite. She asked my roommates if I was there. They said I was out.

When she left, I wrapped a towel around my waist, leapt down the stairs to the common room and pounded my chest in exultation because she cared.

A few days after our first kiss, I found her in a dining room, having fun with the usual poseurs. I asked her if she'd take a walk.

"But I'm not wearing white pants!" she replied sarcastically, "And this tartan skirt is the only clean clothing I have left."

"I promise we'll keep it clean," I muttered.

"No thank you," she replied coyly. "I'm seeing a movie."

I squeezed her arm. "Please," I whispered urgently. "It's important."

"Oh well, since it's important," she laughed.

In the brisk autumn dusk, students with bent shoulders ambled to the library, their sweatered torsos aimed like projectiles at the bright monolith. Cerise and I were more resolved, if less directed. We knew what we wanted but not where to get it. We kept a brisk pace, not daring to hesitate or question our objective. I heard the cinematic click of her black heels on pavement, the sizzle of the match firing her cigarette and her soft, quiet exhalations. Her raincoat brushed my sleeve. I was afraid to speak. Talk was a bomb that would obliterate our intentions. One word would commit us to react, to calculate and to return to ourselves—*our cells*. By walking in silence and collaborating without a plan, we had our intimate paradox—the excitement of closeness in the freedom of solitude.

When it was dark and we tired of wandering, we stopped at a powerhouse where steam rose from the pavement. The mini-industrial eyesore was an anomaly for the rustic campus. We sneaked in through a backdoor and went down a long metal ladder to the floor 100 feet below. The generators were going *chung a chung a chung*. I laid my dilapidated suede jacket on the concrete surface like a picnic blanket and we stared up at the dome of shadows overhead. Our bodies quaked with each *chung a chung* and tensed in the intermittent pauses, when we heard the squeaks and clunking echoes of heavy objects opening and closing, and imagined someone finding us.

But no one came.

"Oh, hell," I muttered and kissed her warm, soft mouth. She moved her loins against me. I reached under the tartan skirt, which she had purchased during one of her earliest teaching jobs in Scotland, and ran my hand up the length of her thin, buttery thighs and inside her panties. She held my wrist.

"Please no, not yet," she whispered.

"Why not?" I groaned.

My genitals throbbed. I was afraid of doing damage to them.

Cerise read my concern. Her hand brushed my cheek.

"I want you, but not yet. Not here."

"When? Where?" I pleaded.

She laughed indulgently. My desperation amused her.

"I am the product of a Catholic education. The nuns at my school walked by our beds each night to make sure our hands were outside the sheets."

"I understand, I do. But I don't know how long I can take this excitement without release. What if it does permanent harm?"

She burst into her ringing laughter of chimes and cigarettes and held my face against her starched shirt and pointy bra.

"You crazy boy! I lived in a convent for ten years. Do you think I'll let you ravish me on a dirty floor?"

We made out until my glands downgraded from sore to numb. When I could take no more titillation, we climbed the metal ladder and walked to her dorm. "Your skirt's clean," I said.

"Thanks," she smiled. On the way back to my room, I detected her scent on my fingers. I didn't wash them for a week.

•

When sleep finally came, I dreamed I was in a supermarket looking for Cerise. She had disappeared. I awoke in a sweat. Was it prophecy or common sense? I told myself that dreams were emotional debris. I had to believe she still loved me but if she was too busy to write she must have found my replacement. She often threatened to find someone more suitable. Her letters were full of names—some familiar, others newly introduced and mentioned in passing—and events—parties, picnics, weddings. Who knew what she'd do? Still, I needed to overcome my fear and suspicion, or this mission would be nothing but a trans-Atlantic *gaffe*.

7

HAMEM

Gray skies never appealed to me until our fourth Saturday in camp, when I woke up without the band of bright sunlight slashing my eyelids. Finally, there was a break in the routine! Clouds gave us respite from the sun, offering a new mood and a cool, overcast day.

It was quiet after lunch so I sat on the porch writing a letter to Cerise. I described the dog tethered to a stake in the yard across the way. Soon the man of the house, "the-dog-and-child-beater," as we called him, would emerge from the house to beat him. Meanwhile, the little boy, who carried heavy pails of water on his shoulders, tossed dirt on the house pet. Soon his father would beat him, too.

I surmised that Cerise would not relish being served such slices of life. They would merely confirm her poor opinion of my location and convince her not to come. I tore up my letter to her and repurposed the case study of the beaten dog and the battered child for my mother, who had a morbid interest in sociology. Anyway, the odds were better that she would respond.

I looked over the letter I had just received from her to put me into the right mindset to write to her.

Dear Rick,

I haven't responded sooner because I attended a seminar and had so much work when I returned that I could not find the time to get around to writing.

The seminar was lovely. I met some fine people. One woman, whose son was a freshman, seemed to know who you were; her son had told her about you. She kept talking about you glowingly.

It was great to be a celebrity, even by association.

You seem upset that your French girlfriend hasn't written. Perhaps you haven't heard from her because she wants to punish you for not going to New York and fulfilling her expectations. It may hurt, but if it's any consolation, these feelings are sure to pass and you will end up the wiser.

I just received the results of my most recent X-rays. They showed benign cysts. Big deal! I was relieved, but angry. Why did my doctor and the radiologist have to make it sound so serious? They stroke your arm, but doctors try to scare you. That's how they sell their services, but it isn't right.

I just walked back from the mall. Fast food wrappers and beer cans were strewn everywhere. What an eyesore! We build more sophisticated bombs and missiles, but we'll be buried in litter before we can attack our enemies or defend ourselves.

Hopefully, you are becoming acclimated not only to your host country, but also to working in a regimented environment, with rules, demands and supervisors. Try to bear up.

Your mother

When writing to my mother, I tried to follow a rule I learned from five years of summer camp: regardless of how bad the situation was, we were supposed to write only good things. Otherwise we were told that our parents would feel terrible and blame us.

Dear Mom,

I'm doing fine. I have not caught a stomach virus yet. Several volunteers have been laid up with high fevers, diarrhea, vomiting and severe dehydration, but the supervisors say it's no big deal. Digestive problems are normal for new volunteers.

The food could be better, but who's complaining? Last week they bought a lot of fish at a bargain. Somebody said it was a week old. They fried it, stewed it, ragouted it—and it tasted okay, except for the tongue-coating after-taste. Otherwise everything is great.

The routine is repetitive but I'm getting used to it. I've made friends. The camp director, Tasha, seems to like me, which can't be bad. I'm looking forward to my first teaching assignment and to living on my own.

Hope all is well,

Rick

I reread my letter and realized that every paragraph was negative. I had not learned my camp lesson well enough. Maybe if I ended on a happy note, it would sugarcoat what came before. I was struggling to compose a cheerful postscript when Fargus came by with a towel over his shoulder.

"Are you wasting another day in the past?" he asked.

"No, I've made it to the present!" I replied. "I'm describing camp life in a letter home."

"You're writing your mom about bad food, lack of sleep and a lot of sick people? You're better off in the past," Fargus said. "It's time to cleanse. Let's crash the *hamem*."

The stone bathhouse in Ayn Draham retained the aura of a pagan temple. The doorman refused our dinars, calling us his honored guests. The baths would be "women's only" in an hour so we had to hurry for our bath and massage.

The *hamem* was a honeycomb of cubic rooms. Straw mats covered marble floors. Clouds of vapor suffused the air. The stone walls streamed with condensation. They seemed to sweat along with the bathers. We stripped down in the hamem's outer dressing

59

room and left our clothes on shelves recessed in the clammy walls. Whereas American men often dangle proudly in locker rooms, inspecting and even scratching their genitals in the presence of their peers, here the patrons wrapped their midriffs with canvas towels before slipping out of their briefs. Did this concealment of private parts signify modesty or shame? Did it relate in some way to women hiding in safsaris?

Under the dome of the central sanctuary a long black pipe fed the marble bath. Very hot water filled the shallow pool and produced steam throughout the *hamem*. An aged man lay in the scalding pool, impervious to the water temperature and the other bathers. His eyes were closed. His arms were splayed along the edge and his legs floated like sticks under the steamy surface. Seated next to the old man, a surly fellow submerged his calves and feet. Only the wrinkles that slashed his brow disrupted the slickness of his bald noggin. Yet prominent as it was, his skull was humbled by his gut, a cupola of hard fat.

The toxic impact of the past month seeped out of me as I lowered my legs into the cauldron. For a half-minute the skin stung badly where air and water met.

Fargus was explaining to me why many volunteers had concluded that I was weird. He offered this advice. "Some people can be themselves," he said. "You can't."

I thanked him and lowered myself into the steaming water until I was submerged to my chest.

"Boiling yourself alive isn't the answer," Fargus said.

"It could make me more palatable," I said. "Ow! Ow! Ow!"

The locals were astonished by my descent into the lobster pot. They yelled their approval and all sank into the steaming depths as I moved my red limbs in a frog kick.

After the hot bath, we washed ourselves with cold water in a tepid room. A harmony existed in the *hamem* between hot and cold, dirt and hygiene. Slime coated the stall floor. I scrubbed down with black soap and rinsed it off under bucket after bucket of cold tap water. Feeling clean and refreshed, Fargus and I padded to the massage room.

The masseur introduced himself as *Boom Boom* for a reason he would later expound upon with sputtering bravado. I watched him work over the bald and dome-bellied man from the bath. Wearing only a canvas cloth tucked and folded over his loins, Boom Boom maneuvered his hulking customer like a sumo wrestler pounding a sack of meal. "Domebelly" looked relaxed, even phlegmatic, but this was evidently a facade for massive tension, which the masseur pulverized with professional pride.

Boom Boom gave "Domebelly" the final flourish. He inserted his feet behind the man's knees and pulled his arms from the crooks of his elbows. This technique made "Domebelly" groan and snort. While manhandling his client, Boom Boom proclaimed his sexual prowess; he had sired twelve children and was still striving for more. "Me work hard at night," Boom Boom repeated emphatically in broken French. "Boom-boom!"

"Maybe he works *too* hard," Fargus whispered.

Once "Domebelly" had dragged his tenderized carcass off of the mat, it was my turn to be pounded into relaxation. With little time left before the women's invasion, Boom Boom put me through his workout in double-time, snapping and slapping my body around as if it were made of more durable stuff than muscle and bone. He stepped on the small of my back and tugged on my arms until my body was as curved as a Viking prow. Then the zealous masseur tucked me in a ball and slammed his bulk across my back. He pressed his full weight on me until the vertebrae snapped like a deck of shuffled cards.

Boom Boom concluded by scraping my skin with an abrasive cloth. He gathered and rolled the layers of epidermis into three snakes, which he laid across my chest like trophies for having survived the Boom Boom treatment. Although at times Boom Boom seemed more intent on dislocating my joints than on adjusting them, the rolls of dead skin on my chest made me feel strangely proud, as if I had achieved a new level of cleanliness.

While I put on my pants, an attendant ran bawling through the *hamem*. The honeycomb erupted in vibrating echoes of shouts and cries, as men dashed pell-mell among the vapors. We followed a crowd to the central bath, where in the steaming pool under the dome by the gurgling water pipe, the old man who had been immersed in the hot bath, floated like a raft of bones. He arms were still stretched along the sides. He was dead.

I returned to the stone bench in the frigidarium and tried to summon the energy to put on my shirt, but the image of the floating corpse lay as heavily over my mind as *Boom Boom* had lain across my back, and it was hard to move. Fargus, already dressed, asked me the obvious question.

"Are you okay?"

I nodded but the rocking of my head nauseated me.

"I never saw anyone dead like that before," I said.

"You never saw a dead animal?" he said, "A squirrel or a dead bird? A chicken on a supermarket meat shelf?"

"It's not the same. He was *human*. He could have been me."

"In 60 years. Come on, Rick. You're getting worked up over nothing."

"Death seems to be stalking me. It's everywhere I look—the vultures every afternoon, the tripe hanging from the butcher's window. The stench is everywhere. There's a reason I'm experiencing this."

"Poor hygiene," Fargus quipped. "We're in a developing country."

"Yes, but I chose this. Why?"

"Man, I wonder myself."

Outside the *hamem*, a phalanx of volunteer body-bearers, with Boom Boom leading the way, trotted out of the bathhouse holding the corpse aloft under a sheet. News of the hamem fatality had circulated fast through Ayn Draham. Women in *safsaris*, with plastic baskets hanging from their wrists, stood in two columns along their path, like spectators at a parade. To avoid the tumult on Avenue Bourguiba, Fargus and I made our way cautiously down the embankment behind the baths, with the stadium ramparts winding like a fat snake on our right.

The coolness and shade of this atypical day had lost their freshness and novelty. The landscape looked sullen when the sky was overcast. The sun was a tyrant, yet its constant glare simulated vitality and joy and made one forget the arid bleakness of the earth, now apparent in its absence.

"That was a funky bath," Fargus remarked.

"It's an anecdote to write home about," I said. "Dear Mom: I saw an old man die like a lobster in the Turkish bath."

"Never seen anything like it," Fargus said. "It surpassed cross-cultural. It was a global experience. Death is part of life."

"Life and death are insignificant without love," I said.

"Get over your fixation on love," Fargus chided. "I did and look at me: I'm miserable but functional."

A pale blue rectangle was waiting on my bed. It was an aerogram from France. Since my roommates were lurking, I pretended to ignore it, so they would not suspect how much it meant to me.

I needed a private place to read, to conceal the emotional

torrent Cerise's words never failed to arouse. When no one was watching, I snatched the aerogram and casually sauntered to the john.

But of course there was a line to use the facility and my effort to be inconspicuous went for nothing. Even at four o'clock on a Saturday I had to wait. The volunteer in front of me noticed the aerogram in my hand.

"Bathroom reading?" he asked wryly.

"Yes," I admitted as I tried unsuccessfully not to blush. "It's short because I'm usually in and out."

When it was my turn, I rushed in. Seated on the toilet, I opened and unfolded Cerise's first letter to me in Tunisia. The moment of inserting my finger into the flap and neatly tearing the sides was one of acute anticipation and intense happiness. It was like removing cellophane and foil from a new pack of cigarettes.

Dear Rick,

Keep your lofty ideals while I cling to my petty ones. Never mind. I love waiting around. Things often happen when you least expect them. For instance, I keep thinking that one day you will tell me when and where we will meet. I only hope the day comes before I book a trip to Italy or Greece, which would be a shame since you chose Tunisia to be close to me.

Admittedly, doing something practical in England would have lacked romance, so V.D.—plagued Tunisia is an excellent choice.

But please don't expend your precious energy on my account or squander your resources on my extravagant tastes.

Do you reread your letters? If you did, you'd despise the girl you describe in them as much as I do. I'm so sick of it. You're so full of crap. What right do you have to tell me who I am and the

pressures I'm under? Why don't you speak honestly about what
you're doing to me?

   Oh, well, I love you.

   Cerise

   As I folded and smoothed the aerogram, I experienced
emotions Cerise's correspondence often stirred—dejection,
frustration and bewilderment. I craved love and intimacy from her
letters, but they exhausted me, instead. I had to rebut her
accusations, assuage her vexations, reassure her of my devotion
and apologize for any bad impressions my statements had made. I
reflected on how I might have offended her and *what I was doing*
to her to make her hate herself.

   Then it came to me: she blamed us for loving one another. By
entering her life and not having the good manners to leave it, I had
done her an irreparable wrong.

   Would she still come to me? I depended on it. Our lovemaking and fighting, living together and existing apart, feelings we
had and ones we lacked, minutes reading letters and hours writing
them and the days and weeks between were my only story.

8

CROSS CULTURAL EXERCISE

   One evening, the high school courtyard was vacant after
Arabic class, a strange omen since every other day the gang
lingered there for a smoke before heading to Slim's. At first I was
bemused, then suspicious, and finally just hurt by the possibility
that I was finally ostracized from a group activity. After the sting of
rejection, I viewed my solitude as a lucky break. It freed me to
explore on my own the Ayn Draham outside our routine.

65

I wandered over to the stadium in the foothills on the edge of town, just under the promontory where the stray dog choir sang every night. It was not so much a stadium as a vast oval plateau of dirt, pebbles and sharp stones girded by a thick wall. It had no seats. It was originally conceived as a garrison, but was only half built when the French colonials realized they had no interests in Ayn Draham to defend.

Near the wide gap in the wall that served as an entrance, a group of small boys played a frantic game, squirming around a red rubber ball in the diminishing light. The ball was half-deflated by the rough playing surface and the manner in which the young players controlled it; they pressed it to the ground with their bare feet before cutting and darting toward the opponent's goal, a furrowed line in the dust between two rusty cans.

The paradox of the training camp was that we were always having cross-cultural training sessions where we discussed the fine points of Tunisian culture, yet we never met ordinary Tunisians to learn how they lived. As I stood on the sidelines of the peewee soccer game, I keenly anticipated that I would finally experience something real about Tunisian life.

Across the field, three teenagers, no doubt starters on the Ayn Draham varsity team, performed standard tricks with a black-and-white soccer ball, bouncing it from their chests to their knees to their insteps and back to their heads. I was watching them flaunt their skills when the ball flew toward me. Was it a deliberate pass to engage my participation or an errant kick? Either way, this was a unique opportunity to interact with real Tunisians. I put myself in the path of the skidding, high-bouncing ball and stopped it inadvertently with my crotch, then kicked a long floating pass back to the players.

They laughed and waved. *"Franceowi! Behi yessir!"*

As the sting in my groin subsided, I wondered if I would be able to have sex again. Would the teenagers appreciate that I had sacrificed my body to make an accurate pass and reward my toughness by including me in their game? My answer came swiftly when one player booted the ball across the stadium and the three teammates jogged after it.

My new friends were gone and the authentic cross-cultural Peace Corps moment was over. Nevertheless, I consoled myself that through the non-verbal international language of sport I had crossed for 60 seconds the barriers of culture, religion and politics. From this Olympian diplomatic moment I shrank back to my usual Peace Corps one-size-fits-all.

I ambled back to the breech in the wall where the small, sinewy boys were starting a new game. They begged me to play by tugging at my shirt and I reluctantly agreed. But I quickly realized that they were way too good for me. The moment my foot touched the red ball, 20 small feet kicked at it and pried it loose. When I lifted my foot to take a shot, a peewee stole the ball.

After my team went down by two goals, the captains conferred. They led me to one end of their playing field and indicated for me to put my feet where the cans were. My legs would be organic goal posts and the space between them would be the goal.

With such a large target, the children devoted ferocious energy to shooting the ball through my legs. As a volunteer, I was glad to do my part, but when the first shot squirted toward the space between my legs, instincts took over—I moved my right goal post and kicked the ball away. The striker lay on the ground, pounded the dust in frustration and yelled, *"Ne bouge pas!"*

By default, I was reinstated as a player. The violent rotating energy of the game, spinning relentlessly toward the unpredictable skittering ball, seemed to repel me further from its core. Like an expelled electron, I dizzily wandered over to the wall near the road to Tabarka, then climbed the stadium rampart and traipsed along the dirt path between the stone and mortar sidewalls.

The sunset's red heart and artery poured across the black horizon, spilling today's blood for tomorrow's hope. As I stood on the earthen parapet, alone but for youthful shouts, I faced the red line that marked a day done and promised one more to come.

Suddenly, a shower of stones shattered my meditation. The peewee soccer game had been suspended by darkness and a few disgruntled players, perhaps seeking revenge because I resigned as their goal, used me now for target practice. I scooped up a handful of dust and pebbles and tossed them at my assailants to obscure my visibility, like an octopus spewing dry ink, but this only incited the children to hurl more stones.

The young soccer demons fired missiles as they pursued me with war cries of shouts and laughter. I crouched and crawled along the rampart on folded legs, gaining speed, as the barrage of stones and rocks intensified. The dirt track I followed was full of ruts and curves. I slipped and sprawled face down as stones whizzed by me, then picked myself up and hobbled quickly on a throbbing ankle. I outran the boys' fire and they gave up the chase. I laughed, exhilarated by my escape.

Under the faint smile of a quarter moon, I walked on the wall, unable to see my feet or the path beneath them. This part of the stadium stood at the edge of the mesa. The wall was 20 feet above a culvert covered by brambles. My ankle twisted in a rut, I lost balance and tumbled off the wall into the ravine below.

•

I might have landed on my head and died, but my life was spared for an unforeseen purpose. My fall was cushioned by dry brush and I bounced and rolled to the bottom of the rift. Thorns turned my face into a pincushion. My clothes were torn, my clogs, the closest thing I had to a trademark, baled out and lay somewhere under the moon's grinning mouth. Groping in the darkness, I located my shoes. When I lifted one, an animal squealed and scampered away—probably a rodent that couldn't believe its luck when a shoe fell on it.

No one was at the house or on the porch. Where was everybody? I looked around and saw a notice taped to the door. Then I realized why the high school courtyard had been vacant and the camp deserted. A cross-cultural session was scheduled for that night.

I ran to the house where the meetings were often convened. It was dark and hot inside. No one was in sight but I sensed a swarming human presence, then heard a click and saw a large, colorful projection of a Bedouin woman's face on the living room wall—it was beautiful, secretive and defiant. Click. The slide was upside down. In profile, two camels' protuberant lips met in a kiss.

"Cute," gushed a woman volunteer.

"We paid the driver ten dinars for that shot," Tasha recounted. "They had chemistry."

Click.

Stuart, another supervisor, embraced Tasha against a ruin.

"OOPS." A remedial click. Then another: Tasha inspected a copper plate at a *souk*. The merchant's glinting eyes were embedded in his thick, leathery facial skin like gems in a geode.

Lights on.

"What happened to you?" Tasha asked.

"Nothing."

"You look like you were dragged by camels," Tasha scowled. "You missed my slide show."

"I'm sorry. I didn't know about the meeting."

"That's bullshit," said Stuart, Tasha's right hand man, best friend and ex-boyfriend.

"What's today?" I asked.

"Tuesday," Tasha replied, narrowing her eyes. "What does that have to do with it?"

"Wednesday is our cross-cultural day. That's why I didn't expect this meeting."

Tasha and Stuart exchanged a baffled glance. Within a moment, they had silently agreed on a course of action.

"Rick, I want to see you in my office tomorrow morning," she said.

"What about Arabic class?" I asked. I was delighted to be excused from language class, but suspicious about the exemption.

"You don't mind missing that, do you?" she asked.

I detected a trick question.

"Of course I mind. Language class is important to me."

"Is that why you've been late 15 out of 23 times?"

"You're keeping count?"

"That's why we're here."

"Where's your office?"

"My room," she said.

9
ATTITUDE ADJUSTMENT

Tasha closed the house door behind us. We turned into a dark, fragrant chamber ornamented with keepsakes. Light filtered through magenta curtains. A Tunisian tapestry draped her bed.

She lifted her sunglasses, revealing warm, brown eyes, and smiled.

"Welcome to my office," she said.

As Tasha opened her arms to present her cozy private quarters and personal effects, I could not avert my eyes from her person. Her lips formed a subtle curve. Her deeply tanned skin featured accents of copper and gold. On her cheek a black mole was embedded like onyx. Her chestnut hair was threaded with strands of henna red and fell below her shoulders.

However, I could not fully appreciate the privilege of beholding Tasha's beauty since the purpose of our meeting made me nervous. So did the fact that I had been unable to brush my teeth or use deodorant before dashing here. A patina of *café au lait*, mixed with baguette-and-butter grit, gave my mouth the taste and texture of breakfast cement. This lapse in personal hygiene increased my vulnerability. If a woman's weapons were physical grace, warm, fragrant skin, a soothing voice and magnetic eyes, how could I spar with so beautiful an adversary in the perfumed confines of her room, when I felt disgusting?

"Is something wrong?" Tasha asked as her lips parted seductively, displaying even, white teeth.

"It's nothing," I lied.

"You seem out of sorts."

"I haven't used the bathroom."

"Use mine."

Was permission to use the camp director's bathroom like a last meal or cigarette, a final rite before execution?

Tasha's towels were neatly folded and impressively fresh, given our primitive laundry set up. This increased her mystique. While I dried my face, I smiled at the thought that within an hour the same terry cloth might touch her hands, press her lips and eyelids. Was I leaving a trace she might later detect? If so, how would she respond to our indirect contact? I even used her toothbrush. My mouth tingled with taboo. Borrowing her toiletries was a casual transgression of intimacy and hygiene. It amused me to speculate how she would react to a stranger borrowing common drug-store items, which once purchased, became intimate extensions of her person. As I returned to her boudoir to resume the menacing discussion, I smirked about my violation of her toiletries. I believed sharing personal products put us on more equal footing.

"Feel better?" she asked.

"You have no idea," I replied, infused with confidence. In my immature and irrational mind, using the camp director's bathroom kit magically protected me against her power. My immaturity defended me, or so I thought. But with each breath of scented air and every moment that her brown eyes studied me, I lost my swagger. Her physical allure and lush environment pulled my masculine bravado down around my ankles and stripped me to my essence—a sex-deprived college graduate.

The exotic character of her room, which suggested the intimate gifts Tasha might share with the man she loved, roused me from my juvenile regressions. The creativity, tastes, desires and experiences of a vibrant woman not long removed from adolescence were in evidence—bric-a-brac, stuffed animals, museum posters, a comforter—like icons on the map of her psyche. Scarves swathed the wall like silk wallpaper and drifted over her bed like tatters of a canopy, torn away in a night of tumultuous lovemaking. Rope incense smoking in a mother-of-pearl ashtray suffused her sanctum sanctorum with jasmine and patchouli. Amid these personal artifacts and sensuous effects, Tasha sat on her bed, like a pearl in a shell, smoothing her thighs.

My agitation returned in force. Digestion and poor grooming

were only sideshows to a more significant psychosomatic event. My facial muscles tightened. My pulse accelerated. In the presence of this sensuous woman I was having an attack of *fitna*, male sexual hysteria—a condition so common in Tunisia that it had its own pre-psychoanalytic, non-clinical term. It gripped me like a taloned harpy. Concentration wavered, guts churned, composure fled. Soon my brain would be submerged in the spume of sexual desire and I would be incapable of decoding a word she said. This was the ultimate test of asceticism that converted all but saints to sinners. It was the dreaded Wall of Abstinence against which sex-starved men crashed and yearned.

Fargus or any well-balanced friend would have advised me to do multiplication tables, ponder Newtonian mechanics, or imagine a bad odor emanating from the desired woman. It was sensible, yet worthless advice. Resistance to raging *fitna* only intensified the passion.

"Do you know why you're here?" Tasha asked.

"I hoped you would tell me," I murmured, as I tried to stifle my inner turbulence. I discerned from her expression how serious this meeting was to her. I had to play my part with a clear mind. Was this going to be difficult—or impossible?

"You're playing games," Tasha replied, crossing her legs and tossing her hair behind her shoulders with a turn of her head, to reveal the shapely curve of her neck. A hormonal surge whipped my spine and made my body tingle, then shiver. Hot, furry sensations not caused by parasites burrowed in my loins and nuzzled my gonads.

"I'm not playing games," I stammered in low groaning voice.

"We're getting nowhere," Tasha replied irascibly. She crossed the room and reached in her straw bag for cigarettes. It was an innocuous act, but to a man racked by *fitna* it was torture.

"What do you want me to do?" I pleaded. "You remind me of a school psychologist, carving my head like a watermelon."

"A school psychologist carving a watermelon?" Tasha repeated slowly, apparently more perplexed by this bizarre utterance than offended by it. She doubted my sanity, which gave her a pretext for terminating me. I had to explain to save myself. The *fitna* flare up subsided. Self-defense was an antidote to sexual excitement.

"You make me nervous," I translated.

Tasha extracted two cigarettes from the soft pack, inserted one in her mouth and offered me the other. So *this* was the last cigarette before execution. Her eyes met mine. Their expression had changed. She studied me differently now, as if I were worth studying, and stood before me at museum-viewing distance—a fertility goddess commanding adoration, prostration, sacrifice—as I sat on her bed, tantalized and paralyzed by her allure. *Fitna* licked up again like a hot tongue.

No, it wasn't *fitna*!

What I experienced was no generalized sensation, but a specific and disturbing feeling I could not admit to myself. I was strongly attracted to Tasha and knew it was wrong for two reasons—Cerise was my girlfriend and Tasha was my boss. Her power over my life and emotions gave her twice the menace—and quadruple the magnetism. This could crush me if I did not fight it.

I blinked at her *bric-a-brac,* looked cross-eyed at my cigarette and tried to meditate my way out of her spell by chanting the mantras, *"Tasha is the boss"* and *"Tasha can terminate you,"* which merged into one—*"Tasha boss terminator."* I needed to overcome Tasha's sexuality, respect her authority and address my social behavior issues. But repeating the possibility I feared most, *termination,* could not save me, because sexual longing and desperation were familiar bedfellows.

Tasha noted my agitated mental state with perplexity. If she knew what was in my head, she would be shocked, offended, or playfully dismissive—the most brutal response. She might point out that my attraction to her was for me another bodily function, like using the toilet, which prevented me from taking the Peace Corps seriously.

I fought the irresistible impulse to tell her how she made me feel.

"*Hold it down!*" I growled at myself. "*Hold it down!*"

"*Murkey, I am not holding you down!*" Tasha replied. She had intercepted and distorted my internal communiqué. Now I had to make sense of it for her.

"Yes, you hold me down. I'm trying to experience something interesting and new. I'm a human being, not a machine!" I cried.

For so plausible a *non sequitur* to have emerged from my addled brain and dry mouth, random selection must have favored optimal design. Without intending to, I said precisely what I meant.

"I'm not asking you to be a machine, but you screw up consistently."

"Isn't consistency a good thing?"

"Not when you're *consistently* late for class. Not when you're *consistently* complaining. Your attitude has been *consistently* poor. You even missed my meeting last night. This is *not* a spa, Rick. You don't make your own schedule."

Now that she chided me for my behavior, she reverted to a role I could deal with, "female authority figure." My disabling attraction to her subsided.

"Rick, do you want to be here?"

"Yes," I admitted.

"You don't act that way. And you shouldn't be here unless you want to be," she said firmly, yet sympathetically. "I know what you were told about staying two years, but life is too short to suffer needlessly. You can do other things."

She seemed to be inside my head like a voice-over in a French movie, telling me what I was thinking, pushing me toward self-termination. Maybe she was right. But just when I was ready to confess what a fraud I was, I realized I wasn't one. I didn't want to go home. I was having fun despite my difficulties adjusting to camp life. I couldn't let her terminate me. I had to see Cerise.

"Tasha, you don't understand. I like being here. I just hate regimentation."

Her jaw was set. Her brown eyes had me pinned.

"You can't continue to play games. No more running on walls and falling off. You have to stop missing meetings and coming late to class. Is that clear?"

How earnest people can be when they tell you to be somebody other than yourself, as if it were even possible!

"*But this is the Peace Corps, not the Marine Corps!*" I insisted. "Don't you see, Tasha, I missed the cross-cultural meeting to do something *really cross-cultural*. Running on that wall, I had a taste of what I came here for. I was interacting with Tunisians and it felt great. I love this country and its culture. Isn't that the main idea? You can't terminate me. I may be poor Peace Corps material, but I have the Peace Corps spirit."

"That's fine," she said, apparently taken aback by my sudden fervor. "I like your enthusiasm. But you have to stop complaining."

"I criticize because I care and want things to improve for everyone. Besides, protest is great therapy and release."

"Have you tried meditating?" she smiled.

"Have I ever!" I said.

She laughed. Did she suspect what had been going through

my mind all this time, how hard I struggled with my *fitna*? She was probably as tired as I was. We had been digging with verbal shovels and found what we were looking for, that thing we had in common.

"Now go to class!"

"Before I go, can I use your bathroom?"

"Again?"

•

For several days, I avoided Tasha and withdrew emotionally from camp life, which paradoxically improved my conduct. I did what was required in a quiet, detached manner; for once, I was a good volunteer.

To repent my criminal trespass into the present, during which I betrayed Cerise with my crush on Tasha, I retreated into our past and worshipped at the altar of our first attractions. Love, I realized, was most easily understood and best remembered as *falling in love*, since "falling" marked the moment when everything changed.

For one month Cerise and I came together most afternoons for protracted foreplay. When I pulled down her panties, she grabbed my hand.

"Please! This is killing me," I said.

"I'm not protected," she whispered.

That was when I extracted from my wallet the red aluminum square with the first condom I ever bought. I had been saving it for the right occasion. She laughed.

"That's like taking a shower in a raincoat!"

How could I argue? She wanted sex with love, tenderness and

passion, not preparation.

It was the middle of November. It felt like winter on the New England campus. The pressure of final papers and exams and the imminent separation of the holidays loomed over the future like the first snows.

Cerise invited me to her birthday party, with a dozen other men, in the basement of a frat house. The long, sleeveless, black dress she wore showed off her shapely, muscled arms that had won several French convent school shot-putting championships. Her black hunting boots made a stunning contrast to the strand of white pearls around her neck. She stormed around the party like a good hostess, winking and rolling her eyes, making her guests feel witty and appreciated. I had a fever and wanted the party to end.

Besides, this was supposed to be *the* night.

At 4 AM Cerise was angry with me; she believed I had conspired to drive every other guest away with my fake coughs and dour expressions. I had not succeeded at cutting the party short, so I outlasted it.

Cerise and I climbed the stairs of her brick dormitory to the third floor. With every step, I moved my hand down her back to feel her contours under the black wool dress.

"You're just like my dog," she reproved me. "He jumps up women's skirts."

She fumbled with the key and I detected her familiar perfume.

"Where do you think you're going?" she asked.

"I have to be with you," I mumbled.

"Oh, you do! Well, you've picked a fine way to show it, trying to sabotage my party."

"I wasn't trying to spoil your party," I said. "I just wanted you all to myself."

She looked at me sternly, then crossed her eyes and laughed.

"Come on then."

She removed her dress quickly, methodically without turning, as if there were a wall between us, unsnapped her bra and stretched, then ran to the bed because she was cold. She seemed intent on making the moment seem ordinary. Or to make me feel it was not so important to her.

But when she slid between the cold sheets and I touched her, I was not prepared for the warmth and softness of her skin. She held me tightly and my fever broke. Afterward, I was never the same.

10

ORACLE

I was on the porch. The dog-and-child-beater next door stood in front of his walled compound watching his son approach from the direction of the well, balancing two buckets of water in his small hands. When the boy stumbled, a little water spilled from a bucket. Perhaps panicking at his miniscule mistake, he lost his balance and fell to his knees. Miraculously, the buckets landed upright and only a little water escaped.

Without crying or so much as wiping the dust off his clothes, the child sprang to his feet, lifted the buckets with his spindly arms and dragged himself faster toward his father, hoping that his diligence and hustle would erase the memory of his misstep. When the boy set down the pails, his father cuffed him across the head. Like a cat, the child anticipated the blow and dodged it, tumbling in the dust. When the dog howled, the dog-and-child beater delivered a swift, violent kick to his bloated, worm-infested guts.

"Hey, Rick, got any spare change?"

Not again. Jann, the bearded supervisor who slept above me, was cadging for coins, as he always did, to play the *I Ching*—an Eastern system he consulted daily to answer questions and make decisions. Jann advised new volunteers while he muddled through his own problems. One of Jann's hang-ups, though he didn't see it as such, was his obsession with the *I Ching*. A man who put his faith in a ritual of flipping coins and interpreting lines on paper prompted my curiosity, but as a counselor Jann did not inspire confidence. His shifting blue eyes and air of detachment made him a perfect spy. Other than when he performed his duties, he was often sitting lotus-style in his bunk.

"Most people misunderstand the *I Ching*," Jann said. "It's not Tarot, or a Ouija board. It's a tool. I provide the questions *and* answers. The *I Ching* just helps."

"So you spend half your life determining how to spend the other half? You'd save time by improvising," I suggested.

"It's about the truth of the present and the possibilities of the future," Jann replied. "Instead of taking the advice of a stranger, I let lines and coins advise me."

Jann aggravated me. His reliance on an apparently random method to solve personal dilemmas forced me to confront my own bewilderment. When I was in school, people warned me about the real world. I feared life as a destructive force out there, harsh and unpredictable. Yet I optimistically assumed that the future would follow my design. I was an exclamation point. But as I moved through college and left the protective shadow of my heroes to compete with peers who stood in line in front of me for the prizes of fame, respect and money, doubts afflicted me. I became a question mark.

I put my pen to the letter paper to write, while my other hand shielded what I wrote from Jann's prying eyes.

"Writing to your mommy?" he taunted.

"My girlfriend," I replied.

"Your high school sweetheart? The only girl you ever loved?"

"She's 27. And she's French."

"*Oo là là!* An older woman! Well! There's more to you than I thought! But hey! Girlfriend, mother, wife—what's the difference? After three years of marriage I know that much."

"That's your problem," I countered. It was no secret that Jann was working at the camp to escape his wife. They had come to Tunisia the previous year in the notorious "couples experiment." Of 23 couples, only Jann and his wife remained—the others separated, terminated and divorced. Jann and his wife also separated, but they were determined to serve out their two years.

"You're right, Rick. And I'm working on it," Jann replied. "There's nothing wrong with my wife—she's great. It's our marriage that sucks. I'm tired of needing someone to make me happy. I have to make myself happy."

The dog rubbed his belly in the dust. The dog-and-child-beater was shouting behind the wall of his compound. A soda bottle fell off the wall and shattered.

"That man's not happy," Jann said.

"No." I stared at my letter, unable to focus during Jann's dark musings. Why didn't he go somewhere and meditate? Failed relationships and spent passion were not high on my hit parade.

"Are you happy, Rick?" he asked.

"Yes," I lied.

Jann's merry eyes probed. He chuckled.

"A word to the wise. I've seen you with Tasha. Clearly, you like her."

"She's all right. What are you getting at?" I seethed.

"Tasha is attractive. In your case, a younger older woman. She's 24."

Jann had inserted the screws in my head and was about to twist. I had been careless to mention Cerise.

"Watch out for Tasha. Don't take her smiles seriously or let her seductive charms go to your head."

His smile suggested that my red face betrayed me.

"Tasha will chew you up and spit you out," he said, curling his forefinger in a "come hither" sign and flicking it with his thumb like a spitball. The gesture was repulsive yet effective in the bitterness it suggested—or the truth it told—but what made it worse was the speed with which it flew into my head and changed my attitude toward Tasha, without her saying or doing anything.

"Thanks for the tip," I said sarcastically. "It sounds like you've had experience."

"You could say that," he said. "Now, what about the coins?"

•

Mon Cheri (A.K.A. Sweetipoop),

I've heard nothing from you for a week. Are you okay? I went to Marie and Rene's wedding. It was what one would have expected. I had my hair done for the occasion and they gave me this atrocious flip. I was nearly in tears, but what could I do? I spent the whole next day rinsing it out. That's what they do to you when you're not a steady customer. These hairdressers secretly despise us and deliberately make us look ridiculous.

Anyway, I looked good enough to be seen by the time of the wedding, thanks to the great tan I got on my parents' farm. The traffic has increased around the house since I've been lying topless in the backyard. I noticed the baker going around that way, which he never did before. Have you kept the picture I sent you, the one that you claim still turns you on?

The wedding was a smashing success: great weather, floods of champagne, loads of bare boobs and shoulders at night. The ceremony took place in a Norman church in a village nearby (Clement's funeral was there, do you remember how horrid you were?) and the party was outdoors in the town square. I enjoyed wearing my "disguise," which earned me the nickname "Calamity Jane." (Will send photos.) However, the costume had the disastrous effect of kindling Gaspard Grognon's—I don't know what to call it!

Fortunately, the crowd was big enough to lose poor Gaspard, but when I returned to my car at 5 AM, there was a love note from him under the windshield wiper.

Meanwhile, Odille Grognon was as emaciated, uptight and miserable as ever. She has finally realized the gravity of her husband's illness and does not know how to cope. She once told me that she could not possibly be jealous of me, but I suspect that she has changed her tune. Odille's problem seems to be that she does not enjoy extra-marital sex as much as Gaspard does, although where he gets it besides a whorehouse is a mystery.

A report on my sex appeal should not require more than one source, but Gaspard Grognon was not the only one under my improbable spell. Another guy would not stop coming on to me. He insisted that we dance. I told him I didn't know how, but this did not deter him. We slow-danced and he got a hard-on. Mon dieu! By six, the party was winding down. I returned to the car and he sprang from the bushes, pleading with me to go home with him. I said that would not be necessary. He made a scene...

I wonder about us, my butterfly. What does the future hold in store for us? My friends don't understand what I'm doing with you and I wonder, myself. You seem so lost. Can this last?

Sometimes I think the one thing you are sure of is my love for you, which makes me feel guilty and sad. At times I think I love you more for the love you give me than for who you are.

Certainly you've made me feel like a woman and for this I'll always be grateful. But is that what love should be? I don't know.

Do you still want me to come to Tunisia? I can book it for some time in August. How's the weather? I've heard the heat is intense. You must tell me your plans ASAP because if you can't see me I can go to England with a French summer camp.

I kiss you tenderly.

Cerise.

Cerise's angry letters typically made me sad and defensive. I would perform verbal gymnastics to mollify her. But when she was in an ebullient mood, as in the letter I just read, I was devastated. Her nagging and insults hurt, but jealousy was her most effective weapon, wounding my pride and wrecking what little security I had. Worse, jealousy was hard for me to honestly express. It always came out as anger, which was the wrong way to respond to this letter. If I fired off a furious comeback to her account of a wedding where two men wanted to ravish her, my jealousy would be pitifully obvious and Cerise would have the validation she wanted. Instead, I wrote a letter addressing her previous one, in which she lambasted me for not arranging her visit.

Cerise,

The mail is slow and you blame me. I'm in the Peace Corps and you blame me. I came to North Africa to be closer to you and you think I'm ridiculous. You imply that I'm poisoning you, but you're thriving and working toward your goals. What have I done wrong?

The first time we separated was torture. All that kept me going was the prospect of seeing you again. You said I'd forget you and the prediction tortured me. Had I sworn my love for nothing?

Our relationship might have been no more than a fluke, but I believed that if we reunited across all that divided us, we would turn a coincidental romance into something real and permanent.

I worked so hard to be with you in Bidonville. But once I arrived, you menstruated for weeks; your doctor said no sex for two months and you complied. Your snide friend asked if I was your au pair boy and you didn't deny it. You complained that I made a mess, distracted you from your work, stole, lied and clogged your toilet. I was your scapegoat and only when another woman showed interest in me did you give me some affection.

You left me in Paris fauché and foutu so you could be a camp counselor. Did you ever go out of your way for me? Now you expect me—and the Peace Corps—to jump so that you can choose between Tunisia and England. Make up your mind. I've run out of arguments. They don't work with you.

Rick

I was satisfied when I sealed this letter that she would be confused and on the defensive. For a moment I smiled at the blow I was striking and forgot how close I was to losing the fight.

11

REEF MADNESS

Classes were canceled on the fifth Saturday of training camp. Our first day off was no gift of compassion or reward for work well done. There were too few students well enough to attend. Thirty-five volunteers, more than half the camp, lay violently ill and quarantined in three houses with shutters drawn. Vultures, on the scent of sick flesh, stood sentry from the rooftops of our compound and soared in slow looping ovals overhead. Their broad wings cast flickering shadows and their crescent beaks deflected sunlight like knives.

Healthy volunteers displaced from their houses, which were converted to makeshift infirmaries, found sanctuary among us. They slept in our dining room on cots, which our landlord, Bechir, rented to the Peace Corps at a significant profit. The influx of new housemates and the absence of our fallen peers reminded us of the microscopic enemy in the grains of *couscous* on our plates, in our *cafe au lait* and in the orange marmalade.

The temporary refugees provided updated infirmary reports in grotesque detail. They described the delirious victims who now occupied their beds, how they were burned with fevers as high as 106 degrees, puked sips of water and stared out at the world with red, glassy eyes, unable to recognize even their closest friends. Dehydration was the greatest risk to their survival. It was said that their lips shriveled to the dark red tint of dried blood and curled like dry hot peppers.

At first, our counselors downplayed the epidemic to boost our morale.

"A little diarrhea never hurt anyone," Rodney assured us.

"We've all had it. It's a Peace Corps rite of passage," Tasha added.

"I read somewhere that it's actually good for you," Stuart adduced. "It's the original colon cleanser."

"Hell, yeah," Rodney added. "Hollywood types pay big bucks to purge. We get to do it for free."

Despite these fun facts, the healthy volunteers were not eager to join their sick comrades. As the epidemic spread, the healthy rarely mentioned the sick, believing superstitiously that the pathogen traveled by words as well as by air, food and water. It was considered bad luck or bad form to dwell on illness, especially at meals, when squeamish diners were likely to blanch and lose their appetites at the thought of their stricken peers. Counselors, in particular, regarded the mention of afflicted volunteers as a breach of positive attitude, which they punished with cautionary looks and veiled threats of bad write-ups and dreadful teaching assignments in forbidding backwaters.

"Be thankful for your health and consider yourselves lucky," they admonished us. We heeded them. The grim prospect of becoming another victim of the scourge made the training camp grind seem more bearable, even pleasant. We worked harder at our tasks if only to reassure ourselves that we were fit.

Our counselors shirked responsibility for the plague. They claimed that it was a normal outbreak of "Bourguiba's Revenge," a sobriquet for traveller's diarrhea that trivialized the disease, but offered no insight into its pathology. They insisted that the outbreak was beyond anyone's control, prevention or cure. Rather than improve the quality and freshness of the food, they offered "helpful hints" on staying healthy.

"Steer clear of fresh, hot bread and fig skins," they cautioned.

When the infection claimed a new casualty from our tables, we asked ourselves if the latest victim had succumbed to the forbidden temptation of hot bread or indulged an inexplicable passion for fig skins. We recognized that such caveats were placebos only.

Courage is called "guts" for good reason: the belly always takes risks. The contagion failed to slacken the alacrity with which we devoured our food. We ate like we worked—our hunger increased in proportion to the threat.

Meanwhile, the disease drew an arbitrary line between the fit and the fallen, which inevitably assumed a moral dimension. For reassurance, those who remained intestinally strong convinced themselves that they were doing "something right," while those who were stricken must have done "something wrong." This was our sole defense, a mélange of positive suggestion and superstition, according to which disease was the physical expression of a failure of will, whereas good health was a sign of righteousness.

To buttress these primitive beliefs, healthy volunteers cultivated odd eating rites. Deliberately, we defied the rules, consuming hot peppers, devouring figs and chewing their skins before spitting them out, to substantiate our invulnerability or to build resistance. We used these perilous provisions as amulets against the evil power of disease. Yet, despite our quirky antidotes, which included smearing *harissa* (hot pepper paste) on our tongues, the disease cut down a new victim each day.

One person in the camp took a more sensible approach to warding off the disease. Raotha, a beautiful Arabic teacher, who had recently taken over my class from Salah, ate lunch in our dining room now, since her house had become a sickbay. With her full, sensuous lips, light brown almond eyes, and a scar on her cheek, Raotha was hard not to look at across the table. I noticed that she ate only bread. For a while, I was reluctant to break the student-teacher social barrier, but I was eventually too curious not to ask her about her austere fare.

"I eat only *hobzeh* because it is very good," she said to reinforce my Arabic vocabulary. "*Wullah*, I have not tasted such delicious *hobzeh* anywhere else in Tunisia."

"But aren't you hungry?" I asked, as I shoveled a large spoonful of couscous in my mouth.

Raotha flashed a smile now that might have glowed in the dark, like that of a fierce and happy cat.

"No. This is all I need. You know I am not a big girl," she replied. "I must watch what I eat or I won't fit through doors—or find a husband."

She winked, the rest of us laughed, and for a moment we forgot our health fears.

Like Raotha, we suspected more plausible reasons for the plague, but we could not voice them, since the counselors addressed our speculations now with threats of early termination. The Peace Corps, they reminded us, was "love-it-or-leave-it." We could not prove our theory that the epidemic was due to tainted food, but it did not require proof: we were immunized against everything but food poisoning.

•

As soon as we heard about the day off, Fargus said, "I hate hospitals. Let's hit the beach." So we hopped on the first bus to Tabarka.

It was packed with humanity until flesh bulged out the doors and windows. The odor of garlic, spices, oil, cooked and spoiling foods, sweat from unwashed bodies and unlaundered clothes overpowered the nose and stifled the air. The motor sounded tortured and uncertain. A large, wailing woman with a stuffed plastic basket pushed her way on to the lowest step, preventing the front door from closing. The driver cursed and swore that the bus would not move until she got off, as the woman pleaded to board.

"Let's get off," I nudged Fargus. "We're not moving."

"We've got seats, are you crazy?" he said.

"We can make a difference by getting off," I urged. "The bus will move if we get off."

"Stop trying to be a hero," he insisted. "It's ridiculous. Why should we get off the bus? We're not taking up more room than anybody else."

Fargus was right. My judgment was impaired by guilt, because I enjoyed good health near so much suffering and pain. I was also not mature enough to take futility in stride, so I indulged a Peace Corps impulse to sacrifice myself for a woman and her basket.

As the bus stopped and lurched over the pass, I wondered when the GI epidemic would claim me. At that moment, I was probably incubating microbes. It was exasperating that nothing was being done to prevent or contain the contagion and that our food might be the source. Fargus and I argued *ad nauseum*. He believed our supervisors' claim that training camp food was no worse than any institutional fare and pointed out that we had no proof to the contrary. I maintained that if volunteers united, we might improve our lot. He dismissed this with his defeatist mantra, "What good would it do?"

"Just be grateful that you're not the one puking and defecating all day," he said. "Or like Dan, with his oozing arm."

Dan was another recent college graduate. A cowlick sprouted from the top of his blond head. It made him resemble a large all-American six-year-old. Black-framed glasses, a pale complexion and a perpetual grin dared you not to like him. As a child, he was cast as *Dennis the Menace* in a movie version of the '60s TV show that was never released.

But that didn't stop Dan from becoming a training camp star. When his arm swelled to three times its normal size, transforming it into a red, scaly club oozing clear, sticky pus, our supervisors exploited his spectacular staph infection to divert us from the gastrointestinal epidemic. Eventually, Dan's staph-infected limb was too heavy for him to carry akimbo, so a special sling was rigged to cradle it like a hammock.

The counselors turned staph-infected Dan into a mascot. He was one of us, but everywhere he went, he seemed to be making a public appearance. He smiled beatifically, as if he were overjoyed about his bulbous appendage. He believed he was a huge success. Dan even invited people to sign his sling.

"How's the arm, Dan?" volunteers routinely asked.

"Just fine," Dan replied, as he beamed tenderly at the suppurating wing swaddled in gauze, like a proud dad gloating over his sleeping babe.

"Dan's a dork," I told Fargus and the busload of Tunisians who did not know Dan. "His staph infection isn't a disease. It's a conversation piece!"

"That's your envy talking, man," Fargus chided. This exasperated me because he was right—I *was* envious. Dan wasn't smart or talented. He didn't earn that staph infection. He was just lucky. I wanted people to notice *me*, to admire *me*, to ask me how *I* was feeling, but I didn't have the right stuff, or in this case, the right *pus*. Who could have predicted that an infected arm could make you a star?

The bus chugged and grunted through the mountain pass at five miles per hour, perfect sight-seeing speed. We passed the village of *Relache les Chiens*, famous for its annual festival, during which domestic dogs were released into the forest to reunite with their wild canine relations. The festival was the Tunisian canine equivalent of "spring break" in Florida. This enlightened custom acknowledged the feral origins of all domesticated pets. The occupants of *Relache les Chiens* clearly appreciated that their pets had lives, affiliations and family ties independent of their masters.

But Ali, a Tunisian neighbor in Ayn Draham with whom I'd become friendly, claimed that the running of the dogs at times had tragic consequences. The previous year, his cousin, napping in a glade, was torn to bits by a pack of reveling dogs and was ordained a local saint.

•

When the large, wailing woman with a plastic basket, who had forced her way on the bus, deboarded on a switchback, she upset the intricate weight distribution that apparently kept the engine running. The bus broke down.

Fargus and I tried to hitch a ride, but only one car passed us, a gold Mercedes with German plates. We were so shocked to see a luxury car that we turned, but the Mercedes kept going and our astonishment earned us no more than a sheet of dust on our clothes and faces. A rescue bus finally came from Tabarka to take us the rest of the way.

At the beach, we hiked to the north end of the crescent shoreline, where white sand gave way to large rocks. To climb onto the rocks we crossed a pile of old lumber and sea deposits, a mound inhabited by every vile predator of the night—spiders, crabs, snakes and rats all made their homes within the shifting timber.

We laid out towels on a flat boulder. In the distance, two fishermen lowered themselves from a boat. Their mates lifted a metal bucket of fish and eased it onto the lapping waves between the fishermen's submersed shoulders. With only their faces visible, the two men bobbed toward the shore guiding their catch between them. I turned to show Fargus this novel transport, but he was splayed and dozing on his back like a mutant of the reef deposited by the tide. I peered down from the edge of the rock at the water below. The reef's vibrant colors shimmered in the heave and suck of the currents. A skein of milky, pink coral was wedged among the urchins, conch and venomous, flexing sponges.

The coral here was highly prized. It could be seen everywhere, dangling from gold and silver chains as sinuous hot pepper pendants, amulets to ward off the ubiquitous evil eye. This was not the best spot to hunt for the stone; hydras waved their poisonous tentacles in false friendliness. Touch one and it would sear your extremity like a hot iron.

The two fishermen walking in the surf with their bucket of fish were now visible down to their knees some 50 feet out. They seemed to levitate on the smooth blue water, until the sea swallowed them up to their necks when they stepped off a sandbar.

"*Fanta! Gini! Boga! Coka!*"

A small boy lugged a metal bucket of soft drinks toward the pilings. His high-pitched cry mingled with birdcalls and the remote murmur of sunbathers, and had the plaintive timbre of a religious chant.

Fishermen's shouts, the pale shimmer of the sea, the boy hawking soft drinks and Fargus on the rock, like a starfish with one blunted point—his head, combined in a hypnotic and harmonious scene both random and ornate. For once since joining the Peace Corps, I had the urge to hold a moment in a bowl of words.

I opened my notebook to the last entry and read it curiously.

Is it possible to be detached in a situation where you are vitally concerned? Inevitably, you fall back on who you are, what you think, your values, habits—even more so when you are not alone.

Among others, you are more conscious of being yourself than when you are solitary and taking yourself for granted.

If you try to be less resistant to "the other" you don't become the other. Your self becomes quieter and more pliant.

I could not recall when I wrote this passage, but it sounded like a relic from my last college semester, when I was always with the same friends and our egos were our most prized possessions. As the last entry in my notebook, it appeared to represent my most recent thinking. It was as if my body came to Tunisia, but my brain stayed behind, or played catch-up with all that was chaotic and new.

I had been in Tunisia for seven weeks, but only truly arrived that moment. I started to write my first Tunisian notebook entry.

I came to this place to live in reality, to know colors and smells, the way things are and not how they appear in daydreams, TV and magazines.

Fantasy seems to offer freedom, but it is a prison whose walls and bars are lies. Fantasy weakens the spirit with distortions. Living in reality provides the only freedom because it allows you to experience life directly and to evaluate it fairly.

Communication depends not on language alone, but on shared experience. Each sign and gesture represents a different time, place and occurrence. To understand a message you have to know its origin. Words alone won't take you as far.

My hand cramped. I stretched out on the rock, satisfied that my mind still worked after a long hiatus. From behind a triangular boulder came a shower of bright sounds, the laughter of a woman. Livia, the volunteer from New York, whose self-imposed uniform in camp comprised a Cub Scout shirt and cap, lifted herself with long, graceful arms onto a nearby rock. She remained steady on the edge before swinging her legs around. Her lean torso streamed water; her breasts molded her soaked tank top to their shapely abundance. She wore a diving mask and a nose-clip and burst from the reef like a mythical creature—part woman, part prehistoric bird—seeking her own myth to be told.

Yet stripped down to real terms, Livia was an experienced narcissist whose nonchalance made her more irresistible.

Still I resisted. I could not cope with more sexual arousal. Cerise punished my love and Tasha flagellated my lust. Did I need one more pinup in my head to fan my overheated libido?

"Not today, Livia," I thought and turned away. But for every man who rejects erotic ogling, another takes his place.

Fargus, aroused after his solar siesta, eagerly fed Livia's ego with his eyes, and she compliantly filled his imagination with her body. They clasped one another in a symbiotic embrace—voyeur and *femme fatale*.

Livia stretched on the rock with legs together and feet arched. Rodney, the procurement supervisor with the deformed hand, hoisted himself onto Livia's rock and started talking to her. *The Procurer*, as some called him, brought Livia here in his official car: the same vehicle in which he transported suspect food for our meals. While he enjoyed the company of the most sensuous woman in camp, 35 volunteers were puking ice chips in dark rooms after eating bad food he bought dirt-cheap.

While Rodney mumbled endearments to Livia, she lay impassively still, as nonchalant to her suitor as she was to our proximity. Rodney glanced at us with an embarrassed smile, put on a nose clip and snorkel, and plunked into the water.

"Can you believe it?" I asked.

"What?" Fargus asked, still enthralled with the sleeping beauty on the next rock.

"She's dating the mass-poisoner because he can bring her here in the comfort of the Peace Corps car."

Fargus shrugged as he admired her glistening physique soaking up the light. "Why do you care?" he asked. It was a valid question. Was I jealous of an attractive woman, whom I barely knew?

"It's a form of corruption," I said. "I'm expressing righteous indignation."

"And I respect you for it," he replied. "Now do me a solid and go for a swim."

"The water's cold."

"It's invigorating."

"There are poisonous animals. I might step on something."

"Tread water."

"Why is it important?"

"Do I have to spell it out? I want to jerk off."

"Can't you wait?"

Fargus shook his head sadly. "I have no imagination. I need the visuals."

Livia didn't hear or didn't care; in either case, she didn't move. To accommodate Fargus, I slid from the rock into the water and did the dead man's float to observe intricate reef creatures expand, deflate and sway in the tidal pool. Diminutive crabs pricked my cheek; a golden star-fish with black tips flexed under the surface and nearly entered the grotto of my mouth. On the rock, Fargus might be dripping sperm on the sea floor like a fish trying to perpetuate his genetic product. Humans could live on land unlike our aquatic ancestors, but in other respects we had not evolved far beyond them.

After what seemed an adequate amount of time for Fargus to consummate with himself, I climbed back on the rock. The boy with the pail of sodas stopped nearby and hailed us with his familiar line: *"Gini! Fanta! Coka!"*

I shook my head, *"Leh!"*

The boy stared balefully, hands on hips, dismayed that anyone would refuse his offerings. Then he turned and glimpsed Livia lying supine on her rock and he stood silent and transfixed. When he emerged from her spell, he hurried away.

The sky had darkened when Fargus and I headed back toward the beach. As we left our rock for higher ground, we noticed that the soda boy had brought with him several of his friends. They all gaped at Livia in silent amazement, as she stretched her arms and folded towels in her damp tank top and cutoffs. When Rodney noticed the little spectators and glared at them, they scattered.

Suddenly, as we walked along the beach, *à propos* of nothing, but perhaps a case of post-masturbation blues, Fargus asked, "Do you think she loved me?"

"Who?"

"This woman I knew in college. She came to my room stark naked under a white fur coat and sat on my typewriter."

I knew how much Fargus wanted the answer, so I took a moment to consider.

"Maybe. Probably."

Exasperation contorted Fargus's round, freckled face.

"Damn it, that's what I thought. I had my head up my ass. All I could think of was finishing the damn term paper. What a dickwad I was!"

Fargus lapsed into plaintive silence, as he attempted to imagine the missed opportunity under fur.

"I apologized, believe me, but she never forgave me for choosing a term paper over her. She told everybody I was gay and they believed her."

We came to pilings of old lumber dividing rocks and sand. As we climbed, a plank slipped down the side and a rat sprang off my foot. In the midst of the wood and debris, nocturnal predators— rodents, spiders and crustaceans—could be heard stirring. I proceeded carefully on all fours, trying not to slip through the cracks, or bring down an avalanche of lumber.

"What did you get on the paper?" I asked. For some reason, I thought recalling the grade would make him feel better. At least it would divert him from agonizing over missed sex.

"I don't know. I think it was an A-," he said.

"So it was worth it."

"That's what I always got! Damn. What a ridiculous school! College was such a waste of time and money."

While Fargus expounded on the pros and cons of sleeping with a woman in his past and the value of higher education, a plank gave way under my right foot. When I tried to right myself, my ankle smacked against another board and I tumbled head first down the other side of the mound. Splinters dug into my hands and ankles as I scrambled from the heap. When my foot touched the sand, I felt an immediate slicing pain in the heel, like an incision of claws or small teeth. I buried the heel in the wet sand.

"What is it?" Fargus asked.

"Nothing. A splinter or crab claws."

"I'd have somebody look at that."

"It's nothing," I insisted.

"It's your life," Fargus shrugged. For once, I was glad of his indifference.

Most people would not have borne this injury in silence. In my mind, it was a coin flip, and I could second-guess either decision. Was I sure the foot wound was "nothing?" No. But I already had three rabies prevention shots and a tetanus vaccine. I also had a history of injury denial. Since childhood, I had walked around at various times with a broken nose, a fractured arm, a deep knee gash and an assortment of sprains and pulls without seeking medical treatment—and with no long-term effects. I had no reason to believe this situation was different. The wound was puffy and tender and had two puncture marks. It was no doubt a splinter or the work of a crab. I wasn't about to take 23 rabies shots in the gut and lose whatever chance I had of seeing Cerise on the remote possibility that the injury would end my life.

12

HOLD THE APPLE PIE

With disease and uncertainty rampant in the camp, the present was no safe place for the mind to dwell. Friendships were put on hold. My sense of community and security were challenged. I lay awake at night worrying what would happen next, and found comfort and refuge in the past. I reflected on my last times with family and friends before coming here.

I thought about my mother. She had always had great hopes for me, which she believed I was wasting.

I reconstructed the last conversation we had before my departure. I stood near the door of her room. It was dark except for the bluish light from the TV whose price tag still dangled from the on/off switch. She had not removed it to keep the set looking new and it would stay there until the picture tube blew.

It was 9:30 PM. She was already curled up in bed, watching a syndicated talk show, her usual sedative. I wanted to show her the new, beige polyester suit I bought with my graduation money. Worn with tan clogs, the embroidered jacket with wide lapels and permapressed pants would set the mark for Peace Corps chic.

"Opening a taco stand?" my mother asked as she erupted in

cackling laughter so intense that her body shook uncontrollably. Tears streamed down her face.

"The price tag is dangling from your arm," she said when she caught her breath. "Is that the latest trend?"

Another discharge of her boisterous laughter rolled over the air conditioner's hum and wracked her frail physique. Like her fits of rage, my mother's mirth was an avalanche that buried everything, including whatever prompted it.

When her laughter had subsided and she wiped the tears from her eyes, she bemoaned that she would be awake all night and her eyes would feel like hot coals in the morning.

"I didn't mean to disturb you, Mom. I'll let you be."

"You're too late, dummy. You already woke me up."

"I'm sorry," I said.

"It's okay, you won't be here much longer."

She clutched her foam pillow to her face as if she had a toothache.

"You're a good boy, Rick, but you're a pain," she said.

Buoyed by this semi-compliment, I said, "You won't be up all night, Mom. I'll be as boring as possible to help you fall sleep."

"You don't have to try hard," she replied and again laughed hysterically. I was the best floor act for my mother. All I had to do was stand there.

I wasn't in my mother's room at 9:30, on a Thursday night because we were especially close. We spent little time together and rarely talked about things that mattered. Even so, I was going far away for a long time and we didn't know if we'd see each other again.

She lay on her back with her hands behind her head and stared at the ceiling.

"Are you looking forward to going?" she asked.

"Yes."

"Rick, do you know what you're getting into?"

"Sure, I do."

"No you don't," she sighed. "Just keep a low profile."

"I will," I promised.

She chuckled, then stared at me and shook her head. "You have no clue what I'm talking about. Your idea of a low profile is the side of a midget's head."

When I asked her to explain, she shrugged. "What's the good of talking?"

"Tell me!" I pleaded.

She peered through the darkness. "When I look at you now, I wonder—what happened?"

Something brushed my hand. I started, believing it was an insect. It was the price tag on the television set, blowing in the air conditioning current.

"*What happened*?" I stammered. "I don't understand."

"I expected so much from you, Rick. It was my mistake. I realize that now. But you were such a bright, little boy, so precocious, so perceptive, so wise—beyond your years."

"And now?" I asked, dreading what she would say. "I'm not *dead*, Mom."

She was silent, as if evaluating this proposition.

"I know. You're not dead. It's just that—I don't know," she sighed, rummaging in her head for the right words. "Peace Corps. Tunisia. A French girlfriend. *What happened*?"

I needed to convince her that I was no failure. There was hope for me. I was energetic and ambitious, and would ultimately succeed. But I knew I couldn't erase her disappointment. I was 21 and she expected a finished product. Since I was no more than a 6'4" embryo, she thought I was just "finished."

As I closed the door, her voice stopped me. "Rick, you know I'm behind you, no matter what you do."

The adrenaline surged, my throat tightened. "Thanks Mom."

"Don't be concerned with material things," she continued. "Keep your health and be true to your ideals. And whatever you do, pay no attention to what other people say. Take their advice with a grain of salt. And never envy them."

With each morsel of wisdom she dispensed, she tried to make me stronger.

"I don't expect you to return for several years," she concluded calmly. "You'll want to see the world and experience life."

"How do you know that?" I asked, stunned by her nonchalance at my imminent and extended leave.

"I changed your diapers, didn't I?"

I could barely hold back tears at this bond that went deeper than memory. Was this what was meant by "American as Mom and apple pie?" She was either the most selfless mother to accept my departure with such equanimity, or happy and relieved to see me go. Unsure which motivation was correct and unwilling to find out, I closed the door quietly between my mother's dreams and my own.

13

HEDGEHOG HERO

For the next few weeks I was the consummate volunteer. I attended classes on time and did nothing to attract the wrong kind of attention.

No, not entirely true.

I cut my hair compulsively in every spare moment. My head never looked right, because it didn't feel right. I had become so immersed in the volunteer routine that my life no longer seemed to be my own, so I obsessed over one thing I could control—my hair. When I cut it, I was the boss.

Acting out autonomy issues on my hair was safe and efficient since follicles could not fight back. The downside was that I had a finite supply.

My private compulsion did not play out in a vacuum. It had an effect on others. Volunteers noticed my ever-shortening mane and thought they also needed haircuts. As I snipped closer to the scalp, my bristles gave a weather report of the anguish many of my peers were experiencing but could not openly express.

I could not sleep. My eyes burned in their sockets but would not close. My mind raced incessantly. The need to live, to do that thing within me that must be done, gave me no peace. I snipped my hair relentlessly, putting my eyes so close to the mirror that all I saw were webs of blood, like window cracks, as I perfected the spiky hedge around my scalp.

"Cutting your hair again!" Moncef, my Tunisian housemate, exclaimed, as he banged on the bathroom door. "You look like a hedgehog."

"I'll be out in a minute." I continued to snip.

"Get some sleep, *Hooyah!*" the Arabic teacher brayed, as he banged on the door. "Nightmares are for sleep, my brother."

"Another Tunisian proverb?" I taunted the man from Sfax.

"*Bara na'ik,*" Tunisian high school teacher countered. "That means '*Fuck yourself!*' in case you need a translation."

I was feeling out of sorts, but I didn't suffer at all times. Whatever my body was going through caused intense mood swings, and I was susceptible to moments of improbable elation.

One afternoon, Jamal, the burly academic director, who

taught physical education in Tunis, approached me during a break between classes. He said he heard that I had played soccer with local boys in the stadium.

I paused before responding. Besides getting me into trouble with Tasha, had my recent stadium misadventure caused an international incident? My refusal to play the goalposts for the peewee soccer players might have prompted a local backlash against the American training camp.

"I kicked a soccer ball with a few kids for a short while," I admitted. "It was no big deal."

I omitted the rock throwing and my tumble from the rampart wall.

"*Au contraire*, Rick. It was very important. I have heard so many stories in town about the tall *Franceoui* who played the goal posts. *Haricot vert*, they call you. It is your sobriquet. It means *Stringbean*."

"Stringbean? I like that. It was nothing, really."

"Do not be so modest. It is highly significant," the former Tunisian handball champion replied. "Sport transcends national borders. It is the global language of fellowship. By sharing it, you made friends between your people and ours. *Behi yessir*."

I had been listless and unhappy that day. Jamal's praise raised my spirits. He had once told me at lunch that I was good looking, but I brushed it off. This compliment opened for me a new possibility—I could contribute to the world through sports and community activities.

My chance to explore this new outlet came in the annual training camp softball game. It had been postponed because so many volunteers were incapacitated by the gastrointestinal disease that ravaged the camp. But gradually the plague abated, people regained their health and the camp was vibrant again. The softball game became more than a midsummer cliché. It celebrated the camp revival.

When I stepped to the plate, I felt people watching. They wanted me to do something special. I was over-anxious and swung hard at a pitch almost head-high. Strike one. Then I fouled off a low pitch, outside. The next pitch I waited on and hit on the sweet spot of the bat. The ball flew far and high—just foul of the right field line. The crowd's cheers turned to groans.

I took a good swing at the next pitch and ripped a hard line drive in the gap between left and center fields. It had a low trajectory and skittered on the dirt field all the way to the wall. No other athletic feat is as exhilarating as a homerun. In football, you need others to help you score. In basketball, the scoring is too prolific for one basket to stand out. But a homerun is the work of one person. It is a momentous hero-maker. Everyone cheered me, even on the other team. I was deliriously happy. I knew I would hear those cheers until the moment I died.

Physically and emotionally off since my heel injury a few weeks before, I started to take risks, not due to courage but indifference to consequences.

My brashness took an unexpected political direction. The afternoon classes had gone from brutal to unbearable. The extreme heat and sleep deprivation made it sheer torture just to keep our heads up in the drone of language repetition. On our way to afternoon classes and during breaks, we grumbled about how tired and oppressed we felt. Did we sign up to be treated like machines? Weren't we all spiritual castaways, a cadre of American idealists and individuals who joined the Peace Corps because we cherished freedom and could not get enough of it in America?

Over the course of several evenings, we planned a protest. It would take place during the break at around 4 PM. I would go down to the *lycée* courtyard and lead the student boycott. We believed ourselves immune to repercussions. Each of us on our own could be terminated, but how could the Peace Corps dismiss our entire cohort?

I stood in the courtyard. In the arcades of the first and second floors of the *lycée*, as in a coliseum, the other protesters waited for me to speak, for the protest to officially begin.

"A time comes when you can't say another word, am I right?" I declared.

"Right on!" the other volunteers answered.

"There are moments when the simplest sentence becomes too complex. Do you hear me?"

"We hear you, brother!"

"And an overworked mind is a mind that will go insane. Are we willing to go insane? Hell no!"

"Hell no, we won't go—*insane!*"

"I don't know about you, but I have reached the point when I can no longer think. My brain needs a break. Are you with me?

"We're with you, man!"

"Then repeat, 'No more class today!'"

"No more class today!" the other volunteers answered.

"Repeat!"

"No more class today."

"This we know, we won't go!"

"This we know! We won't go!"

We did the call and response for several minutes, pumped our fists, clapped and laughed. We stood our ground. It was not that we were sure of ourselves; we did not know what to do next. We were waiting for management to react. It was a genuine Peace Corps student strike be-in; teachers grinned with embarrassment while students relived their campus protests. Suddenly, camp authority responded in the person of Jamal, the educational director. The strapping, handsome coach, textbook author and universally beloved good guy approached me in the center of the courtyard with his warm and easy smile.

"When I said you were good looking, Murkey, I never thought you would do this," he quipped, his light green eyes beaming with mirth. Everyone laughed.

The demonstration had reached inertia. We were right to let management know how we felt, but we remained Peace Corps employees. Could we overthrow the American government in Ayn Draham and establish a separatist republic among the wild dogs of the cork forest?

A leader must know when to seize the moment and when to let it go. Our moment was over, but before we dispersed and returned to class, we had to be sure that no one was punished. To indemnify the protesters from the Peace Corps version of a court martial, I appealed sincerely to the educational director.

"Jamal, we appreciate that you and the teachers are preparing us to live on our own, which means speaking your languages. We know there is a lot to learn, but we can't learn it all at once. We're only human. We need time off to rest our brains. As the Tunisian proverb says, '*Shweah b'shweah.*' Little by little, right?"

Jamal laughed. The volunteers and teachers joined in.

"*Behi yessir,*" the educational director said with a courteous nod. "So the hard work is paying off. *En tous cas*, your suggestions have been duly noted. We will respectfully consider them."

The volunteers applauded and returned to class. Meanwhile, I reverted to my morose and introverted self. But as I ambled slowly toward our classroom, Raotha, my beautiful Arabic teacher with bright almond eyes and high cheekbones, smiled at me. "*Bravo.* You spoke for all of us. The teachers support you, too."

I enjoyed that afternoon class so much that I could not recall why I had protested being in it. The praise of a beautiful woman can do extraordinary things.

14

A NIGHT IN TUNISIA

When class was over, Tasha waited for me at the bottom of the hill. She wore aviator shades and flashed her teeth like a lifeguard. Tasha did not swim.

"We're going to the beach," she said. "Wanna come?"

At the start of training camp, I often socialized with Tasha and the other supervisors. They seemed to include me for political reasons, in the belief that I was a VIP, because I had been invited to the Ambassador's Residence. But after my disciplinary meeting with Tasha and Jann's warning, I avoided the camp director and her coterie.

"I don't have my swimsuit," I said.

"Swim in your underwear."

"I don't have a towel."

"Let the breeze dry you—or use my towel."

"There's no sun."

"So you'll stay white as a sheet. You'll have fun." She pointed at the sky. "If we hurry we'll be in time for sunset."

"I guess I'm going then."

"Only if you want to."

I did not know why Tasha invited me. Was it my reward for leading the student protest and then dispersing it? Or had I been so quiet and unobtrusive of late that she worried about me?

On the mountain pass to Tabarka, I lay in the back of the station wagon with my feet sticking out the window. Stuart, Tasha's right-hand man and former boyfriend, interrupted my meditations. "Sounds somber back there."

"Murkey's morose again," Tasha complained. Stuart stepped on the gas. The tan clogs spun on my toes like windmills. I pulled in my legs to prevent the shoes from flying off.

"No melancholia allowed in this car," Stuart proclaimed. "All brooding and other forms of philosophical mush are *interdit*."

"Great. More mind control," I said.

"Damn right," Stuart countered. "We're gonna kick some conformity into you, boy!"

We followed a narrow, dirt road, overgrown with vines, cacti and low-hanging mangroves, and came to the dunes guarding the beach. Among the rushes and gnarled tree trunks, animals crept from their lairs to hunt in the early evening coolness.

"Isn't it beautiful?" Tasha intoned as she guided the wind through her chestnut hair with open palms. "How do you like my spot?" Face upturned, eyes closed, etching the sky with her lovely profile, Tasha received the twilight breeze.

With our backs to the sunset, we faced its reflection in the flickering waves. Beneath our feet the dune shifted and assumed a new shape so gradually that we couldn't be sure it changed, even as we watched. It was pointless to try to reconstruct a prior pattern. Still life is an illusion.

Tasha stretched her arms and wrapped her hands behind her head to be embraced by this place she called her own. What first may have seemed an egomaniacal gesture was actually a genuine and natural response—our discoveries are completely our own.

"Rick, what is it?" she asked. I was silent, preferring not to share my misery. The pincer marks on my heel had scabbed, but I was often depressed and irritable. It occurred to me that I had been mistaken not to have the wound examined.

"You're brooding," she said.

"Who does it hurt?" I replied.

"You!" she replied. "There's a world of beauty out there."

"Yes," I thought, "but not for me. Can't get too attached. I'm leaving soon."

I wanted to cry out that I might have incurable rabies, but indulging in emotional excess would be admitting it to myself, which was unbearable.

Suddenly, sand poured all over my face. Tasha was applying Tunisian sand torture to my state of mind. Yet even this extreme measure did not work. My mood was immovable.

How could I tell her about the innocuous but potentially lethal wound on my heel that I failed to treat while there was time? Should I tell the camp director that I could be sliding toward a violent, ugly death? Faced with such dire prospects, I felt entitled to feel like life's injured party. Sunset was another villain, a liar and a romantic delusion, beauty and light yielding to darkness.

"Let's go in the water!" Tasha pulled my arm, as if she could physically drag me from my destiny. I wondered why she coaxed me. Did I need to be explored, analyzed and modified?

In the gentle sea, the others in our party were chicken-fighting. Women rode on men's shoulders. Riders and steeds alike comported like water-wrestlers. They rammed each other and butted heads, grabbed each other's limbs and hair, all to make their competitors spill into the water. If splashes and raucous laugher were reliable indicators, they were all succeeding beautifully.

Suddenly, a body lunged out of the dark sky and fell on Tasha and me in the dune. Stuart rolled in the sand, smacked his hands, barked like a seal and made strange faces.

"You two haven't been frolicking!"

Tasha and I waded into the surf. I burrowed my knees in the

wet sand and she climbed on my shoulders. As a voluptuous rider on a scrawny mount, we were a vulnerable fighting force and needed superior tactics. Rather than ram and grapple like the others, we leaned on our opponents, then backed away. They toppled. We toppled. Everyone claimed victory and we went to eat.

A cool breeze refreshed the clientele at *Heshmi's*, Tabarka's best three-crescent restaurant, a thick-walled, open-windowed villa on a cliff over a grotto.

Stuart plucked an eye from a roasted fish splayed across his plate and popped it in his mouth. He proclaimed this to be an age-old Tunisian custom. After flipping the fish on his plate, he stabbed the other eye and thrust it under my nose. His eyes were inebriated, yet solemn.

"According to timeless ritual, two men at the table swallow the eyes of a fish. This act wards off the evil eye from all who witness it."

I inspected the viscous, glistening eyeball stuck on the fork and came to a firm decision. "I'm not eating that."

"Your birthright as a man is to eat the eye of a fish!" Stuart badgered. "It's your obligation! You want to protect your friends from the evil eye, don't you? You're a man, aren't you?"

Who knows what manhood is or when it begins? It is marked by a boy's first erection when he sees a naked woman? Is it his first wet dream, his first intercourse, or his first paycheck? Is it when he sprouts pubic hair, falls in love, or risks his life? No one knows, which is why rites of manhood are always there to fill in the blanks.

"Whose sacred custom is this? The Barbary Pirates or Sinbad the Sailor?" I inquired. To my credit, I did not need to eat a fish eye to know I was a man. In this respect, I was still sane.

"It's *his* sick custom," Tasha interjected, "Stuart, if you were a real man, you'd find better ways to prove it."

Moved by this rebuke, Stuart stuck out his tongue. Turning to me, the bespectacled California beach boy philosopher said, "Rick, you must eat the eye of the fish, because you *have* the eyes of a fish."

A proposal to eat fish eyes may be distasteful, but being told you have them is traumatic.

Stuart was not done. He explained that fish, called *hoot* in Arabic, symbolized spiritual redemption, predicted the future and protected one from evil.

"Can you forego this once-in-a-lifetime, three-in-one cross-cultural activity? Consider that prophecy, protection and redemption can all be yours for swallowing a morsel the size of a shirt button. Where's your anthropological curiosity, man?"

I would not test my manhood, a trait too fundamental to doubt and too elusive to prove, but the chance to participate in an authentic Tunisian ritual was irresistible. It might finally help me put aside western logic and see things magically.

As I lifted the fish eye to my mouth in performance of the solemn animist rite, a tray loaded with cold, sweating *Celtias* arrived. Tasha lifted her bottle for a toast. "To men, what pigs you are!" Then turning to me, she winked. "Exception granted."

I did not deserve an exception. If Tasha knew what was in my mind and heart, she would have put me near the top of the pig list. Jann's warning still whispered in my head. Were her warmth and kindness a tease? I averted my eyes in guilt, opened my mouth and popped the fish eye down my shirt.

The waiters had been shaking hands and whistling the whole evening, weaving about the room slowly and methodically at the end of a long shift. Our waiter alighted from the kitchen and stood before the swinging doors. A tuft of black, glistening hair swept over his forehead like a question mark. His mouth became a dark circle and he started to sing.

The waiter's bulldog face conveyed a child's eagerness to please. His jowls trembled and his nostrils flared. He used the hollows of his face to shape his sound.

Stuart was impervious to this nuance and hostile to the recital. He grabbed his head and slumped over our table like a man condemned to entertainment. "No, not again! I won't give this guy an extra *millime* for this!" he swore.

When the singer warbled on, Stuart renounced pacifism. He clanged his plate with his utensils and dropped a plate to disrupt the performance, but the spontaneous singer was impervious to the clatter, believing it to be percussive accompaniment. His eyes crossed and closed as his song rose, swooped and soared to its conclusion. His colleagues applauded, uttering praises, and praising God. *"Woolah! Woolah!"* they cried. The *artiste* bowed, stepped back and disappeared behind the swinging doors.

"We had to come on amateur night!" Stuart lamented. "I came to Tunisia to escape buskers and Fritos!"

"Cool it," Tasha admonished him. "You're not in your room with the stereo full blast. You're in public in a foreign country. Decorum, please!"

"I say, 'No!' to being an audience. It's too great a burden to listen and appreciate. Talent is tyranny!" Stuart raved, waving his bottle and tossing a stream of beer down the front of his shirt.

"You have nothing to worry about," Tasha replied.

15

BOUDOIR CONFIDENTIAL

We returned to camp at midnight. Tasha and I headed down

the camel-humped road to the dust bowl, where we lived two houses apart. Dogs sang on the ridge and Tasha's heels smacked her sandals like castanets, keeping time with the canine chorale.

"Want to come to my place for some brandy?"

"What does she want?" I asked myself. Since puberty, I had developed a bad habit of reading women's signals wishfully, rather than realistically, resulting in painful embarrassment.

But now that I had persistent symptoms and faced the possibility of death, such scruples were un-exchanged currency—useless and wasteful.

"A nightcap, Rick?" Tasha asked as we approached her house. "It will relax you."

"Do I seem tense?" I asked nervously.

"Oh, Rick!" Tasha marched ahead.

Then an invisible hand slapped my face. I had to accept Tasha's invitation without presuming her intentions. She had the power to smash my plans. I could not fall in love with her, but I had to respect her. If she liked me, I didn't want her to stop. I caught up with her.

"Don't be mad," I said.

"I'm not. I don't want to stand in the dark."

Tasha lit red candles and poured brandy in paper cups. The amber liquid soaked my throat and stung my gums. Was this a symptom of tissue necrosis? I put down the drink.

"You don't drink much," she said.

"You're observant."

"I was a barmaid in college." Tasha's lips curled in a shrewd smile. "A barmaid's like a nurse, at least I felt like one. Customers come to a bar to feel better and forget. You bring them a drink and they're grateful. You're their best friend." She paused to reflect. "Hmmm. I rarely talk about my pre-Peace Corps existence."

Tasha sounded happier after discussing her past. She described her experience as if it happened to someone else. Maybe I was wrong about her seducing me. She seemed to want a friend.

"Everyone thinks their story is unique, but they're all pretty similar. A barmaid listens and smiles. That's how you earn tips."

"You must have heard stories," I said.

"You know what they say: 'Heard one, heard them all.'"

Tasha swirled the cognac in her cup, gazed in my eyes and smiled.

"You're still not drinking."

"I don't want to be another guy who tells you stories."

"So I'll tell you one. My parents got divorced after 22 years. My father had friends, a job. It was a new life for him, but my mother had nothing left. Her children were all grown up."

Tasha smoothed her hair. "That won't happen to me."

Her face froze as she stared in the candle at an enemy only she could see. I had seen that look before. Cerise had it.

Jann's observation echoed. *Tasha is another older woman, a younger older woman. She's 24."*

Across the footlocker coffee table, Tasha lifted the glass to her lips and tilted her head to stare at me from a new angle. Her arm stretched across the bed.

"You fear commitment, don't you?" she said.

"No."

"Most men do," she said.

"I can't speak for most men or take the blame for them."

She patted my shoulder. "Life isn't fair. Get used to it. Excuse me."

While Tasha was in the bathroom, I perused the medical dictionary on her shelf, hoping I would find information there to dispel my worst fears.

Incubation may last from ten days to two years. But it is usually 3-7 weeks. The virus travels in the nerves to the brain, multiplies there and then migrates along the efferent nerves to the salivary glands. Rabies is uniformly fatal.

If a wild animal is captured, it should be euthanized and its head shipped on ice to the nearest laboratory to examine the brain for rabies.

I dropped the medical dictionary on the floor. To die in this forsaken place, where the *genius loci* consisted of an open sewer, vultures performing daily aerial shows and dogs howling moonlight serenades, exceeded my worst nightmare.

Tasha returned to the room. "Are you all right?"

"Nothing, nothing," I mumbled, sliding the book on its shelf. "It must be the brandy."

"You only had a few sips."

"I can't hold my liquor."

Tasha resumed her seductive pose on her bed, while I sat on the floor across the great divide of the trunk.

"I asked you about commitment because I feel like we've met before."

"We've never met," I insisted anxiously. I had to prevent Tasha from thinking we shared a destiny. Cerise was my destiny. I was here for her.

Tasha's small arched foot ran along her other leg. Like an animated icon from the *Kama Sutra,* it traced her smooth and shapely calf. It was erotic and tender—and beautiful to watch.

"It's hard being one of the few women and having the top position makes it worse," she said. "I don't mind the responsibility and power, if you want to call it that. What I hate is having to be a bitch to get things done. It's not my strength."

"What is your strength?" I asked.

Tasha stroked the length of her hair before sweeping it behind her neck. "You have to ask? Love."

All of my facial muscles tightened. I gulped. I felt Tasha tug at me from across the room, like the moon pulling the tides.

"Still, I'll take being a bitch any day of the week over guys hitting on me like they've done most of my life."

"Down boy!" I told my hyperextended manhood.

Did she want to be lovers or friends? I was stuck. If I flirted with her we could not be friends and my love for Cerise would be a joke; but if I said, "Tasha, I'm in love with a French woman!" she would hate me for presuming her intentions and rejecting her.

I knew from experience that when someone dropped an H-bomb on me, as in, "I have a boyfriend," or "You're not my type," I never saw her again. Honesty killed more relationships than it saved.

"Irving and the others respect me. But then Irving will make a comment about a woman's ass, like I'm one of the boys."

"At least he's not talking about your ass."

"He does that, too. He once told me I had it all—a sharp mind and a great ass."

"He meant you're well-rounded," I opined. "In a crude way."

"I could be less well-rounded. I have to curb the couscous."

Each time Tasha mentioned her ass I felt a twitching in my pants. I couldn't stop thinking about it. I even tried to look at her butt when she was sitting on it.

I ached from being attracted and knowing it was wrong. Was it too late for simple feelings? Of course it was.

But then my "worthless" education rescued me. Finding myself in a tight spot in the present, I framed the moment in the prehistoric past, or even better—in mythology.

Under the cotton blouse and short flowered skirt, Tasha was a lovely woman wielding power. She was Circe turning men to swine by attracting them.

How often had Lauren rebuked me for staring at her breasts while we discussed Kierkegaard? "I'm sorry," I said, "but they're so beautiful."

"Don't even think of taking a leap of faith," she chided. "Just look in my eyes!"

Circe had two powers—sex and intellect. If I focused on sex with Tasha, she would destroy me. But if I kept my eyes on her eyes and listened to her words, we might become allies.

Tasha stretched. She stroked one arm with the other hand and her torso twisted. She pulled her shoulders back. Her hard nipples pressed against her blouse.

"Circe!" I muttered to resist her sensual power. "Circe!"

"Rick, are you okay? I don't even know why I ask. Are you mumbling Circe?"

"Oh, that. It sounds crazy but you sort of remind me of her."

"So now I turn men to swine?" Tasha stared at me with narrowed eyes, as if trying on this idea like a flea market *fripe*. "Don't worry. It's not my style."

"It's not that. You're a strong and beautiful woman and that combination has always threatened men. It's too much for us."

"You're probably right," she laughed.

Then words and ideas poured from her. Her eyes glowed with images she had seen and her hands danced with their shadows in the candlelight.

If I made a move on Tasha, Cerise and I would be finished with no goodbye. The most important relationship in my life would be expunged, and this expedition would be an exercise in meaningless self-extinction—unless Tasha was the love of my life, and my purpose in coming to Tunisia was to meet her. Romance can be a cancer of the mind, replicating scenarios out of control.

"I don't know what's next for me," Tasha said. "My tour is over but I might stay. I'm good at this and I love Tunisia. I don't know."

If she didn't know what she was doing and I didn't know what I was doing—then what were we doing?

"Do you know what you want?" she asked.

"What I want?" I repeated fatuously.

What should I tell her? That I was drinking her cognac and thinking about her ass while I loved Cerise? That I was in her bedroom at 2 AM with no other desire than to be her friend?

Was it time to make a move? I needed a love-choreographer. What if I stretched, lost balance and fell conveniently on her bed? Or I could lower my eyes, pucker my lips, wrap my arms around her legs, kiss her feet and plead for compassion. But that would mean lunging over the trunk and putting her scented candle and painted ashtray at risk.

What if I explained to Tasha that in this life I was reserved for Cerise, but in a parallel life I would be with her? What if I said nothing? What if I had two girlfriends in training camp? If rabies didn't finish me, that would do it.

All you owe another person is honesty. All you owe yourself is happiness. If you feel something, you should show it. But I was too tired and conflicted to know what I wanted. I struggled for clarity.

I was going to tell Tasha something, anything, when a miracle occurred. Tasha yawned and sighed. "It's two o'clock. Don't you think we should go to bed?"

By "we" did she mean "together"?

She led me to the door.

"I haven't talked this much in years," she said. "I enjoyed it."

"That was easy," I said, standing under a cold shower, celebrating how well I handled Tasha's nightcap. My two primary male-female relationships remained intact. The plan to see Cerise might still work.

While I tried to sleep, I scratched my pubic hair and felt a bump above the groin. It was like a hard button. Was it a hookworm, roundworm, fungus, a melanoma lesion, or a bubo swelling on my lymph glands?

Rabies and now plague: was an angry deity tossing another disease my way for good measure?

The one infection I was sure I didn't have was syphilis. The growth was not a chancre because I had had no sex in months.

I raced to the bathroom and switched on the light, only to close my eyes in fear. When I opened them, I found a mole above my pubic tuft, perfectly formed and hideously complex. Before I touched the growth, it slipped from my skin and hit the floor. It was the fish eye I had tossed under my shirt at dinner. I laughed. It had saved me from the evil eye, after all. By falling, it removed the threat of cancer and plague, and even put rabies in doubt.

The dogs howled from the ridge with hoarse and breathless voices a dirge of loneliness and desire.

•

I returned to bed but couldn't sleep. After spending so much time with Tasha, I had to give equal time to Cerise. I was either motivated by guilt or a need to understand the hold she had on me, that prevented me from loving anyone else.

I remembered the November we had, the one guiltless month of love.

I chased Cerise up the stairs and down the halls of the brick dorm to her bare room on the third floor.

We were laughing. The room had a ceiling bulb, a brown floor, pane windows and two single beds head to head.

Was love possible in such a cold, empty place? The room seemed to disapprove of our nakedness.

We didn't care. We ran to the bed and slid under the white sheet, made love and slept entwined to keep warm.

December came. Finals and a separation loomed. One morning, she came to my room with doom in her eyes.

"I'm pregnant."

"Are you sure?"

"I'm absolutely sure that I'm positively pregnant."

The alliteration made her laugh, but her laughter made her cry.

"I knew it would happen. It had to happen. Twenty-five years without sex and I get caught the first time."

I tried to reassure her that my sperm was immotile, infertile and as lazy as I was, but she didn't believe it. Freedom must be punished. The nuns had told her and she rebelled. But now she believed them with self-flagellating certainty.

"You could be late," I said hopefully.

"No, don't you see? I'm always on time. On time! And now I'm ten days late."

She spoke with dismal cheer. The world made sense again. She was a sinner whipping herself because heaven needed hell.

"How can you be sure?" I could not accept that we were sinful. I wanted heaven alone.

"My grandmother said I'd know by my pregnant eyes."

"Did she tell you what pregnant eyes look like?"

"She said I'd know. And I do. I have pregnant eyes, Rick."

She opened her eyes ridiculously wide, as if a flashbulb went off in her face. We laughed.

She would not make love. I understood and accepted this act of contrition. Our belated abstention was our sacrifice to God. Maybe he would show mercy.

That Christmas break, I hitchhiked home 400 miles to save money and considered dropping out of school to support our child. During interterm, I bussed tables at the dining hall to prove to no one in particular my humility and responsibility.

I waited for news as she trekked across the country in borrowed cars with her friend, a rich leftist bisexual journalist.

A week before spring semester, I a postcard came from Miami.

"My worries ended last Tuesday. You should be as happy as I am."

SAVED!

16

SO HOT

I expected a sanction or reprimand for my role in the student protest, suspension from classes for a week or probation of some kind. Nothing happened.

Making me wait for my punishment was probably a more insidious penalty. Or conversely, following rules was an overrated virtue in the Peace Corps. Here, like elsewhere, risk taking was rewarded.

A few days after our nightcap, Tasha invited me to dinner in Tabarka. She and the other counselors were entertaining Bill Dozier, the Peace Corps Associate Director, whose firm grip had nearly crushed my hand at the airport.

It was what I expected. The *brique à l'oeuf* was deliciously warm and runny, with a soft-boiled egg, tart capers, and a salty chunk of tuna. The conversation was an oral anthology of Peace Corps "war stories." Dozier recounted how he successfully started a basketball program at his high school in the *bled*. When the basketball he paid for out of his own stipend arrived deflated, he inflated it with his own breath. "It took me 20 minutes," he boasted. "A Guinness World Record."

"Why am I not surprised?" I muttered.

Tasha recounted her attempt to start a cheerleading squad at her high school, which was thwarted when one girl's *safsari* came off and another cheerleader tripped on it. Stuart reminisced about playing touch football in the ruins of the amphitheater at El Djem.

Unexpectedly, Dozier turned his attention to me as I bit into the soft egg in my *brique à l'oeuf*.

"Murkey, you have an unusual haircut. Did one of the barbers in town butcher your head?'

"No, I did it myself."

"At least you didn't have to pay for it," Dozier laughed. "Murkey, you're quite a Renaissance man."

"Not really," I replied with caution, not modesty.

"Don't be modest. You've already written quite a résumé since coming here—airport art critic, sports diplomat and radical student leader. Is there anything you don't do?"

"I stink at ballroom dancing," I admitted.

Dozier nodded, smiled thinly and assumed a somber expression. Suddenly, he reached into the dish of hot peppers on the table and announced the *filfil-eating* match, a mainstay of the Tunisian dining tradition. He challenged me one on one.

"Wasn't the fish eye bad enough?" I muttered to Tasha. "How many Tunisian food rituals are there?"

Tasha bowed her head and kicked me under the table. She was

not about to laugh at her boss.

Dozier stared at me with cold intimidation, raised a fiery red *filfil* before him like a dueling sword, brought it slowly toward his mouth, bit off the stem and masticated the pepper slowly with apparent relish. He smiled smugly at me. A superior look covered his face like moisturizer as he slid the dish of peppers toward me.

While I scrutinized the hot red and green peppers, he remarked, "A future hairdresser probably wouldn't be interested."

That was more insult than I could abide. I did not view myself as a hairdresser. I cut my own hair to relieve disturbances in my brain. *Filfil* eating was an unlikely marker for masculinity, but I was not going to let Dozier misrepresent my sexuality or impugn my intestinal fortitude. I could handle any hot pepper he dished out. Since Dozier had selected a red pepper, I chose a green pepper to oppose him. I raised the *filfil,* guided it into my mouth and chewed it in the same he-man style the assistant director had demonstrated. Within seconds, heat seeped into the lining of my mouth, burned my throat, pressed against my rib cage and ripped open my jaws.

"AHHHHHHHH!" I pointed in my mouth to indicate my agony. Others at the table offered water, but Dozier suggested bread. Water would only intensify the pain. The assistant director's eyes took a break from their usual whipped dog beleaguerment, as he revelled in my predicament.

The competition continued. Tears streamed down our faces. Finally, we had swallowed ten *filfils* apiece. The main course arrived. Dozier offered me a draw, but I declined. I had not eaten ten hot peppers only to tie my nemesis.

"You're being childish," he said, as I popped the eleventh hot pepper in my mouth and swallowed it whole, in the hope that it would sneak by my stomach. Dozier admitted that he couldn't eat another pepper and conceded victory to me.

But my triumph, however sweet, was evanescent. Within moments, my stomach expressed acute distress. Chemical knives were slashing my gut. I could not sit. Then, I could not stand. I could not even look at my dinner, much less eat it. As we left the restaurant I was doubled forward. The *maître d'* asked if anything was wrong.

"He's humble," Dozier explained, to which the Arab host bowed to express reciprocal humility.

The other volunteers lifted me and placed me into the back of the station wagon, where I lay curled like a bloated fetus. As the others sang "A Hundred Bottles of Beer on the Wall" we heard sirens behind us. Officers of the *Garde Nationale* demanded our identity cards, but only Dozier had one. Despite his mastery of Tunisian Arabic and his frequent mention of his position as Assistant Director of the Peace Corps, he could not persuade the patrolman to let us go. Finally, wracked by severe stomachache and cramps throughout my digestive tract, I pleaded, "We're all cousins."

Tasha and the others laughed inadvertently because it was a typical Tunisian rejoinder. The policeman, however, wasn't laughing. He detected inappropriate flippancy and asked me to step from the car. The volunteers helped me out in the same manner that they had inserted me. I was still bent and cringing, with my head waist-high.

"So you're a funny man, eh?"

"I wasn't trying to be funny, sir. I'm in pain. My stomach hurts."

"Why does your stomach hurt so much, young man?"

"Too much *filfil*," I said. "My stomach is going to explode."

"How many *filfil* did you eat?" the officer inquired.

"Eleven," I said.

"I eat 20 *filfils* every day," he boasted casually, "That is how I expel impurities and stay strong. We Tunisian men all eat 20 *filfils* a day, minimum. But you are an American man. You do not have the experience eating *filfil* that we Tunisians have. I ate my first *filfil* before I had teeth."

"*Monsieur,* if you do not let me go home, there will be an accident that has nothing to do with cars."

The *Garde Nationale* officer patted my back and laughed. "Eating *filfil* is not a game, *jeune homme.* What you need is milk, ice cream or yogurt. I just bought a cup of Dannon. I would be glad to give it to you to relieve your suffering. But you must promise me that you will not do this again."

"I promise. Never again, Officer."

"If you eat that, you will feel it is the best thing for you. And you will know for the future. *Tfath'l.* Take it."

The officer tore off the top of his yogurt cup. "I have no spoon, but it is like milk. Drink it down."

I followed his order. He watched me attentively, like a father, as I took the remedy.

"*Ça va mieux?*" he asked.

"*Oui, merci, monsieur.*"

"*Pas de quoi. Allez. Bislema. Tisbalakhir. Bonne nuit!*"

After this show of gentle authority, the officers strutted away. They waved at Dozier to drive on.

All the way back, the dinner party expressed relief and amazement at how kind and understanding the policeman had been.

"Your *filfil* binge was childish, Murkey, but your stomachache saved us," Tasha said.

"What saved us was that you won his sympathy," Dozier

pointed out. "If you can touch people's emotions here, they will do anything for you."

17
THE HUMBLE WOODWORKER

A few evenings later, we experienced unusual humidity. I was on the porch, writing a letter to a college friend, as part of my outreach to the past, when the sound of distant bells and percussion wafted from the town on the ridge. The air reeked of rotting fruit and burning flesh. A finger-snapping crackle was in the air.

"A boy was killed in the forest," Ali, our neighbor, reported.

He pointed toward the procession that coiled down the road. A phalanx of solemn mourners bore torches around a dark, inert shape on a pallet—a child's corpse.

Ali was a sallow man with large, shallow-set eyes. Some volunteers dismissed him as an oaf because of his constant grin, his halting French and the way his blood-shot eyes protruded. Yet there was nothing stupid about our shy neighbor's wistful, elusive smile. It suggested not that he was oblivious to pain, but intimately aware of it.

I once asked Ali why he smiled so often. *"Me-na-a-r-a-s-f-sh!"* he replied. *"Je ne sais pas."*

"You don't know? Is that possible? Maybe you're just happy," I replied.

He grinned wistfully. *"Menarafsh!"*

I conceded the point and thought Ali was remarkable for making it. In an age dominated by overbearing know-it-alls, his admission of ignorance about why he smiled showed exceptional candor, for which the gentle Tunisian deserved respect.

To explain his relationship to Allah, our neighbor fingered the glass buttons of his checkered summer shirt and recounted bashfully the story of his marriage to a woman his mother selected for him. For years Ali had remained single for fear of marrying the wrong woman. He prayed everyday to Allah that he would find the woman of his dreams.

Finally, realizing that Ali would never wed on his own, his mother found him a wife. "Is she beautiful?" Ali asked his mother. "Please, don't condemn me to unhappiness." His mother guaranteed that his arranged bride was lovely and took Ali's money to pay for the marriage contract. Ali prayed to Allah that his bride would not disappoint, but when his blessed day arrived and he lifted the veil, it seemed that his mother—and perhaps even God—had betrayed him.

"Allah, is this what you call a face? Is this what you call a woman?" The woodworker demanded silently.

Since the brothers of the bride were policemen from Tabarka, Ali was compelled to go through with the wedding to uphold her family's honor. Later they divorced, but after so many years Ali was still afraid to go to Tabarka.

"Allah promises love, but is there love? Allah promises beauty, but is there beauty? Allah promises happiness. Where is it? I want to know!" Ali asked agnostically.

The funeral procession drew near. The mourners pounded their chests with fists as the drum slowly hit the off-beats.

"The boy was bitten by a dog of the forest, on the far side of the stadium," Ali said. "I didn't see it," he admitted truthfully, "but they say his lips and tongue were swollen and his body turned gray, and his skin was covered by many scabs as big as one hundred *millime* coins. Of course, this is not what I came here to talk about, my friend."

"No? What did you come to talk about?"

"I want to invite you to my house for lunch."

The Ambassador was scheduled to visit the next day and I was invited to eat the midday meal at his table. However, since food portions were generally small, I believed that I could easily double-book lunch. After all, this was my chance to be an ambassador on my own, to build a friendship with a Tunisian and witness his living conditions. It was also a rare experience, since Ali was our only Tunisian neighbor who showed an interest in talking with American men. Other Tunisians in town focused on the women, whom they ogled, harassed and regaled with sucking noises usually reserved for prostitutes.

I could not refuse my only Tunisian friend, whimsical downtrodden Ali, although I knew his mother's house sat at the foot of the steps of Ayn Draham, with the river of sewage flowing by—not a location conducive to appetite. The direction and intensity of the breeze would no doubt be a factor in the success of our social occasion.

"*Hooyah,* my brother, I will see you tomorrow at your mother's house," I confirmed.

Ali's eyes widened. "*C'est ça!*" he said to confirm his satisfaction.

Jann came out on the porch, stroking his beard with peculiar fixation. Noting Ali's presence, he asked, "Hey, what are you doing here?"

"Mr. Jann," Ali replied, grinning. "I did not see you."

They shook hands.

"Yeah, I'm invisible these days." Jann laughed dryly, then turned to me. "So, you've met the eccentric *artiste* of Ayn Draham. I warn you he's insane."

"He's a nice guy," I protested.

"You must have a ball around mental hospitals," Jann said. He turned to Ali. *"Tu sais que tu es fou, n'est-ce pas? You* know you're crazy, right?"

Ali grinned. *"Oui, je le sais. Mais toi aussi.* You are crazy, too." Jann pretended to be shocked. "Hey, don't say it so loud. It's top secret. I thought I could trust you."

After pointing out my weakness for insanity, Jann attempted once again to exploit it. "Got any spare change?"

"No."

"No?" Jann repeated with incredulity and pain.

"If you play *I Ching* everyday, you should make sure you have enough coins," I reproved him.

Not one to dwell on disappointment, or to take sensible advice, Jann turned to the next closest mark. "Ali, *mon vieux*, do you by any chance have some coins?"

The gentle Tunisian, eager to accommodate, pulled a coin from his pocket, which Jann perused suspiciously, bit and spat on, to determine its value.

"I'll be damned!" Jann shouted, "One millime! In my 14 months in Tunisia this is the first one I've ever seen!"

"I'm sorry I cannot give more," replied the humble woodworker of Ayn Draham, who had already offered me a salad fork and spoon of finely finished corkwood as a gift, "I would have been rich, but Allah put a hole in my pocket."

"I thought he put one in your head," Jann cracked and patted Ali on the shoulder to show he was teasing. Then Jann turned to me and said, "Ali's a good man. He also separated from his wife. He gave me good advice."

I could not imagine what that was.

Jann flipped the coin. It was very light. "I wonder what this will buy you," he mused.

"Everything and nothing," Ali replied paradoxically.

Jann nodded significantly and rolled his eyes. He determined that the coin was too light to flip and tossed it back to Ali. The Arab bowed his head and put the one-millime piece back in his shabby pocket.

"*Shokran*," he said, "This way I will not tempt bad luck. I carry this one coin, not to buy anything, but only to protect me from the evil eye, for it is written that one should not cross a deserted street with empty pockets."

Ali bowed, repeated the time of our appointment and walked toward his house near the steps. Jann watched him disappear in the darkness.

"He's certifiable but harmless."

The funeral procession had stopped at the house next door and the crying and wailing were now excruciating. The dog-and-child-beater fell to the ground and pounded the dust. The dog, now tied to the stake by the compound, was howling. The litter that the mourners had carried now lay on the ground. The dog-and-child-beater pulled a gun from his belt and aimed it at the back of his mutt's skull.

After the gunshot, the dog lay flat. Bits of its brain were splattered on the ground. It was so quiet that I thought I heard the blood flow from the wound and pool around the dog's body. The dog-and-child-beater must have heard it, too. He pumped all of the bullets in his gun into the dormant animal. Then he picked up his son's lifeless body and dragged himself into his villa.

18

AMBASSADOR AND SPECIAL GUEST

A cortège of black Lincoln Continentals drove by the high

school as we walked to lunch the next day. The convoy wound its way down the dusty road by the stadium and headed toward the camp. The Town Cars maneuvering on the rough road among ruined structures looked like a surreal commercial, demonstrating the off-road capabilities of the top-line luxury sedan.

These elegant Town Cars were as strong and indomitable as tanks and suggested a power that no topography could deter. Regardless of the ideals that may have brought us here, these sleek sedans represented the true reason and purpose for our presence and for the Peace Corps, itself. Our service was a sideshow.

The limousines stopped on the dirt path where most of the houses were clustered. Three burly security men stepped out of the first black car. They wore sunglasses and surveyed the entire town with grim faces. A tall, elegant man, with white hair and a white suit stepped out of the second car. Ambassador Ardsley was an impeccable diplomat, lean, fit, tanned and wiry, a hybrid of intellectual and swashbuckler. Hollywood could not have cast anyone better for his part. After the Ambassador, one other guest alighted from the back of his chauffeured car. It was Lauren, looking resplendent, yet businesslike in a white blouse, a long black skirt and flats. Her only adornment was a gold chain belt.

Why was she here?

Irving P. Irving and Bill Dozier emerged from the third car. They shook hands with the Ambassador and Lauren. Though they had driven for two hours in the same caravan, the Peace Corps executives seemed to be meeting the Ardsleys for the first time.

Lauren exchanged pleasantries with Tasha and the other Peace Corps managers, including Rodney, the mass-poisoner, who said something that made her laugh. Of course. Suddenly the whole event, which I had eagerly anticipated, made me sick. The Ambassador would never know what actually went on here. This was an official visit to boost the morale of "the little people."

It was disappointing, but not surprising. Lauren's appearance, however, was perplexing. Why was she in Tunisia? Did she return or never leave? Wasn't she now a big-time, fast track young TV correspondent?

The security detail and Peace Corps hosts quickly engulfed Ambassador Ardsley and Lauren, as they moved in a protective scrum toward the compound. The pressure of having Lauren on the premises subsided. It was doubtful that she would even see me, or seek me out. As the mass of volunteers turned and scattered to lunch in their respective houses, a hand squeezed my arm.

"So, you're giving me the cold shoulder? That's not the famous Tunisian hospitality I heard about."

"I'm not ignoring you," I replied, as my face burned with embarrassment. "I'm just a volunteer. I didn't want to be presumptuous or out of line."

"Since when?" Lauren laughed, as she linked her arm in mine. "Oh, that's a good one—a decorous Rick Murkey. There must be something to this Peace Corps."

Lauren's presence, her fragrance and her physical contact took me aback, albeit she touched me in a gentle and friendly manner, with no sexual overtones. Even so, her mere proximity was closer and more intimate than I was used to, *Boom Boom* the masseur having been the only other person to touch me for the past few months. I was also acutely aware that others were watching us.

"I'm happy to see you, but surprised," I admitted.

"You're even thinner than when I last saw you," she remarked.

"Yeah, well I eat less. Why are you here?" I asked.

"That doesn't sound very welcoming, but I'll forgive you."

"It's not what I meant. I just thought—you said—you were

going to New York, to launch your TV career."

"Oh, that. Yes, I went to New York, interviewed, did all of these tests—and *voilà*, I'm on TV. You're talking to the Mediterranean correspondent for America News Network."

"That's great," I replied. "So what brings you to Ayn Draham?"

"You, of course. I wanted to check up on you."

"Oh, come on!" I said.

"Well, it's true!" she winked. "Okay. I'm also looking for a story."

The party had stopped in front of my house, where the dining room was judged to be spacious enough to accommodate 15 diners. As we waited to enter, I continued to feel the eyes of other volunteers on Lauren and me. She was right. I had changed. She made me self-conscious. I wasn't as interested in being different.

"So," she whispered. "What do you have planned this afternoon?"

"Planned? Why do you think I have something planned?"

"Just a guess. Have you met local people? Can you introduce me to your Tunisian friends?"

"What makes you think I have Tunisian friends?"

"Because I know you! I'd be disappointed if you didn't."

"It so happens that a Tunisian neighbor invited me to lunch this afternoon. He lives on this street."

"There, I knew it."

"He does little corkwood carvings."

"A craftsman. Oh, that's superb. Can I come along?"

"But your dad is here. He's the Ambassador. What about respect? I even thought I shouldn't just leave."

"That's ridiculous. Daddy won't mind. He won't miss us at all. There's already a long line to kiss his ass. It'll be chapped before he's back in Tunis."

Our midday meal was familiar to my first lunch in Tunisia at the Ambassador's Residence. Couscous shared the plate with hamburgers and hotdogs, which Rodney procured to Americanize the meal. He even found ketchup, mustard, pickles and buns. Or Dozier and Irving probably brought their own supply from Tunis.

After a half hour of empty banter, a camp record, lunch was over.

"It's been great meeting you," Ambassador Ardsley told the new volunteers at his table as he clapped his hands like an emcee concluding his show. "You're doing important work. Let's hope we never meet again. It's not personal. The Embassy won't hear from you unless you're in trouble. So please, let's not hear from you."

The lunch party laughed politely before bursting into applause. Then we all got up from the table. The camaraderie and good manners quickly dissolved as the important people prepared to leave, taking their importance with them. The Ambassador, his retinue and luncheon guests headed toward another house, where he would make a formal presentation for the entire Peace Corps cohort.

The procession moved slowly against the annihilating sunlight and the pungent waft of the open sewer of Ayn Draham. Maintaining their dignity, the Ambassador and his cadre ignored the stench and walked to the main event without flinching or covering their noses. Lauren and I dawdled, slipped to the back of the crowd, then stopped walking altogether, until we fell behind and sneaked off to Ali's house for a second lunch.

19

ALI AND THE ART OF OVEREATING

"This is so exciting," Lauren said as we tried to find the gate of

Ali's walled villa.

"Why don't you meet Ali before you say that?"

I liked the gentle woodworker but he was no celebrity, just a local guy who didn't do much of anything. I was trying to manage Lauren's expectations, so that she would not be disappointed.

When we found the metal door, I turned to Lauren. "Listen, I don't know how this will play out. You know Tunisians. Men and women are pretty segregated. Ali may be embarrassed."

"Doesn't he have a wife?"

"He lives with his mother."

"Perfect. Mothers love me. And I dressed for the occasion: white blouse, dark skirt. All covered up and hemline below the knees."

"Right. But remember, you don't speak or understand French."

"Yes, I do."

"Not here. A sophisticated woman may fluster him. If he knows you speak French, he'll clam up. There goes your story."

"You win."

"If you have to say something, speak English. I'll translate."

We entered the courtyard, a garden of infertility, disused vineyard staves entwined by brittle wisps of vegetation.

Ali sat on a bamboo chair on the porch of the main building, every inch the master of his impecunious domain. Our host was whittling corkwood. On closer examination, it was the figure of a slender woman with round breasts, sharply delineated nipples, a fragile clavicle, a long neck and a small head with protuberant eyeballs. It was Lauren's body and Ali's face. Had he predicted my unexpected guest?

As Lauren approached, I thought Ali's eyes would pop their sockets and roll down his cheeks.

"Who is this? Your wife, Rick?"

"No, this is my friend, Lauren. She is a television reporter from America."

"*Enchanté, Mademoiselle.*" The woodcutter grinned and bowed. "I am glad you have come. My mother always makes too much food. You will help me finish it."

"Relax. She doesn't know French," I reassured Ali under my breath.

He smiled and exhaled. "That is good, because I would not know what to say to her."

Just then Lauren noticed the figurine in Ali's hand and leaned closer to examine it. "It's extraordinary," she whispered.

Ali fumbled nervously with the female figurine and enclosed it in his fist. He had no idea that his artwork was admired. He may have believed that it revealed a shameful pornographic tendency that offended the lady. In his panic, he brought his hands together behind him, forgetting that there was a knife in one of them.

"*Je me suis piqué!*" Ali cried in pain. Instinctively, he inserted his cut finger between his lips to stop the bleeding, but, realizing the gross impression he might be making on his guests, he removed the bleeding digit from his mouth.

"I should not drink my blood," he said. "It is not an *apéritif.*"

He grinned at his riposte. We laughed and he appeared to relax—but not entirely. He was still clutching the naked female figurine, which bore a general resemblance to his female guest.

"Take it," he whispered as he thrust the amulet in my hand. "When you have no woman, this will keep a woman in your mind."

"His finger is still bleeding," Lauren said. "Here, I think I have something." She removed a Band-Aid from her purse and covered Ali's cut.

"*Merci, Mademoiselle,*" Ali said. "Your friend is very nice,

Rick."

"That went well," I whispered to Lauren.

A massive woman swathed in silk and chiffon tatters appeared in the doorway leading to a back room. Her mouth was divided between east and west of her remaining teeth. Ali's mother held a platter piled high with pasta. She exhorted us to eat, eat and eat!

But first she asked who Lauren was, hugged her and played with strands of her golden hair.

"Behi yessir!" she repeated. *"Très belle."*

As soon as Lauren and I took our seats at the Formica table, Ali's mother ladled out piles of *harissa*-coated pasta on our plates. Pasta was not considered a typical Tunisian dish, yet we often ate it in camp and it was also a standard side order at the *le restaurant populaire*. Pasta turned out to be as integral to Tunisian cuisine as the baguette, and no wonder since Italy was geographically the closest European country to Tunisia.

A fatty chunk of stewed lamb was embedded in the soft, twirling strands. *"Hamdulleh!"* My carnivorous nature flared as I speared the meat at the end of my knife. Submitting to a primordial urge, I tore into it with my incisors. Juices squirted in my mouth as if from a loaded sponge.

After the intense pleasure of the succulent meat came the towering pile of dry spaghetti. Because Mrs. Ali cut the strands in half, they would not stay on my fork when I tried to twirl them into thick spools to stuff in my mouth. Bowing my head over the plate, I used my fork like a shovel and pushed the noodles in.

Overeating was one sport Lauren knew nothing about. She glanced at me several times with mounting concern. Her fork moved lightly around the pasta as if she were dancing with it.

"I can't eat this," she whispered as she smiled charmingly for Ali and his mother.

"You have to. You're a guest. You want your story, right?"

Lauren took several bites, chewed thoroughly, swallowed and groaned. Ali and his mother interpreted this as appreciation.

"Your friend loves Tunisian food," Ali observed.

"Oh, yes, it's her favorite."

"I must lose weight," Lauren whispered. "I've gained ten pounds at this meal."

Ali's mother must have read Lauren's expression, because she expressed concern to Ali in Arabic.

"Is something wrong?" I asked.

"My mother thinks Lauren does not like the food."

"No, no, she loves it. She wants your mother's recipe."

Mrs. Ali smiled when Ali translated my lie. His mother regarded us beatifically from across the hut under a terry cloth tapestry depicting a sultan petting a lion under an electric blue sky. When our plates were fairly clean, she offered seconds.

Lauren stared at me as if she would rather stick a fork in me than eat another bite.

"This is the best *meklah* we have had in Tunisia. But overeating is unhealthy," I said.

Ali appeared to read my meaning and Lauren's distress.

"*C'est ça!*" Ali agreed. "*On y va?*"

He was halfway to standing up, when his irrepressible mother brought a Bundt cake to the table. It looked deliciously dense and we knew that even a portion of the sponge cake would absorb everything else we had consumed, inflate in our guts and prevent us from moving—ever again. Mrs. Ali cut a large wedge for me.

"*Shokran.* You're too kind," I said. "It's wonderful, but *wullah*, my stomach is not big. And Miss Lauren's is smaller than mine."

"My mother will be offended," Ali said. "You must honor her by eating her cake."

Mrs. Ali cut our pieces into smaller morsels to make them fit in our small stomachs. We tried to resist, but our implacable hostess held the dessert to Lauren's mouth; we struck a compromise and fed ourselves.

It is unnatural to want to be hungry, but as I crammed dense cubes of sweet cake into my dry mouth, I longed for a pang of hunger that would help me clean my plate without regurgitation.

20

FOREST SPIRITS AND DEMONS

I had chewed through half of my dessert and Lauren a quarter of hers when Ali proposed a walk. His mother lamented that we had not eaten the entire cake, but Ali explained that Americans ate less and it would be bad manners to make us eat more.

We climbed the stairs of Ayn Draham, our first test in keeping down our lunch, then up the main road toward Tabarka. Ali then guided us up a steep side path into the cork forest.

This was not a generic Peace Corps experience, but a personal discovery. I had been driven through these woods several times, but had never walked in them. Yet Lauren and I could not immediately enjoy our luck. We focused on keeping our heads straight and moving slowly just not to vomit. Eventually, the fresh and fragrant air and the forest's intangible power restored us and we quickened our pace.

The cork trees were long and slender, with tortuous trunks of delicate, white bark. They were tightly clustered, but did not just stand together—they interacted. Their gnarled trunks appeared to lean toward and away from another, as if engaged in lively repartée. They splintered sunlight into flickers. Here one did not need to hide from the sun; the trees put one in harmony with it.

"You and Miss Lauren are lucky," he said. "You are Americans. You have freedom."

"No, you are lucky because you know who you are and what you will be. You don't have to find your way," I replied.

"We're all lucky," Lauren said in English, as she belched and covered her mouth. "For different reasons."

Weariness and sorrow came over the face of the woodworker of Ayn Draham. His protuberant eyes shone with a curious light.

"Only remember this, my friend," he said. "God knows, time shows and the wind blows it away."

"Are you listening?" This man is amazing!" Lauren whispered.

By what quirk of fate had I come upon the Khalil Gibran of Ayn Draham?

"This wood," Ali intoned, as he drifted into the formulation of an idea. "I can't put in words how it makes me feel. My whole life I have come here to be alone with God. This is where life is best. Of course, this is all I know. I wonder if there are more beautiful places." He turned to us. "You have traveled. Have you been anywhere more beautiful than this?"

"I've lived most of my life in big cities. They're beautiful in a different way," I said. "I went to school where there were woods, fields and hills. That was beautiful, but this is better."

"They say there are *djins*, spirits and demons here and you never know what you'll find," Ali replied. "God is in the forest, but not his justice. Sometimes I am afraid when I come here."

We were tramping through a thicket when a fast, violent thrashing in the brush shook my balance. A snake was attacking a rat. Ali touched my shoulder and guided me away.

"Sometimes I think I made a mistake not to leave Ayn Draham," Ali said. "I thought there was no better place."

"Maybe you were right," I replied.

I understood his regret and wanted to console him, but Ali was not satisfied with my reassurance. He regarded me with helpless frustration, having come to the edge of what he wished to say, without saying it. When he was able to phrase his thought, his eyes widened and he raised his bandaged finger.

"Life is like *Oomo*, the Tunisian all-purpose detergent—we hope that it is pure, but can only guess its contents," he said.

"He's like the Poor Richard of Tunisia," Lauren remarked. "I wish I had brought my tape recorder."

Ali grinned sadly at Lauren and me. He hoped that we could read his meaning in this domestic adage, but it eluded me.

"Time is heavy for me," he said with watering eyes. As we crossed the rift and walked among tall, delicate white bark oaks, Ali stooped. Time seemed to be a stack of bricks on his shoulders that rose higher than the clouds.

Ali was on the verge of putting more feelings into words that would carry them like a caravan out of his mouth, but they were lost in the desert of his dejection. His lips parted in a silent cough, as he struggled to expel an adage that nearly choked him.

"Time is not sand in a clock," he said. "It is the sand on the beach, under the sea and in the desert. I try to build my life on it, but it will not stay; it blows away."

I felt something crawl on or under my skin. It may have been an insect, or my brain shedding ignorance to make room for enlightenment. We hiked silently, depressed by Ali's despair and his struggle to articulate it.

"This is beautiful," Ali said. "But I ask, *'C'est ça, la vie?' C'est tout? Il n'y en a plus?'* I know when I die I will ask, 'This was life?' There will be no more. And yet there was already too much."

He pounded his fist into his palm as if to smash the conundrum of his life with his hands. This gesture appeared to relieve his dejection. He smiled. "When you were eating my mother's *patte*, I laughed inside, because that is my life."

Ali's doubts exposed my own. I believed I wasn't making the most of my life, because doing so required insight and skill I had not developed.

"*C'est ça,*" I said in the manner of Ali. The master wood-worker chuckled at my mimicry. We shook hands and exchanged "*Hamdullehs!*" to express the tragic silliness of life.

Lauren had recovered from her massive effort to digest and the cultural correspondent in her was ecstatic. She found Ali intriguing as a local character, and thought our friendship was a touching angle.

"He's exotic, yet so real," Lauren said. "No one has ever seen anyone like him on TV. Do you think he would agree to an interview if I came back? Or we could pay for him to come to Tunis."

Suddenly, from the brush close by, we heard a woman gasping and the grunting of a wild beast. Could it be the fabled wild boar of Ayn Draham?

"*Zoobi, zoobi, zoobi,*" Ali cursed. He had found the origin of the arboreal noises. In a small clearing in the dense undergrowth, Bechir was having his way with Saida, the pretty maid. Bechir's body lay on hers like a heavy black sack and the only thing moving was his wide, hairy butt up and down like a sturdy old machine slightly out of whack. Saida's legs were splayed to the side, long and slender and fragile like broken wings.

"The woman I love, fucked by a dog!" Ali growled. He loaded a sharp rock on the end of a thick rubber band he used for shooting birds, pulled it back and fired. Bechir's body jerked for a second, then he screamed hoarsely as he rolled off his sexual captive.

We bolted as gunshots cracked the silence. To stay out of

sight, we crouched as we ran through the tall grass, not looking back. We leapt into a ravine and scampered for our lives up the other side, then sprinted upright through scrub and forest, until we reached the ridge above the stadium.

Such a narrow escape should have made us laugh with relief, but Ali looked so forlorn that Lauren and I could not exult in the adventure as we caught our breath and gazed down at the training camp from our wild dog's perspective. The woodworker's revenge had not mollified his pain.

"I'm sorry," I said.

His eyes revealed a deep and permanent melancholy and bespoke a misery that belonged to him as surely as his face. But suddenly, from under the suffering, his eyes lit with an insight that brought him pleasure.

"Where loves come from and where it goes, I cannot tell you. It passes through," he said. "The tree takes root and grows. The fire burns the tree. Yet the tree remains. Where does it take root to reach the sky? In you and I? In a forest of dreams or a thicket of lies?"

"In Bechir," I said.

Ali laughed and patted my arm. "Not in Bechir. Bechir is a fungus on the tree." The woodworking philosopher broke into his familiar grin.

Lauren and I thanked Ali and hurried back to the camp. We were late. She was excited.

"That was unbelievable," Lauren said. "I wish I had brought my camera and tape recorder. Ali is a bona fide folk hero—a Tunisan craftsman, a poet and a prophet. And he's good with a slingshot."

"It's too bad it's not an Olympic event," I said.

"Rick, you're so cynical."

"And you're a mess," I pointed out. Her skirt and blouse were dirty and covered with twigs and straw. Her shirtsleeve was torn. "The others will think we went to the woods to have sex."

"Will they?" she asked indifferently as she inventoried the damage to her clothes. "Damn! I've ruined a perfectly good pair of Guccis. *Pecato!* A fine excuse for buying another pair in Rome."

Ambassador Ardsley's visit was over and his entourage clustered around the caravan of black luxury vehicles. Lauren's father was chatting with Dozier and Irving. His security detail shuffled anxiously as they surveyed the area, no doubt for signs of Lauren.

"Seriously, don't tell anyone you were with me. They'll think I did something to you."

"Don't worry," she said.

"What *will* you tell your dad?"

"He probably didn't notice I was gone. But if he did, I'll tell him I was following a lead. Maybe he'll finally take me seriously. But I wouldn't bet on it."

"We should split now or they'll discharge me from the Peace Corps and incarcerate me."

"Okay. I had a great time. Let's keep in touch."

"Right."

After digesting Mrs. Ali's spaghetti and Ali's profundity, watching Bechir get laid and shot in the ass, and fleeing the scene at top speed, I could have used a siesta, but there was no time for sleep, and I was so tired anyway that rest would not have helped.

21

DOG FIRES

At first, the pile on the corner of Avenue Bourguiba and the crooked drive leading to the *lycée* looked like standard garbage. But a few hours later, after our morning classes, the defunctive stench and swarm of flies made us examine it more closely. It was a mound of dead dogs, covered in a crust of blood, their skulls and brains scattered in the dirt like soft pebbles. Their fur seemed to vibrate—a swarm of insects permeated their bodies and streamed from their orifices.

At lunch, anxiety ruled. The *mechoui* was that evening, but the dead dogs had slackened enthusiasm for the event, at which two freshly slaughtered lambs would be roasted. The air carried a haze of portent, a dull hum like labored breathing, as if its molecules were sighing. Many of the volunteers had pets at home; some had even made friends with local rodents and fed them crusts of old bread from the wooden bin. These animal lovers were the most affected by the slain canines.

"I say we take over Ayn Draham in the name of the ASPCA," Stuart said. "We'll declare martial law and put dog-killers to justice."

Tasha gave Stuart a silent rebuke, but she too was clearly shaken by the acts of carnage that were beyond our control. She was not one for grandiloquence. She communicated best one on one and established her authority to the group with her presence and decision-making. Yet now she spoke with purpose and conviction.

"We've worked long and hard this summer and I won't let the killing of wild dogs ruin a party I've been planning since day one of training camp. Volunteers are coming from all over Tunisia. Sure, the Peace Corps is about doing a good job and helping the host country. But it's also about having fun and appreciating the people you're with. So everybody rest up because tonight's going to be the best party ever," she said.

"Right on," was the dismal response, as shouts and whining amplified outside. I couldn't help thinking, "A party's a perfect place to die."

Rodney "the Procurer" patted me on the back with his pink-fingered claw and cried, "Hallelujah, Murkey, don't you see it? ASPCA Worldwide. Like the Red Cross. We could go anywhere, expenses paid." Rodney grinned madly as he mulled this profitable though improbable angle.

"No, I hadn't thought of that," I said as Rodney scuttled off, his legs sausaged in Livia's black jeans. It was their subtle way of saying he was in her pants.

In the mirror of the long, dark latrine, my face was drained, my eyes rimmed with pink. Were these the final signs of the disease that had been gestating in me for weeks since the mysterious claw piercings in my heel? I had already noticed more than the average of number of vultures circling overhead.

Thoughts of my poor mother rolled into my mind like a dark nimbus. After all the years she supported me, with doctor's appointments, summer enrichments and college tuition, what a failure I was. Dead—right out of college!

"Cretin! Ignoramus!" I taunted the ashen face in the mirror.

Lying in my bunk, I crossed my hands. Thoughts buzzed like gnats, then slowed, as my mind uncoiled. Dreams came in a vague, listless sleep—a montage of faces, places, and events from my life, and one long highlight of running home from school in torrential rain, laughing, my clothes soaked through.

"Rick, get up. It's four o'clock." I felt a hand on my shoulder shaking me. It was Tasha.

I wanted to tell her to let me sleep, but couldn't. No last minute ravings. I had to face my consequences quietly, or my mother would have to pay my burial costs out of pocket.

"I swear, Rick, I'm recommending you for Metloui!"

This was a remote spot in Tunisia, where few westerners lived and even fewer were likely to visit or return from sane or alive. Tasha expected me to trepidate.

"No problem," I replied, "Can't wait." I giggled and broke into a deep-throated laughter, like a goofy Dracula. Tasha couldn't resist laughing, too. What else could she do when the stench of decomposed dogs polluted each breath and shellacked your face with disease and slime?

Clouds appeared overhead; they seemed to arrive from nowhere to squat over Ayn Draham. They brought with them a peculiar, moist breeze, the first sign of rain in several weeks.

"It better not rain, Allah, you hear me?" Tasha pointed her finger to the sky. "I'll never forgive you if you rain on my party!"

By the *lycée*, the dog pile was now a pyre, with flames yielding a brown, acrid smoke. Local men in white tunics surrounded the blaze. A car pulled up. Rodney jumped out, wildly waving his deformed hand.

"Stop! You can't do this!" he fulminated against the town elders. "This stinks, do you understand?" He pinched his nose to demonstrate, but the local citizens were motionless before the smoke. Their silent intransigence further incensed Rodney.

"You can't burn these dogs here, do you hear me? It's disgusting! We're having a party over there! People will be eating, drinking, dammit. You can't make us breathe this filth! It's a violation of international law. Do you understand?"

Rodney thrust his pink claw in an elder's face. The man let out a piercing cry and recoiled from Rodney. Moncef, the Tunisian teacher, urged Rodney to back off. He explained that the townspeople were burning the *djins* in the dead animals.

"Make them stop!" Rodney cried. He was wild now, swaying

and waving his thalidomide claw in every direction to frighten the local people with his deformity. The mullahs fell back from the fire, believing, no doubt, that Rodney was the evil *djin* they were trying to expunge from the corrupted dogs.

"I'll show you what I think of your Tunisian hospitality," shouted the camp quartermaster as he shoveled dirt hyperactively on the flames. "You ignorant zombies!"

The leader raised his arm again and issued another piercing cry. Suddenly, townspeople pelted Rodney with stones and drove him to the ground, where he lay curled in a protective ball. A group of us ran interference between Rodney and his assailants, and closed ranks around him. We kept our heads down and our hands up to show that we did not intend to fight. When the elders felt that their pyre was safe, they dropped their ammunition. As we carried Rodney from the circle, a dog skull rolled from the top of the pile, fire sizzling between its teeth.

22

PARTY TIME

Disease and death do not appear in every frame, in every moment of life. You perceive them in flashes before they disappear. You sense their proximity, and since you can't see them, their closeness is always in your head.

"Welcome to my party," Tasha said, as she pulled me into the crowd. The camp director was dressed as a Bedouin woman, in an array of skirts, sashes and kerchiefs purchased at her beloved flea markets. The back of the *K'sar Haddada* house, the one closest to the stadium, was now set up with a stage of milk crates and wood planks propped up against the back porch. Agricultural workers and well-digging crews had driven in from all over the country. Their CARE and AID trucks and vans now circled off the makeshift amphitheater. Coolers stocked with wine and beer were everywhere in violation of Bourguiba's recent "get tough" edict banning the purchase and consumption of alcoholic beverages on the Muslim Sabbath. This measure was widely interpreted as the liberal strongman's ploy to seem religiously-minded in response to critics who accused him of pandering to western thinking and tourist dollars. Whatever the impetus for the new policy, our party's liquor stock suggested that it was mainly for show.

Two trucks beamed their headlights on the stage at the emcee—none other than Bechir, the wounded lecher, who had rolled out of sight for the past few weeks, no doubt nursing his punctured rump. He stood before us with a thick wad of rumpled padding around his flanks and waved his arms for quiet. He introduced the musicians. Five wraiths in white *jebbas*—loose tunics that went to the middle of their calves—stepped on stage to tune their traditional Andalusian instruments—the *ud (guitar),* the *mizwad (bagpipe),* the *nay (recorder),* the *kanun (autoharp)* and the *darbuka (clay drum).* Their first plucks, squeaks, strums and pops started, paused and twisted before they gathered in one powerful hypnotic sound.

When the five lean men first appeared, they seemed to float down from heaven, but once they started jamming, they were not too ethereal to swing the party to life. The *nay* wailed, the *ud* twanged a hot, driving riff, the *kanun* made the rhythm surge like a string section and the *mizwad* whined like the original synthesizer over the palpitating, ground-shaking *darbuka* beats.

The *mizwad* was an intricate instrument, a large, goatskin sack with two pipes jutting from one end and two little tips like animal teats for pitch on opposing sides. The *mizwad* was a versatile instrument. It could sound like baby elephants, beep like car horns, or chatter and chirp like besotted birds.

The maids, restrained by their need to be modest in front of men, moved with sensuous subtlety under *safsaris*, their ankles and wrists jingling with bells to embellish the Malouf beat with the furtive movements of the forest. A great tension was building in the party, as the music raised the energy to unbearable levels that only dancing could release.

Suddenly Tasha and Livia, wearing *sinj* on their fingers and *jallalil* around their ankles, spun around the stage. They had hennaed the bottoms of their feet and now kicked high with red soled frenzy. Each dancer took her turn toward the *mechoui*, luring flames from the spit in her direction. Smoke curled around the smoke-charmers like vapor snakes. Livia was sinuous and limber, smoke incarnate, while Tasha's oval face made her resemble a spirit doll in nomadic beads and sashes.

Compact and powerful, Tasha pirouetted to the fire, then shimmied down from the shoulders, limbo-like, until she arched back on folded legs, with her shoulder blades nearly brushing the floor. She had mentioned in passing that she minored in dance in college and that the chance to study folk dance drew her to the Peace Corps. This was her ultimate creative statement.

A lick of smoke followed Tasha down and settled on her skin like a sheet until she disappeared under it. The music increased in volume and tempo to a febrile crescendo. Tasha voiced a long, aspirant, "Ahhhh!" and a jubilant shriek. The smoke dispersed. She sprang up from the shoulders and hips and back to her feet. Then, with a distant gaze and a rapt smile, she cut a twirling, spinning path through the crowd, as if dancing in open space.

Bechir, transported by the succulent sounds and the dancing women, forgot his place in the Peace Corps order and chased Tasha around the circle, clicking his fingers, as he tried to engage her in a mating dance. At every turn she eluded him. When the self-appointed Peace Corps bouncers realized that this was not part of the act, but improvised lewdness, they rushed to stop Bechir. The lascivious landowner, who was losing his butt padding in the midst of his hip thrusting and gesticulations, finally lost his balance. He fell on the ground, where he rolled and foundered, as volunteers laughed and splashed him with beer.

"Why did life have to end so beautifully?" I wondered. I was weak, feverish and freezing, yet the music and dance made me happier than I'd been since coming here. The musicians started another *mezwad* melody and more dancers with towels wrapped around their hips gyrated around the *mechoui* like flashing human tops, their eyes wide and mouths open to the fire.

"Rick, are you all right?" Tasha asked, her hand on my arm, her eyes probing.

"Sure," I choked down a sob. I couldn't tell her now about the disease that would soon transport me from the party.

I thought about Cerise. What a fool I had been to swear my love—and two months of chastity—to her! What good were these fine sentiments now? How much I wanted to tell Tasha everything, to make love to her and coax my manhood to its final glory.

The music had lured the dogs out on the ridge, where they howled for the first time that evening. They had found the wailing of the *mizwad* irresistible. Accompanying the organ music with their plaintive vocals, the dogs comprised a magnificent choir, improvising an oratorio of pain.

Suddenly, gunfire cracked on the horizon. The lead dog, whose body had been arched in consummate self-expression, flipped in the air and dropped as his companions scattered, barking and yelping in terror. The townspeople were on the prowl and determined to exterminate every last canine in the vicinity.

Meanwhile, the Peace Corps crowd was losing patience with

the slow-cooking feast. The mood was ugly. The lambs were not roasting fast enough. They had just begun to have dark crusts on their fat jackets. The meat was not sufficiently done to kill a tapeworm, but the supervisors, determined to keep the party going, gave the signal for the *mechoui* to be served.

Machetes were deployed to hack the lambs into raw chunks and ragged slices. Since utensils were scarce, revelers tore at the raw lamb flesh with their teeth. I tried to eat my portion, perhaps my last, but it was riddled with gelatinous fat and gristle and I could barely chew and swallow it.

I was flushed, my head was pounding and I was shivering hard. Regardless of how much I drank, my lips were parched. My eyes burned in their sockets. My throat was swollen and my legs felt as rubbery as the lamb-fat on my paper plate.

I staggered to the house, stripped down to my nylon briefs with the red racing stripes and collapsed in the narrow bathroom. My mouth tasted nauseatingly greasy and my breath stank of fever and red wine. I knelt before the dark bowl, trying to purge the disease by vomiting. After dry heaving for several minutes, I took a break. My head hung over the bowl. I wept and started to pray.

"Whoever you are up there, how could you let me die this way—without cause or reason, in this place you, yourself, have forsaken—to eat a last supper of uncooked meat while dogs are massacred in the moonlight?"

"Oh, great Whatever-Name-You're-Going-By-These-Days, must I die as a silent casualty, a secret statistic, an underdeveloped life in an underdeveloped country?"

There was silence, then a gurgling of pipes. I unfolded my arms and stared down into the black profundity of the toilet bowl. Above my genuflection, through the narrow window where I'd first watched and heard the dogs serenade, torchlight wavered as more gunshots cracked from the ridge.

My body trembled so violently now that I could not lift myself from the bathroom floor. I tucked myself in a tight ball to absorb the shaking. Before I had tried to expunge the disease, but now I tried to put myself to sleep, to have this end quickly without detection.

There was a rapping at the door.

"Who's in there?" Tasha asked. When I tried to answer, my teeth were chattering too hard for me to make a coherent sound. Tasha tried turning the handle, but I had latched the door shut due to natural modesty.

"Who's in there?" she repeated, pounding on the door.

"It's me," I croaked.

"Rick? What are you doing?"

How could I explain? I crawled to the door and released the latch.

"Rick, are you all right?"

I had sworn at the party that if she asked me this again I'd wring her neck, but now I was too ill to follow through.

"I'm all right!" I shouted hoarsely, as I tried to stand. My legs buckled and I fell in a heap. Why did she have to see me this way?

She placed her hand on my forehead. "You're burning up."

I laughed feebly. "Burning up? I'm dying."

23
DELIVERED

Tasha helped me to my feet and walked me slowly to her house, where she laid me on her bed and covered me.

I woke up in the late afternoon. I was alone, seemingly for the first time since I arrived in Tunisia. I had not died, just contracted an intestinal virus. When I returned from the bathroom, Tasha was in the room, changing the sheets.

"You're awake!" she smiled. "You slept for two days."

"Thanks for helping me," I said. "I thought I was going to die."

"Not even close," she said.

"Did I say anything embarrassing?"

A smile curled on her lips. "No more than usual. Oh, you said you loved me."

Heat returned to my face. I was in an embarrassing spot between admission and denial. "I did?"

Her brown eyes locked mine. "Relax. I didn't believe you. You were raving so it doesn't count."

"Thanks, Tasha," I replied gratefully. It swiftly occurred to me that I sounded way too happy about not being in love with her and she might be offended. I tried to compensate. "I mean, you're wonderful, but I *was* delirious."

That too sounded so loutish that I stopped talking and let my hapless grin misspeak for me.

Tasha smiled. She apparently found my awkwardness and discomfort amusing, if not endearing. She reached in her pocket and extracted a blue paper square. It was a familiar aerogram.

"I brought your mail. I believe it's from your girlfriend."

Tasha holding Cerise's letter in her hand struck me with the violent force of a nightmare. They were meeting for the first time without an introduction. Their symbolic proximity was not all that took me aback. I had believed that Tasha and Cerise were bleach and ammonia—combining them would surely explode in my face. But nothing happened. My hand reached for the blue rectangle reflexively but stopped in midair.

"How do you know it's from my girlfriend?" I asked. "How do you even know I have a girlfriend?" My face was burning again but not from a virus. I needed to shift the focus from my intrigue to her intuition.

"I know more about you than you think," she said with good-natured candor.

I accepted the aerogram from Tasha reluctantly. It was a token of what had made me stiff and uncomfortable with her. She knew me, despite my effort to be mysterious. Yet, she was a benevolent despot, no petty tyrant. I felt great tenderness for her, so maybe my delirious ravings were true. I wanted to tell her so, but the blue paper square in my hand kept me from speaking. Tasha smiled enigmatically as she unfurled another sheet and let it float onto the bed.

24
I'M NO EINSTEIN AND THE BEACH

Rick,

I received your letter and was both pleased and astonished at how practical you've become. I didn't know you had it in you. As a result, I've planned to come to you in Tunisia. I took the only flight available on Saturday, the 24th of August. I realize that you may be unable to leave on Saturday, so I am prepared to wait for you at a hotel. Would you book me a reservation? Thank you. If you do not come by Sunday, I will be forced to wander the streets for a Kasbah gangbang. But I hope you will be there. It's been 13 months since I've had any sex and I am more than ready. I love you madly, incredibly, impatiently and incurably...

Cerise

It felt so great for Cerise to be happy with me even for a moment that I believed my mission was as close to success as she thought it was. But there remained one significant step to take.

I had to ask Tasha for permission. And I couldn't do it.

For two months, I had tried to hold onto my pre-Peace Corps identity, to keep my emotions constant and my goals intact, but living in this commune had changed me, and now that I was close to my goal it felt too close.

When Tasha had teased me and peeled away my attitude, layer by layer, I eagerly anticipated asking her to authorize my tryst with Cerise in Ayn Draham. I wanted to show her and everyone else that I was not just a mixed-up kid, but a double agent for love and America—seeing Cerise was always my first priority, the Peace Corps was just a cover.

But now I avoided asking Tasha, no doubt because I dreaded that she would say, "Yes." I cared about her. I knew she deserved love and that she cared about me, if only as a friend. I also knew that asking Tasha to see Cerise would mean the end of something. It would preclude our ever knowing each other better—and I pre-grieved this loss.

Yet, the question had to be asked. Cerise had bought her ticket to Tunis and I could not strand her there.

"Sure, your girlfriend can come and you can meet her," Tasha said when I stammered my request. "Jamal's driving to Tunis next Saturday. You can go with him."

Tasha smiled reassuringly. Was it sadness I detected in her eyes or my own dejection reflected in them that made it hard to thank her? Nothing had happened between us. I had behaved correctly and eluded the snares of lies, false promises and vain pursuits. I ought to have been satisfied with my conduct. This was how life should be lived—without complications, confusions or regrets.

Tasha's swift approval of my plans was so unexpected that I was in euphoric disbelief. Was life ever this easy? It gave me confidence. I convinced myself that I had handled everything perfectly.

But soon after this glowing self-assessment, I fell into a funk and was miserable for days. I did not look forward to seeing Cerise; I even hoped that she would not come. I started writing poetry—a bad sign. After resisting my feelings for Tasha, here they were, banging inside my brain. I felt cheated. I had started to build a life here despite myself, and Tasha was part of it. Now it was ending.

I could not be around Tasha, but I could not stop thinking of her. She was in camp, two houses down, as she had been for nine weeks, but I did not see her, until she handed me a folded note.

"Did you lose this?"

I unfolded the math sheet and read the lines I had written in perplexed introspection. I never even knew the paper was missing.

"Do I love her? Do I need her?
Am I fooling myself, am I leading her on?
Do I feel the things I should feel?
Is it a fantasy, or real?"

I blushed. "I guess I wrote it. Did you read it?"

Tasha regarded me frankly. "Yes. It's interesting. It's a poem, right? Or maybe a song lyric. You're more sensitive than you let on, Murkey," she said. "You should develop it."

Even while she held damning evidence of my confusion and emotional fraud, Tasha chose not to question or discuss the content of those lines.

"Thanks. I mean I guess I will. Writing things down is how I try to deal with them. I'm no Einstein with emotions."

"Nobody is," Tasha said. She swept her hair off her face and assumed a friendly tone. "We're going to the beach. Do you want to come?"

She was letting me know that we could still be friends, that she understood my situation and did not consider me a two-timing traitor.

"Sure. That would be great."

"Get your swimsuit and towel and let's go."

It was a flawless day with transparent sunlight and a fresh breeze. Tasha and I lay on the deserted beach while our companions swam 200 feet out. They waved their arms and shouted to flaunt their feat, but their voices mingled with the waves. From a distance, Arab women in white *safsaris*, with children in tow, walked toward us on the beach, laden with baskets.

Tasha lay prone by my side. Her round buttocks in a faded flowered bikini were domed cupolas calling me to worship. My body tingled. I was filled with desire, but what could I do?

"Tasha," I whispered, in so low a voice that I could barely hear it. My heart jumped as she moved. "Tasha," I whispered more boldly. What would I say if she answered? Should I propose that we walk down the beach to a more secluded spot or behind some rocks? Was I insane?

I looked around. The other volunteers were frolicking and waving, exhorting us to join them in the cool blue. The Tunisian women in fluttering white sheets settled their plastic baskets a short distance away, as their nearly naked children gamboled. Two Arab men in rolled-up pants sauntered aimlessly toward us.

Tasha lay still. Was she sleeping? I had an impulse to lie next to her and whisper in her ear, "I love you!"

I swore under my breath that I was a fool. My girlfriend was arriving in a few days and others were watching. Tasha would be angry if I woke her up.

"Don't ruin it now, idiot!" I berated myself. "Just lie here."

But the longer I tried to cool my passion, the hotter I got. Her firm round buttocks and shapely thighs belonged to a fertility goddess. I ached for her. We would probably never go farther, but at least at that moment I needed to express what I felt for Tasha, *to* Tasha.

The swimmers were splashing toward the shore and laughing—apparently at my dilemma. Suddenly, I realized what I should do. I crouched over Tasha and whispered her name.

No response.

Still kneeling, I found a slender blue vein behind her knee that ran along a beauty mark. On a map of Tasha, this vein was a river and that mole a state capital, or at least, a county seat. I drew closer, bending until I seemed to be genuflecting, and kissed the county seat.

Tasha didn't move. I prostrated myself again, kissed the same place and ran to the sea.

25

CERISE IN THE SUPERMARKET

I dreamed of wandering through a suburban supermarket. Silent strangers pulled grocery products off of shelves and tossed them in carts along wide, air-conditioned aisles. I looked everywhere for Cerise and called out for her, but she didn't reply. It was useless asking anyone if they'd seen her. I was the only one who knew her and she was gone—forever.

I woke up in a sweat; it was another supermarket nightmare. Why was I fixated on supermarkets? Was it homesickness? A yearning for more food, or more choices?

Agitated and perplexed, I reminded myself that I was meeting Cerise in 12 hours after not seeing her for 13 months. Could I not relax and enjoy the day that I was reuniting with the woman I loved after coming 4,300 miles for that purpose?

"Think!" I told myself. "Tonight you'll make love to Cerise!"

Yet on the brink of this deferred dream, the message of the nightmare haunted me. Every rendezvous entailed a separation, which postponed the ultimate separation. One day I would return to a world without Cerise that was as cold and bland as the one before she arrived, but worse because of the memory and the longing she would leave behind.

26

DRIVING WITH JAMAL

Jamal, the handsome, barrel-chested education director of the camp, was a congenial travel companion and a seasoned driver. Although he would later be exposed for plagiarizing our innovative language text, the education director's tact and friendly disposition made him seem exceptionally trustworthy. He was indifferent to the "dirt" that grabbed most peoples' attention, untroubled by bad moods and dark thoughts, impervious to perplexity and doubt and endowed with an unequivocal exuberance for life.

After three hours of driving, we stopped by the stand of a roadside vendor whose *shishkabob* Jamal had frequently savored on road trips between Ayn Draham and Tunis. This was part of what made Jamal special—he was aristocratic in his bearing but had a gift for enjoying simple pleasures. He extolled the savory cubes of grilled lamb laced with long red *filfils*, then tore one from the stick with his incisors and chewed it with enthusiasm. He lifted the *shishka-stick*.

"I will eat the fat of no other meat," he proclaimed to me and to the empty streets of Medjez El Bab, where squat blue and white buildings appeared to float in a sea of dust.

With pale, green eyes, a warm smile and a light, athletic gait for a large man, Jamal carried himself like a living master—*a master of living*. Life was a game for him, but rather than play it, he lived it playfully. He wore authority not as a skin but as an accessory, which he easily removed. At that moment, he was no longer the educational director and I was no longer the student; we were two *copains*, standing by the road to Tunis, devouring chunks of broiled lamb, guzzling sodas and squinting in the white sunlight.

"It is good, no?" Jamal asked. He raised his *Fanta* bottle and I raised my bottle of *Gini*, as he made a toast. "Savor the meat and the moment!"

These were billboard words worth living by. As we chewed the succulent meat and fat and peered into the glare of pale sunlight, we heard bells shaking, *darbukas* thumping, a *mizwad* moaning and a *nay* wailing. In the blinding light and sizzling heat, it was possible to visualize a caravan of dancing dromedaries—was this my first auditory mirage?

"*Écoute!*" Jamal whispered and turned to the food vendor. "*Shnoah, Sidi?* What is it?"

The food vendor patted his chest and waved his hand in rapid circles as he launched into a lyrical speech in Arabic, full of passionate bursts and pauses, about the otherworldly sounds emanating from the town square.

"*Tu es chanceux, mon jeune ami*," Jamal said. "You are a lucky man. We have come just when the great singer Karim Hambowi is in Medjez-el-Bab. *The Desert Lark* is giving a public rehearsal. If you love music, you are in for a treat. *Fisa fisa!* We must go quickly. *Allons-y!*"

In the center of the square, circumscribed by squat blue and white buildings and dominated by three two-story edifices—the post office, the police station and the municipal building—an ensemble of musicians in white *jebbas* was playing. A modest crowd around the artists swayed in total silence, more like light waves than assembled bodies.

In the middle of the small orchestra, a gaunt figure in a black suit and tie and black-framed sunglasses was singing. He clutched the microphone-stand so tightly that he seemed to be using it to stand upright. The great Hambowi's frail body twisted and his face trembled as his protean voice moaned lyrics with exhilarating and excruciating emotion. Two violins swooned in accompaniment, while *darbukas* tattooed a feverish beat and an *ud* and *kanun* super-zither reinforced the rhythm with lush chordal swells.

"Hambowi is very sick," Jamal whispered. "His lungs and eyes are nearly gone from an illness he contracted as a child. Shistosomiasis."

I had read about this debilitating scourge in the Peace Corps handbook. It came from infected snails in standing water. Worms crept into the soles of the feet, migrated to the lungs, laid eggs and often left victims blind and breathless.

"What is he doing here?" I asked.

"He was born in Medjez-el-Bab. This is his hometown," Jamal replied. "He is here to attend his cousin's wedding. One finds greatness in obscure places."

Karim Hambowi sang as if every word of every lyric contained a treasure within a geode of casual meaning. The struggle to reveal the truth in his song played on his dark, handsome face. His voice by turns lulled, comforted and pierced the ear. He was so engrossed in his music that scales and octaves fell away from him like old skins and dry husks. His voice rose to a lofty pitch, warbled, screeched, broke and lowered to a deep-throated baritone. He bore an expression of exquisite anguish and sublime transport; his voice was a bridge between two worlds. His body trembled under the stress. His hand fluttered over his chest. He dropped his head and the music stopped.

The square was silent, Medjez-el-Bab was silent, the sun and the air were silent. There was no sound until several vultures took flight and drifted overhead like kites, making echoes with their flapping wings. The crowd erupted in sudden, motley applause—clapping, hooting and yelling. Women cried, gasped and ululated. Hambowi humbly acknowledged his audience by bowing, smiling weakly and removing his shades. His irises were white, obscured by cataracts.

Jamal and I returned to the car and resumed our journey. We were both stunned by the music and the aftershock of sun and heat. Finally Jamal broke the silence.

"Hambowi's song was very sad. It is painful to know of death and disease," said the wise and burly Jamal. "We live, so we must die. Between the beginning and the end, we make what we can of this life, something true and beautiful if we can. Life is not always good. There is enough pain, unhappiness and despair in each life to fill seven, but when you believe even for a moment that life is not worth living, remember that there is nothing we can ever make or imagine that is as lovely as the fragrance of jasmine. Life gives us this—and so much more."

There is no free lunch or free ride. Jamal's philosophy 101 was the course requirement for the drive to Tunis and I should have accepted it as a bonus and a bargain. On the verge of reuniting with the woman of my life, it seemed natural to have exhilarating thoughts, acknowledge my luck and the goodness of others—but I didn't. Jamal's glorious four-star lamb-fat and *filfil* had given me reflux and his gospel of joy made me anxious. I lapsed into sullen silence.

Jamal might have been bored with my company, or felt he needed to dispel the bad vibes I circulated. He turned on the radio. A man was warbling as violins screamed toward a tumultuous crescendo.

"*C'est incroyable!* Do you recognize the singing?" he cried.

"I know it's not Pink Floyd," I joked.

"That is correct. It is Hambowi, *the Desert Lark.* We just heard him in the town square. Is it luck or is it fate?"

I was going to ask if I could check another box for "headache," but Jamal was such an amiable companion that I could not break it to him that my cross-cultural interest stopped at musical appreciation. After he sang a few verses with *the Desert Lark,* he asked, "Do you understand the words?"

"No," I admitted.

"*C'est dommage,*" he said. "It seems to have been written for you."

"Anything is possible," I said. "But what could *the Desert Lark* and I have in common?"

"Because you have the curiosity to pose this question, I will give you an answer," Jamal replied. "I will translate the song."

"I went to have my teacup read.
An old woman in gypsy rags sat before me.
She watched my tealeaves swirl in the cup.
I thought I would die waiting for the leaves to make a sign,
She read them and smiled,
'Fear not,' she said, 'for love will come to you in time.'
Then her face turned to stone—

There was sadness in her eyes;
'Death awaits you,' she sighed.
I cried and fled.
I ran down streets, afraid to stop,
Afraid to accept the sign in my cup.
I walked for miles. Fear was my only friend,
I was tired and lost.
I could see no beginnings, only the end.
I stared into the dark,
Sadness overpowered me.
I lay down and wept,
When a hand touched my shoulder.
I turned, but no one was there.
I heard the woman's voice:
'Death is far away. Leave your fear behind.
Find your love today.'
Dawn came and my fear was gone.
I see death on my horizon,
I know my fate
But my soul is free.
Death has set me free."

Jamal's voice-over translation of the lyrics faded as the song played on. It was a live recording and the tune might have continued for hours. Listening to Hambowi after learning about his life and hearing his lyrics was like being in the ocean after having only seen it from the shore. When Hambowi moaned, sighed and burst into a fervent chant, I thought of his mortality and the young man's simple destiny, to love and die. As I listened, I felt a pressure on my chest. Tears filled my eyes. I was ashamed of the incontinent feelings that rushed out of me. I squinted at the windshield to hide my tears. The song abruptly ended and the wild applause that ensued made me swallow and cough to muffle a sob.

"Did you like the song?" Jamal asked eagerly.

I nodded and mumbled incoherently, attempting to conceal my reaction.

"It was great. Very powerful. Thanks, Jamal."

He glanced at me and smiled benevolently. He understood the effect the song had on me and was pleased.

"You're welcome," he laughed in his gracious, indulgent way and turned his attention to the road, so that I could compose myself.

"You know, there are only two important questions," Jamal interrupted the silence in a casual tone. "'When will I die?' and 'How will I live?' We cannot answer the first, so we must answer the second. To know how to live, we must answer yet another question, "What is true and what is false?"

"It sounds simple," I said abstractedly.

"*Mais c'est très difficile!*" Jamal replied, "Regardless of how much we know, it is impossible to know everything. In a moment, when someone tells you something, you must ask, 'Is it true or false?' Everything depends on guessing right. If you are deceived, you can waste time or lose your life."

Success and survival being reduced to an endless sequence of "true" or "false" tests confirmed my bleakest expectation of life, but being mentally prepared for this truth did not ease its impact on my fragile confidence and somber mood.

"*Ne t'en fais pas, jeune homme.* Don't be sad or worried," Jamal said. "You will learn *shweah b'shweah.*"

"How can I not be worried? Do you expect me to be happy about living in ignorance and uncertainty?"

"*Bien sur!* Be happy," Jamal laughed, exposing the gap

between his large front teeth. "This is what life is—and you are alive!"

"But I can't read minds and it's impossible to know everything," I protested. "Guessing true or false every moment is like going through life blindfolded."

"You need faith," Jamal said. "Relax. As we say in Tunisia, *In sh'Allah.*"

Tunis reached out to motorists with its metropolitan tentacles—wide, urban highways skirted by billboards and redolent of motor oil and seawater. At a remove of ten kilometers, we inhaled the putrid tang of Tunis Lake. Jamal dropped me off on Boulevard Bourguiba in a throng of white sheets and teeming cafés at the epicenter of Tunis.

"Thanks for the ride—for everything, Jamal."

"*Pas de quoi,*" he replied, nodding his head. "*Bislema,* Rick, *et bonne chance.*" With a wave of his hand and an easy smile, the big man jockeyed his little Fiat into the jitterbugging traffic.

BOOK 2
TUNISIA, WITH LOVE

1

HOT NIGHT IN TUNIS

Six o'clock and no Cerise. Did I go through all of this for nothing? Scenarios of shame piled high in my imagination—a fertile field of paranoia, even on a good day. Getting stood up at an airport was pathetic. If I returned to training camp without Cerise, at best I would be viewed as a romantic loser. Worse case, people would say I made up an imaginary girlfriend.

In elementary school, I did not always listen to instructions. When a teacher told us how to take a test, I listened up to a point before zoning out. When the teacher stopped talking and we had to start our task, I looked frantically at the next child to ask what I missed. I had the same anxiety now as I waited for Cerise. Did I recall the right date, time and place? My doubts deepened with each passing second. I started to convince myself that I had bungled the rendezvous. How could I be so dense?

A tap on the shoulder interrupted my anxious musings.

"Hello."

She stood behind me, deeply tanned, smiling tightly through bright teeth, looking smaller and more fragile in person than I remembered her. She shook her head wistfully. Her eyes were as moist and bright as a sun shower.

"As usual, standing the wrong way," she teased. With a catch in her throat, she added, "You're so thin."

"So are you."

The cab driver in the red and white Renault was jazzed on the spastic rhythms of traffic and the vibrations of the old four-cylinder engine. This must have been a fringe benefit of his grueling job. No matter how fast he drove, he couldn't be making much *floos* with fares so low and the meter ticking so slowly.

Cerise and I made out in the back with long soulful kisses, our legs entangled with her bags. Her lips felt incredibly soft.

"Did you miss me?" she asked, holding my face between her hands as if it were a crystal ball. She drew me back to her and kissed me tenderly on the mouth.

"I want to be a whore to the man I love," she murmured in my ear and began proving it by clutching my penis with a firm and delicate hand. Her spontaneous lust in the backseat mingled with the intense evening street action wafting in through the open windows. In one moment, her touch excited me more than my imagination could do. The intimacy and directness of her desire became more powerful and real to me than the sum of her letters, and overpowered memory, longing and control. I remembered the time I tried to lose my virginity in a Volkswagen—the contorted limbs, tangled clothes and steaming windows. If I did not pull away from Cerise and restore decorum, there would be an accident resulting in significant damage to the romance of our encounter.

"Can we wait until we get to the hotel?" I asked.

"I don't know," she intoned seductively. "I've been needing it badly."

The Hotel d'Amilcar squatted behind a dingy red awning that sagged like a frown of exhaustion. I gave the driver a *dinar* tip. He was so grateful that he pulled away with my foot in the car. The back door flapped open as he turned the corner, like a wave goodbye.

Our room was dark and airless. Asphyxiation was a noted aphrodisiac.

Desire filled the room, expelling all that was extraneous to physical sensation. In a silence not lacking words but beyond them, like a peak above the tree line, Cerise stood naked before me, long and slender, her skin nutty brown but for her red nipples and black pubic hair. Her eyes fixed on mine, then lowered shyly, as she offered herself to me. After one year of separation, we were pilgrims returning to a sacred place, divided from innocence only by the distant recall of the pleasure we again expected to receive.

Cerise approached me on arched feet and stopped just beyond my reach. In this way I might encounter her from a tantalizing middle distance, enter the atmosphere around her and inhale her perfume. She stepped closer still and reached to stroke my cheek, her tearful eyes fixed on mine. Each diminished distance was a lowered veil revealing a greater intensity of intimate rediscovery.

As we stood almost touching, my jaws tightened, my skin tingled, my entrails hummed. In the year we were apart Cerise had existed to me only through her letters and her absence. Now her form, fragrance and warmth poured over me and filled me, expelling her absence. I closed my eyes. My sensations of her were so intense that I could barely breathe.

"My love," she gasped.

Seeing and touching her, I was awed by her reality and all of the emotions she stirred in me. She was not only the object of my lust, but a miraculous *Galatea* come to life from the ether of desire, paper and ink.

When Cerise was close enough for me to taste her fragrant skin, I pulled her down on me and touched her all over, to introduce myself to every part of her. The softness of her skin was beyond anything I remembered or imagined. To hold her close and feel her flat belly and the forest of pubic hair against my cheek and her buttocks in my hands was more than sex; it was freedom from words, from writing, from the endless test of will and imagination to recreate feelings and desires from decaying memory. It was release from the captivity of longing. It was absolutely real.

We could not do enough, feel enough and enjoy enough to fill the emptiness that had come before, or match each craving with its complementary satisfaction. Like a flood, the need engulfed the moment in frenzied appetite.

"Was it good?" I asked.

"Oh yes."

"For me, it's never enough. I wish I could go all night, without stopping, always just on the verge of coming. Like the figures on Keats' *Grecian Urn*."

"We can, my love. We have three weeks."

As she said this, a wave of doom enveloped me. For her, three weeks was a long time, but I heard a ticking in my ears like a swarm of second hands sweeping me toward another ending and more bitter craving.

I was parched with thirst. The tap coughed and dribbled brown water. I jerked the spigots back and forth to prime the belching pipes, but they only drooled.

We let the tap run, took splash baths by the scoopful, swigged *Johnny Walker*, smoked *Gitanes* and stared at the ceiling. The room was stuffy and unbearably hot. The air wrapped us like an invisible textile, heavy and densely knit. It stuffed our noses and lungs, irritated our skin, scratched our throats and made us gasp. It was like breathing yarn.

"Do you love me?" she asked.

"Yes. Of course."

As soon as I had spoken, I was stunned and perplexed by what I said. "Of course!" sounded too much like "maybe." It seemed to qualify, rather than emphasize my feelings. I hoped that it would be dispersed and forgotten in the ensuing silence, like an involuntary stomach noise. A whiskey glass on the night table tipped and smashed against the floor tiles, extending my remark by punctuating it. Then came the scraping of the lighter flint and the glow of her cigarette.

"Is that all?" she asked.

I was ashamed. How could I feel equivocal about my love for Cerise? It couldn't be true. I wouldn't let it happen.

"I love you but this feels like a room in hell."

"I know, but we're here. That's all that matters, isn't it?"

"Yes, you're right," I said, as I smacked a mosquito on my cheek. "No. It's not all that matters. We could be in a better place."

A loud truck screeched outside our window like an elephant in Le parc du Belvédère, adding a grace note to my misery. I could not expect Cerise to alter my destiny. I turned to face her, but she was obscured by the dense, sweltering darkness.

"I know this is hard for you. Stay as long as you have to. Then we can be together but not this year, not now," she said softly, as if she read my mind and knew the source of my resentment. "The test. I have to work doubly hard, my love. It's for our future."

She caressed my face. It was hard to know which to believe— her calculating words or the ardor of her touch. Knowing her as I did, I had to believe both. That was my problem.

I surrendered to her caresses and my desire. We made love again. Only then was fatigue strong enough to extract sleep from the suffocating heat.

2

CERISE MEETS TUNISIA

We checked out the next morning. I settled the bill with the Arab concierge behind the counter and complained about the lack of water. His eyes were deeply embedded in his large-boned, thick-skinned face, yet they engaged me with casual amusement.

"There are plumbing problems all across Tunis," he said. "It is tourist season and Europeans take many showers. The Hotel d'Afrique alone consumes most of the water available to the hospitality industry. But, *Monsieur*, please look on the bright side, that there was any water at all."

I probably should have thanked him for the spray that came with his rebuttal; it contained more water than our sink.

The concierge's attitude was too vexing for me to engage it further. I stood in the lobby and realized I had to relieve myself. Since I had already officially checked out, he pointed to a Turkish toilet in the airshaft. No toilet paper was provided, only a spigot to wash one's hands. I thought it would be funny to tell Cerise this bit of local color, but if I did we'd never hold hands again.

When I came down with the bags, Cerise was standing in the lobby. My beloved did not look as happy as she had been when she was applying her makeup in the room. Her face was strained as if she were suppressing a dark secret. When we were inside a cab and away from the Hotel d'Amilcar, Cerise burst out laughing. "Did you notice anything perverse about the hotel concierge?"

"Yes, but he seemed fairly normal."

"While I waited for you, he was staring at a map with a peculiar smile on his face. When he stepped from behind the counter, he was holding his penis in his hand and smacking it against his trousers, moaning, *'I can make you happy.'* Can you believe it, *Mon cheri*?"

"Unfortunately I can. That's taking hospitality too far, don't you think?"

"It was awful, really, my love. It was discolored. And *huge*." She drew her hands apart to show the length. "And when he smacked it, it looked like a dead eel."

Cerise's knowledge of aquatic life was impressive, but her account of the flasher assault disturbed me. On one hand, I was jealous of the massively endowed desk clerk for making such a vivid impression on my beloved. The insertion of his penis in her mind imposed on our intimacy almost as if it had been inserted in other private parts.

But I was angrier with myself for failing to be on the spot to deter or punish his perversion. I felt like the little boy who accompanied his mother down sordid streets, trying to be brave while knowing he could not protect her from the catcalls of Ripple-swilling winos leering at her ass from flophouse stoops. I wanted to be Cerise's heroic lover, but instead I was the bungling husband, holding the bags while a hotel clerk was holding his dick.

Cerise had been a victim of similar deviant acts in her past, which never failed to torment me when she recounted them at Brockwurst or in letters from Bidonville. Was it her fate to encounter flashers—or was it every woman's fate because there were so many sexual predators? I wanted to protect her, but how was it possible? I couldn't be everywhere. At any rate, it wasn't clear that she wanted my protection.

The more I thought of the concierge smacking his priapus against his pants in front of my girlfriend, the more indignant I became. The taxi was hurtling along when I blurted out, "Let's go back to that hotel! I want to make a citizen's arrest of that desk clerk pervert. Or at least punch him in the face and kick his groin."

"*Arrête*, Rick!" Cerise exclaimed. "Stop! Let it go. Do you want to go to prison for assaulting a Tunisian? Have you heard what Tunisian jails are like?"

"You want me to stop?" the taxi driver inquired in confusion. We were in the middle of a gas-fume belching boulevard.

"*Non, Monsieur.* I was yelling at my husband."

He grinned. "*Behi yessir. Très bien, Madame.*"

"I have no idea what Tunisian prisons are like," I admitted.

"But as Thoreau says, in an unjust society, prison is the place for an honest man."

"Thoreau was in a New England village, not Tunisia!" she hissed.

We stopped for breakfast at a *restaurant populaire* on a side street close to the depot. It was clean by "popular" standards with vinyl padded chairs and linoleum checkerboard floors. We ordered *briques*, the crispy folded crêpes containing poached eggs sprinkled with capers. Cerise loved the folk delicacy and ordered another, declaring it to be extraordinary and without doubt one of Tunisia's national treasures.

The emaciated waiter rejoiced at her effusive praise. He lingered by our table and engaged her in a halting dialogue about France, where his cousin worked as a subway sweeper.

"Do you know my cousin, *Madame*? You must know him."

"Well, maybe. What is his name?"

"Abdul."

Cerise tapped her cheek and assumed a pensive expression as if scanning her mental files for a subway sweeper named Abdul. Was it at a dinner party? Or during one of her shopping trips to Paris?

"No," she concluded after her rigorous memory search. "I don't think we've met."

The waiter hovered over us with his mouth agape. His eyes were wide and doleful. It was as if Cerise's lack of acquaintance with his cousin portended evil and even his death.

"Are you sure, *Madame*? Are you certain you never met him? Abdul. Abdul Ali. Please try to remember."

Cerise was growing alarmed. She shook her head briskly and exhaled a nearly silent, *"Non, non. Je suis desolée, Monsieur."*

The waiter kindly offered to give Cerise his cousin's address for when she returned to France. I suggested to him that France was a large country with 50 million people. It wasn't unusual for two strangers not to know one another. The waiter nodded blankly, but was too distraught to assimilate this concept.

Cerise quickly reassessed the situation. She studied our waiter, tilted her head, squinted and tapped her forehead.

"Excuse me, *Monsieur*. Does your cousin Abdul have dark eyes and black hair?"

The waiter's eyes sparked with hope.

"Yes, he does."

"Well, then I do know him. I met him in Paris."

"You did? *C'est magnifique, Madame. Merci.* Is he in good health?"

"*Oui, oui.* He feels fine and he's doing great. *En effet*, when I am in Paris I am always sure to stop at the station where Abdul works. It is the best one in Paris. He keeps it so clean. He is really very good at his job."

"He is? Oh, thank you, *Madame*."

"And he always mentions you. He's very proud of his cousin."

"He is? Oh, thank you, *Madame. Vous êtes très gentile.*"

He brought Cerise a *brique à l'oeuf—gratuit.*

As we trudged toward the bus station, Cerise was full of praise for the Tunisian waiter.

"You led him on," I remarked.

"That's not true. I just made him feel significant. Isn't that what we all want?"

"You didn't know his cousin and you knew it."

"How cynical you've become, my love," she reproved me. "It is quite normal for these people to ask about relatives. Families are important to them. What should I say? 'No, idiot, I don't know your cousin.' That would be rude. And perhaps I knew him. You never know."

"A Paris subway sweeper? You don't even talk to your neighbors."

"Perhaps I should."

We boarded the bus and found abutting seats. When the bus left the station, I fell asleep. When I awoke, Cerise was leaning in the aisle, talking to a portly Tunisian man with a shock of hair teased up like a cotton candy mountain. He called himself Hedi.

"This kind man offered me water," Cerise said. "Isn't that nice?"

"Nice," I yawned, peeling my tongue from my palate. "Can I have some, too?"

Hedi forced a smile and thrust the canteen into my hands. The price of the swig was to hear about *his* Tunisia. Cerise, who had just arrived in Tunisia the day before and would be a tourist for three weeks, was determined to get her money's worth.

She assumed the serious demeanor of a seminar student, pretending to take notes of all he said. It was her French flair for diplomacy to listen attentively and uncritically to his rant against France, the U.S. and the imposition of western values on Tunisian society. Cerise sat passively through the Tunisian's monologue and never challenged a word. It was mystifying: was I the only one she argued with?

Hedi was a teacher at Ayn Draham high school.

"So you're one of the Americans," he said mockingly. "Why are you here?"

"We're training to teach in the schools," I explained. "To learn about Tunisian culture while we represent our own."

"What for?" he asked. "To spy? To undermine our customs and our self-esteem?"

"No, to teach English."

He shook his head with a wry smile.

"No, no, my friend. You are deceived. You may not like the news I have for you, but it is accurate. We need your English like we need sand. We have more than enough English teachers and we don't speak the language anyway. You are here for one reason alone: you would be unemployed in your own country."

"That's not necessarily true," I replied, though the sinking sensation in my gut corroborated his claim.

"*Oui! Écoute.* Our government needs your government's money, so we are obligated to take unemployed Americans in the bargain. It's a fact. Don't deny it."

Hedi's logic and aggression infuriated me, but I drew back from the temptation of retaliating with an insult. Instead, I suggested a solution. "It's your right to object to the Peace Corps, but you should voice your rage more constructively. You can petition your government, lead an anti-Peace Corps movement and picket the Peace Corps office or the U.S. Embassy."

"We don't want your English," he cried. "Why don't you go back where you came from?"

Rather than mollify Hedi, my advice inflamed him. He knew that public demonstrations would do nothing but land the protester in jail. My personal heckler did not wish to become Hedi David Thoreau, when it was easier and safer for him to practice uncivil disagreeableness with me.

Maybe Hedi was right that I was a useless turd passing time in Tunisia. But that was why I signed up and endured training camp. I wasn't going to let him or anyone send me home with "parasite" stamped on my passport.

"I'm staying here and working here—and I don't owe you an explanation," I replied indignantly, without considering the implications of my self-righteous declaration.

"Oh, yes, you must explain to me why your government supports Bourguiba, who does nothing but fill his pockets with your so-called foreign aid. And you—yes, YOU—are part of the problem."

Suddenly, Hedi stopped and lapsed into eyeball-flaring silence. He felt safe when his attacks were anti-American and personal, but once he invoked the name "Bourguiba," he knew he had gone too far politically for a public place. However, his damage, as far as I was concerned, was done. The Peace Corps might be the harmless tip of a foreign policy whose primary feature was to support stable governments, regardless of how backward or corrupt they were. As a volunteer in a foreign land, I needed to see my impact on the economy, politics and culture of the people I came to serve.

When we arrived in Ayn Draham, Hedi said, *"Bislema,"* and wished me a good year. On our way to Slim's Hotel, Cerise berated me.

"Honestly, Rick, did you have to incite that argument with Hedi? You embarrassed me."

"So now you're on Hedi 's side? He provoked me!"

"It's his country," Cerise pointed out.

"I won't apologize for being American, and I'm sick of hearing how bad I am for being here. Everybody runs to America, but when an American goes anywhere else to work it's like we've committed a crime."

"Control yourself," Cerise advised. "Be diplomatic at all costs. You don't want to start a war every day over everything."

"Of course not. I'm in the Peace Corps."

At the hotel, I watched the brisk, mechanical way Cerise removed her clothes, how she pulled the dress over her head, unsnapped her bra and let the cups fall from her breasts, as if I weren't there.

She noticed me watching her and stopped.

"What are you looking at?"

"You. Getting undressed. You're really good at it."

She gave me a long, bemused smile and shook her head.

"*Qu'est-ce que tu as?* You have a problem."

"I like looking at you. Is that a problem? I can't believe you're here."

"That's sweet." She smiled wanly. Her face was drained and her eyes trained wearily on the next step in her routine, as if she were climbing a ladder. A cigarette smoked by her side while she sat at her mirror, wiping makeup from her face.

When she slipped into bed next to me, I kissed her, but she pulled in her arms. "It's my period," she said.

I continued to nuzzle her cheek.

"It'll relieve your cramps," I said.

She chuckled as her body contracted. She folded her arms in front of her in a "do not enter" sign and tucked herself against me.

I kissed her goodnight and lamented the wasted opportunity to make love. I counted down the days in our interlude: 18. Tomorrow there would be 17, minus three or four days for her period. That meant we had 13 days of sex after 13 months of none. What bad luck that she had her period now; if only we could have planned our rendezvous around it.

But her period wasn't the problem. Time was the problem, or more precisely, the lack of it. We were under pressure to pile more needs, feelings and events on a brief interlude than its fragile platform could support. As Cerise lay with her back to me, protecting her sleep, her absence returned and lay next to her presence.

While I tried to lose consciousness, I deliberated the pros and cons of masturbating in the sink to relieve my yearning, when she whispered, "My love!"

I thought she was inviting me to make love and I turned to her, but it was a false alarm. It was her love, not lust, calling me across the chasm of sleep.

"Rick, what will happen to you? How will you survive here, being so crazy and getting into fights?"

"I'll find a way," I said.

She sighed deeply and fell into a deep slumber.

3
CLASS ACT

Our Peace Corps training entered a new, decisive phase the next morning. For eight weeks we were students; now we would learn to be teachers. It was our rationale for being here and the start of the school year was a month away. I faced teaching my first training class with trepidation.

Most of the pressure was in my head. This was only a ten-minute demonstration and the students were volunteers like me. It was not all or nothing: I would have more student teaching opportunities in Tunis, along with professional coaching. Besides, I had already been assigned to an adult education program in a town called Menzel Bourguiba, so my performance with high school students was irrelevant. No matter, I was scared.

I had taught English in a summer foreign exchange program and as a one-on-one tutor, but these jobs didn't count because I was a student and no one expected me to be good. The stakes were higher now. This was my first full-time position and I had to be professional. Yet despite my limited experience and immaturity, Cerise believed I could succeed.

"If you can convince a young person, you can convince anyone," Cerise said. "Young people are more uncompromising and they demand honesty."

That first morning, we all piled into the living room of the largest house for teaching orientation, which amounted to Dozier preaching on the "science" of teaching.

"The best antidote to class disruptions is preparation," he claimed.

"My arse!" Cerise whispered in my ear. "Students are not as predictable as lesson plans."

"You must first be firm, make your rules and be certain that they are obeyed," Dozier averred.

"Ugh!" Cerise whispered. "Typical pseudo-respect."

"If anything, be stiffer and more detached than you would usually be," Dozier commanded.

"Yes, by all means," Cerise giggled softly. "So they can laugh at you and turn you off."

The seminar proceeded in this way, with Dozier pontificating in one ear and Cerise contradicting him in the other.

After the meeting, I went to Cerise's hotel room for our conjugal visit. I still lived in the camp; Cerise thought it was "more diplomatic." As I worked on my model lesson plan, she blew intently on her nails. I fretted over the stilted, corny student-teacher dialogue dignified by the term "lesson plan" and finally tossed my papers on the floor.

"This seems so phony I can't believe it will work."

"Are you sure you want to be a teacher?" she asked.

"No, I'm not. But why are you asking me that now?"

She sighed.

"You're such a child. How do you expect to make the transition from disruptive student to authoritarian teacher?"

"Good question," I muttered desperately.

Cerise took a long, vise-lipped drag of her cigarette, as if determined to decapitate the filter.

"You will have to resolve this dilemma," she said.

We argued over many things, but Cerise's teaching expertise was indisputable. She was right that identity confusion was the most significant potential disaster on my pedagogical horizon. After years of defying, denying and undermining teachers' authority, my new self faced my old self. Sins of the disruptive student were replayed for the student teacher—joke telling in the back, peals of laughter, rhetorical questions, non-sequiturs and scornful stares. I drove teachers to numb indifference and enjoyed every moment. Most disturbing to me, as I assumed my new incarnation, was that I could not recall specific teacher behaviors that incited my insubordination. My rebellion was impersonal and indiscriminate, not a rejection of individuals, but of authority. Now I would have the authority.

My only hope was to execute a brilliant lesson plan—a dialogue so stiff that it could be etched in cardboard.

"You can't hide behind a lesson plan," Cerise warned. "It's pure knee-jerk regurgitation designed for morons." She paused to blow on her nails. "The French system is a rhetorical device. If the students want to play along they will. If not, *tant pis pour toi*. The students will decide."

The practice class, my first performance as a professional teacher, was the next morning at 9 AM. It took place in a room where I had been a student repeating Arabic expressions only a week before.

When I entered the room, 30 students were already waiting in their seats. I walked in with my head slightly bowed, as if I expected a spitball or eraser to be thrown at it. I strode to the blackboard, stoked on nervous energy, shook the adrenaline from my legs, glanced out the window and turned to face my class.

I had worked through the night, refining my lesson plan and delivery like an actor rehearsing alone before a mirror. Now I faced the entire cast, my first students in my first class. True, they were supporting actors receiving a stipend, yet I would never forget their faces. A first can never happen twice.

The students stared at me with curious expressions. A wiseguy with narrowed eyes and a tilted head sat to the left. Sexy girls with teasing, flirtatious expressions sat on the right. There were the shy types, a cool intellectual or two in black-rimmed glasses, eager beavers, cool dudes in the back with their legs stretched and ankles crossed. Had I really gone halfway around the world? I recognized all of these kids. This was high school as I remembered it. Nothing had changed but me.

"Madeleine eats cheese," were the first words from my mouth.

"Madeleine eats cheese!" they replied in one thunderous voice.

"Good. They're with me," I thought.

"You—," I said.

"You eat cheese." They were following. Great. I was glad I chose 'cheese' as a word.

"Yesterday—Past tense." Grammar point #1. Come on, you can do it!

"Yesterday you ate cheese." Bravo, class!

"Where did you find it?" rejoined one of the cool dudes in the back.

"I do not know," said the class clown. "The store had no more cheese."

The class laughed. Cheese had been in short supply in the local stores, so it was valid social commentary. But we couldn't sidetrack the lesson.

"The store will have cheese tomorrow," I replied. "So we—eat. Future tense!"

"We will eat cheese tomorrow."

"Very good!" I replied. "*Behi yessir!*"

They had rewarded me for responding to their joke, so I acknowledged their language by translating my praise into Arabic.

Surprised by hearing an American use a Tunisian phrase, the students laughed again. They were still with me. We needed to keep the lesson moving, so I waved an arm and commanded, "Repeat. We ate the cheese from the *market*."

"We ate the cheese from the market."

"Present progressive!" I barked.

"We are eating the cheese from the market!" they repeated.

"Future tense!"

"We will eat the cheese from the market."

"By the way, *store* and *market* are the same—*kif-kif*." Students smiled and nodded at hearing the familiar idiom. "*Kif-kif. The same*. Store and market are the same as *hanoot*," I explained.

They repeated *store*, *market* and *same*—their bonus words.

"*Barakala a fik!*" I cried out, pumping my fist. "*Merci bien!* Thank you very much!"

"*Barakala o fik!*" they called back and laughed. "You are very welcome!"

This was fun. It was almost too easy.

But now the distinction between *much* and *many*, countable and uncountable modifiers, lay ahead.

"*Much* is for things that can't be counted individually," I said. "Much sugar, much salt, much pepper, much cotton." Staring out at the many eager and attentive faces, I thought my explanation had the brilliant simplicity of 2+2. "*Many* is used for things you can count—many cups of sugar, many grains of salt, etc."

But smiling faces can lie, especially about what they know. The drills would prove how well I had conveyed the lesson.

Their silence made it clear that they understood nothing. I was patient and persistent. I repeated the explanation and drew stick figures on the blackboard. Yet no matter how many primitive pictures I drew or examples I gave, they were nonplussed. I moved on to 'a little' and 'a few.'

"A little sugar, a little salt..."

"Sugar and salt are both little," quipped one of the boys in the back. The class laughed. Did they already know this grammatical point? They seemed to be toying with me. I was not in control. Cerise had been right—the students were deciding my fate. Communication breakdown was crashing down on me and I was desperate. I had dreamed of going to school without my pants on and now I was living the dream.

Then the door opened and in walked Dozier and Tasha.

"A little music, a few songs, a little time, a few minutes, a little food, a few *casse-croûtes*," I raved.

Casse-croûtes evoked another large, warm laugh. The French word for 'snack' had been translated by Tunisian culture into a cold, doughy cheeseless *focaccia* garnished with capers, anchovies and olives. Tunisian *casse-croûtes* were sold in every bakery and pastry shop and were a local favorite. The students rewarded me for knowing one of their favorite words by showing that they understood the distinction between 'much' vs. 'many.'

I was relieved, even euphoric, when the trial was over. I thought it had gone well. Then came the critique.

"You broke the first rule of TEFL," Dozier censured me. "Never resort to the student's native language."

"Never translate," Tasha added.

"But it worked!" I exclaimed. "They got it, didn't they?"

My teaching critics exchanged familiar glances of mutual reinforcement. I had seen authority figures resort to it when challenged. It implied superiority of knowledge, judgment and numbers. I knew I would not prevail against it.

"Beside the point," Dozier huffed.

"The challenge is to teach within the rules," Tasha chimed in.

"Believe us, it really works."

•

I dashed to Cerise's room when the critique was done. It was my first siesta to truly relax. I had mastered fear and my first class, and expected a hero's welcome. But when I knocked on her door, there was no answer.

"Cerise?"

The bath was drawn, but Cerise was gone. It wasn't her way to leave a tub full of water. Maybe she went out for a bar of soap.

While I waited for her, I devised a special greeting. I stripped naked and draped a towel on my penis as I had done at Brockwurst when our love was new. When she arrived, I would be standing there like a horny *kouros*.

It was hard to hold a towel that way for ten minutes. When she did not walk in, my high spirits decomposed to panic. Suspecting foul play, I searched the closets, balcony and hallway for her body, and listened for muffled noises. Was she abducted, raped, or sold into prostitution? As I peered under the bed, the door slammed and I heard the clickity-clack of Cerise's clogs.

"Where were you?"

Her nose was twisted and her lips pinched in a circle of pique as she tore and unfolded the foil on a pack of Tunisian cigarettes.

"Oh, shut up!"

"Shut up? You left the water running."

"When can we leave this barbaric place?"

"Ayn Draham? Saturday."

"Not before?"

"What's wrong?"

"I went to buy cigarettes and must have walked to the end of the earth, but I couldn't find *Gauloises* anywhere. And the people! They looked at me as if...I can't stand it."

Her fingernails sank into my arm, as she pressed her face against my chest.

"I have to leave here. It's so awful. I can't bear the hostile eyes. The poverty. The beggars. The filth. This is no place for me."

She was nearly hysterical. I hugged her to calm her down. It worked—too well. She broke our embrace with a curt, "Excuse me," and extracted a cigarette from her pack.

"Were you critiqued?" she asked.

"Yes, how did you know?"

"I'm a teacher. What did they say?"

"I used French and Tunisian words in the lesson."

"It's against the rules."

"Who cares how people learn, just as long as they learn!"

"Tunisia is run on the French system. You have to learn it. You can't fight institutions."

Cerise lit another cigarette and stuck it in her mouth.

"There's already one lit," I pointed out.

She glared in fierce defense of her sanity. "Some people chain smoke, I gang-smoke. What difference does it make?"

She got up and folded her green blouse with its pointy collar. I came up behind her and bear-hugged her around her breasts.

"I have a geyser of semen that yearns to be free."

She looked at me with casual indifference.

191

"Have you considered masturbation?"

I rubbed against the bumps under her towel.

"I'm irresistibly attracted to you."

"How nice," she said, wringing out her underwear.

"Cleanliness is next to godliness, but I'd trade it for a little passion," I complained.

"Is that so?"

I took the towel off my penis peg and wiped my forehead.

"What's the use?" I lamented. "I need a woman who craves my body."

"When you find that lucky woman, what will you offer her?"

I sank into the bed. "If you have to ask, you'll never know."

4

THE SILENT WAY

On Thursday, after we'd done our practice classes, Dozier demonstrated a new teaching technique—*Words Without Words*, or W3, a silent method. He introduced sticks of various colors and lengths representing sounds and raised them in sequence to produce words. When someone produced the sound represented by the rod that Dozier was showing, he pointed at that person emphatically like a maniacal charade player. When someone erred, Dozier shook his head vigorously, making his bristle mustache scrub the air like steel wool.

The demonstration agitated me. We would be unable to use rods or silence in our lesson, so like any theory that could not be applied, the W3 technique taunted me with untestable hypotheses. Imposing rods and silence on a teacher complicated his task. It also raised one more barrier between teacher and student, along with stale role-playing and a sterile classroom environment. It seemed to me that such barriers ought to be lowered and props and gimmicks removed, so that teachers could respond directly to students. I believed that the objective was not to induce answers, but to prompt questions; not to teach, but to encourage learning.

As I composed motivational speeches in my head, something more immediate and disturbing than the prospect of holding up sticks and pointing at teenagers brought me back to the here and now.

Across the crowded room, I felt Tasha's eyes roasting me with reproach. I resisted her gaze by watching Dozier as he thrust rainbow rods in people's faces and coaxed phonemes from unwilling mouths. Finally, I glanced back at Tasha and our eyes locked. Her face, normally warm, animated and confident, seemed cold and bleak. Her large, brown eyes accused me of disappointing her; they asked me to acknowledge her pain. Worse, they showed disbelief that I was with another woman. I turned away.

I couldn't bear to look at Tasha. To recognize her loss meant to accept mine—that we might have loved each other. I sacrificed that chance to be with Cerise.

Tasha's dismay and disbelief put Cerise's ambivalence in a cold light. If Cerise did not accept me, it was my own fault for living in the past and bringing a relationship close that thrived best at long distance, if at all.

I finally summoned the nerve to meet Tasha's gaze and tried to reason with her visually.

"I'm sorry, Tasha!" My eyes pleaded, "I tried to be honorable. I said I had a girlfriend. Why didn't you believe me? It's not my fault, Tasha. It had to be this way, don't you see? It was over before it started."

But her eyes still swore that I betrayed her and that she despised me for it. I should have been able to reply, "What's wrong, Tasha? Stop looking at me that way. You didn't want me anyway." But I wondered, "*What if she did?*"

Back at her room, Cerise asked aimless questions about various people in the camp, trawling for gossip, before pouncing on the only information she really wanted.

"Who is that woman you were staring at?"

I blinked in bogus bewilderment.

"You know." Cerise splayed her fingers to admire the fresh varnish on her nails. "Shall I describe her? The pretty one with the deep tan and long hair. A little plump."

"Tasha isn't fat," I said.

"So you *do* know who I'm talking about," Cerise said. "And you're defending her. How gallant."

"You shouldn't insult her. It's because of her that you're here."

Great, I thought. I had given Cerise grounds for suspicion. She gazed in the mirror as she twisted a curl with her finger and let it fall along her face, angling her head one way, then another, with the self-engrossed stare of a cover girl.

"That woman gave me a look. Why do you think she did that?"

"I have no idea," I said.

"No idea," Cerise chuckled. "There was nothing between you?"

"We were friends."

"That's all?" Cerise smiled to herself as she admired her nails.

5

THE POINT IS NO RETURN

Cerise let this remark pass and dropped the topic of Tasha and me. Maybe she was being good to her word about not caring whom I befriended or slept with, so long as it did not interfere with us. But I didn't believe it. Cerise was expert in cultivating guilt. Now that she knew about Tasha, she let remorse take root and grow in the fertile, anaerobic soil between my ears.

And grow it did. I spent more time with Cerise in our last days in Ayn Draham, as if making amends for implicit crimes. Hanging out at her room felt like detention. I was in self-imposed exile from the camp, isolated from my peers when we should have been bonding before dispersing to our respective locations. I was missing out because of Cerise. She had been my secret from the Peace Corps, but now after ten weeks, I had a secret from her—the Peace Corps was important to me.

Distances tormented me—between the camp and me, between Cerise and me. From the distance of a few weeks, I realized now how close I came to falling in love with Tasha. If that had happened, Cerise and I would not have been in a room together. Our love was a contingency of Tasha's good will. When I looked at Cerise I was no longer amazed at her miraculous presence, but fearful of her lasting absence. What would happen in the coming year when we continued to be in limbo between yes and no?

It was our last night in Ayn Draham. Cerise was contentedly reading a fashion magazine as if this moment were *terra firma* on a turbulent sea and we could drift on it forever. Her serenity was so at odds with my agitation that I viewed it as a declaration of war.

"I don't know if I want to stay," I said.

No answer.

"I don't know if I'm cut out to be a teacher."

"You'll get used to it."

"You said you don't like it here."

"I don't. And neither do you. But you're here. What can you do?"

I swallowed hard before suggesting the alternative; but I

couldn't. I knew what she'd say. Then she read my mind and said it anyway.

"Us living in Bidonville is out of the question. You know that."

Yes, I knew it, but hearing it was still aggravating. She believed a woman should come to a man. But she also claimed that we were different—until she decided that we were the same.

"It wasn't so bad that year," I remarked.

"It was awful," she contradicted. "I failed my exam."

"If you hated living with me, why are you here now?

"I didn't hate living with you. You were a distraction."

"According to Pascal, distractions are the essence of life."

"Not if I want to succeed," Cerise rebutted. "Why are you rehashing this? Are you picking a fight? If you are, I refuse to participate. This is my vacation."

"I'm not fighting," I said. "I'm discussing our future. If we have one. We'll be separated another year. Things can happen."

"What kind of things?"

"I don't know."

"Darling, are you worried that I will lose interest? That's sweet. But you know I will always love you."

She flipped coolly through her *Marie Claire*.

"This fall's fashions are a joke. I don't think mannequins would wear these clothes—it they had a choice."

"You're changing subjects again," I replied. "I'm talking about how easily we could fall apart and how we might prevent it from happening, and you're talking *prête-à-porter*."

She blinked at me as if I were a strange man in a train station babbling in tongues.

"How much is the Peace Corps paying you?" she asked.

"Ninety dinars a month," I said.

"That's slavery," she said. "I'll be making 4000 francs per

month next year."

I stared at her in familiar disbelief. It was Bidonville revisited. We quarreled over things like sex, love and respect, and she always turned the argument to money.

"What difference does it make?" I challenged her. "It's the starting pay of a Tunisian."

"But, darling," she replied, flipping her magazine pages with one hand as she held her glass of *Johnny Walker* in the other, "Tunisians live with their families. You are an American in a foreign country. You must pay rent and buy food."

I had never questioned my subsistence salary. It was part of the Peace Corps experience. Now I was at a loss to justify it. She noted my exasperation and touched my head. "I wish you'd never come."

I detected tenderness in her voice and attacked it.

"What should I do?" I pleaded, to overwhelm her with her own sympathy. "What will we do?"

She picked at the polish flaking off a nail.

"Do what's right for you." Cerise pulled away adroitly. She loved me, but my life was my business.

"So you feel no commitment to me," I said. "You don't care about us."

"If that were true, I wouldn't have spent my vacation in Tunisia. But living with me wouldn't work, Rick. You'd get bored and we'd hate each other."

She stopped chipping at her fingernail and looked at me. Her eyes were moist.

"My poor lost love."

"I came here to be with you," I said.

"No!" She replied with a cold stare. "Nothing could be farther from the truth."

"It *is* true."

"No Rick. That's false and unfair. Don't try to make me feel guilty."

"I don't want your guilt," I replied. "I want you. And not just for a few weeks. I want you all the time."

6

NOCTURNAL ADMISSIONS

Camp broke that Saturday. After months of idling in the eternal present together, volunteers wandered off to their respective futures.

Our first mission was to secure accommodations in the middle of a housing shortage. Menzel Bourguiba, my next location, was a mystery. A volunteer nobody remembered had been posted there years ago and no one had visited him then or gone there since. Menzel did not attract tourism or prompt curiosity. There was no information about the town except that it was called *Little Chicago* because it was on a lake, *Little Pittsburgh* because it had a steel mill and *Little Paris* because it had French traffic circles, kiosks and architecture.

After breakfast, Tasha told me there was no room for my suitcase in the Tunis-bound truck.

"But you promised."

"There's just no room. We can't take everyone's."

"Do you expect me to lug all my luggage around Tunisia?"

Tasha looked at me in the same angry way she had done at Dozier's teaching demonstration. Tears filled her eyes. She turned away and waved her hand, more disgusted with herself than with me. "Okay," she said and walked off in her flip-flops.

The bus sat in the middle of the dusty depot like a sacrificial animal, its luggage compartment gaping like a gash in its metal flank. The *fellaheen* and women in sheets, laden with plastic baskets, surged toward the doors of the shrine that opened to receive them. Cerise and I pressed forward, reaching with one arm to rudder to the front. The money for the trip was in the breast pocket of my bush jacket. When we approached the dispatcher, I grabbed for my wallet to pay for our tickets. The wallet was not there. I fumbled through the other pockets. It was gone. I was *paumé, fauché, foutu*, dead broke.

"What's wrong, my love?"

My chest heaved and my face burned. I felt like I was imploding. I had saved 50 dinars to prove to Cerise I was now mature and independent, but in one second my life savings and new identity vanished. Despite my frugality and self-sacrifice, I was back to being a parasite.

"It's gone. The money was here, and it's gone," I stammered. I looked down at my body as if it were playing tricks on me. I kept my head down to avoid facing Cerise, but she touched my shoulder and kissed my cheek.

"It's all right, my love. I have money."

"But I wanted to pay, I saved 50 dinars and it's gone. How could this happen?"

"I don't mind helping you out. Let's not let this spoil our vacation. I meant to spend the money."

"Are you sure?" I asked. For the first time since she arrived, I realized that something had changed between us. Two years before, while we were traveling, she called me a "thief." Clearly we had come a long way since then.

"Yes, of course, you've been so good to me."

"I have?"

With glistening eyes, Cerise nodded her head and kissed me.

There was an "us" after all.

•

A cab in Tabarka rescued us from a sudden downpour that blurred the Christmas lights hanging over every intersection and lacing the walls like electric snakes. The red-capped driver had a penchant for sexual innuendo.

"*Madame, Monsieur*, shall I perhaps take you to *Le Dar*? You do not know Le Dar? I will tell you. It is remarkable, a national treasure. Le Dar is on a cliff. If we had something to dive for in Tabarka, we would dive from *Le Dar* into the sea. But what am I saying? You did not come here to dive. *Non, non! Le Dar* was once a pirate's castle. The pirates left and it became a bordello."

He raised his eyebrows and lowered his voice. "Please accept my apologies, *Madame*. I do not wish to offend your delicate ears, only to state historical facts. Now Le Dar is a ten-star pleasure hotel. I say ten stars because five stars are not enough. It is *pas cher, très intime*, you see? It is ideal for a honeymoon. You know? Of course you do. *Oh là là!*"

"You don't offend me at all, *Monsieur*," Cerise said magnanimously. "And please do not curb your use of *bordel* on my account. I have used this swear word at least three times today."

When the driver heard this, his eyes bulged, his head snapped back and his red *kefia* flew off his head. Cerise meant to tease him, but shocked him instead. Groping for his cap, he jerked the wheel. When the car swerved, he hit the brakes. The car spun like a top and came to a stop, facing a sign that read "*Le Dar* straight ahead."

"*Allah y berek*! It is a sign from God. You must go to Le Dar!" our driver exclaimed, adding revelation to sexual insinuation. "It was meant to be. I'm sure you will be very happy. Heh heh."

•

The dining room at Le Dar was dark and murky. Old nets dangled from the ceilings like hemp beards. Candles flickered in stained glass sconces along the stucco walls. A waiter poured gasoline in an urn in the dining room and tossed a match to ignite a fire that put our faces in red light.

This was a pirate's lair without passports or boundaries. The world outside, with its details and restrictions, could pull us apart, but here the world was a shadow.

"Let's go to bed," Cerise said with a furtive smile.

In the room, she caressed me, removed my clothes with the slow graceful gestures of a dance and pinned me on the bed. She moved on top of me until I spun her over. As we made love, our bones collided painfully, but when I stroked her thighs and buttocks with their miraculous softness, she cried, "Oh Rick! Mon cheri, my love!" I delighted in the way she said these simple words, the child's cry and intimate whisper of her voice, how she turned my random, monosyllabic name into a charm and the endearment into a holy chant. She called me to her and her words meant more to me than sex alone. They gave me identity and purpose and brought me into existence like nothing else.

Afterward, Cerise stared at the ceiling and blew smoke at a remote thought. I stroked her arm and moved close to her, inspired by a potential sex marathon. But Cerise was otherwise engrossed.

"What is it?" I asked her.

"I was thinking of something I often do in Bidonville when I'm driving home from the university."

"What is it?" I murmured, kissing her playfully.

"Oh, it's nothing, really. I just get so horny sometimes. There's a billboard on the road of a man in his bikini briefs. It's so silly but I fantasize what it would be like for him to come off the billboard and fuck me in the car."

"Why are you thinking about that?" I asked. My lips lost their pucker. Blood drained from my stump. "Are you saying I'm second best to a billboard?"

She smiled remotely. "You can't be jealous of a billboard, can you?"

"I probably shouldn't be, but I am! It didn't happen, did it?"

She smiled inscrutably and dragged on the cigarette.

"No, my fantasies never do. They're safe."

Now it was my turn to stare at the ceiling. My lust was blunted by the disappointment of being runner-up to a gigantic underwear model. I also experienced rising fear about an unavoidable psychological catastrophe.

"But your fantasy is coming true, isn't it?" I asked hopefully.

Silence. Cerise kissed my cheek and chuckled. "My love, do you need reassurance?"

"No, but, well actually yes, always."

"All I meant was that my sexual fantasies are of the kind that cannot be fulfilled and that's what keeps me honest. If I wanted to fuck other men, I would, but I don't. You're the only man I want."

I brightened, "Really?"

She blew another trail of smoke at the ceiling.

"What was the problem with Tasha today?"

"She said they had no room for my luggage."

"Why the scene? Was there something between you?"

"No," I said. But I knew a simple "no" would not persuade Cerise, so I added, "We're friends. She liked me."

"Friends?" Cerise sneered, "You don't need to use euphemisms with me."

"It's true. Why would I ask her to let you come here if we were having a relationship?"

"She gave me looks all week."

"We spent time together, that's all."

To my ear, it sounded true. And it was, in a way. Cerise's laughing eyes suggested that she found my words and whatever I had done amusing.

"I know you too well, don't treat me like an idiot," she said.

Her smile reassured me that if I confessed, all would be forgiven. But I had worked too hard all summer at being virtuous to accept half-absolution.

"I never made love to her!"

Cerise returned to her smoke rings and I thought about Tasha. Had we done enough to warrant jealousy? Cerise's cigarette was done and so was my time to confess. She curled up to sleep. I put my hand on her shoulder. "What's wrong?"

"It's bad enough that you betray me, but your lies are unbearable."

"I swear that nothing happened with Tasha," I insisted.

Cerise laughed coldly.

"Rick, by nothing you mean sex. Do you believe sex is the only thing that can happen? Did you have good times with Tasha? Did you smile and laugh and keep her good company?"

"Yes. We liked each other, but we didn't have sex."

Cerise turned toward me and smiled.

"Why didn't you, my love? You should have. You did everything else."

Cerise was a blackbelt in recrimination. She knew where to strike. I tried to conceal the pain her blow inflicted while she studied my anguish and confusion over Tasha. She must have found it odd that we had spent so much time alone without sex.

There was a Tunisian saying: when a man and woman are alone together, the devil is the third party. Cerise held me accountable for sex, real and potential. Her suspicion demanded full disclosure, so I resolved to be completely honest.

"There was something—once," I began.

Confession is illumination and emits heat. Sensing that I was ready to open my wicked soul to her, Cerise troped toward me. Her body uncurled and brushed against me, as if she were seducing my dark self. Her eyes were sad but resolute as she braced for the terrible truth she craved.

"On the beach once, I kissed the back of her knee."

Cerise's face tightened. "You kissed her knee? That's so intimate. No wonder she thought you loved her!"

"Of course!" I cried inside. I had desired Tasha all summer and she must have known it. When I kissed her knee, it was clear. What a fool and hyprocrite I was.

I pleaded with Cerise that we only had 12 days left, but she was cold to reason. I cried with frustration as time cracked under our struggles and complications. I tugged gently on her arm and whispered entreaties for love and tenderness.

She turned and punched my face, showing her years of experience as a champion volleyball player.

"You call that tenderness?" I shouted, dabbing the blood that dripped from my nostril.

"You deserve it, *salaud.* You pig!"

"But why?" I cupped my nose to contain the blood. It had been broken on one side; did Cerise break the other one to satisfy her love of symmetry?

"Okay. Assume that I wanted to sleep with Tasha! I gave up that chance for you. You should feel good. Where is virtue without temptation? What is triumph without competition?"

I was in a rhetorical rhythm when Cerise put her hand over my mouth.

"You don't love me. I'm just an experience for you. Just another goddamned experience. That's how you dance through life, from experience to experience."

"How can you say that?" I asked. "You're not just an experience. You're the greatest experience."

"*Con! Salaud!*" she flailed her arms against me and sank her painted talons into my shoulders. As we wrestled, her rage was tempered by playfulness. We fought and made love intermittently through the night. It was a grueling love—the only kind we knew.

•

The next day, Cerise read a book for the upcoming year's examination. Slouched back on the beach chair, lips pursed, eyes square voids in dark glasses, she forbade conversation and made me ache for the closeless she denied.

At sunset, mosquitoes swarmed upon us, buzzing in our ears, keeping us awake while they ate us alive. I smacked myself to deter their assaults but by morning, my face was swollen and inflamed, my eyes shut to slits, my ear lobes bloated to twice their size; I was one big burning itch.

A dotted line ran along the four white walls like a perforation. They were mosquitoes, sleeping in formation, black bubbles on thread legs, sated and inflated after a night of feasting. One by one, I smacked them and watched our blood squirt and trickle down the walls.

7

THE ROAD TO ZARDOOK

For a week we toured Tunisia, stopping for an afternoon in the town where I had been assigned. We were relieved that it was not as primitive as we feared and left in haste in order not to disturb this first impression.

Otherwise, we wandered aimlessly, seeking something we could not identify or find. In lieu of what we did not have, we assumed the quiet guise of traveling companions. We were neither distant nor intimate, neither happy nor hostile. We seemed like a normal couple, comfortable and familiar. It was the worst we had ever been.

I stared at Cerise's profile as we bumped along the *Sahel* in a battered bus. Her once-radiant face was forlorn. Her eyes were resigned. I was her martyrdom. I had not done much to induce this effect, but I was hardly innocent. In her mind I was more than a bad influence; I was intrinsic to her condition, woven into her pain, like an emotional addiction.

But what could I do? I was addicted to her as well.

"Be kind to her," I told myself as she drifted off into neck-twisted, mouth gaping naps.

If I had calculated how to make her suffer, I could not have done a better job. Yet, the torture I inflicted was unpremeditated, based on personality and fate. I was an instrument, not a perpetrator of her punishment, and could neither prevent nor undo the damage.

Only six days remained. Surely, time would demand the best of us and we would extract from our last days the sweetness of our happiest moments, rather than wallow side by side in quiet misery.

We headed to Sidi Bou Said. I hoped that the most beautiful, serene and tolerant place in Tunisia would inspire us with its harmony and beauty.

•

I was always skeptical of the affective powers ascribed to famous locations—can a Parisian skyline or the roar of Niagara Falls enhance a relationship or save a broken one? Yet I found myself hoping for the renowned healing magic of Sidi Bou Said.

Sidi Bou Said, the fabled maze of white walls and blue doors, of date palms and stone stairs, of birdcages and Andalusian tunes, sat on a steep cliff over the blue sea.

However, when Cerise and I left the station, we were not in a paradise of white honeycomb walls and azure sky, but on a tree-lined asphalt road at the foot of a steep hill.

We asked an old *fellah* where the town was.

"Not far, not far," he muttered, as he headed in the opposite direction.

"*Not far, not far!*" Cerise mimicked. She glowered at me as if it were my fault that we were carrying four bags up a steep hill under a hot sun.

"Let's climb," I said with as much conviction as I could muster from the blisters on my feet. We had come to the name of a place that was nowhere in sight. The bags grew heavier with each step and gored my legs with their metal edges. I decided to take bold action and stuck out my thumb.

"I'll bite it off," Cerise snarled. "Do you want me to be sold into slavery?"

The hill leveled, the road narrowed. Trees and hedges gave way to white walls and small windows. We heard the whisper of miniature saws. Birdcages and baskets of differing configurations hung in display—pale, woven pagodas and strange balloons.

"Basket-weavers," Cerise muttered. "This is where you belong."

We had come to the pristine medina, with its white walls and blue doors. Soft human voices harmonized with chattering birds.

"Where is the hotel?" Cerise asked. "I hoped you would know—*for once*—where we were going."

•

A small sign for Zardook indicated a sharp ascent.

Would it lead us to the fabled palace converted to a modestly priced hotel? We trudged up the shady street that ended in a bluff 200 feet above the sea.

On the promontory, sea and sky merged like a fathomless blue Rothko before our eyes. A sweet, jasmine breeze gave succor from the heat. I reached for Cerise to share this sublime moment, but grasped at molecules of air.

"Cerise?"

She was chugging down the path. Her bags bowed her shoulders and rocked her from side to side.

"Cerise!" I cried out but she did not break stride. Suddenly, her adrenaline ran dry. She stopped for a smoke, extracted the last cigarette and crushed the pack in her fist.

"What's the matter?" I pleaded.

"Why did we come here?" she asked as she exhaled black smoke like a seizing engine.

"To gaze at a sight of miraculous beauty?" I asked.

"To find a hotel, *imbecile!*"

She jabbed the stubby *Gaulloise* in her mouth and resumed her defiant march, as her bags slammed her hips and thighs.

"The hotel is nearby," I said.

With each fierce stride, a nicotine cloud hovered before her overheated face.

"Show me."

I looked for the marker, but all signs of Zardook had vanished. We were back in the center of town.

"It's here somewhere," I pleaded. "There was a sign...I swear!"

"Somewhere!" Cerise snarled. "Clearly you don't see the signs."

She dropped her bags and tossed the burning filter. The lapels of her chartreuse blouse, normally crisp, were curled and wilted. Her lips quivered. Flecks of eyeliner spattered her cheeks.

"Have you asked anyone? Rick, I just don't know."

Her head bowed and she giggled. Was she having a nervous collapse or was she lightheaded from hunger? If only we could sit in a café or restaurant and have refreshments. But it was siesta and nothing was open.

"I have an idea. I'll ask someone," I said.

The only open business was a *tabac* down the block. An old man counted cigarettes behind the counter.

"Where is Zardook?" I asked.

He stared blankly, crossed his wrists and pointed in opposite directions. Was he ambivalent or warning me to get lost?

"*Sidi,* where is Zardook? The hotel?" I implored.

"Amilcar," he said, waving toward the station.

Amilcar was one stop before Sidi Bou Said. A luxury hotel had just opened there as part of the international conspiracy to make all places look alike so that tourists always felt at home. Before I left the *tabac,* I looked over the food selections. There were various confections in packages with Arabic writing. I didn't think Cerise would eat their contents. But there was a tube of *Smarties,* the

209

European equivalent of *M&Ms*, so I bought it.

As I approached her, Cerise detected a lack of answers on my face.

"Did you learn anything?" Cerise asked tremulously.

"No. He was ambiguous at best."

"*Merde! Merde! Merde!*" she shouted and burst into tears, then skittish laughter. In this tranquil town of artisans and poets, Cerise was having a breakdown.

"But look what I found!" I showed her the tube of *Smarties*. Cerise regarded the candies with revulsion and refused to pop even one chocolate pill in her mouth. "*Smarties!*" she sneered. "That's child's food!"

I tossed a handful of *Smarties* into my mouth with sugar-loving relish.

"It's not a *Hershey's Kiss*, but it's better than nothing," I said, offering her the tube again.

"You're hopeless," she said. "I don't know why I'm with you."

"The restaurants are closed," I pleaded. "Anyway, what's wrong with being a child sometimes?"

"Oh, eat your *Smarties!*" Cerise snapped and walked off.

Was there not one hotel in the most beautiful town in Tunisia? Cerise would never trust me again. I searched for a manhole to fall into. Not finding one, I looked up and there it was—the sign!

"*Zardook!*" I cried, "*Zardook!*" I pulled Cerise by the arm. "If we don't find it, we can always jump off a cliff."

We retraced our steps to a street lined by white walls and dripping with red and purple bougainvillea. We came to a black wrought iron gate and a stately villa.

"*Zardook!*" I fell to my knees in gratitude. The mustachioed concierge was discreetly pleased to accommodate us. A disheveled cleaning woman guided us to our room. There we enjoyed a view of the courtyard with its white columns, arched trellises and squat trees with bulbous trunks around a circular pool of black water. The serenity and romance of Sidi Bou Said would finally be ours.

8

DREAM SEX, NO FOREPLAY

In the hour before sunset, we descended the rocky escarpment to the beach, a patch of brown, gritty sand littered by sticks and debris.

"It isn't paradise, but it isn't hell," I said.

"What profundity!" Cerise jeered. "Why don't you write it in your notebook?"

"I left it in the room so you'd have me all to yourself," I said.

"How thoughtful," she replied.

Cerise peeled off her tee shirt casually as if she were intimate with the world and stood above me in her bikini. Watching her sent a tremor through my loins. Sex on a deserted beach at sunset was finally an accessible fantasy. When I stroked her calf, she sidestepped my hand, cast the towel on the sand and lay down.

"Let's swim," I said. Cerise did not respond. I dove into the calm water, swam and shouted out to Cerise to join me. When it was clear that Cerise wasn't coming in, I returned to the shore and lay next to her. Feeling peaceful and stimulated, I put my hand on her buttock. No response. I moved my hand along her creamy thigh. She smacked it.

"What on earth are you doing?"

"I was being amorous. We're alone on a beach."

"No, we're not. Those perverts are no doubt watching us and masturbating. I just want to lie in the sun, if you don't mind."

If Cerise had simply said "perverts," I might have shrugged.

But "those perverts" implied that she had specific ones in mind—though she had been in this town for only a few hours, scarcely long enough to compile a list. I lost my erection and peered at the cliff for imposing eyes. Not even small mammals were in sight, yet I remained on alert. The weed of paranoia Cerise had planted was in full bloom. The harmonious convergence of sun, earth, water and a nearly nude woman had made me a healthy hedonist, but now I was inhibited, frustrated, depressed, angry and uptight—my usual self.

We dined at Le Café des Nattes, an old-style Arab restaurant with pillows, low tables, and benches along the walls. The ornately woven rugs and mats provided the perfect ambience for our reconciliation. Besides, there were signs posted all over town that Andalusian music was featured here, as part of a music festival.

"Music in July. No more music now," the waiter declared with exceptional finality, apparently to rebuke me for naïvely thinking there could be music at any other time.

Cerise stared morosely across the candlelight, as if I had died and she were holding a *séance*.

"Why did you come here?"

"I thought there would be music."

"Not the restaurant! Tunisia."

"To be closer to you."

She sighed.

"Okay. I'll come clean. I came to see you in that dress."

She *was* lovely. Her candy-stripe frock was tight and low-cut, with a tapered waist and spaghetti straps across her tanned shoulders. But my compliment aggravated her; I was obstructing her justice.

"You came to get away from me," she said. "We would have been closer if you had stayed in the States."

212

"And found a steady job with a good future?"

Her eyes were imploring. I had turned a valve and now the emotions flowed.

"I could have come to you, not as the older woman, but as an equal."

"Equality is in the mind." I inserted a *filfil* in my mouth for comic relief. "I feel equal to you now."

As she often did when I upset her, she extracted the compact from her bag and touched up her face.

"Would you like me better if I were boring like everybody else?" I asked.

She snapped the compact.

"That's crap. You could never be like anyone else."

The waiter placed tall glasses of mint tea between us. His mocking glance made it clear that *he* thought I was like anyone else.

"A nine-to-five job would have killed me; I didn't even know what kind of job to get."

She shook her head hopelessly. We were back to normal. I admired her smooth arms and her soft breasts heaving against the crisp, white cloth.

"I love you." I stroked her arm.

She shrugged.

"You don't have to say these things."

"I want to say them because I mean them."

"Of course your love is a privilege. My friends all ask about my darling *au pair* boy."

"They're envious." I said.

"*C'est ça. Tu sais que tu es idiot parfois!*"

She sneered as she flicked her cigarette ash. In the candlelight, her face had the mystical glow of a de La Tour, but she was insulting me in French, a sure sign that she was about to explode.

"You are beautiful, I wish we could make love now," I said.

She cocked her head and smiled. "How can I thank you? That is the highest compliment you can pay. And since you get hard, you can't resist."

I threw up my hands. "Is that a crime?"

"It is when you put it in every hole!"

"That's not true or fair!" I replied.

Apparently Cerise thought it was more than fair, because she bolted from the table as the supercilious waiter arrived with our *couscous royale*. He gloated over my misery, as I wondered how to translate *doggy bag*.

When I walked into our room at *Zardook* with two bags of Tunisian take-out, Cerise was in her nightgown reading a book. She was oblivious to me. I could not draw from her so much as a hello.

"Us" might be over. Still, there had to be a graceful way to handle our remaining days; I had to sleep on it. What I needed was a primer for falling out of love, a *Death and Dying* for breaking up, to figure out which phase we were in. Denial? Absolutely. Anger? Constantly. Buying time? Mainly wasting it. Depression? We were in it. The problem was that we were in all four phases at once— every one but acceptance. Out of sequence, there could be no progress, only congestion. Would we make it to acceptance?

Yes, but first I needed to improve my behavior, to forget my selfish needs and most of all, to stop begging for sex. In other words, I had to stop being myself. I must act less like a lover and more like a friend.

Once I resolved to be someone else, I peacefully drifted to sleep. I dreamed that I was on a beach. A woman appeared in a long shirt. She smiled. I followed. She lay on a patch of white sand protected by the rocks. I lay next to her, caressed her leg under the dress and discovered that she had no underwear. I heard a buzz in my ear: a narrator's modulated voice-over echoed from another place.

"You made love to another woman, didn't you?"

But the voice-over did not awaken me. Suddenly, the woman in the long dress was naked. She pulled me onto her and we rolled in the sand clinging so tightly that our hearts were humping. She guided me inside her as she whispered, "I know it was just a passing thing. You couldn't help yourself. She forced you."

I surged inside the woman on the beach. Something was wrong. I had never had sex in a dream and now I was consummating. Was this the fabled wet dream we learned about in 9th grade health class? I opened my eyes. Cerise was writhing on top of me. Her eyes were fixed on mine. She dug her fingernails into my chest and cried out. "Oh, God!"

Cerise lay on my chest and held me close, gasping, crying, whispering, "My love! My love!" Then she kissed my neck and rolled off of me.

"What happened?" I asked inanely as she curled up beside me.

"You were sleeping," she said before she passed out.

Now I lay awake, excited and perplexed about her unprecedented passion. I wracked my brain to analyze its causes. Was I irresistible when I was asleep? Despite her claim that she wished to be a whore to the man she loved, Cerise was often distant and repressed; yet she had just brought me to an erotic wonderland. Sleepwalking was established, but dream intercourse was a new frontier. No doubt, our conscious minds were too conflicted for us to have uninhibited sex, so we had to have it in our sleep.

Yet, the more I considered this theory, the less it satisfied me. Certain details of our lovemaking were puzzling and incongruous, yet oddly related. Who was the dream woman on the beach–Tasha, Cerise or a fantasy female? And how did the dream sex relate to Cerise's eruption of lust? Did she make the dream woman appear when she mounted me or did they come separately?

Then I realized that I had to stop using dreams to clarify my life; they were just as confusing.

9

TWO TYPES OF RESIGNATION

It's hard to put love to sleep, to say, "It's over." Everybody wants to be lucky and bridge the gap between two human beings. I tried to merge with Cerise, but something prevented it and trying harder did not work. I was the wrong man for her. That was what she thought, and I had to accept it.

The next morning, the humidity that had oppressed us for a week was gone. Cerise and I ambled through town like dutiful vacationers in the famous public gardens of Sidi Bou Said.

When we returned to Zardook to check out, Cerise noticed a few hundred francs were missing from her suitcase. We searched everywhere, but the francs were gone and probably stolen.

"It won't do any good to report it," the portly manager told us with the smooth "professional" sympathy of one who had seen enough crime to be at ease with it. He touched the tips of his waxed mustache to test their points, shrugged and spread his forearms on the counter as if preparing to levitate.

"Believe me, my young friends, the police can do nothing. It is sad that such crimes occur, but there is never proof." He presented himself as an expert with a long résumé of experience: colonial constable, retired colonel in the French Foreign Legion, importer of bottled water and a lifelong resident of Tunisia. But we insisted on justice, so he summoned the maid, who denied everything.

"*C'est comme ça,*" the manager sighed. "Enjoy your firm young bodies and forget about it."

The manager's mustaches were pointed like clock hands at 10:10 AM but it was already one in the afternoon. We left for the police precinct. It was harder to find than Zardook, so we took a train to La Marsa, the favorite beach of the beautiful people of Tunis.

10

SEX AND THE SUN GODDESS

The beach at La Marsa exuded the glamor of Tunisia's most exclusive bedroom community, where Destour Party officials and bureaucrats, ambassadors and technocrats lived and loved. Young sun-worshippers on the white sand had the bored detachment that the alchemy of wealth transforms into a cool attitude.

The Tunisian Love Brigade was out in force. Dark, handsome men with toothsome smiles kicked sand, burst into short sprints, stretched their arms and torsos, put each other in half-hearted half-nelsons, dangled soda bottles, joked boisterously and prowled for loose women. Love soldiers strutted to our blanket, armed with superficial smiles, to ask about our health, guess our nationality and offer eternal friendship and companionship.

Cerise conspired with these intruders by smiling warmly and responding with her bright voice to their generic queries. She basked in their attention and contemplated out loud about living a fuller, "more interesting" life. I knew what that meant. When she praised the Tunisians' smiles, I had had more than enough.

"Smiling is their job," I explained. "I'd have a great smile, too, if I practiced. But who can practice smiling with you around?"

Contrary to its desired effect, which was to motivate Cerise to treat me better, my remark enraged her. Like a sexual semaphore, she made distant eye contact with a platoon of love soldiers, who trotted to our towel, threw themselves on their knees and lobbed questions at us.

Cerise, always the teacher, would not deny their intellectual curiosity, or leave unquenched their thirst for knowledge.

I fended off the social onslaught of these sexual predators by distracting her.

"You're just trying to get even with me for imagined infidelities."

"I don't know what you're talking about, my love. You're too fair-skinned to be in the sun so long. You imagine things."

"*Madame*, do you like *Coka* or *Fanta*?" a beach boy asked.

"I feel daring. I'll try both," she replied with a flirtatious smile.

"But even if I were unfaithful—which I'm not," I persisted, "there is a huge difference between a discreet affair and this public humiliation you're subjecting me to. I'm like Hester Prynne and you're the Puritan elders."

"You are so *merdique*," she turned to me. "You are no Hester Prynne. You are Nestor Prick!"

"Do you want to see my country?" the crouching Tunisian love soldier asked Cerise, as he attempted to seize the initiative.

"Yes, I must see *everything*," she replied with a lingering look.

Meanwhile, I continued to disrupt their flirtation with literary references.

"Why don't you just write a scarlet 'R' on my chest with your lipstick?" I demanded.

"Maybe later, Rick. But now I'm trying to live a fuller life. I only have a few days left and you're interfering with my fantasies," she taunted me.

"*Madame,* do you like to dance?"

"Yes, of course. How nice!"

The Tunisian man stood up and started to dance. He reached for her hand.

"I just read a CIA report that the population density of horny gigolos per square foot is higher in Tunisia than anywhere but Monte Carlo," I declared. "They pay attention to all women— young, old, attractive, unattractive—so if you think I'm a lying cheat, these guys are no improvement."

"Still, don't you think it's healthy to yield to impulse?" she asked, her face so angled that she could smile at me and the Tunisian love soldier simultaneously. "I feel so kinky."

"Would you like a massage?" I asked haplessly.

"I want a gangbang," she said.

I could try to be all men to her—but not at once. Cerise lay on her elbows, vulnerable and provocative, her shoulders curved and delicate, her head tossed back, black hair falling to the sand. Smiling skyward with lips parted, she awaited her stated desire. I might have dissuaded her from a gangbang by citing the increased risk of disease, but nonchalance seemed a smarter response.

"Nobody's stopping you," I said.

"No," Cerise snapped. "You're so perverse that you'd probably condone it. Why shouldn't I do it, after all you've done behind my back?"

"By *all,* you mean *nothing?*"

"Ha! You've done a lot. Not now. Not lately. But you have and you will."

"Whatever I might have done when we were apart, I could not have done if we were together," I said, using modal auxiliaries to state the truth without self-incrimination.

"Yes, yes! I know all about it!" Cerise cried. "You came to Tunisia to be with me— so HERE WE ARE!"

A shadow fell across our grim, sunbaked conversations. Another smiling love soldier had come to shoot more bull. He pointed his index finger and snapped his fingers at me as if I were a contestant on his game show. "Swedish, right?"

"No."

He tilted his head, squinted suspiciously and pointed at his temple to indicate that he was concentrating on his next guess.

"Russian."

"Closer," I answered, trying, despite myself, to help him, since he stood there haplessly clinging to a game he played poorly.

"American!" he shouted, clapping his hands. "Of course, of course! I knew it all along. And you, *Madame*, you are—*Belgian*?"

Cerise shot me a conspiratorial look. If there was one thing a French woman found insufferable, it was to be called "Belgian." She made the face of a hay fever sufferer—staring cross-eyed at the tip of her nose as she prepared to sneeze—and told the love soldier, *"Je ne suis pas Belge,"* in a Belgian accent.

The Tunisian stud was alarmed by Cerise's facial contortions, but he was poised enough to bow his head and grin.

"You are having a good time in my country? She is beautiful, my country, no?" he asked.

"Yes, lovely," I said. "We're having a wonderful time. Just this morning we had 150 francs stolen from our bags and a week ago all the money I had in the world was taken from my pocket while I waited for a bus. *Hamdulleh!*"

The young Tunisian beachcomber forced an embarrassed smile, looked nervously down the beach, shouted to a friend and left us alone. Cerise and I laughed—for the first time in a while.

11

A RAMADAN GOOD TIME

Our final days passed swiftly. We took a commuter train to Tunis, where I had one more week of teacher training for my new employer, the Bourguiba School for Lifelong Learning.

Cerise and I crashed at the *lycée* by Le parc du Belvédère, the scene of my first days in country. We slept in a narrow cubicle abutting the dormitory where *pions*, student monitors, watched over boarding students during the school year. When we were naked, we crouched below the glass partition to avoid performing a live sex show for the volunteers in the main room.

It was *Ramadan*, the month of fasting. Tunis was a writhing paradox—by turns agitated and gracious, starving and roasting, frenetic and phlegmatic. The reek of urine and trash mingled in the nose with sweet jasmine. Beggars glutted the streets. Women squatting in airy *safsaris* and men in ragged togas held out their palms with more success, since *Ramadan* was a month of almsgiving. Their cajoling filled the woolly air like songs, accompanied by coins rattling in their cups.

At first, the days were solemn and brutal. Physical strain was palpable in the buses and trains and on the streets, as God and the Devil played in parched mouths and empty stomachs. Tempers flared and faces grimaced; most people seemed to be on the verge of weeping. But as the days passed, fasters fell into the rhythm of abstinence; they appeared to suffer less and triumph over hunger and thirst.

At 7:30 every evening, a cannon boomed from the *medina* wall, marking the end of fasting. The city stretched and sighed. Firecrackers smacked the ear and gunpowder hovered in the air. Lights went on and candles kindled as earth imitated sky.

221

After teaching classes, volunteers strolled down Rue de La Liberté, a dark, serpentine avenue that meandered across Tunis, to feast at L'Andalouse on cold squid salads and piquant fish bisques.

At 11 PM, Tunis poured into the streets to celebrate the day's conquest over collapse. The medina was the magnet and no place was "hotter" than the celebrated *Bab Souika*, the Times Square of Tunis. Its block-long all-night cafes were packed with raucous men playing cards and dominoes.

We went to see the best *Ramadan* show in town: *Walid's Woman Trouble*.

A scrum of hot and eager Arab men in red *kefias* marked the spot. Again, we were thrust into Tunisia's most popular aerobic sport—crowd jostling. It required quick feet and an instinct for narrow spaces. I let my hand rove over Cerise's back to guard her from gropings. It was an unnecessary precaution since the *fellaheen* had one objective in mind, which they pursued with single-minded fervor—to squeeze through the club's narrow doors, which became for them gates of earthly paradise.

We were thrust into a dark room littered with folding chairs. Obscured by a heavy veil of smoke, four musicians in dark suits, sunglasses and white bowling shoes occupied the stage. As the crowd spilled in, the band started blowing their *noubas*. The music lowered to a whisper. A burly man with large, liquid eyes and a dark, caterpillar moustache appeared onstage and began to moan and gurgle in a deep baritone. This was Walid. He wore a white *jebba*, black socks and white pointy-toed slippers. In his white shroud, his body seemed amorphous. Between his hem and his socks, his legs were bare and hairy.

The barelegged baritone strutted and swayed, as he crooned his *Maghreb* Blues about the women in his life. His primarily male audience shouted and laughed enthusiastically, while puffing emphatically on cigarettes. Walid clutched his head in his hands while his eyeballs rolled in their sockets. Women were driving him mad, he complained. In a moment, we understood why.

The *Bedouin Brides*, three ample dancers in desert regalia, emerged from the wings. They shimmied around Walid and thrust their hips against him in time to the mesmerizing music, then tightened their circle around the star until they enveloped him.

After receiving several robust butt-thrusts, Walid crumpled to his knees. The *Bedouin Brides* leered at the fallen star with exaggerated lust and closed around him in a "harem body slam." The *fellaheen* in the audience in matted turbans and soaked shirts watched this blend of sexual gladiatorial and farce with hoots, yells and backslapping alacrity.

Walid trembled between bravado and fear, impotence and lechery, as the circle of Maghreb mamas closed around him. Suddenly, he shot to his feet, swung his arms like sabers and sidestepped the *Bedouin Brides* with a bullfighter's bravado.

The *Bedouin Brides* uncoiled into a chorus line, thrust their hips frequently at the frenzied crowd and shimmied off-stage.

After the show, Cerise and I strolled down the stone-paved, sparkler-lit streets of the *medina* and discussed what we had seen, as we had often done after watching a film.

"That was extraordinary!" Cerise remarked. "If I had not seen it, I would never have believed it."

We passed crowded cafés where shouting men slapped and pointed frenetically at cards on tables.

"What are these men doing here?" Cerise, the amateur anthropologist, inquired, as she waved her arm like a wand over the throng of café patrons. "Don't they have families?"

"Maybe they prefer gambling, swilling sweet tea and shouting at each other to family life."

"But they stare at women so hungrily!" Cerise observed. "And here they are, staying up all night—*with men!*"

"Religion and poverty prevent them from pursuing women," I said. Although it was probably true, it sounded like a cross-cultural platitude and I felt obliged to supply other options. "Male bonding? Group psychosis?" I suggested brightly.

12

MONEY BACK GUARANTEE

My second priority after student teaching was to be reimbursed for a portion of the money I lost at the bus station, so that I could repay Cerise. Stealing was so prevalent in developing nations that the Peace Corps provided theft insurance to mitigate volunteers' losses. But the reimbursement process involved a massive effort and a long cross-cultural field trip to police headquarters. I spent hours there completing forms and having them stamped by a gauntlet of cranky officials.

Not that I was complaining. I would have gladly mummified myself in Tunisian red tape to pay back Cerise. I anticipated the satisfaction of putting the money in her hands and watching her suspicious face soften with relief. She never called me a sponge, but I noted her discomfort whenever I borrowed money. She thought she was acting like a mother, not a girlfriend. I explained to her that my mother would never lend me money, but this did not reassure her. Until the borrowed dinars were in her hand, she would not see us as equals.

Seven offices and four hours after my arrival, the ultimate police official put the last stamp on my certificate of loss. I was so patient throughout the ordeal that the functionaries treated me kindly, plying me with sweet tea, which Ramadan forbade them to drink. Jazzed on caffeine and sugar, I traipsed across Tunis to the Peace Corps office for phase two of my money and manhood recovery—to induce Irving P. Irving, the Peace Corps Director, to sign off on my reimbursement.

Irving's signature on a check might prove harder to obtain than the Tunisian police certificate. The director was reputed to be tough and ruthless. He was the Peace Corps' globetrotting hatchet man, notorious for slashing bloated budgets of overspending, underachieving overseas offices.

I had not spoken with Irving since he extracted me from Italian police custody in Rome. After herding us to Tunisia, he handed us off to Tasha at the airport. This was consistent with his "prime mover" managerial style. Irving viewed himself as the omnipotent administrator who set things in motion, delegated to subordinates and let the system run itself. Meeting volunteers was not in his job description. Tasha claimed he was averse to it.

"Come in. Sit down," the gruff Peace Corps director beckoned. "What can I do for you?" I sat in a thick leather chair in front of his massive desk and stared at a blown-up vacation photograph of Irving in a blood-smeared apron, holding up an animal carcass. The portrait sported a caption, "I eat what I kill."

Before I saw them, I felt the director's flinty, blue eyes drill into me. As a former sergeant in the army's elite Komodo Dragons division, Irving claimed that he could size up a man in five minutes or less. His eyes widened with recognition. "You!" he wagged his finger at me as if he were flipping memory cards until he came to the right one. He snapped his fingers, "The airport!"

He recognized me from Fiumiccino. I had to lie—and fast. If he identified me as the toilet terrorist suspect the Italian police arrested, I would not only leave without my lost dinars, but be terminated on the spot.

"I was at the airport, sir, but so was everybody else."

The director tilted his face to observe me with one squinting eye, as if he were peering through a telescope at a remote asteroid. "The men's room, right?"

"Sir, I can't tell a lie. I used the men's room at the Rome airport. But we were there for eight hours. I would have been a freak not to use the men's room at least once."

Irving could not dispute my point, which meant that he could not terminate me. This appeared to perturb him.

"I don't have time to discuss the men's rooms in your life," Irving snapped. "Why are you here?"

Irving's putdown of men's rooms as an appropriate topic of conversation was ironic, given what I knew about him. When training camp nights were as slow as vultures coasting under a hot sun, the counselors told "Legends of the Corps." According to one myth, Irving was hired as director after he encountered a Peace Corps crony in the State Department men's room.

"I'm here for you to sign my theft insurance claim, sir," I said.

I handed him the certificate of loss, which he scanned brusquely and tossed on his desk.

"You did that in record time."

"Thank you, sir," I answered proudly to show how much his compliment meant to me.

"Don't thank me," Irving snapped. "Your victimization costs the Peace Corps money."

"Sorry, sir. It happened when I was getting on a bus. You know what that's like."

"We're on a tight budget. We can't afford your mistakes!" Irving lambasted me.

"No, sir," I replied humbly. As Irving's refusal to sign the form grew as a possibility, I fought back tears. I imagined the disappointment in Cerise's eyes and lines of concern forming at the corners of her mouth. I had to fight for us.

"Sir, it's my right to be reimbursed."

Irving cocked his head pugnaciously and leaned forward. "Did you say *right*? What's a right?"

I wondered nervously if this was one of Irving's Komodo Dragon Battalion commando questions I heard about. Was he testing my patriotism, measuring my manhood, or appraising my ability to respond to a Tunisian challenge of our core values? I had no idea what he was thinking, so I took him literally. I sat straight in the chair and extemporized on the meaning of rights, including the Magna Carta, the social contract, Locke, Montesquieu, John Peter Zenger, the Bill of Rights, the Gettysburg Address, *Brown v. Board of Ed*, Miranda, *Miller v. California*, *Roe v. Wade* and other rights highlights. Irving cupped his face in his hands and listened with amusement, amazement and finally void-eyed stupefaction. When I had exhausted my knowledge of rights as well as Irving's patience, the director leaned across his desk and growled, "Your rights are what I say they are!"

After asserting his despotic power, Irving benevolently signed the reimbursement check and pushed it toward me. I would have grabbed the money and made a swift exit, but no one received 21 dinars from Irving P. Irving without earning 25.

"When I was your age, I was like you, a shiftless, little know-it-all punk hanging out in pool halls," Irving reminisced.

"Pool halls, sir? I don't play pool."

"ONE DAY—," he steamrolled my biographical objection, "I woke up and realized I'd spend the rest of my life in a pool hall if I didn't shape up and make something of myself. I enlisted in the army and served six years. When I was discharged, I had a family. I worked days to support them and attended college at night.

227

When I earned my engineering degree, I joined the Peace Corps and served two two-year tours. I haven't done badly for myself. Do you want to know what I learned after all that?"

My eyes were transfixed on the check. Would he smack my hand with a nightstick if I reached for it?

"That you don't miss pool?" I guessed.

"THAT THERE ARE NO RIGHTS, EXCEPT THE RIGHT TO WORK HARD!" Irving bellowed.

"That's very edifying, sir. Thank you, sir." I snared the check with such conviction that I was lucky not to mutilate it. I was nearly out the door when Irving's voice cut me short.

"Rick. Nobody wears tank-tops in Tunisia but tourists and fags. From now on, wear button-down shirts. It's the Peace Corps image."

"Peace Corps image? Nobody told me. What is it, sir?"

"Rick, if you're walking down a street with a seductive French woman—that's *not* the Peace Corps image. Walking down the street with young Tunisian men, *that's* the Peace Corps image."

"Sir, let me make sure I understand you: walking in a tank top with a beautiful woman is homosexual and not the Peace Corps image, but walking in a buttoned-down shirt with young men is heterosexual and the Peace Corps image. Thank you for setting me straight."

I nodded profusely because I was hyped on all of the tea the police had given me. Yet I was also thinking that despite Irving's Peace Corps experience building bridges in Bangladesh, he had public images all mixed up.

"Have a good two years and for your sake, don't let me see you again." Irving dismissed me with a peremptory wave of his hand.

As I raced down the *Avenue de la Liberté* to meet Cerise, I envisioned what her expression would be when she saw the check.

Waves of exhilarating vindication were coursing through me when my reverie was cut short by a *thwop*. A mutilated rat carcass lay in a hairy pancake in front of me on the broken pavement. It had been dropped from a roof. But even that could not dampen my anticipation of Cerise's reaction to my successful mission.

I met Cerise at Le Café de France and waited for her to ask about the reimbursement, but she never mentioned it. When I waved the check, she was less excited than I was.

"It's the money I lost!" I proclaimed.

"Oh, good, my love. I'm glad you got it back."

That evening at dinner, a veteran volunteer explained that the roof-tossed rat I encountered was a common form of protest. Reflecting on Cerise's cool response to the reimbursement I worked so hard for, I wondered where I could find a rat and a roof.

13

GOODBYE—*AGAIN*

On Cerise's last day we explored the *souk* for fine leather bags. In one well-stocked *hanoot*, a young merchant tried to pet Cerise's ass while she circled a cluster of clutches. As his hand approached for landing on her soft bottom, I grabbed his shoulder and spun him around to meet my fist. Cerise's scream broke my spell of jealous anger. I grabbed her arm and we ran down several winding, stone-paved streets to avoid pursuit, until we emerged from the medina through a small arch in the wall.

"Why did you do that? Are you insane?" Cerise asked when we stopped at a French-style café on Boulevard Bourguiba.

"I was defending your honor. He was going to touch your ass."

"Excuse me, but my ass is no honor. You are so naïve. It's just part of the price one pays for a chic handbag."

"You can find another bag, but your ass is one of a kind."

"That's sweet of you to say, but I promised myself a nice leather bag and now I'll have to go home without one."

"I'll send you one. Or bring you one next time I'm in France."

That evening, we met Fargus and other volunteers for dinner at the only Vietnamese restaurant in Tunis. Hair was the topic of conversation. Fargus praised blondes and Cerise agreed as she stroked my hair. Fargus smirked and shook his head.

Later, in our glass-walled cubicle, I asked Cerise, "What color is my hair?"

"It's blond, *cheri*." She stroked my hair and kissed my forehead.

"It's not blond, Cerise. It's brown."

"To my eyes, it is blond."

She frowned and withdrew her hand from my cheek. "What difference does it make?"

"I don't have blond hair, that's all."

Seconds after raising the point, I wondered why the mistaken hair color bothered me, because it was clear that by raising it, I ensured that our last night would be an explosive culmination of arguments that began three weeks before, went unresolved, and would now be recapitulated.

But since I could not retract what I had said, I continued on the path of destruction. "If you think I have blond hair after four years, I'm afraid that one day you'll be disappointed that you're with the wrong person."

She pulled my hair and sat up, with her breasts swaying in the window. "*Alors!* Have it your way. I am with the wrong person, so now I'll find the right one."

"Don't make a scene," I pleaded, as she stood up naked in the glass window. Outside our little room, I heard people moving around in the cavernous dormitory.

"I'm not making a scene," she hissed as she slipped on her bra. "I'm merely getting dressed like an ordinary human being. Of course, it only seems strange in a high school dormitory!"

She dropped a loose sweater over her head, slipped into tight jeans and smoothed them over her narrow hips. Puckering her lips to distribute the gloss evenly, she ignored me, as she prepared for an event that she doubtless visualized in novelistic detail.

"Where are you going?" I asked.

Outside, the elephants in the cageless zoo shrieked in perpetual fear of molestation.

"Oh, I don't know," Cerise replied breezily. "I thought I'd walk through the park and pick up a stray rapist."

I swallowed hard at the strong possibility that it might happen. I didn't want to beg, but I had to stop her.

"Don't go," I implored.

She patted her hair in place, slung her bag on her shoulder and waved goodbye. "Write about it in your notebook."

Her derision stung my pride. I wanted to come back with a mordant retort, but my problem was that she was right—I probably would write about it in my notebook. Anger, futility and sadness took turns at beating me as the clicking of her heels faded.

"It's over," I told myself repeatedly. I picked up the yellow notebook and an idea came to me.

"Love without acceptance is a beautiful useless thing."

Unfortunately, nothing followed. I tried to write by applying pen to paper, but my words degenerated into doodles. I tossed the notebook in the suitcase and lay on the bed, staring at the abject light bulb dangling from the ceiling. Suddenly it was eclipsed by a shadow.

Cerise stood in the doorway, smiling.

"You looked so sad when I left that I couldn't leave you."

After wounding me, she would now play the Red Cross. I could not smile or feel triumphant. She turned off the hanging light bulb, took off her clothes before the window and slid into bed next to me. We made love and talked freely through the night about everything that mattered, just like the friends we were when we were at our best. We explained our thoughts with the same care and elaboration that we devoted to our letters. Only this was much better because we could see and touch each other, and hear one another whisper. We asked each other what we meant and did not have to wait for answers to forgotten questions. By holding on to each other and to the sound of our voices, we tried to forestall the dawn and make each moment last longer and matter more than it ever could.

"I want you to see the world," she whispered, when I closed my eyes before succumbing to sleep. "But I've done my wandering and I don't want to go through it again. I only hope that I'm still around when you grow up."

When I awoke the next morning, Cerise was gone. I was alone again and dazed from a lack of sleep. My body's first responses were familiar—a tight throat, the sensation of being truncated and only partly there. I drifted through the day feeling numb and distracted. Her presence had been amputated from my life.

That night in my single bed, in the main room of *le dortoire*, I opened my notebook and found a message on the last fresh page penned in familiar, round script:

I promise I didn't read anything before this. Goodbye, my love. Take care and be as happy as you can and know that I am yours. I am more convinced of it than ever. XXXX Cerise

I touched the words on the blue-lined paper. They were all I had left of her. My fingers traced the indentations where she had applied pressure to the pen point, as if they were the curves of her body. I tried to release hidden powers in the words, so that the ink would turn to blood and the paper to flesh and the words would come alive and become her.

But the message lay cold on the page. I was back in a familiar place—absence, in the state of longing. Cerise had sprayed cologne in the notebook to delay my arrival, but she could have spared herself the trouble. We were closest in Absence. Physical proximity complicated our feelings. Distance made them clear.

I read her message repeatedly. Everything else we had said to one another seemed peripheral to it. Her words embraced and encouraged me, and I loved her as much as I ever had. Yet I wondered if this note explained all that had passed between us in the last 20 days, or belied it.

Later that week, volunteers from across Tunisia reconvened for our induction ceremony. A staph infection had inflated my foot to twice its size and transformed it into a red, suppurating club. At the induction party, I hobbled with a crutch and someone splashed wine on my new cream-colored suit—the one my mother said made me look like an ice cream vendor. Now I looked like a drunken one.

When I turned in at the *lycée* dormitory, the only married couple in our group occupied the windowed cubicle where Cerise and I had been days before. Like a child touching a painful wound, I stared at the narrow room from my dormitory bed. The couple had draped a white sheet over the glass partition.

Then I realized how different Cerise and I really were and I missed her more than ever.

BOOK 3
MENZELMORPHOSIS

1

FIRST ENCOUNTERS

Mission nebulous, foot swollen to twice its size, I hobbled down Avenue Bourguiba toward the vertical red Monoprix sign, passing wrought iron street posts, boarded kiosks and immaculate traffic circles, familiar in design but curiously out of place. A column of pink smoke wafted in the horizon from *El Fouled*, Tunisia's only steel-mill. At first impression, Menzel Bourguiba was a good place to begin, an urban *tabula rasa,* whose disparate energies and ambiguous identity matched my own.

The driver pointed this way when I asked about a cool drink. I entered the narrow pastry shop in the shadow of the Monoprix sign. The proprietor was an aging man with sallow skin and a red *chachia,* a Fez cap perched on a crown of wispy hair. His gossiping eyes asked 1000 questions and answered 999 as he poured lemonade in a glass.

"Are you a tourist?"

"No," I replied.

"I didn't think so," he replied, as if he knew all along. "Menzel Bourguiba has nothing to see."

He poured a second glass of lemonade. As I drained it in one gulp, I thought it was an odd remark for a local businessman to make.

"I'm from the *Sahel*, not from here," he responded to my silent observation, "Ten years ago, I came here on business, but there is no business. Half the town is unemployed; the other half works in France. I made too few dinars to leave, so I had to stay."

His plight was paradoxical and oddly American. He was like a pioneer prospector who, when stranded in a boomtown mined clean of precious metals, opened a general store.

The man in the red cap spoke with great authority about Menzel Bourguiba. He seemed to know everyone and everything in town. But when I asked him if he knew of an apartment to rent, he squinted, shrugged, put his finger in his cheek and let his eyes wander to the corners of the ceilings, chasing elusive trains of thought. "Is the apartment for you?" he asked.

"I'm the new Bourguiba School teacher," I replied grandiosely.

"Bourguiba School?" A doubt fluttered in his voice. An instant of recognition illuminated his yellow face, but faded into stupefaction, when he realized he had mistaken this institution for another. Then he remembered something.

"Yes, yes," he said, wagging a finger. "Only a year ago, or maybe two, there was an American *jeune homme* in Menzel. I believe he, too, was an English teacher. He disappeared."

"He probably went home," I replied to ward off the omen.

"I don't remember the details, *jeune homme*." The old man raised an eyebrow and laughed dryly. "All I know is that he is gone and you are here. That will be 500 *millimes*."

It was definitely time to go. The pastry shop owner's innuendoes were aggravating, especially when he called me *jeune homme*. He made "young man" sound like an endangered species. I paid for my three lemonades and five fudge bars, and walked out.

"The high school is not far, *jeune homme*," the pastry merchant said, but "not far" from the mouth of a senior shopkeeper was not the distance I covered under the broiling sun with three suitcases and a typewriter in my hands and a laundry bag slung across my back.

Through the dusty, deserted, sun-blasted streets I staggered on one swollen foot to an uncertain destination. I tried to devise a plan as sweat dripped from my hair and burned my eyes. Where would I stay that night? There was no hotel in sight. I stumbled, dropped the bags and tumbled on the ground. After panic and desperation had failed, anger produced a strategy—I would go to the high school and stay there until I was expelled.

I occupied the bench in the principal's office for one hour. I had not sat on a bench like this since junior high school, when I was sent to the principal's office routinely for talking in class. It was never a good place to be, and now that I was a teacher, it was no better.

The office was suffused by harvest hues. Yellow light streamed through the tan window shades, making the stacks of green file folders glow like enchanted hives of advanced insects. As she buzzed back and forth in smacking flip-flops, *Madame* Zaza, the perky secretary, efficiently ignored me, after informing me more than once that the *proviseur*, Monsieur Hamahama, was not around and was too busy to see me even if he was.

Perspiration poured down my face while discharge from my staph-infected foot dampened my sock. I felt disgusting and those who saw me probably concurred. For this reason, I did not press *Madame* Zaza for an interview with the principal. Camping out in the school was a bold tactic, but I failed to predict the poor impression my red face, sweat-soaked shirt and unlaced sneaker would make on school workers, whose expectations of teachers I must have violated. With each moment that I sat in plain view, mouth breathing and probing for clues with restless eyes, opinions were being formed that might doom my mission to teach continuing education in this or any other town where my image became known.

After two hours on the bench, I was prepared to spend the night on it when a lanky French man with thick glasses and wild hair burst into the office, foraged in his mailbox and asked *Madame* Zaza if the new teacher had arrived. When the secretary pointed to me, the Frenchman blinked, shook my hand, kissed my cheeks, embraced me warmly and offered a place to stay.

Though I wanted to believe in people's innate kindness and my charismatic effect on them, instinct told mw that this was a case of mistaken identity. But I could not set the matter straight. Good will is a fragile thing that a moment's hesitation can destroy.

Even as we lifted my bags into his *Renault Cinq*, I detected the first symptoms of inconvenience and perplexity shade Antoine's face. When he learned that I was an American, his letdown was complete. By that time, however, my bags were in the car and we were en route to his apartment.

When the door opened, a honking noise greeted our ears. Suddenly Antoine's wife was wrapped around him, her lips planting lusty kisses over his bearded face. Embarrassed by his wife's effusive affection, my benefactor reached for me with his free arm and introduced us. When Nunu registered my presence, her mouth went slack. Returning to her feet, she assumed a more discreet pose. Behind thick glasses, Nunu's eyes were buttons. Her chin jutted like an elbow. Her mouth was a puncture hole. She spoke with sloshing sounds.

During a meal of radishes, soup, meat, fried potatoes, cheese and salad, Antoine told the romantic story of how he and Nunu met at a church picnic days before he was to leave for Tunisia.

"It was love at first sight," she honked. Antoine blinked in apparent disbelief, like a man awakening from a strange dream.

Antoine was tuning his guitar when the bell rang. Pierre Planque, a burly teaching veteran, stood at the door, tugging at the cut-off shorts that bit his gut. A French bachelor, the young man for whom Antoine had mistaken me, was arriving any day and the local *coopérants,* overseas French workers, were looking for a place for him to live. Pierre, a cross between Errol Flynn and

Orson Welles, was delighted to see me. "It will be easier to find a place for two bachelors than for one," he remarked.

We piled into Pierre Planque's car, shouted *"Allez!"* and screeched and skidded though the grid of boxy villas comprising Menzel Bourguiba. We stormed realty offices and raised clouds of dust as we chased down leads. Between stops, we went by Jean-Claude Colombi's place. Colombi, like Pierre, was a veteran *coopérant* who had served in Tunisia for nine years. An elfin man, with long hair, a waxed moustache and a needle-like goatee, Colombi was a celebrated poet, whose sonorous pronouncements lent a dramatic flair to our pursuit of housing.

Rolling his world-weary eyes, Colombi summed up each over-priced, green-walled, urine-reeking dive we reconnoitered with his trusty maxim, *"C'est l'angoisse, mec."*

That evening, after playing his songs and showing off his prized collection of comic books, Antoine led his bride to their bedroom. I sank into the living room couch by the oil heater and flipped through the comic saga of *Epinard*, a French superhero who was a cross between "Popeye" and the "Jolly Green Giant." *Epinard's* line to victims and villains alike was *"Reste tranquil!"*

I wondered if this had been a good first day of being on my own halfway around the world when I heard a long groan, a diphthong of sexual exaggeration, followed by yelps and cries. Rising in pitch, then subsiding gradually like an express train bypassing a local station, Nunu's passion faded in a trail of breath catchings, sighs, coughs, moans, a snort, then silence.

A week passed and I was still crashing with the newlyweds. Housing was tighter than expected. The *coopérants* surmised that the landlords were hoarding their properties to drive up rents.

For Antoine and Nunu, socioeconomic explanations offered no solace. They sullenly observed me soaking my staph-infected foot in a pot of salt water. At meals, Antoine stared in his soup; Nunu inquired anxiously about the fried potatoes. At bedtime, Nunu's moans were shorter and less inspired, until they were supplanted by Antoine's snores.

One night, I awoke in a violent coughing fit as I choked for breath. The room was pervaded by sweet smelling kerosene that leaked from a second-hand heater. I crawled to the door, fumbled with a police lock, nearly impaling myself, and crawled into the hall for air.

Antoine burst from the bedroom, holding his guitar by the neck like a club. *"Qu'est-ce que tu as?"* he demanded. "We give you our couch and food and now you wake us up! What's wrong with you?"

I gagged and pointed at my throat. "I can't breathe."

When the situation was clear, Antoine and Nunu shared a guilty look. They noted my bluish pallor and feared my suspicion.

Contrite for what they might have done, the newlyweds made a special effort to care for my infected foot and continued to suffer my presence.

The long-awaited French bachelor finally arrived. He and I rented a white-walled villa two kilometers from the center of town, on a dusty, rutted side street off the main road. Half naked children scampered around, throwing cans and bottles.

The house was freshly painted and well-appointed. The owner, an assembly line worker, whose job in a French stereo factory had made him deaf, took pride in the newest amenities— mosaic floor tiles and black monkey tail window bars. A plump, flowering azalea bush pressed against the wrought iron bars. Its delicate magenta flowers clustered in the spaces between them like notes in a vertical score.

The *coopérants* and I stood in front of the house, feeling

victorious and relieved. Jean-Claude Colombi, the Corsican poet, clapped his hands and offered a fluted bottle of *Sidi Rais*, the sparkling rosé fermented under the supervision of the Tunisian First Lady, who was French.

Colombi lifted the bottle. "Ritual is the wine of routine," he proclaimed in resonant cadences. "So after our exhaustive exploration, we consecrate your new habitation!"

Having forgotten his corkscrew at home, Colombi cracked open the bottle close to the cork. Without pausing to inspect the jagged edge, he placed his lips on the neck and took a long, thirsty pull of the fragrant wine. Colombi wiped his mouth with a flourish and passed the broken bottle to Pierre Planque, who eyed the jagged neck with caution, poured rosé in his mouth without planting his lips on the bottle and splashed his shirt.

After each of us had sanctified the house with a swig, Colombi handed me the broken bottle to place among the others that stood on the white walls surrounding the property, as totems of drunkenness or a primitive home security system.

Living for the first time in a place of my own, I needed furniture. My needs were simple, and my employment uncertain, so the only items I bought were a woven *natte* with ensigns of purple, red and green, a used mattress and planks to set it on. I put my books on the floor along the green walls, hung my clothes on a laundry line suspended between two nails and lived like a nomad in a bourgeois villa.

Colombi showed me *le marché au puces* across the road where brass samovars, Ottoman spittoons and all *bric-a-brac* known to man were on display, but the celebrated poet thwarted my spending impulses before I purchased a spoon, fork and knife.

"*Mon jeune ami*, if you buy everything that appeals to you, you will have no *flous* for food," Colombi said, before raising a finger to utter one of his maxims. "In Tunisia, *mec*, you must learn one thing, if nothing else—*'Shweah b'shweah'* as the Tunisians say. Or as you say in English, *Leetle by leetle.*"

2

SCREAMS FROM A MARRIAGE

Call it insecurity but I was convinced that most of the French community despised me. They invited me to their homes to eat five-course meals and watch slideshows of their past vacations, but while they passed the peas, they passed judgement. For these high school teachers and agricultural specialists, I was alien and immature—in other words, American. They told dog stories in their dialect of grunts and stops, but when I tried to interject a story on another topic, they stared at me with bafflement. No doubt, my French was not as good as it could have been.

One couple was extremely provincial. The Poumidors believed that America and New York, in particular, were the Devil's world headquarters. When they learned that I was born in New York, *Madame* Poumidor reared back in her chair, blanched horror-stricken and held her hand between us to shield her virtue from my evil emanations.

Jean-Claude Colombi and his wife, Armelle, were exceptions to the French rule. They were an unusual couple to behold—she as tall and stout as he was short and slim. A Corsican by birth, Colombi had the penetrating eyes and dashing style of Napoleon. He spoke with an Italian inflection in mellifluous cadences that could make a dog-story, a genre in which he was expert, sound like a Racine soliloquy. Colombi was a Frenchman unfettered by French restraints. He did not require five courses at every meal or feel threatened by American culture.

Au contraire, Colombi was always eager to discuss the U.S., ask questions and toss American slang into the *repartée,* like "R-a-a-t on" and "Aw-kay" for an exotic verbal spice.

Armelle was a Lyonnaise for whom culinary genius was a genetic trait. She was gracious with everyone but Colombi, on whom she would turn acrimoniously, regardless of the occasion or location, with loud *engueulades.* Armelle ranted at all that Colombi did and said, but her petty annoyances were symptoms of a larger complaint: after 15 years of wedlock, work, children, house and husband, she was exhausted.

Armelle resented Colombi's hobbies most of all. He had purchased a ten-speed bicycle, which he rode for hours everyday after school.

"*Alors,* Colombi!" she shouted, "*Ça suffit!* I cook and I supervise the maid and all you do is ride your *petit vélo.* What if you fall off? I suppose you'll want me to play your nurse, along with your wife, your housekeeper, the mother of your children and your whore. No way! *Va te faire foutre, idiot! Con! Salaud!*"

"*Mais, mon choux, ma douce!*" Jean-Claude replied with flamboyant tenderness and tried to nuzzle her neck, but Armelle swatted his cheek with her broad hand.

"Don't *mon choux* me. You mustachioed worm!"

Colombi rolled his eyes, gave a forbearing look and mouthed his favorite proverb: "*C'est l'angoisse, mec.*"

If the Colombis had only argued, their relationship would have been simple to predict, take distance from and discount. But they were no stock old couple quarreling from hostility and boredom. When Armelle did not revile Colombi, she praised his poetic genius and promoted his publications with doting admiration. They appeared to care for each other, yet their affection was buried under a callus of familiarity and stress, which made their bickering painful to witness. Their relationship was not hate, but ravaged love.

I went to Tunis to see Dr. Mamooni, the Bourguiba School Director, to seek his help in starting the program in Menzel, but he was attending a conference in California. As I meandered in downtown Tunis, waiting for the next bus, I ran into the Colombis, who were shopping after leaving their children at the French School in La Marsa. They hailed me warmly and offered to drive me back to Menzel.

I never doubted their kindness, but they may have also wanted me in the car as a referee since they squabbled all the way home. Armelle scolded Colombi for being rude to the headmaster.

Colombi proclaimed, *"Je m'en fous!"* Winking at me in the rearview, he added in English, *"Ah don't ca-a-a whot zot os-ho-o-l z'inks."*

Armelle was linguist enough to know what he meant.

"Cochon! Quel espèce d'idiot!" she screamed.

Colombi patted her thigh, *"Eeet's awrat, bab-Y!"*

Her face reddened with indignation.

"They will make our children suffer because of you!" she lamented.

"Rela-a-a-a-x!" Colombi cooed.

"I can't relax. You are a *voyou*, a juvenile delinquent who never became a man. It's my fault!" She turned to me. "You see, Rick, Colombi went from his mother to his wife, with only three months on his own. That is why he is such a spoiled child! Yes, Colombi—you are *gaté*!"

"But those three months between Mama and Armelle—what I didn't do!" Colombi replied.

He recounted his job on a banana boat that shuttled between

West Africa and Marseilles. He worked in the hold, shooting at tarantulas when they crawled out of hanging bunches.

"Stop!" Armelle cried, cupping her ears, "Nobody believes this crap, least of all your wife, who has heard it for 15 years."

Colombi, aroused by Armelle's exasperation, pursed his lips and leaned toward her, cadging for a kiss as the car swerved to the side of the road. "Oh, my little cabbage," he said. "Fifteen years of heaven on earth!"

Armelle screamed, while Colombi described his tactics for controlling the tarantula population by shooting into bunches of hanging bananas. These preemptive strikes, which Colombi claimed to have learned from America's bombing in Southeast Asia, were effective, but messy, since they resulted in more splattered bananas than dead tarantulas.

One day, Colombi fell asleep on duty. He was awakened, not by a supervisor, but by a tickling sensation moving up his leg.

"*Arrête!* I can't take anymore!" Armelle cried, "For God's sake, stop this verbal masturbation and drive!"

"What can I do but masturbate since you will not let me make love to you? *Mec*, it was not my hand crawling up my leg, as my dear wife would have you believe," Colombi said, "but a black tarantula with red stripes on its legs."

He smiled gleefully in the rearview mirror to gauge my revulsion. I flinched to appease him.

"I didn't move a muscle," Colombi whispered. "I was so c-o-o-o-l, you know? I just let the creature crawl all over me until she was bored and walked off. What else could I do?"

"*Mais quelle espèce de merde*," Armelle huffed. "What crap. Now tell us that it was the most satisfying sexual experience of your life!"

"No, my dear," Colombi corrected. "It was far more spiritual

247

in nature. This spider was *extraordinaire*! She crawled off my lap and down my leg and walked away. But before she disappeared, she turned to me and spoke—in perfect French!"

"*Mais alors!* A French tarantula! He's hallucinating!" Armelle agonized.

Colombi's voice descended to a murmur.

"Actually, spiders are highly intelligent invertebrates, *tu sais*. This one must have been a genius. Do you know what she said? *'You cannot look in the eyes of a spider without resembling one.'* It's remarkable, no? A tarantula has eight eyes, you know, so I see things in eight ways. Believe me, *Mec*, it has given my writing an edge."

Concluding his tale, Colombi thrust his flexing fingers into his wife's thigh. She shrieked and slapped his five-fingered tarantula.

"No, no, no!" Armelle wailed, *"Je ne peux plus le supporter!* I can't take anymore! Let me out of this car this instant!"

"You can't leave now. We're going 50!" Colombi pleaded.

The Colombis were an exhausting couple; now even they were exhausted. The car was silent, but not for long. Jacques recounted the story of their love. They met as students. She was "the older woman" with whom he fell madly in love.

"It was really not as romantic as it sounds," Armelle commented. "I had money and a place of my own."

"Who needed money?" Jean-Claude replied defensively.

I liked the Colombis and felt grateful for their friendship, but their relationship depressed me.

I hoped to wed Cerise, but for the present I was lonely and alone and viewed every married couple with envy. The Colombis' togetherness intensified my aloneness, yet their squabbling warned me of what I could expect from matrimony. My mind distorted the Colombis' voices until I heard Cerise's and mine.

Would we fight this way over time? Didn't we already?

Colombi told another tale of his brief and momentous bachelorhood. While he waited for his girlfriend to come home, he made love to her roommate. While they were in bed, his girlfriend arrived, so he hid in the closet until she went to the bathroom, then slipped out the window and leaped onto his Vespa.

"Must we hear your insipid fantasies?" Armelle squawked.

I saw myself with Cerise in 15 years, trying to feel virile and arouse her jealousy with old bachelor stories, only to elicit similar invective. In my case it could be worse, since Cerise would believe my tales of sexual conquest and avenge herself with infidelities.

When we were back in Menzel, Colombi dropped off Armelle before driving me to my new house. Sensing that his marital turmoil had shocked and depressed me, he patted my arm and smiled ruefully, *"C'est l'angoisse, mec."*

•

My Dearest Love,

I miss you no end.

Back at school I have the shittiest schedule imaginable. On Mondays I teach from eight to five, and the same on Tuesday, the only advantage being that I can take off Friday afternoon and have a long weekend. Still, the situation is quite hopeless. The teacher's union is holding a rally across the street. Jobs are being cut to save money. The result: more kids per class in worsening conditions. My classes range from 30 to 40 students. It's ridiculous, and the big losers are, of course, the kids.

I went to the university to check the results of the last test. Only one passed—the ugly redhead I wrote to you about last year. Marie failed for the third time. I really wonder whether I am wasting my time to even try again, but since I have started, I will follow through, just this once.

I was so worried about your foot. Thank God you did not get gangrene: you must promise to take better care of yourself. Yes, your health is just as important to me as your fidelity. (Honest.)

I find it hard to communicate with my old chums. I'm not quite here yet.

Our lime trees along the boulevard have gone brown. The sky is cold, dreary and gray. I am in my fluffy blue bathrobe and knee-socks (and nothing else), busy spinning our four weeks together into tender memories. Even the soap, toothpaste and mosquito quarrels, my jealous probe into your infidelities and your always getting us lost are now delightful sorrows!

Rick, mon amour, mon cheri, quand serons nous enfin ensemble pour longtemps? J'ai besoin de toi, de ton embrasse, tes bras autour de moi.

Now that I've talked to you, I feel a little better. Please write. Your letters are all I have to keep me warm. As long as I have them, how can I be bored?

> *Love,*
> *Cerise*

3
AUTUMN IN TUNISIA

Autumn replaced the languorous heat with a restless breeze. Fresh fall air, which signified beginnings in the States, here imparted the sadness of departure. Autumn in Tunisia was not so much a break in the temperature as a loss of it. In leaving us, the sun made it clear how much we needed its embrace.

Like foods, places need certain ingredients to be enjoyed. The recipe for Tunisia was sun, water and stir. The sea rendered coral and cool breezes, seafood and history. The sun gave blue skies, white light and bright colors to sand, rock and prickly plants. Even if the summer sun was a scorcher, without it you felt abandoned to the fall chill, as the earth slipped into darkness for which you were unprepared.

However, change stirred in the faint warmth. *Ramadan* was over and children disappeared from the streets. Autumn had always meant the start of a school year, the excitement of old friends and new encounters. In Menzel Bourguiba, school had also started. Everyone I knew—my housemate, the French *coopérants*, Fargus in Bizerte—was immersed in classes, meetings, lesson plans, papers to grade and names to learn. Except for me.

Despite the fact that I was hired and trained to teach, this was the first fall since I was six when I was not in school.

I tried to join the workforce of Menzel and play the role I was given: Bourguiba School teacher. Twice a day, I stopped at the high school to retrieve my mail and schedule a meeting with the *proviseur* of *Lycee Mixte*, the elusive Hamahama. Each time, doll-faced *Madame* Zaza flashed her charming smile and delivered her all-too-familiar lines.

"*Non, non, Monsieur. Je suis très desolée.* No, I'm very sorry, but the principal is not here. So, what can I do about it? He cannot see you if he is not here, am I wrong? *Il est logique, n'est-ce pas?*"

"Yes, very logical," I said. "But the Bourguiba School is logical, too. English lessons are logical, too, no? *Le proviseur* is my boss and I still have not seen him. Is that logical?"

"Tomorrow, perhaps," the secretary replied, her smile revealing deep dimples in her round cheeks.

For two weeks I let myself be thwarted, beguiled, diverted and sedated by *Madame* Zaza's frisky smile and promise of "tomorrow." What choice did I have?

I recalled Dr. Mamooni's speech for the Peace Corps teachers at the Bourguiba School headquarters in Tunis. With a shaven head and dark glasses he never removed, Mamooni crushed words in the monotonous jackhammer of his jaws, as he boasted about his pedagogical empire, and the miracle he performed, by bringing adult foreign language education to the masses across Tunisia.

"I am the Bourguiba School!" he proclaimed. " I determine the books you use and how you teach."

To underscore his authority, Mamooni pounded his fist on the desk like a gavel and tipped a glass of bottled water, which he scowled at as if the object had defied his will and must be crushed.

"Students will pay in full before they appear in your class. If they fail to pay in full, they will not remain. Is that clear? We are not doing this for love. The Bourguiba School is an international success because we are profitable." Again, Dr. Mamooni brought his fist down on the table. This time he slammed a puddle of water, splashing his face and making his wet goatee resemble a rat's tail.

Was Mamooni deluded? I would have welcomed the problem of dealing with non-paying students, because in Menzel I didn't even have a director or a school. The Bourguiba School was not an empire, or a vital institution with an international reputation so much as a small medieval kingdom in Tunis, with a few outposts in prosperous towns. By assigning me to Menzel, Mamooni had condemned me to a wilderness.

4

HAMAHAMA

After a month in Menzel, I was still waiting for my mission to begin. Meanwhile, 15 miles away in Bizerte, Fargus's classes had started and his Peace Corps life had taken root. He lived in his own apartment, was flirting with a flight attendant in his class and had sex with a prostitute.

"Did she wear a sheet?" I asked. I was so accustomed to seeing Tunisian women covered that I could not imagine them otherwise.

"Not when she was working," he replied. My naïve comment was so obtuse that it made him blush.

We strolled Bizerte's quaintly shuttered streets with their specialty stores, loitered in the palm-lush parks, maundered in the *medina* and drank mint tea by the Claude Lorraine style lagoon, watching the bobbing skiffs moored to the jetty.

Fargus had an authentic, émigré existence, beautiful and gritty. He could only speak a few words of French, but he knew how to survive and was a successful volunteer. I spoke fluent French, but fulfilled no needs beyond eating and sleeping.

"Murkey, get your program going and make it viable," Fargus advised.

"I'm trying. The principal won't see me."

"Talk to Mamooni. He'll help," Fargus said. "Oh, wait, on second thought, don't talk to Mamooni. I heard Rodney walked out on the phosphate company to teach English in Kuwait. Mamooni will grab anyone to replace him—including you. He'll cancel Menzel and send you to Metloui. You don't want that to happen, right? You'll be in the desert screwing sheep instead of counting them."

Metloui was such a dreaded assignment that none of the new volunteers were even considered for it. But now I was surely a leading candidate. I resolved to deal with the Menzel program more aggressively. I continued to press for a meeting with Hamahama, only to receive *Madame* Zaza's smiling apologies, curt dismissals and habitual deferrals.

Another week passed and Hamahama still eluded me. It was a dilemma. If Hamahama, the local mogul of education, refused to cooperate, what could I do? As a volunteer, my role was to serve, not command. The facilities were in Hamahama's hands.

One afternoon, Colombi stopped his car to give me a lift from the market.

"*Alors, mec.* How is the Bourguiba School? When do your classes begin?"

"It's not starting. The principal won't see me," I said.

"This is outrageous. I know Hamahama. I will introduce you to him myself!"

We cruised the neighborhood where the *proviseur* lived and tracked him down as he walked sedately home.

Colombi slammed the brakes and I jumped out to accost Proviseur Hamahama, who stopped in his tracks and threw up his arms in fear and self-defense, perhaps believing that I was a terrorist or kidnapper. The school principal was relieved when he realized that I was only the English teacher of the Bourguiba School. He shook my hand and welcomed me belatedly to Menzel. Hamahama admitted that he had *his* doubts about the Bourguiba School and was unaware that he was the director. The program had closed the previous year, he confessed, for lack of attendance and Mamooni dismissed him. In effect, there was no program.

I realized that Mamooni set me up to fail, but I might get even with him. It soon became clear that Hamahama hated Mamooni even more than I did, so I seized on our common animosity toward the turgid tyrant of Tunis to bond with the principal. I admitted to the principal that I found Mamooni to be a pompous blowhard, with an abrasive, abusive manner and a talent for belittling colleagues, subordinates and students.

It was a calculated risk based on a behavior I had seen while growing up: a shared hatred can be more potent than love, since it is longer lasting. A person welcomes the confirmation of his personal loathings because it elevates them to the level of truth. Proviseur Hamahama agreed to promote the program and register students. He also promised to contact the factories in the industrial park outside of Menzel to gauge interest there and to put the word out about adult education in a general way. However, Hamahama concluded his pledge with a cautionary finger pointed skyward. *"Shwea b'shwea,"* he said.

"Little by little" seemed too little with a month gone, but I was ecstatic at the results of this first meeting. I had been successful at obtaining the support of the top educator in Menzel. For once, I seemed to be doing something real.

5

TAHAR, INC.

My mother had recently sent me a letter in which she referred to a practice class I taught in Tunis that went brilliantly. These student teaching experiences now belonged to my ancient history. Yet when I reflected on my early classroom successes, I recognized that I was wasting my talent. Seeing Fargus flourish made me angry about my unemployment. I blamed it on myself. But what had I done wrong, besides reporting to Menzel Bourguiba in good faith for a position that did not exist?

At least Hamahama was now aware of the program. He had posted a registration sign-up sheet at the high school.

By this time, I had been in Menzel for six weeks. According to Moktar, the emaciated *surveillant* whom Hamahama assigned to help with registration, enrollment was "right on target:" four were signed up for my class. Moktar was optimistic. He insisted that word of mouth would increase our numbers, *shweah b'shweah*. Still, how fast and far would the words of four mouths travel?

I circulated handwritten flyers that read, "Be more effective—learn English!"

Walking door to door, I distributed the notices and introduced myself to the townspeople. Returning to the pastry shop, my first stop in Menzel, I reconnected with the old proprietor with the red cap and met his friend, Tahar, an insurance broker, who promised his support. He assured me that he would speak with a well-placed executive at *Soljitex*, the local mattress factory. Who knew? Maybe they'd spring for a company-wide English program.

After this positive first contact, I checked back with Tahar on a regular basis, but he never repeated or referenced his generous offer. When I mentioned English classes, he snapped his fingers, smacked his broad forehead and apologized for forgetting to contact his friend. He blamed his busy life, yet whenever I dropped by his office, he was at his desk, pontificating to someone on an impressive variety of topics—birth, death, life, love, happiness and household furniture—in which he claimed expertise.

Tahar was fond of spouting proverbs. Among his favorites was, "Man is like a cheese: he must mature to have good taste."

One afternoon, the insurance broker gave me a long look and nodded gravely.

"Do you know what you need?" Tahar asked as he wagged his finger.

"More students?"

"Life insurance."

In light of the epidemic at Ayn Draham and my recent staph infection, Tahar had a point, but I couldn't afford more insurance on my monthly stipend.

"No thanks. I'm covered," I demurred.

"*Misedish*," he replied, "You can never have too much insurance. It's like I always say, 'Insurance is immortality; he who pays now, plays in paradise.'"

"That's poetic," I admitted. "Is it from the Golden Age?"

"If you mean the golden age of Tuni-Mutual, then yes. It is our new advertising slogan," he said. His eyebrows wiggled with enthusiasm. I had unwittingly triggered his latest theory. "My clients do not understand what I bring to them. Tell me, *jeune homme*, what you think of this slogan? *Insurance is a miracle; the more you lose, the more you win.*"

Tahar gazed upward. His eyes were luminous with revelation. In the pause after this epiphany, I bolted for the door, but Tahar insisted on hearing what I thought of his slogan.

"It's a paradox," I admitted.

"You are persuaded?"

"In the abstract," I said. "But I don't need more life insurance. A fortune teller guaranteed me long life."

I thought I had ended this discussion, but had only raised a question in Tahar's mind. He grimaced.

"Tell me, *hooyah*, was she licensed?"

"I didn't ask to see her license," I admitted. "Does it matter?"

"It makes all the difference, brother," he replied. "Many fortune tellers work without licenses, misleading the public with false futures."

As I tried to make sense of this baffling information, megaphones honked down Avenue Bourguiba.

"Bourguiba's coming! The President for Life is on his way!"

6

BOURGUIBA AND THE BASTARD CITY

It was an important day for the *gouvernorat*.

The president-for-life was dedicating three new tourist hotels and a gas station in Bizerte to highlight his government's economic program and it was rumored that he would pass through Menzel on his return to the capital. Banners were draped over the streets and sidewalks were festooned with flags and posters bearing Bourguiba's avuncular face. The town was astir: Bourguiba would make his first visit to the town that bore his name.

"Our president is coming!" Tahar cried, as if announcing the birth of his child. His body trembled as he grabbed my arm. "This will be the first time he is here, in this town named after his magnificence."

"You sound excited," I said.

"*Hooyah*! Don't you realize the magnitude of this occasion? Our Supreme Warrior is finally seeing the town that bears his name, but which he has ignored for years like a bastard child."

"What took him so long?"

Tahar giggled nervously. "*Franchement*, I believe he feared it would be unworthy of his name. But today could mark his change of heart. Today our town's father may embrace his loving child."

To punctuate this fervent hope, Tahar reached into the cavernous jacket of his shiny, undertaker suit and extracted a red packet of cigarettes. *Habibs*.

"Let us smoke the cigarettes bearing our President's name to honor this historic moment," toasted Tahar as he lit our butts. It was a first for me: I had toasted with wine, champagne, and even beer, but never a cigarette. Was it a peculiarly Tunisian way to pay homage, or Tahar's personal foible? Either way, it converted cigarette smoking from an unhealthy habit to an opinion-polling device.

Later that afternoon, I stood by the main road with the rest of Menzel to salute the President-for-Life. A phalanx of belching motorcycles, mounted by snarling cops in lavender uniforms and visors, led the parade, spewing plumes of smoke with proud disdain. A convoy of black Mercedes sedans raced behind them. We waited for Bourguiba to wave from the back of a limousine, but all windows were tinted and sealed. After an hour, the crowd dispersed.

I walked home. Colombi had stopped on his bike in front of the house.

"Bourguiba! Bull-sheet Bourguiba, *supreme merde de la republique!*" he cried. Colombi was making me anxious with his declamatory candor. If the neighbors heard such subversive talk, I might be called in for questioning and have my visa revoked.

Colombi said not to worry; most people knew all about old Habib. Over cups of instant coffee, he related stories of the President for Life.

"He's a clever man, he knows his people, like every great politician," the Corsican began. "In 1962, there was a major economic crisis. Ben Salah, a Socialist and Bourguiba's second-in-command, nationalized industries and collectivized farms. Previously, wealthy landowners and peasants with small plots had controlled the land.

"The farm collectives were a disaster. To be productive, peasants needed to own something, even if it was only a small property. Without that, they were lost.

"There were riots. Ben Salah was disgraced, tried and condemned to death. After playing the scapegoat, he escaped into exile. But Bourguiba's prestige was tarnished. He had gambled and lost. Still, he would not retreat. He delivered a speech on radio. He declared that he had blue eyes, a French law degree and a French wife. If the Tunisian people did not want him, he did not need to be the Tunisian President."

"'What I do,' he proclaimed, 'I do for Tunisia.'

"Bourguiba was reelected without opposition.

"Several years later," Colombi continued, "there was malaise. High Inflation, massive unemployment and limited enrollment to the country's one university made people see that government reforms would not relieve their misery, that education would not feed their bellies. Again, Bourguiba went on the radio to restore faith in his policies and governance. He swore that Tunisia would overcome its underdevelopment. To illustrate, he recounted in a quiet, even intimate voice that when he was six years old, doctors discovered that he was born with only one testicle!

"'My family was in despair,' Bourguiba told his people. 'They wondered if I would be more than half a man, if I would ever be a father. I also wondered.'

"*Mec*, shepherds, peasants, workers, the simplest people were in shock that their leader revealed such a terrible secret about his manhood. In one swift confession, he brought courage to the level of taboo and made himself a tragic hero. Bourguiba followed his own pregnant silence by reassuring Tunisians that he had married, fathered children, fought for freedom and led his infant nation—and if he could do all of that *with one testicle,* they could overcome their economic distress.

"Of course," Colombi concluded, "you can guess the results of *that* election. Bourguiba won 99% of the vote—all by comparing the economic underdevelopment of his country with his genitals!"

7
BEING IS NOTHINGNESS

While waiting for my school year to start, I faced the hardest challenge of my life—doing nothing. It went against all that I was ever taught. Western philosophy weighed against me: from Aristotle to the Existentialists, we are what we do has been how humans define ourselves. By this criterion, I was nothing.

At first, I viewed being without doing as an experiment. By living without deadlines, duties, roles, commitments, constraints and the other mental clothing in society's wardrobe, I might touch the bottom of life and create an original identity.

As days passed without change, I felt isolated and craved purpose. How could I unlearn my personality and what would replace it? My self-esteem had depended on what others thought or said—teachers, schoolmates and family. Without them, I viewed myself in terms of my situation: a volunteer without a job, imprisoned in cultural walls.

Gathering my past like a pharaoh, to ensure passage to the next life, I wrote letters to anyone I considered a friend. They were diaries to an imaginary audience. Scratching unlined pages with a cartridge pen, I conjured up a world—college, home, the U.S.— where I was defined, where the recipients read my words with interest. Each letter was a beam into the void, a verification of my identity and value.

I sent many letters, but received no responses. The college world existed only in weightless memory. I had passed out of that life; a new one was taking form.

Only Cerise consistently wrote. With the skill of a psychic apothecary, she wrote words I needed to read, conveyed emotions I needed to feel. She was the one person from my past still present, to remind me that the stagnant recluse in Menzel Bourguiba was an imposter of a dynamic man. Cerise's letters were identity injections. As long as I received them, I knew who I was.

•

Mon cheri,
   It is a gray day. The sun sulks and it is very cool outside on the balcony, where I have just smoked my after-breakfast cigarette. After a week of heavy coughing and sniffling I am at last getting well. Beware the tenacious Scottish flu!
   I felt better yesterday, so I went for tea at the home of a girl who teaches English at my lycée. The girl is agrégée. She went to "Normale Sup," is a tiny brunette, lively, but slightly "Vielle France," if not old-fashioned, in dress and appearance. She lives in an old building near City Hall and her place is amazing.
   Her furniture is all Empire. She bought it in Blois, where her family is no doubt wealthy bourgeois. There is a complete encyclopedia on her Empire shelves. Sitting in her Empire chair, surrounded by her Empire décor, she looked Empire herself, whereas at school she looks insignificant at best.
   I enjoyed this culture shock and have since been pondering this: how much more than clothing, furniture and apartments are people anyway? Claire's and Jeanne's apartments are interesting for what they reveal. I wonder how people pigeonhole me after they see my horrid furniture, which I never chose.
   This amuses me and I hope you like it, too. You can be sure that I'll be more involved in furniture inspection from now on!
   If life has in store awakening experiences of this kind, it can be wonderful; if it can make me love you more as it did this summer, it is all this and more.

Love,

Cerise

•

I took stock of my décor. Browned paperbacks lined the damp, green walls like derelicts. Shirts and pants hung on a clothesline along the cracked walls like flea market rejects. Straw mats etched with white mold covered checkered floor tiles. I stared out the windows striped with black bars. What conclusions would Cerise draw from these furnishings?

After reading her letter, I enjoyed an immediate and temporary sense of belonging, which her declarations of love induced. Cerise understood better than I did the wilderness I was in, that my life was static and isolated.

But fresh, intimate love was for holidays, too good for daily consumption. For daily use, I lived on canned love, cured in memory, sliced thin in onionskin airmail, sweet and dry as potpourri. I might see her again during the winter holiday. For now I had to live without her.

Still, my longing for closeness was intense. I fantasized about it and tried to extract it from letters without success. There was always Lina in the magazine, but I took her for granted. When I looked at the magazine after days of neglect, Lina seemed to reproach me, "Where have you been, baby? Don't I turn you on?"

One dreary Friday afternoon, I realized I had not had an erection for days. I tried to imagine what women were like under their *safsaris*, but had nothing to go on. Sight is the erotic pathway and mine was blocked by "sheet blindness." I visualized the shapes and curves of women by naming every female part that stirred my senses—buttocks, calves, thighs, breasts, nipples, belly and vagina. But such magical referents to female sex required verification.

Pages from the dusty catalogue of memory were too faded to excite. At 21, I was aging rapidly and prematurely.

For some reason, I thought a film would cure me. I walked to the Menzel Theater, across the *oeud,* a dry creek bed near downtown that divided the nice area of Menzel from the shantytown. An American western was playing. The hero, a mixed-race ranch-hand, was cheated, degraded and railroaded out of town after he made love to the ranch owner's daughter, in a scene upstaged by mating horses. The movie house was packed with howling, chatting, *glibbet*-spitting adults and children—many sunflower seeds landed on the back of my neck. When the film was over, I headed home. As I crossed the *oeud,* I heard a rasping voice, *"Aide moi!* Help me, I beg you!"

An old man lay in the ditch. He had stumbled and fallen on his face. He was drunk and dirty; an empty bottle of *Thibar* wine lay nearby. When I helped him to his feet, he did not thank me, but asked what my favorite vegetable was.

It seemed an odd question to ask a stranger, but hoping it would reveal a new facet of the Tunisian character, I said I liked eggplants. He asked if I didn't prefer carrots. "I like carrots," I conceded, "but not as much as celery, squash and potatoes." He repeated his affinity for carrots and giggled.

His produce poll apparently had a wide margin of error. He beckoned me with a hand wave and grabbed his crotch. His cry for help was an act and his "vegetable" question was a pick-up line like, "What's your rising sign?"

I had done my good deed, so I said, *"Bonne nuit,"* and walked briskly in the opposite direction. "I need a better a social life," I thought.

8

FRENCH COOPERATION

Although Colombi was the only French volunteer to befriend me, other French couples occasionally invited me to their homes for *de rigueur* five-course dinners starting with *hors d'oeuvres* and concluding with a slideshow.

The price of a free meal was the entertainment. I never saw so many boulders in my life.

Regardless of where the pictures were taken—Madagascar, Norway, Fiji or Yucatan—people squinted under trees and held indigenous fruits with embarrassed smiles on their tilted faces. Another stock feature of the vacation slideshow was the sidekick couple. Blurred on the edges, heads cropped at the mouth, bodies chopped at the elbow, they were convenient characters for anecdotes about gastrointestinal disorders.

We were at Pierre Planque's villa. His wife, Paulette, a charming, gap-toothed woman with ringlets of chestnut hair cascading down to her shoulders, had prepared a *cassoulet*—franks and beans Toulouse-style. When I complimented her cooking, Paulette responded with a broad, flirtatious smile and a high-pitched, *"Merci."*

Was that a tingle in my loins I felt? As I speculated on a miraculous rejuvenation, the lights went out. Pierre narrated another amazing Mexican vacation—palms, petting a donkey, a Mayan sundial. The lights went on. I opened my eyes and realized I had dozed through the entire show.

I was disgraced by my rudeness to the man who had helped find my house and to his wife, who had fed me delicious food and briefly awakened my dormant libido, and apologized profusely to both of them for my *faux pas*.

"*Ne t'en fait pas*," they took turns telling me. "Don't worry about it."

However they seized on my remorse to gain a swift advantage. The eight couples were bored with their typical Saturday nights of grading papers and devising lesson plans. A party was proposed for the next Saturday. It was agreed that it would be held at our house since we bachelors had nothing of value to be damaged or destroyed and no children to get underfoot. *Quelle idée!* Everyone was happy. My crass nap was forgotten.

The theme for the *fête* was French folk dance. *Gavottes* and *minuets* would abound. During the afternoon of the party, the *coopérants* came by to install a sound system and decorate my living room. They sent me on an errand to buy candles for ambience and a potential power failure. When I returned from the store, the living room—my room—was empty. My books had been swept from the floor, my clothes removed from the walls. The straw mats and suitcases had disappeared. My plank bed was gone.

Despite my misgivings about the whereabouts of my personal effects, the party mood infected me. Crêpe streamers floated from the ceiling, tickling joviality out of the spare décor. I admired the ingenious, festive French. This would be my first *soirée* in over a month. It promised to be an exciting alternative to the usual American western at Menzel's decrepit movie theater.

At the same time, I was anxious about being a wallflower among married people. The most fun I could hope for was that a wife would get drunk and flirt with me. However, this was only likely to arouse a husband's jealousy, motivating him to make passionate love to his wife, while gaining me nothing but ill will.

In my ambivalence about the bash, I had forgotten about my vanished possessions. I went to the bathroom, but couldn't open the door. After pushing it enough to squeeze through, I discovered the cause of the obstruction. The toilet was buried under my belongings.

What a total loser I had become! I was a single man hosting a couple's party for people who treated my worldly goods like garbage. I was incensed but determined to control myself. After all, I owed a lot to my French allies. They had taken me in and found me shelter. It was a delicate situation. I needed to assert my rights, without offending them or disrupting the *fête*.

The party planners were taping balloons to the ceiling and testing dance tapes, when I approached Pierre Planque, the captain of the local rugby club. "Pierre, are you aware that you have put all of my worldly possessions in the toilet?"

The burly bruiser from Narbonne stared at me in bafflement.

"My friends, you haven't thought this out," I continued in a calm manner. "How can anyone use the toilet when my stuff is in the way?"

"Jump?" interjected Dombrowski. The teacher of animal psychology at the agricultural high school in nearby Mateur was deftly applying his expertise to my problem, and his comrades found his solution *très rigolot*. They laughed long and hard.

"*Mes amis*, you are showing no respect for me by dumping my things in the toilet, but my objections are not entirely *égoiste*. We will be drinking all night. What if someone misses the bowl and relieves himself on my bedding or mats? What if someone throws up on my clothes? Will I be compensated for my loss?"

While my French *copains* pondered these revolting scenarios, described with diplomatic calm in squalid detail, Colombi arrived, spinning on one foot, snapping his fingers, and shaking his hips.

"Let the dancing begin!" he proclaimed. The other Frenchmen guffawed. Turning to me, he declared, "At last, *mec,* you will attend a party in which you do not merely participate but which participates in you."

"Colombi, tell these guys to remove my stuff from the bathroom."

He stared at me with frank astonishment as if the water closet were the most appropriate place to store one's possessions.

"Let me put this another way—would you want *your* personal property in a toilet?" I asked.

"No, I am not that spiritual," the Corsican poet confessed. "Whose idea was this?" he inquired, scanning the faces of his countrymen.

Dombrowski explained that my roommate had denied access to his room and since the kitchen was the staging area for refreshments, the bathroom was the last resort.

Having reasonably accounted for their actions and motives, my French friends believed the matter resolved and resumed hanging balloons.

"Get my things out of the bathroom in five minutes or there won't be a party!" I cried.

They looked at me, then at one another and relocated my personal effects in the hallway and kitchen.

That evening, the small French community returned in elegant dress and a party mood, transforming our quiet, empty house into a small ballroom with music, dancing and laughter. A festive spirit washed away the preliminary turmoil and filled the space with fellowship and fun. Plain women were beautiful, jerks were gallant, and all conflicts of the day were forgotten.

For many weeks, I had been a parasite living off of the largesse of the French *coopérants*. They entertained me in their homes but I could not reciprocate. Now, my primitive lifestyle finally had value. I gave them something they needed more than a meal—somewhere they could let loose. I felt content to watch, listen and enjoy my French allies enjoy themselves, but they were as generous with their fun as with their refreshments; they insisted that I dance. Paulette Planque, who was especially gorgeous in a low-cut blouse and a tight skirt, pulled me onto the dance floor and taught me some folk steps. Then we slow danced. How great it felt to be physically close with a woman again. Paulette was so lovely that I almost forgot that Pierre, her burly husband, was close by.

The next day, Colombi and I went for a hike on *Ras Jebel*, a lonely mountain north of Menzel, to work off our hangover. He told me that last night's confrontation had been regrettable and perhaps unforgiveable.

"You were immature last night, *mec*. You should have never made that scene."

"Was I supposed let them urinate on my stuff?"

"Those people are stupid," he said. "They didn't know what they were doing."

"So I let them know."

"*Mec,* when someone who is petty does something mean to you and you respond in kind, you are the loser."

"My mother taught me to stand up for myself and fight back if I had to," I replied.

Colombi sighed, "Your mother hurt you by telling you that."

I was annoyed at Colombi for challenging my mother's wisdom. I fortified myself with her parting words of advice: "Don't believe what others say, follow your instincts." But Colombi was my friend. Why would he deceive me? I believed that my outburst was justified, but I might have overacted. It occurred to me that I did not how to behave in many situations, so I improvised. If only I had a guidebook or a role model. I would have liked to see Colombi react to a similar provocation.

We climbed the treacherous face of *Ras Jebel* to the summit. Colombi stood on the precipice, with legs apart and arms akimbo, and stuck his puffed chest over the abyss. Reaching high to embrace the cosmos, he improvised an ode to fresh air, which he punctuated with vigorous inhalations.

"Ah, Nature, it is you I love. Come closer. Embrace me, nature. Let me fuck you."

He thrust his pelvis, then gripped his belly. His arms coiled around himself as he doubled over and puked over the edge. "*Je suis fichu, mec*. Nature has embraced me too hard, I fear. My body is exploding. How will I get down?"

A prime minister of France once died in coitus, was it possible to expire from a pelvic thrust? There was no time to reflect on this medical conundrum. I pulled Colombi away from the edge.

"*C'est l'angoisse mec*," Colombi gasped, curled up on his side shivering, as bile dampened his mustache. "If I were a lion, a mountaintop would be a perfect place to die," he stammered. "But I am a high school teacher."

We were 20 miles from Menzel. I could not leave Colombi on a crag while I searched for a rescue party. If I did not get him off that mountain and to a hospital, he would die. We struggled down an incline with Colombi's arm wrapped across my shoulder and finally made it to the car. Between groans, the poet instructed me how to drive a stick shift and I managed to get him to the hospital.

The physician on duty, Dr. Michel, was a French *coopérant* performing alternative military service. He diagnosed Colombi for acute appendicitis. The witty Corsican admitted that he had experienced abdominal pain for a while but a Tunisian *t'bib* assured him it was only acid indigestion. Colombi tried to avoid an ulcer by imbibing containers of milk, but this only aggravated his condition.

While a surgeon operated on Colombi, I waited in the emergency room and attempted to calm Armelle, who was hysterical. By turns, she deplored Colombi's self-neglect, bewailed his possible demise, and screamed at the doctors to save his life.

Meanwhile, a Tunisian worker in drab blue pants and shirt entered with his teenage son, a slim adolescent boy who looked meek, rather than sick. The father handed Dr. Michel a rumpled piece of paper, which the physician perused with embarrassment. He told the father that he could not help, but the distraught worker finally prevailed on him to examine his son.

Five minutes later, Dr. Michel returned with the boy and insisted that he could not sign the paper that the agitated father waved in his face. After wailing, pleading and shaking his fists, the father dragged his son from the emergency room.

Afterward in private, Dr. Michel explained the situation. The father wanted a doctor to sign an official medical affidavit verifying that the boy had been raped. This document could be used to press criminal charges against the alleged rapist and avenge the family's honor. However, traces of rape were impossible to detect several weeks later, so Michel declined to sign the form.

Dr. Michel shook his head. "It's a pity. I wanted to help, but I couldn't. Of course, sexual assaults occur too frequently, particularly in boys' dormitories. Maybe this was a case of rape, but the evidence was gone. I want justice, but I can't swear to what I don't see. *En tous cas*, I'm here for a year. I would like to avoid involvement in a blood feud if I can."

9

LEMONS, LUST AND LONGING

I didn't want to leave the hospital that night, but Dr. Michel promised to come by my house the next day to tell me Colombi's condition. He was good to his word and showed up at noon wearing a safari jacket and a white fedora.

"Everything went well. Your friend is fine. He will be discharged tomorrow," Michel said.

"That's great. Let's celebrate with a glass of *Thibar!*"

We drank a bottle of wine in my backyard. There wasn't much ambience with the weeds, sand and walls, but the sunshine was a warm and pleasant interloper in the cool, dreary fall. It was a melancholy afternoon, since we knew the weather could not last.

After I drained the dregs into our glasses, I made a toast.

"It's a perfect day to do anything—even to die."

"That's a bit farther than I would go," Dr. Michel said, as he anxiously stroked his goatee and gulped the last of the *Thibar* in his cup. Smacking his lips, Michel praised the wine, glanced at his watch and said he had to go to work. He suggested I come along.

"Doctor, I don't have to go to the hospital. I'm fine. I only said it was a good day to die for effect," I protested.

He laughed.

"I wasn't suggesting that you go for psychiatric observation. *De toute façon*, no one there is qualified to evaluate you," he cracked. "But you are a writer, no? Something of interest might occur. At the very least, you may see a transfusion."

We were driving toward the hospital when I saw her by the lake with two bags of groceries clasped to her red tube-topped breasts.

"Stop the car," I said.

Dr. Michel prided himself on his roadster's handling and slammed the brakes. The screeching tires startled Paulette. When she saw me, her brown eyes smiled. Dr. Michel chuckled. "This should be more entertaining than the hospital."

"I haven't seen you since the party," I said bashfully. She giggled as dimples formed like whirlpools on her round cheeks.

"It was only a few days ago. So why have you come?"

I paused to devise a ruse.

"I wanted to see Pierre. About rugby."

"Do you play?"

"Not really, but I'm interested."

"He's still in school, but he should be back soon."

"Great. I also wanted to thank you. I haven't stopped thinking of—how much fun we had dancing."

"Yes, we danced well together."

Her full lips curled, revealing the gap between her teeth. We stood in the road. A cry erupted from her house nearby; it was her one-year-old.

"Paulette!" a deep female voice called out sharply.

"Come," she said. I followed the graceful sway of her hips into the spacious villa. Paulette's square-jawed mother-in-law, watched as she knitted a sweater sized for a buffalo. Her silence was more violent than virtuous. In another time and place this stone-faced, steel-haired matriarch might have sewn the first flag of her republic, or smuggled guns under her petticoats to incarcerated kin. But she was the mother of Pierre Planque, hulking expatriate, so she gave me a dirty look.

Paulette returned with a basket. "We know you can dance, but can you pick lemons?"

"Of course, it's my specialty," I said.

"Good. Then help me. I'm not tall enough for the highest

branches."

The lemon tree stood near the picket fence at the far end of the sloping lawn. I was sure of myself, since I had picked figs at Cerise's farm. Paulette warned me to be careful but her warm, brown eyes told me she was impressed by how fast and high I climbed the tree. I reached for clusters of brilliant lemons and dropped them in a basket that Paulette held to her breasts. *Thwop. Thwop.* When Paulette smiled, her dimples curled like commas.

We were working silently, smiling at one another, when we heard a bullhorn voice from the house.

"Paulette!" *Madame* Planque cried and waved. "Paulette! The cassoulet is burning!"

"Oh là là!" Paulette muttered. Her brown eyes were slick with tears. As she strode toward the house to stir the beans, I followed her pear-shaped buttocks with my eyes as if my eyes had legs, squeezed them as if my eyes had hands.

To justify my presence, I attacked the branches with both hands, grabbing and dropping lemons with style, as if fruit picking were my true vocation. I had nearly filled the basket when Paulette returned.

She was sucking her finger. She had burned it on a pot.

"Look at how much you've done! You're a hard worker," Paulette said.

"It's a fun job," I replied.

"Too bad you can't make any money at it."

Paulette smiled. Her luminous smile and the poignancy of her pendulous breasts inspired me, but her acknowledgement of my hard work boosted my morale. Being unemployed had made me feel worthless of late, so working hard at this simple task yielding tangible results was exhilarating.

Meanwhile *Madame* Planque continued to rock and knit on

the screened portico, her suspicious gaze choking the moment like a condom.

"Your mother-in-law never smiles," I whispered to Paulette as I hoisted myself into another tree. Her playful eyes were now sullen. She pouted as I dropped more lemons.

Paulette grew pensive.

"Do you know what you want to do with your life?" she asked.

"I'm happy now," I replied evasively.

Paulette squinted and put her hand to her forehead. She seemed to be searching for me in the sky.

"You can't live on fleeting happiness. There's another happiness, something solid to build a future on."

"I can't explain my plans to you in one sentence," I said. I was afraid to tell anyone what I wanted. Language gave life to thoughts and feelings and exposed them to extinction. I worried that putting my dreams in words might kill them.

After being idyllically happy moments before, we were now quiet and subdued. I needed to restore our jollity. Closing one eye, I dropped lemons in the basket with exaggerated aim. Paulette laughed. That was all the encouragement I needed. I tossed a lemon and it went into her tube top between her breasts.

Paulette screamed and dropped the basket. She frantically ran her fingers inside her top to remove the offending citrus, and her breasts nearly popped out. *Madame* Planque stood up and squinted, as if to say, "Just as I suspected!"

This was precisely what I had tried to avoid. Now everyone would think I had done this on purpose. I dropped from the tree to help her round up the rolling lemons on the lawn.

"I'm sorry. I didn't mean it," I said.

"I know. Let's pick them up," Paulette replied.

Just then, Pierre's crunching footsteps on the gravel driveway announced his arrival. He was a teacher but he plodded like a laborer, lugging a satchel as it were a sack of coal. Had he seen his wife lose her top under the lemon tree? Would he take revenge for my role in this breech of modesty? I tried to be calm and look innocuous.

Children slammed the gate and splashed gravel over the driveway with dashing feet, giving me a momentary reprieve.

Paulette and I had refilled the basket with rollaway lemons.

"I should leave," I told her, by which I meant that I should escape by the road and avoid Pierre.

"You wanted to speak to my husband, no?"

"It can wait."

"Will you bring the lemons to the house?"

I carried the basket to avoid looking suspicious. As I passed Pierre, I kept my head down. Pierre was glum, but he grunted hello to his wife and to me, slung the briefcase on the picnic table in the yard and sat down to mark student papers. He apparently had no suspicions or concerns about my adulterous lust.

"I'm going to the market. Can I give you a ride home?" Paulette asked.

She drove the jeep down Menzel's pot-cratered streets with reckless speed, attacking every rut, catapulting from the bumps and slamming into the dips, bouncing on her seat like a cowgirl at a rodeo, transforming the third world suburban grid into an obstacle course.

"This is so much fun," she laughed.

We reached the house. She cut the engine.

"Thanks for the ride and for the lemon-picking," I said. "Do you want to come in? I can make coffee."

"No, I can't," she said. "I must go to the market before it closes."

"Maybe some other time," I replied.

Silently, she reached for my hand. My heart raced.

"Take this," she said. "Thank you for your help."

She pressed a fat yellow lemon in my palm.

I squeezed the memento and grinned. Her large brown eyes lingered on me; she smiled, exposing the dark space between her front teeth to give me a last look at her. Then she leaned toward me and kissed me gently on the lips, more as a consolation than a come-on, walked back to her car and sped away.

10

PASTRY PUNKS

Paulette proved that I still had a sex drive. In fact, it was in overdrive. Hormones that were seemingly shut off now surged. I slept with the lemon to recall the promise of Paulette's last flirtatious glance. The lemon was a token to be redeemed by her reappearance, but it also made the sheets smell unusually fresh, postponing the need for a laundry.

I waited for Paulette for several afternoons in a vigil of palpitating anticipation, on alert for engine growls and screeching tires. I paced the areas around the house, as if I might find her crouching among the rocks, seeking a backdoor. Not finding her there, I looked for her in town with exaggerated secrecy.

Paulette did not visit the house and I did not find her in town. Our time together was a spontaneous accident, which was all that it could be. She teased me, but with three children, a husband and a mother-in-law, what else could she do? It was easy to lead me on. I should have worn a collar and a sign on my back: HORNY BEAST, PLEASE TEASE.

I told myself I deserved to suffer for lusting after another

277

man's wife. I interpreted Paulette's avoidance as an act of supreme love to save my life. Pierre, the rugby captain, probably confronted her with his suspicions of our mutual attraction, which his mother's report of our lemon-picking intimacy exaggerated.

This speculation soothed my ego and satisfied my emergent cross-cultural perspective. In Tunisia, all wives, regardless how free they were in their own cultures, became *Tunisian* wives, subject to mistrust, surveillance and restrictions like their native counterparts. Taboos and constraints were as pervasive as the air.

To get Paulette out of my head, I threw myself into my work. But this was like throwing myself into a dry swimming pool, since my job did not exist. Only eight students had enrolled in my classes, not enough to sate Dr. Mamooni's enrollment lust—so I did another wave of Bourguiba School advertising, by posting handwritten posters all over town.

When these *affiches* ran out, I stopped by the pastry shop under the shadow of the red *Monoprix* sign to see the old *patissier*, have a demitasse of espresso and hopefully meet new contacts.

What drew me to this narrow shop with a pile of cold pizza *casse-croûtes* on the counter and an old man with jaundiced skin and matching attitude? The *patisserie* was the one place in Menzel where you could hang out and have a bite; more importantly, it was my personal superstition to frequent the first place I visited in a town. I believed "the first place" was a personal shrine that would determine my experience.

The pastry shop was also a magnet for a crowd of unemployed local tough guys for whom the old man was a father figure and treat-sheik. They always shook my hand and greeted me with *"Shnoa wellek? Labess? Hamdulleh!"* before switching to French. During our perfunctory conversations, they usually suggested strolls in the woods near the lake or visits to the *hamem*.

To gain a detailed cross-cultural perspective, I might have accepted their invitations. Unfortunately, I had met the degenerate old man on my way home from the Menzel cinema, who polled me on my favorite vegetable before grabbing his crotch. That sordid encounter taught me the value of staying in central, well-lit locations.

"I heard about an apartment," the old pastry shop owner now confided to me. *"Pas cher."*

I told him for the fourth time that I lived in a house. His eyes drooped behind his thick lenses as if he were sad and offended that I had found lodging without his help.

The door opened and *les voyous* entered. Mahasin and Abdul were the gang leaders. Mahasin was a lean and agile street philosopher; Abdul a short and menacing bull, whose shaded eyes and phlegmatic manner epitomized the surface blandness and incipient violence of Menzel Bourguiba.

Underskilled and underfinanced, *les voyous* paced downtown Menzel like frustrated big cats in a zoo, aware that one false move or word could be their end. Their vulnerability exaggerated their tough swagger.

These pastry punks should have been enrolled in my English classes. Continuing education might have made a difference for them, providing at the very least a constructive alternative to the boredom and vice of loose-ended living in unstructured time. But they could not enroll in the Bourguiba School since they could not pay tuition.

"Aslema, Haj-baby! *Shnoa!"*

"Haj" was an honorific indicating that the pastry chef had been to Mecca. He saluted them with a bowed head and his hand over his heart.

"Allah gives me one more blessed day," the old man replied wistfully, with eyes upturned, as if Allah had double-crossed him.

"*Hamdulleh,*" Abdul hissed.

Mahasin leered. He had pointy teeth, a gleam in his eyes and a deep scar on his face. One of his two bandannas was wrapped around his head; the other covered his left hand, which was missing two fingers. Mahasin had lost them in Tunis when he lit a firecracker at an international rally for world peace.

"A rich *Franceowi* stopped his big Mercedes to ask the way to Tunis," Mahasin said.

"So what did you tell him, *jeune homme?*" the old *patissier* asked as he dropped capers on a cold focaccia.

"Nothin'," Mahasin grinned, waving his stump-hand in circles, like a flag. "Like they say: a man on a bicycle don't talk to a man in a car and a man on foot don't talk to nobody."

He brought the stump hand down against his other hand as if applauding himself. The gang laughed. The old man smirked, as he laid an anchovy on each square of harissa-coated *casse-croûte.*

Mahasin imparted more breaking news. A young man they all knew had killed his brother for 50 *millimes.* The old man shook his head sadly.

"It's stupid. I wouldn't do that. See this?" Mahasin moved his finger along his facial scar. "I got that in a knife fight. It was dumb. I didn't know what I know now, that '*tout depend de tout.*' What happens to a stone can change our lives."

"You're a fine young man. You have made great progress," the pastry shop owner said, beaming with pride. Mahasin's rhetoric was impressive, but it was unclear how having his face slashed taught him that all things were related. Still, he spoke with such conviction that I believed his insight without understanding it.

Moments before, I had been an outcast leading an uninspired

life; now I was connecting with my Tunisian peers. We apparently had more in common than our differences in appearance, language, culture, religion and education suggested. We were the same age.

"So—," Abdul looked at me like a street hustler, his eyes on a remote target. "You want to take a walk in the woods?"

"No."

The pastry shop proprietor offered me a health tip, as he did whenever I entered his store. He advised me to eat more *harissa* to thin the blood, improve breathing and dispose of "impurities." I agreed diplomatically, but wondered what made him think that my blood was thick, my breathing poor and my body contaminated.

Swiftly he changed subjects.

"I bet you like the girls, eh?"

"Sure I like them—where are they?"

The young toughs laughed. Even the shop owner chuckled.

"Our life is different from yours, *jeune homme*," the old man explained. "Here women do not go out dancing. You cannot date them and kiss them in doorways. You must marry them. And marriage is expensive."

"*Mais oui.* A young man needs *floos* for a wedding contract, an apartment and furniture," Mahasin said, grinning bitterly.

It was a coin flip for which was more depressing: The 50-cent fratricide or Tunisian sex relations. I wondered if the two were related.

"Marriage *is* a business, right, *Haj*? Like a pastry shop!" Abdul said.

As *les voyous* laughed, the *patisserie* owner looked sternly at his *protégés*. It was his store—he alone could make cynical jokes.

"Laugh, young *voyous!* Only last week, I paid off my bedroom set and my wife died five years ago, God bless her soul!"

This incited more laughter. Even the old man bowed his head to hide a smile, before he glanced to the heavens and laid his palm over his heart, pleading for absolution for his irreverence.

11

FITNA

I headed for the open-air market on the way home. The conversation about marriage stirred up thoughts about Cerise. Her impatience focused on my instability and unsuitability as a mate. The Tunisian checklist of requirements for marriage was remarkable for its candor. In a culture of poverty, every institution, including marriage, had a strong economic component. Yet in Tunisia, as elsewhere, the underlying purpose of marriage was to raise a family. I wasn't ready for that; yet I was involved with a woman and perpetually thinking about sex.

Now I was lusting for another man's wife and fantasizing about forbidden babes hiding in their white *safsaris*.

As I ambled into the market, I bumped into Colombi. I had not seen the goateed troubadour since his appendectomy. He seemed startled to see me and unsure how to react.

"Hey, *mec*. How are things—how do you say—*shaking*?"

"Still surviving and trying to work."

He looked beyond me, as if he were on the look out.

"You know, *mec,* it was not, how do you say, cool what you did with Paulette," Colombi said.

"Pierre Planque's wife? We picked lemons in her front yard."

"What were you thinking, *mec*? Everyone is gossiping about it—and Pierre is extremely angry with you."

"But it was in broad daylight. Her mother-in-law was watching."

"Precisely my point! You know how old ladies exaggerate."

"But it was innocent. It was nothing!"

"*Au contraire, mec.* Lemon picking is a highly seductive act. There is a body of erotic literature about lemon picking that goes back to the Middle Ages. Troubadours sang of lemon picking from their beloved's tree. As you can imagine, it was a metaphor for sexual intercourse. This is why troubadours could not stay anywhere too long—jealous husbands were an occupational hazard."

The eroticism of the lemon seemed implausible to me, but I was not going to challenge my only friend in Menzel on this arcane point. It did occur to me that there might have been a course offered at Brockwurst on erotic troubadour literature of the 11th century, but I enrolled in "sociology of the boudoir" instead. What did that do for me? Nothing.

"Oh man, if I had only known," I said. "Does this mean I will never have another home-cooked French meal in Menzel Bourguiba?"

"It could mean much worse than this, *mec.* It could mean that you will have a black eye, a bloody nose and missing teeth if Pierre gets his hands on you. An angry rugby player is very dangerous. Even now, I am taking a risk by talking to you in public."

"He's that mad?"

"He thinks you have put horns on his head, you know—*cocu,* made love to his wife? Look, *mec,* I like you. We are the same, you and I—poets and lusty peasants. But Pierre is my colleague and compatriot. We are in the same community. We see one another everyday at the high school and we, how do you say, *chow down* at the same dinner parties."

"I'm sorry, Jean-Claude. I understand if you can't talk to me."

My anxiety and contrition aroused Colombi's sympathy. He

regarded me as if I were his naïve, younger brother, who made the same mistakes he had made, but not as well. Colombi had once leaped from a married woman's second floor window onto the seat of his *Vespa* to escape her husband's wrath—without harming his private parts and pelvis. He was a master of sexual intrigue and I was barely a beginner.

"Baa! I don't *geev a sheet* about these cretins. You are my friend. So don't, how you say, give yourself a wedgy about it. *Mais fais gaffe!* Be careful. If Pierre sees you, he is a rugby player, who knows what he is capable of doing!"

"Then I'm already as good as dead," I said fatalistically. "He knows where I live and I'm always alone."

"Don't be so tragic. He won't come to your house. Just avoid him. He is fond of horse meat, so skip the horse butcher and you will be safe."

"Thanks, Jean-Claude. I am grateful for your wisdom."

"Take it. At least someone can use it. I am so deep in *la merde* that my wisdom is worthless to me," Colombi said ruefully. Unwittingly, he gave me the opening I needed to ask him about my mental state. As a poet, he was an expert in emotions. He may have even written an ode on my problem.

"Jean-Claude, I have not been myself. I have a sickness. I feel like a 13-year-old boy."

"You are not sick, *mec*. You have *fitna!*" he replied. "In Arabic, it means challenge, also struggle. But in your case, it means male sexual hysteria."

"Male sexual hysteria? I've heard about that, but I don't believe it. I'm not hysterical, I'm horny."

"*Exactement!* You wish to merge with the universe, to make love to all moving things, which you express by picking lemons with the rugby captain's wife. *Il est très logique.*"

"Yes, that's it. So what can I do?"

"I think you know what you can do. What you s*hould* do is control yourself. *Ça y'est!* I must run! So what have you learned today? Steer clear of other men's wives—and horse butchers! *Bon! Aller!*"

Colombi left me with a potential life-and-death decision. Would I risk encountering a jealous husband by going to the butcher on the chance that he did not sell horsemeat?

The meat market was in the old French cavalry stable behind the general market. If I met Pierre Planque there, I would be trapped. But my craving for protein was worth the risk. I walked into the stall tentatively and asked the butcher if he sold horsemeat. *"Non, monsieur.* No pig, no horse. Only beef, lamb, veal, chicken, donkey and quail!" he said.

"Magnifique!" I said. This butcher was a craftsman. Like the butchers in Ayn Draham, he cut steaks in meat brassieres—two slabs of beef connected by a tendon that curled into cups when heated—but his meat brassieres were succulent and delicious. I needed one now because this was as close as I would get to a woman's breasts. As I paid for a steak, I heard a "Pssst" behind me.

12
X-CULTURAL

Brawny Abdul strutted stiffly toward me with deceptive speed, springing from the balls of his feet. Mahasin, the one-handed philosopher, was striding with him.

"You want to go to the house?" he asked in his low, shifty voice.

"The house?" I repeated as I tried to decode this message. "*Your* house?"

Since he had already proposed that I walk with him to the woods, the baths and the lake, he seemed on schedule to invite me to his house.

"You know—the house of women—*le bordel,*" he whispered excitedly. "*La maison close.*"

"Oh, that house!"

A spike of excitement shot through my loins. Finally I had the chance of a lifetime—to visit the infamous Menzel bordello. Once the biggest French garrison in Tunisia, Menzel had a venerable tradition of pay-for-pleasure. A social climber could not have been happier to be introduced into high society than I was to be invited to the Menzel bordello.

This was not just about sex. It was commercial fornication in a repressive society. I was going after major taboos now, having my sex and anthropology, too—and *nothing* went better with sex than anthropology. True, I had promised Cerise that I would forego bordellos and venereal disease. But paying for pleasure offered a simpler, more acceptable solution to my *fitna* than lusting after a rugby player's wife. Abdul and Mahasin led me to the former French military headquarters, an unremarkable two-floor chateau on a residential street two blocks from downtown.

Inside a spacious hall girded by a balcony, a growling woman in leopard print underwear snapped out her arm at me, flashing long fingernails and toothsome grins.

"Ten dinars," the man said inside a ticket booth, which had been salvaged from a gutted movie theater. The sex worker in leopard panties gyrated, her breasts popping and jiggling in her spotted bra.

"The sign near the door says one *dinar,*" I told Abdul, making him the intermediary, since I did not want to start a dispute with the proprietor and cause Abdul to lose face. The leopard panties girl flicked her tongue sideways like a lizard.

"It's one *dinar* for students, senior citizens and regular customers," Abdul explained under his breath. He was becoming agitated. "For adult men, it is two *dinars* and foreigners, ten."

"Do they have to work harder for foreigners?" I asked, furious at the discrimination. I was a volunteer, trying to get by on less than the minimum wage, and they were charging me 16% of my monthly stipend for ten minutes of loveless sex.

"I won't pay a *dinar* more than anyone else," I said. "You're right to close your trade deficit, but not at my expense."

"Will you pay five?"

The dialogue had downshifted from ethical business practices and equal treatment to the familiar haggling over price. The question was no longer if I was being overcharged, but by how much. "I'm a man like you. Two *dinars* is a fair price!"

The ticket-taker was intractable. Abdul's jaw tightened with disappointment. I was about to walk away when a small voice suddenly spoke to me: it was the spirit of Ali, the humble wood-carver of Ayn Draham, "*Hooyah*, it violates the law of Tunisian hospitality for you to pay more because you are a foreigner. But is it fair to make your new *copains*, Abdul and Mahasin, suffer after they have brought you to the doors of delight? You are poor but you have more money than they do. Pay the inflated price gladly to subsidize your Tunisian friends."

Lina blowing her bubble on the cover of *Stud* magazine flashed across my mind. The excitement this image failed to stir in me made it clear that I could not afford to miss an experience like the Menzel bordello, where the woman in leopard-print intimates now writhed and hissed like Cleopatra's asp.

My *fitna* was out of control and my convictions collapsed. I forked over the five-dinar bill showing the face of *Madame*

Bourguiba smiling with matriarchal dignity. Abdul and Mahasin slapped me on the back, *"Barakala o fik, hooyah. Shokran a la wejib! Hamdulleh!"* ("Thank you, brother, thank you so much and praise to to God!")

My Tunisian companions knew their way around and disappeared. No doubt, they had special girls they visited, whom they courted with their affections as well as their gonads. But I was unschooled in whorehouse protocol, and stood in the parlor, not knowing what to do with myself. I was lost, but not for long.

A tall striking woman in her 40s, who appeared to be French, with a solemn face and thick, long white hair, approached and discreetly asked if I spoke her tongue. When she discerned that I had the minimal linguistic proficiency to ask for sex, she gently inquired if she could assist me. She had a long, languid body, draped in a low-cut, loose-fitting China silk dress. Her large almond eyes, cold and lovely, were encircled with kohl. Her high cheek boned pallor, blackened, prominent eyelids, airy whisper and the sweetness of her lavender cologne gave her the sensual aura of an erotic corpse.

"Viens avec moi," she said quietly.

A sense of quiet purpose and continuous industry pervaded the house, punctuated by opening and closing doors. The dignified madam led me upstairs and down a hallway, and directed me in a genteel whisper to enter the last door on the right.

When I knocked, a strong, rich voice said, *"Entrez!"*

I entered a room resembling my living room, with bare walls oozing brown mildew through many cracks. A young woman in a camisole stared in a mirror. She wore a ponytail, which she flipped over on one shoulder, then the other. At first, I believed the uncanny resemblance I saw in her was a misperception. Could this be Raotha, the beautiful, dignified and haughty Tunisian teacher from Ayn Draham? Impossible. This had to be another woman with a full, shapely mouth, brown eyes as luminous as magic lanterns and black hair pulled back from a sleek widow's peak to a ponytail. In the training camp, Raotha seemed exotic, but she might have possessed a typical Tunisian beauty. Many women might have resembled her. Had I seen enough Tunisian women to know for sure?

But the scar on her cheek, like a laugh line turned sideways, was indisputable proof. Our best features do not distinguish us like our flaws. I did not want to recognize her, but she glanced at me from her self-study and her eyes widened. The gum she had been chewing dropped from her mouth.

"My God!" she cried in English. "What are you doing here?"

She was using a tactic I wanted to learn—using questions as a defense. Although Raotha had taught French and Arabic to the volunteers, she was qualified to teach English and spoke it fluently. This reunion displaced us violently. In one another we could acknowledge what had become of us. I told her how I been led to this place, about Abdul, my teaching job. It was more than I needed to say. I spoke for the same reason that I might have covered a naked woman with my coat—to protect her modesty. If I used enough words, we might forget where we were and our memories of one another would be safe and intact.

Finally, my words subsided to a stutter. I had no heart to ask her how she had come to this. It was not like asking her how she spent her vacation. For all I knew, this was her secret life and she had been doing this for longer than I knew her. But silence had the force of a thousand questions that crashed down on her. She slumped on the bed, her head bowed, and cried. She did not seem to bear a weight, but to be trapped in a net. I stood across the room from her, unsure of what to do. If I physically approached her, she might suspect that I was exploiting her desolation.

"Help me," she cried softly.

That was all the permission I needed to sit next to her and put my arm around her. She became calm—and practical.

"I'm working, so what can I do for you?"

It might have been easier for us if I had withdrawn from our mutual recognition, touched her, and pretended that this was a business transaction. But I knew it was wrong. She was a colleague, a fellow teacher, and it was clear that she was not selling herself, but being sold.

"Tell me," I stammered, bracing for more tears. "How did you get here?"

"I don't want to waste your money. I know how much they made you pay. It's horrible. It's against Tunisian hospitality."

"I know. I was thinking the same thing."

We both laughed.

"What do you expect? It's owned by Bulgarian gangsters," Raotha said. "We sell them cheese and they sell us."

"You ask why I am here, so I will tell you. I wanted to study in Europe," she began. "But there were no scholarships, so I looked for work in various countries. France was impossible. There were already too many Tunisians there and the jobs were in factories. Then I saw an ad in the newspaper for opportunities in Bulgaria. The headline read: 'Seeking French Language Teachers.' It seemed authentic. After all, French-born teachers would never go to Bulgaria for the money they were offering. But it was good for me because I could work on my masters degree in Russian and international affairs.

"So I called the phone number and received an appointment. It was at the Hotel L'Afrique. You know, the blue ice cube, the gleaming 50 story blue skyscraper in downtown Tunis. I had only been there once and I was excited.

"But I should have known there was something wrong when the director of the institute met me in the lobby and told me the interview was in a suite in the hotel. His name was Boris. He had good manners and was quiet and gentle. He told me that he was a jazz guitarist by training, but times were hard for musicians—the Communist regime was cracking down on weddings, so musicians were out of work.

"We went to the suite. It was actually a room, but a nice one. Boris was a gentleman. He asked me questions about my background. He offered me a bottle of *Fanta* orange soda out of the bottle. He even proved that he was a jazz guitarist. He played 'A Night in Tunisia.' You know that song? He was good. I was relaxing. *Off my guard.* Is that the right idiom? Yes. At least, I haven't lost my English. I went to the bathroom. When I came back, everything looked the same. I drank more of the soda and my eyes lost focus. I felt weak. Then I blacked out.

"When I woke up, I was bound, naked and in a fog in a small, dirty room. I thought I was in a medina, but wasn't sure in which city. I was alone for a long time. Then a man came in. He was coarse and ugly and had a thick mustache. He raped me and said that now I was working for him.

"He brought me here and warned that if I tried to escape or said anything to anyone, they would kill me and no one would care. Who would believe a prostitute? We don't even officially exist. Anyway, the police are involved. They are bought and sold like we are."

Raotha told me that at least five of the 20 women who worked at the house were "recruited" in the same manner. They had all applied for positions, some as teachers, and others as barmaids or nannies.

"Is there any way you can leave?" I asked.

"If I could, don't you think I would?"

"I mean, can you leave even for a short time?"

"I could sneak out, but it would be dangerous," she replied.

"I have to help you."

From that moment, I knew I was committed to Raotha's escape, but I had no idea what I would do.

There was a gentle knock on the door.

"That's the signal you have to go. Look, you must wipe that expression from your face, or they'll think you had a bad time and I'll be in trouble."

"What can I do?"

She squeezed my hand. "Don't worry about me."

"Don't you want to go home?"

"Yes, but how? Go!"

"I'll be back. I'll get you out of here!" I whispered and gave her a five-dinar bill. "If you can escape the house, this should be enough for food and a *louage* to Tunis."

"Goodbye," she said, stroking my cheek and kissing me. "Now smile, look happy."

The white-haired madam was at the door when I left. She asked me in her whisper if I was satisfied.

"Mais oui!" I said emphatically.

"Please come again," she replied.

I wandered the grid of streets around "the house," a maze of parallels and perpendiculars that disguised each particular in a general uniformity, making everywhere look like everywhere else and nowhere at all. Here it was possible to be lost not in twists, turns and *cul-de-sacs*, but in straight lines and right angles. I was rendered oblivious by a cacophony of emotions. Nothing was familiar. I could not find my way home.

Raotha's story exploded this living grave of a town. Everyday life was irrelevant. These houses and streets were props in a vast cover-up for crimes—kidnapping, prostitution and murder—that flowed like molten rivers under the crust of everyday life.

It must have been early evening. There were still lights on in houses that I passed. I walked briskly, aimlessly, in a straight line that I broke only with an occasional, arbitrary turn, as I pretended to go somewhere. The streets were tied in a knot; by walking them I might unravel it.

"*Salut, mec!* Are you *aw*-kay?" Colombi pulled up beside me on his bike.

"Yes. Fine," I said blankly. Colombi stopped my inertia; I slowed my stride so that we could talk. Then I realized how tired I was.

"My class is too large even for one of my theatrical talents, *tu sais?*" he said. "*En effet*, too many students are like a watery soup."

"And too few make no soup at all," I said, alluding to the Bourguiba School's dismal registration numbers. But I didn't care about teaching at that moment and neither did Colombi. He had just had a long workout on his bicycle. Standing at rest over his tilted bike, Colombi exuded freedom and fitness in his headband, tee shirt and shorts. As he pulled a loose strand of black hair behind his ear, he ceased to be the reluctant teacher and harassed husband, but the dashing mischief-maker of his many stories. I saw him not as he was, but as he had been, the ideal collaborator in my mission to liberate Raotha from sex slavery.

I told him about the pastry shop, about Mahasin and Abdul, the bordello, Raotha and the Bulgarian sex trafficking syndicate.

At first he regarded me with deep concern, as if I were too crazy, even for him, but gradually, he believed my account and assumed an expression of outrage, which gave way to sympathy.

"You know, it is ironic, *mec*, that a town of this modest size has a bordello infamous throughout Tunisia, *vraiment*! It is a sign of great sophistication—and yet, such barbarism, you know?"

"It is a clean, well decorated house," I pointed out.

"Yes, evil often dresses well and keeps clean," he said. "So, what can we do, *mec*?"

"We have to rescue her, extract her from the house and bring her back to Tunis."

"That is kidnapping, *mec*."

"But she was kidnapped to work in that house."

"Ah, but those kidnappers have police connections. We don't. We would be arrested and thrown in prison for life and she would be returned to the whorehouse, or be killed—and who would be helped?"

All that he said was logical and accurate, world-weary and wise, but I was disappointed. My agitation and energy were pitched so high that I felt I had to return to the bordello, make a mad dash with Raotha to a waiting car and speed down to Tunis in the dead of night. Colombi offered me my only chance and he was not inclined to swashbuckling, so it was not going to happen. The issues he raised were important to keep in mind. We walked back to our neighborhood.

"You have a good heart, *mec*," Colombi said. "You want to be a hero. But can I give you some advice?"

"Do I have a choice?"

"The next time you want to make love, masturbate," he said, as if it were his original idea. Then his eyes widened and narrowed, as he recalled some urgent information. He angled toward me to whisper, "By the way, *mec*, avoid Pierre at all costs. He has been saying things about you. Perhaps he looks for you, too. He is angry.

He thinks you have been with his wife."

"But I didn't—"

Colombi laughed with sonorous enthusiasm. He patted my arm and winked. "You don't have to explain or excuse yourself, *mec*. I know what it is to be young—and hot. Heheheheh." Then his face became serious. "Just *fais gaffe*. Watch *yaw* step."

If Colombi did not solve my problem of saving Raotha, at least his common sense brought my inflamed imagination in line with my real life. I was able to recognize my street and my house. That night, once I settled down in my bed, I realized that in all of the turmoil, I had not had sex. I looked at Lina, winking and blowing her bubble, which formed the apex of a triangle with her erect nipples in the *décolletage* T-shirt. I noticed the lines around Lina's mischievous eyes and their cynical glint. I flipped to her pictorial: Lina standing, sitting, on hands and knees, petting a butterfly on her breast. I closed the magazine.

13
DEATH OF THE DICTATOR

When I opened my eyes, the purple flowers in the window were missing. For six weeks the delicate purple flowers of an azalea bush had been the first things I saw each morning. They were splayed across the black iron monkey-tail bars of the window grill, like G-clefs singing musical notes. They gave me incentive to get up. But no more.

The azalea bush had been hacked. Its stems lay black and soggy on the ground. In grief, I tried taping the stems to the bush stump. When they flopped over and I accepted that they were dead, I carried the amputated stems into the kitchen and washed them gently in the sink. But seeing them clean and dead depressed me no less. I buried them and asked myself who had mutilated the beautiful plant. Suspects abounded: a mischievous child on the block or the local 'voyous'—Abdul, Mahasin and their cadre. Or maybe Pierre Planque was giving me a warning to pick no more lemons with his wife.

With so many plausible suspects, and no way to prove the guilt of any of them, I interpreted the botanical mutilation in metaphysical terms as an omen of tragedy elsewhere. My thoughts turned to Raotha. Perhaps last night had been my last chance to save her, and now it was too late.

To allay these grim speculations, I made coffee and strained to hear the BBC broadcast, a tenuous chord of coherent sound amid kettle whistles of interference. A sudden crash against the kitchen window left a web of cracked glass. I opened the door. A cat sprang stiffly against the screen, as if electrified. Its claws pierced the mesh. Spread-legged, it rubbed its belly against the metal netting and sprayed over it, secreting droplets through the holes.

Startled by my presence, the cat sprang backward, scampered over the wall among the shards of bottles and vanished.

The BBC finally came in clearly in time for the Nursery Hour.

"Mary had a little lamb, her fleece as white as snow."

"Oh no, please, not this!" I groaned. It was the "English for Foreigners show," with reading and repetition. A kindergarten teacher articulated each word in a ringing voice at the rate of five words a minute.

I cupped my ears and cursed the radio, but the genteel woman's voice relentlessly recited nursery rhymes. As my brain plummeted to record depths of depression, I tried to grasp how I had come to be here at this precise moment in this mildewed kitchen, listening to nursery rhymes in the middle of a bleak, brutal nowhere populated by bush murderers. I put my head in my hands and tried to cry, but I couldn't even do that properly.

Then, in a serious voice sounding far away, a news announcement interupted the nursery rhyme. "It has just been learned that Francisco Franco is dead."

Was the Spanish dictator really dead? Since my childhood, he had been one of life's certainties. He occupied a black hole, all power and no light. I was not aware of Franco's personality and never heard his voice, yet his sunglasses and uniform were icons of brutality and repression that made me shudder. He personified evil. His power and longevity were mysteries at the core of human nature that defied justice and justified paranoia.

El Caudillo's existence had made the world dangerous and inhospitable. If I had lived under his regime, I would have been dead. Only now *he* was dead. After torturing, liquidating, and oppressing his countrymen for the principle of authority, he joined the rank and file of his victims. I grasped what had moments before eluded me—that hope exists.

The BBC children's hour returned with Mother Goose. But I did not have to sit alone and listen to it. Having rediscovered hope, I was filled with manic energy. I slammed the door of the dark house and went into the world to celebrate.

14

CULTURE CLASH

I stopped by the high school for my mail. There was none. I had written to my college friends, but nobody wrote back. Was Brockwurst the coherent, happy world my loneliness made of it, or an emotional addiction? Whatever my alma mater had been to me, I no longer belonged there. This was my new home.

Again, the pastry shop was my destination. The gang of *chomeurs* was there—One-handed Mahasin, Abdul the Bull and their sullen retinue of silent followers. I pulled a fudge bar from the ice chest by the counter and lifted the confection for a silent toast. "Did you hear? The Great Dictator is dead."

The old man was perusing a newspaper. He looked at me with vague disgust.

"Yes. But what about the rest of the world? What about us?"

He slapped the paper with the back of his hand.

"The generalissimo is dead but Israel still lives."

"Damn Israel!" Abdul shouted.

"May vultures defile their graves!" Mahasin cried.

The young toughs cheered loudly as they added their own stylized epithets, while I ate my dessert in diplomatic silence. The Peace Corps had warned volunteers in person and in print about this situation and ordered us to avoid political arguments, which we would only lose. Even apathetic street hustlers conceivably hated Jews, Israel and America. Yet I was stunned and disappointed by this sudden expression of prejudice; I thought I was making friends with the local *chomeurs*.

"So how's the soccer team doing?" I asked to defuse the potentially volatile argument with a timely non-sequatur—a social technique we learned in a training camp workshop titled "Political Argument Avoidance."

The old man was neither his avuncular self, nor preoccupied with *croissants* and *casse-croûtes*. World affairs lay heavily on his little red *chachia* and inflamed him with hate.

"You Americans help them!" he cried, slapping the newspaper on the counter.

I shrugged.

"*Sidi,* I don't make foreign policy. I am here to teach English."

He looked me over and nodded, conceding the point.

"Still, it is your government and you work for it."

"You're a Tunisian. Are you responsible for everything your government does?"

He paused to consider and nodded.

"No, you are right. No more politics," he said. "It's bad for the appetite. This means it is bad for business. Would you like a pastry, *jeune homme*?"

This vitriolic discussion was unforeseen and I was relieved that it was over. Tunisia was a liberal Muslim state and the president was a friend of America. Even so, Tunisia had once declared war against Israel. A battalion was dispatched on foot. When it reached the Libyan frontier, the war was over and the soldiers returned home.

But the discussion was not over.

"We hope Israel will be destroyed and a Palestine state erected in its ashes, that the Zionists will be killed to the last one and sent to hell," Mahasin proclaimed, like a mullah addressing a crowd of thousands. He waved his handless sleeve as his friends cheered.

I had tried avoiding political confrontation, but here it was, and it wasn't going away. The eyes of Mahasin, Abdul and the others were on me, grinning with the hot intensity of stage lights.

"I already said that I can't discuss politics," I said. "At any rate, what difference does it make? It changes nothing and it only makes people angry."

"He is right. *Misedish!* It makes no difference what we say or think," the shop owner sighed. "I hate many kinds of people, Jews are only one of them."

The old man made peace by pouring cups of thick, sweet tea.

We were all in a good mood and seemed to be friends again, but not like before. Although a diplomatic blow-up was averted, I was guarded. I finished the tea and left the pastry shop.

15

PREDATOR AND PREY

As I walked past the traffic circle that separated downtown from the rest of Menzel, Abdul, Mahasin and their crew caught up with me and tagged along.

We walked for a while in silence.

"*Hooyah*, did you see the lake?" Abdul asked.

"No," I said.

"You have to see it, *hooyah!*" Mahasin said. "It is the only beautiful sight in Menzel Bourguiba.

"It's getting dark."

"Not so dark," Mahasin said.

"I should get home."

"What? You have a family? You are free. Come. You're near Le Lac de Bizerte. You must see it," Mahasin insisted.

"Is it far from here?" I asked.

Le Lac de Bizerte was not mentioned in any of my guidebooks. It wasn't one of the natural wonders of Tunisia, but I continued to walk with the gang. They were not behind me anymore but to either side. I didn't know what else to do. If I ran now, I could never leave my house again.

We passed a field where Pierre Planque and the other Frenchmen were practicing rugby in the blue sunset. Seeing Pierre unexpectedly startled me, but I felt protected by my Tunisian bodyguards. The lake appeared suddenly through a stand of trees. The last daylight streaked the dark, placid water in shimmering hues, like the scales of a fish.

"You were right. It's beautiful," I said.

"Are you Jewish?" Abdul asked, grinning coldly. The gang stared intensely at my face, hands and knees, looking for fear. I smiled but scanning their eyes, I guessed that a cool attitude might not save me. I had not walked into a forum on comparative religions—but a set-up.

"When I took this job with the U.S. government, I swore not to discuss religion and politics," I explained. "If I break my oath, I may not only lose my job, but face punishment."

"No, no, *hooyah!*" Abdul said. "We will not tell your government. You can trust us. Are you Jewish?"

"I'm American."

"But are you Jewish?"

Violence seemed not only possible, but an inevitable outcome of this discussion. I had a *déjà vu*. I was back in fourth grade and it was another Friday afternoon. Neighborhood boys were walking nearby or waiting ahead, on the way home. They would all form a circle when I approached. One boy, often the youngest among them or a newcomer to the group, had to fight me. No matter how hard I tried to avoid the bout, the circle enveloped me. My designated opponent started the fisticuffs by taunting me or by throwing an object— a book, a lunchbox or a shoe—before charging at me.

Yet, the two situations differed in significant ways. Fighting afterschool when I was nine had no repercussions, whereas fighting now might result in injury, death or termination by the Peace Corps.

"Are you Jewish?" Abdul repeated, smiling to gain my confidence. He was pretending that my answer did not matter. He knew I wanted to avoid conflict, so he tried to make me believe they liked me despite their hostility for my nationality and suspected ethnicity.

I resisted the reflex to respond truthfully, ignored the weakness of my position, forgot about my fourth grade fights and focused on the motivation of this hostile cohort. They were predators; I was prey. To defend myself, I needed to mimic them. They were angry, so I had to be angry. I thought of my azalea and convinced myself that these men had butchered it.

With eyes narrowed, head down and jaw clenched, I took a step toward Abdul and the gang, then cocked my head and glared.

"Why are you asking me that?"

Abdul was grinning. Until that moment, I had backed away from him and he thought I was intimidated. But now that I spat his question back at him, he was confused and his momentum stalled.

"We only wondered, *hooyah*."

"Wondered what?" I taunted him. I was working myself into a self-protective fury that fed off of his bewilderment. I wouldn't let them scapegoat me for their problems. I pointed a finger at Abdul. "Are *you* Jewish?"

Astonishment clouded Abdul's eyes. He shook his head in disbelief. "No, not me."

He was not the smartest in the group, but the biggest and most aggressive. Ignoring the others, I strode forward and wagged my finger at Abdul like a knife.

"I think you're Jewish." I stared Abdul in the eyes and waved my extended arm over the group. "You're all Jewish. I can tell!"

"No! It isn't true, God's my witness," Abdul stammered, as if he were pleading with the Gestapo. "Not me. I'm not Jewish."

"None of us are Jewish, *hooyah*!" Mahasin added.

The gang recoiled. Their circle widened and snapped. Each of the bullies cowered alone at the thought of being a Jew, leaving gaps between them. I felt like a cop accusing them of murder. The word "Jew" was more threatening than a gun.

"Are you sure? You don't have to lie," I scowled as I scanned their faces. I exhaled and relaxed. "Okay. I believe you. But if you're not Jews, why did you ask me if I was?"

Abdul looked relieved that I was no longer on the attack.

"We were curious, *hooyah*. I didn't want to offend you, Brother."

"That's okay," I said. "You wouldn't know a Jew if you saw one."

They were subdued. Their heads were down. I remained still for a moment and trained my eyes on them.

"I'm going now," I said. *"Au revoir."*

I passed slowly between their scattered lines and had gone several paces beyond them, when I felt a hand on my arm. I shook it off. Then I felt the hand more firmly. I spun around.

"Brother," Abdul said, "What's wrong? We are your friends."

"I don't like my friends touching me."

"The last American who was here let us touch him."

The gang laughed. My spell had worn off. I recalled the pastry shop owner's reference to the last American *jeune homme* in Menzel, who disappeared. The old man might have known more about it than he revealed. It also became clear why no one in training camp knew much about Menzel Bourguiba.

"Not all Americans are alike," I replied.

One of the *voyous* hit the middle of my back. Another lunged at me from behind to bring me down. I stumbled, but slipped his tackle. Then Abdul grabbed my arm and tried to put me in a headlock. I swung my fist and staggered him with a blow to the mouth.

The others converged on me and threw wild punches. It was my unexpected good luck that I had attended a rough high school, where muggings, fights and bomb scares were the norm. Six students once jumped me in a hallway and I came out of it uninjured. I knew what to do. I threw my elbows fast and hard to clear space among the bodies, slipped between the scrum, rolled on the ground like a rugby ball and staggered forward until I found my balance to run.

"*Bara na'ik!*" Mahasin cursed me.

"We know where you live!" Abdul threatened.

As I ran through the woods, I looked over my shoulder to see if the gang was in pursuit. It was dark and I was scared and exhilarated. I had deprived *les voyous* of their victim, but it was just a skirmish in a war I probably could not win.

I staggered out to the road and walked as I speculated on what was coming next. I wondered if the Peace Corps office would hear about the incident. If they did, would they terminate me, or let me face the consequences alone? Would the thugs come after me and break into the house? As Colombi often said, "*Quelle angoisse!*"

A car approached from behind. I was in its headlights. When the vehicle passed, it screeched to a stop. Did the driver mistake me for a hitchhiker? I had not put out my thumb. The car suddenly sped in reverse and headed toward me. Did Abdul, Mahasin and the gang commandeer a car to seek and destroy me?

When the car skidded next to me, I dove into a gap in the hedges.

"*Mec*, where are you? It's Colombi!"

I crawled out of the hedges. "I thought you were a kidnapper."

"*Mec*, I believe your paranoia is getting worse, if this is possible."

I told Colombi the story of my day. It poured out of me in a jumbled epic—dead flowers and a dictator, a political standoff and an international incident with *les voyous*. Colombi looked baffled and amused by my torrent of emotions, but he modulated his response in a code of nods and furrowed eyebrows.

"Everyday is a struggle for you, *mec,*" he said. "But it is a good struggle. For most people life is so predictable and boring that they cannot stay awake for the whole thing. But you are always going here and there, looking, seeking, questioning, trying to make sense of this crazy life. Will you have dinner with Armelle and me?"

Colombi had just published a cycle of poems in the most prestigious literary journal of France and Armelle was in a jubilant mood. They wished to celebrate with me.

"What happened was not your fault," Colombi said, as we drank our white *Pernod* and water. "Those boys are ignorant. Their minds are useless to them and to everyone else. I know you believe you might have done things differently and avoided the situation, but eventually they would have tested you."

"I'm an outcast, Colombi. I realized it today. I was trying to fit in with those guys, but how could I do that?"

"We're all misfits here, *mec.* Your fit may be a little worse because of your country's foreign policy."

"Exactly. I'm so naïve!"

"Ridiculous!" Armelle replied with maternal irritation. "Stop scolding yourself. You were fishing for students, trying to make something happen. That is what you should do."

"*De toute façon,* you're not too old to be naïve," Colombi chuckled.

"I should have been writing," I said.

"Ah, but you were writing, *mec,*" Colombi said, "Do you think writing is only putting words on paper? This is how my students think, which is why it is pure torture to read their papers. It is not so simple. I celebrate tonight this thing I love, but I must admit the truth—writing is hard. You write even when you don't know what *zah fawk* you are writing about, *n'est-ce pas?* Writing is sculpture, but first you must create the stone before you find the form in it."

"*Mais quel genie! Je t'adore!*" Armelle cried. She rewarded Jean-Claude's metaphor by moisturizing his beard with exuberant kisses.

"All I write is letters," I said. "And no one responds."

"Letters are like talking," Colombi replied, when he had recovered from his wife's outburst of affection. "You want to talk to someone who knows you. But you are a different person than the young man your friends knew. Maybe they do not recognize you in your letters and this is why they don't reply."

It was an interesting theory, but it didn't make me feel better.

"I'm doing everything wrong," I said. "All I do is get in trouble and make people hate me."

"But you do it so well, *mec,*" Colombi laughed.

16

THE HUNTED

For the following week I lay so low that I was more lizard than man. I rarely went out. When I made my daily foray for mail and foraged for groceries, I moved cautiously behind indistinct enemy lines drawn helter-skelter by my illiterate fear, to avoid Abdul and his gang, Paulette's jealous husband and anyone else enraged by my presence.

When I passed the pastry shop on my way to the *Monoprix,* I accelerated to keep pace with my palpitations and escape the gravity of that dark shrine. I kept my eyes locked in a forward gaze, afraid that merely glancing at the hangout could suck me in to its black hole of hate.

Colombi's claim that I was a writer, even if I only wrote letters, consoled me. Feeling flat and uninspired was now a sign of progress, not disaster. But instead of writing one more unrequited

306

letter, I sat in a cold room and wrote down everything I knew.

This exercise yielded self-knowledge—that I was both determined and confused—but since I did not know how to apply these insights, they were as useless to me as rare minerals without tools of extraction. In this sense, I was as underdeveloped as my host country.

Dread enveloped me like a vine and choked my survival. Even visits to the high school and market became too perilous. I felt as useless as my white suit on its hanger on the wall.

Yet I could not stop thinking of Raotha, raped and imprisoned at the bordello. In my endangered state, I felt closer to her than to anyone. I also felt responsible for her, because she relied on me. But fear held me captive and I could not help her. It was cruel that she put her hope in me when I was hopeless.

Finally, I had to see her.

I walked to the brothel in sunglasses, as if they made me inconspicuous.

The spectral madam did not appear to recognize me. When I asked for Raotha specifically, she seemed moderately surprised.

"You know Raotha?"

"I've been here once before."

"Very good. I'm glad you were pleased."

She brought me to a different room at the end of a hallway. When I entered, Raotha was staring in the mirror, as if struggling to recognize herself. Was she being drugged? When she saw me, her eyes widened and filled with tears. I was relieved that her mind was still sharp and her feelings intact.

She raised her arms and collapsed against me. Her body throbbed with convulsive sobs. We held each other and our bodies trembled in a slow-dance of agony. Her passionate nature, which came out at the training camp in her brilliant smile and lively teaching style, accentuated her misery.

"*Aja* is next week and I cannot go home. It will be the first time in my life that I will not be with my parents. I feel so terrible for them, worse than for myself. And my sister!"

"There must be a way out of here," I said.

"I'm afraid not. They say the business is best now. Nothing brings out lust in men more than family holidays."

This wry observation reminded me of the wild *Ramadan* scene at *Bab Souika,* the congested club where men howled at large women in Bedouin dress.

"Do they ever let you go out for any reason or length of time?"

"Never."

From the window, I saw a potential escape route. The corner room was over a courtyard, enclosed by a wall that joined the house a meter from the window. A service lane was on the other side of that wall. If we could make it from the window to the wall and jump 12 feet into the alley without being seen, Raotha would be free.

She gave me a letter to send for her and I kept her company until my half hour was up, so as not to raise suspicions about our relationship.

I stopped at the market on my way home. In the street, each crunching footstep foreboded the next—in every shout, call or infant's cry, I heard a signal to an ambush party. When I entered the dusty arcade of the outdoor market, the crowd made me nervous. I glanced over my shoulder, dodged suspicious jostlers and stumbled into a peddler's potato stand, causing an avalanche of spuds.

When I was calm enough to stand at a produce stand and assess the worthiness of a turnip, a voice behind me said, "I know turnips are healthy, but they give me gas."

I turned in the direction of the remark, spoken in deadpan American English. A pale-faced man with gold-rimmed glasses and a wispy mustache stood before me in a long, black *bernous*. A broad smile imbued his small, blue eyes with fiendish intensity. He looked like an assassin.

"You must be the American Fargus told us about," he said, offering his hand from inside his coarse, custom-made woollen cape. "I'm Dennis."

Just when I believed myself marked for extinction, an American in a Berber *bernous* appeared to save me. He and his group of well diggers had just arrived in town to finish projects in the Mateur district before the back roads were impassable quagmires and the ground was too cold to dig.

I was so relieved to see Dennis that I wanted to hug him. My personal siege was lifted.

"What took you so long?" I asked as I reached to shake his hand.

17

WELL DIGGERS

The well diggers, Jake, Cary and Dennis, were Peace Corps volunteers in the last months of their two-year stint, digging wells for CARE-MEDICO in the Mateur district. Fargus had mentioned them when I visited Bizerte.

The well diggers tapped subterranean water for a parched land. It was a challenging, important mission, which they ran like a business. They drew up budgets, hired and paid workers, managed machinery, construction and logistics, supervised work on site and made deals with vendors. They were generous, impulsive, down-to-earth, ordinary men, but their jeeps, vans and trucks made

309

them seem like demi-gods, free to go anywhere in Tunisia.

Transportation determines a nation's size more than its borders or topography. The well diggers' mobility made Tunisia small. They could drive you down muddy back roads to a forgotten Roman ruin in the *bled,* then disappear for days, returning with stories about the desert.

The well diggers worked and played in mysterious ways. It was unclear how long they would live in town or when they would actually be there, since they often worked in the field. They rented a blue house near the *oued,* only blocks from the bordello.

"The owner knows us," Jake, the top well digger, said. Physically solid, mentally tough and the oldest in the crew, he wore a walrus mustache on his ruddy face and swaggered bow-legged like a wrangler. "He gives us a discount since we fixed his plumbing."

They laughed about the last time they got drunk and went to the house. I asked if they had seen a beautiful woman with a scar on her cheek, but no one recalled seeing her; they had been too drunk to remember much.

"Say, guys, Murkey here's a pay-for-sex virgin. You have to come with us," Jake said. "We'll set you up. The owner owes us."

18

EXTRACTION TEAM

My plan to rescue Raotha was barely an outline. I had no experience extracting anyone from anything. *Id al Aja* was closing in. I had to devise tactics, assemble a crew and secure a getaway vehicle.

I approached the well diggers for help a day before *Id al Aja.* It was strange weather, warm and damp, with such a cool, gentle breeze that you barely felt it bite your neck.

When I entered the well diggers' house, they were cooking, baking and slaughtering for their Halloween party. I complained about the heat.

"Sounds like you're horny, man," Cary said. "Take two aspirins in case it's something serious."

That year, two holidays and two cultures converged at the end of October. *Id al Aja* was a solemn feast, commemorating Abraham's faithful sacrifice of his only son to God, whom God mercifully spared. Tunisians celebrated this event by roasting a lamb and eating its eyes as delicacies.

Halloween, *wallpurgisnacht,* was an annual reunion of demons raging at night, roughly coinciding with the Mexican *Dia de los Muertos,* but it had little religious content for Americans. It had become our secular fall carnival, when children filled bags with candy and adults revived their childhoods at costume parties.

The well diggers appreciated the ironic coincidence of two holidays, Muslim and American, sacred and frivolous, and were throwing a party to marry the traditions. They slaughtered two turkeys for a Halloween barbeque to match the *Aja mechoui* and invited every volunteer in Tunisia to feast with them.

When I walked into their house to appeal for help, I found Cary, a lanky farm boy from Iowa, holding the turkeys by their limp necks as he grinned through pink Ben Franklin sunglasses under the shade of a cavalry officer's hat.

"Don't worry, dude. They're already dead. I twisted their fucking necks," Cary said.

"Wish I'd seen it," I replied. "I once saw an old man castrate a pig."

"Now that's entertainment," said Dennis, the pale, blue-eyed well digger I met in the market. In his wireframe glasses, Dennis looked like a lunatic from the Age of Reason. "Where'd you see it?"

"My girlfriend's farm."

"Was she sending a message?" he quipped.

"No!" I said. "Maybe."

Cary was already getting a head start on Halloween in his blue revolutionary war coat with silver buttons and epaulets. As the youngest well digger extracted a sword from a scabbard in his belt, he raised the turkeys' necks with one hand and in a swift horizontal motion, severed their heads from their plucked bodies with the other. The bodies dropped with a wet plunk on the floor.

"I wish I could do that to Ahmad ali-Fuq-Fuq at the *gouvernorat*," Jake said as he warmed his butt by the gas heater and read a paperback.

Dennis emerged from the kitchen with a yellow disk on a bronze platter.

"Shnoa?" I asked. "What is it?"

"I bought it at the bronze *souk* in Tunis," he said, referring to the plate. "Paid 50 *dinars*, down from 200."

"I meant the yellow thing on the plate," I said.

"It's a cake," Jake said, without raising his eyes from his book. "The icing has lemon peels. Dennis thinks fine food means lemon peels."

Mabruka the maid, who had a gold tooth and wore a flower-patterned dress, swept and dusted near Jake with exceptional diligence.

"I warned Jake not to screw the help," Dennis said. "Now she's in love."

Cary was now speaking respectfully to the turkey heads. He had read somewhere that primitive tribesmen begged forgiveness from slain foes and slaughtered animals to appease their vengeful souls. "I'm sorry I had to kill you guys. But you should know you're going to a better place—our stomachs."

"Their spirits should be happy with that," Jake cracked.

I chose that moment to ask the well diggers for help.

"A woman who taught us French and Arabic in training camp was kidnapped and is now a sex slave at the bordello," I said.

"Oh, yeah? What does she look like?" Cary asked.

I described Raotha's almond eyes, her full lips and the scar on her cheek.

"Hey, I saw her. She's got a nice ass."

"Don't tell me you had sex with her."

"Okay, I won't."

"I promised to get her home by *Aja*. Can you help?"

"*Aja's* tomorrow. We're having a party."

"My plan would take a few hours. And Halloween's in a few days. You guys would be perfect for this."

"That's flattering, man, but we're lovers, not liberators," Cary said, as he flung the bird heads in the trash.

"What do you say, Dennis? Extracting English teachers from whorehouses for the holidays is your department," Jake snickered.

"It's a good cause, but we can't get openly involved," Dennis said. "We're one of the biggest employers in town. Anyway, the bordello people know us. We've helped the manager out more than once."

"If we show up when his property disappears, he'll think we stole it," Jake added.

"Listen, I love a job like this, but Jake's right. What we *can* do is provide a van if you need it. And I'll drive you out of town," Dennis said. "*You* have to get her out."

19

THE MASTER OF PLANS

I had hoped the well diggers would lend their muscle and *savoir-faire*, but they were right that their high profiles would make them suspects and undermine the mission. Who else did I know with the experience to spring Raotha from a sex-fortress? It was soon clear that only man in Menzel Bourguiba could play this role—the poet, Jean-Claude Colombi. He had the right résumé for this mission: in his youth, he had jumped from second floor windows to escape angry husbands. He had shot tarantulas on banana boats. He still rode a bicycle around Menzel Bourguiba. More importantly, Colombi had the right attitude for this undertaking. He had an instinct for risk-taking and trouble making. But the Corsican's most important qualification was his total commitment to all he said and did. I had to find him.

It was mid-afternoon. He might be home, but I had little hope of finding him there. I had been to his villa, but in the anonymous grid of Menzel Bourguiba, houses looked alike and street signs and number addresses were sporadic. Driving to the Colombis' place involved a series of turns familiar only to themselves and frequent visitors. I might have walked for days without locating it.

At any rate, Colombi was rarely home. He was usually out on his bike or in his car, in the market or on a sandy patch in the park, practicing *petanque*, the Provençal version of Bocci ball. But I couldn't wait for a random encounter, so I showed up at the *lycée* at the end of the school day to intercept him.

As it turned out, the great poet was walking out with Pierre Planque. I flinched when I saw the rugby captain and stayed back. I was not afraid of the burly Planque at his workplace; he needed his paycheck too much to assault me there. I stayed out of sight

314

because my appearance at the high school was strange enough to be remarked upon and remembered. I did not want anyone to connect me with Colombi, if he agreed to join this mission.

From just outside the gate, I watched them leave in their respective cars. Pastèque was the first to pull out. Colombi was close behind. When Pastèque had passed, I accosted Colombi's vehicle and rapped on his window. His head flinched when he saw me and he slammed his brakes.

"What are you doing, *mec*? Have you gone mad?"

I jumped into the passenger side and he drove on.

"Jean-Claude, *écoute!* I told you that a Tunisian English teacher was kidnapped and is now a sex slave in the Menzel bordello. She is losing hope. I promised to get her home by *Aja*. Please help me."

When we stopped at one of the few traffic lights in Menzel, symbols of progress that rarely worked, Colombi turned to me with a smile.

"*Mec*, have you been drinking all day? If so, *bravo!* It has lubricated your imagination."

"Colombi, this is real. I think I can get her out of her room, but I need time to get her clear of the house and out of town. And I need your *savoir-faire* to set it up."

"Let me be clear, *mec*," Colombi said. "You want my help to free a teacher from a whorehouse."

"*Précisément.*"

"And you believe I am uniquely qualified to mastermind this plot?"

"Yes."

He navigated the anonymous Menzel streets in silence. When we arrived at his house, he said, "You have come to the right man, *mec*. But to succeed, we must discuss the plan over an *apéritif.*"

20
ESCAPE FROM THE BORDELLO

The next morning, Colombi and I met Dennis at the well diggers' house to discuss the final details. Colombi arrived on his bicycle. It was an integral part of the plan—he believed that his transportation to and from the whorehouse on a bicycle would make it impossible to connect us.

"You know the Tunisian proverb," Colombi said. "The man in the car never speaks to the one on the bicycle."

Dennis said he never heard that aphorism and disagreed with the bicycle as a getaway vehicle.

"It's too conspicuous," he argued. "It will be too easy for someone to pursue you."

"Dennis, you are clearly an intelligent man, but in this instance you are in error," Colombi said. "For one thing, I am extremely fast on two wheels. More importantly, a man on a bicycle is never suspected of vice. In fact, he is rarely associated with sexuality of any kind. I don't know why."

Such a far-flung theory begged to be disproven, but Dennis and I just shot each other a look and continued to review the plan.

Colombi would cycle to the whorehouse. Meanwhile, Dennis would drop me off at the end of the block and I would walk the rest of the way. While Colombi and I were in the bordello, Dennis would circle the block and idle in the alley next to the bordello, waiting for Raotha and me to clear the courtyard wall. Five minutes later, Colombi would leave the brothel and ride his bike to the well diggers' house, ditch it there and walk to Avenue Bourguiba, where we would pick him up. From there we would drive to Tunis.

There was one last detail. We needed clothes for Raotha.

Colombi had brought a shopping bag with a woman's dress and shoes. "I took them from Armelle's armoire," he said. "But she will never miss them. She has not thrown away anything in 15 years."

Before we left the house, Colombi went over our bordello script one last time.

"We argue over your friend. When *la maquerelle* intervenes, I concede the girl to you and keep *mère maquerelle* entertained while you free the bird. You have ten minutes. After 15 minutes, I will tell *la maquerelle* that I must leave briefly to make a business call from the nearest payphone."

It was 1 PM. Dennis and I sat in an old *Citroen* half a block from the bordello. We watched Colombi ride by on his bicycle. Instead of stopping and locking his bike across from the brothel, he turned the corner.

"What's he doing?" Dennis asked irascibly.

"He wants it to feel spontaneous," I said.

We waited for Colombi to come back into view. Finally the Corsican turned the corner where we were idling, pumped his fist and applied his brakes, nearly flipping himself over the handlebars.

"Is he insane?" Dennis asked.

"He's doing this, isn't he?"

When Colombi tied his bike to a pole, I left the car and walked to the whorehouse. He loitered in front, letting me enter first. The French madam approached us both, but addressed Colombi. "What do you desire, sir?"

"I have come all the way from Mateur for Raotha," he said.

"A fine choice, sir. She is one of our most popular girls. *Très rafinée.*"

"Wait. I came for Raotha, too," I said.

The madam assured us with great solemnity that we would

each have a chance.

"That's unacceptable," I complained. "I was here first and I'm in a hurry."

"Ah, you young men are always in a hurry. You should take your time," Colombi replied. He smiled at the madam, who returned his smile.

"*Jeune homme*, this house is for loving, not fighting, *n'est-ce pas, Madame?*" he mocked me. "*Vas-y, alors.* And take your time!" The wraithlike madam smiled, charmed by the poet's incongruous gallantry. She reassured Colombi that the girls were lovely, hygienic, fit and worth the wait.

"*Mais bien-sûr, Madame,* I expect no less from such a first-rate establishment."

Since Colombi had relented, the madam allowed me to go up first.

As I climbed the stairs, Colombi continued to chat with the madam. Although she was no doubt jaded by male sexuality, she was susceptible to verbal seduction—Colombi was a master of it.

When I entered Raotha's room, I covered my mouth so that she would not launch another emotional outburst that could spoil our plan.

I glanced out the window. The station wagon was parked in the service lane outside the wall. I whispered to Raotha to gather her things. She said she had nothing but the silk tunic on her body and the slippers on her feet.

I squatted on the sill, slowly rose to my feet, clasped the roof gutter with my left hand and twisted until I was flush against the house. Easing one foot at a time onto the courtyard wall, three feet to the left, I found my balance and reached for Raotha. She sat on the sill, rigid and afraid. If we stayed too long in plain sight, neighbors, who never considered reporting a brothel next door, might view it as their civic duty to call the police about an escaped prostitute.

"Come on, Raotha," I pleaded. "It's all right."

"I was never good at gymnastics," she gasped.

"I'll catch you," I reassured her, holding out my palms as if inviting a bashful girl to dance.

She closed her eyes, took the short leap and landed against me. We nearly tumbled into the courtyard, but I pulled us toward the outside of the wall. Clinging to one another like inebriated dancers, we swayed, stumbled, writhed and struggled for balance until gravity had its way.

"Jump!" I whispered superfluously, since nothing held us on that wall but our resistance to falling. Holding hands, we leapt onto the car roof, slid down the windshield and landed on our feet on the pavement. We slipped into the back of sedan, and Dennis drove away.

To avoid suspicion, Dennis waited on a side street for Colombi to ride by on his bicycle, but after five minutes the poet still had not appeared. What was keeping him? We needed Colombi to clear out fast. The madam might give me a half-hour with Raotha, of which 20 minutes remained, just enough time to be on the road to Tunis.

While we gripped the upholstery with nervous fingers, Colombi appeared behind us on his bike. He circled in front of us, twirled his mustache, and waved as he passed, then peddled fast to the well diggers' house. He opened the gate and left his bike inside, before walking slowly toward Avenue Bourguiba. We followed in the car at a safe distance, then drove by him and stopped at a corner. When Colombi reached us, he made sure no one was watching and slipped into the car.

"Man, we were worried about you. What did you do, get a

quickie?" Dennis asked.

"No, no. This word is not in my sexual vocabulary," he said. "*Enchanté, Madamoiselle,*" he said to Raotha.

"*En effet,* I was a victim of my own success," Colombi explained. "My charm was too potent today. I could not lose the hostess. When I said I had to leave, she started up the stairs to check on Rick. I begged her not to bother and I promised to wait the full 30 minutes. I had to make small talk to reassure her. *Franchement,* I think she wanted me for herself. I only managed to free myself by telling her I had to call my wife and tell her I would be home late to do the laundry. *La maquerelle* was never married, so *naturallement* she believed *zees boolsheet.*"

Dennis cruised slowly through downtown Menzel. After several familiar blocks of stores, we were outside of town. Avenue Bourguiba turned into the highway to Tunis. Dennis gunned the engine and we were off.

Raotha opened Colombi's duffle bag that contained Armelle's dress and shoes. She stared at them, stroked the fabric of the dress and cried.

"I'm sorry if they are out of style or the wrong size," Colombi said. "They belonged to my wife when she was your age."

"No, it's not that. They're fine," Raotha apologized between sobs. "I can't believe I'm free. I hoped for this for so long. I'm so happy. Thank you."

Did her cries express injury or relief? Regardless, Raotha's tears affected us like a persistent rain. They made us reckon not with the present liberation, but her prior captivity. In her rescue, we witnessed her shame. Unable to separate the two, we granted her the privacy of our silence. We looked away and pretended to be strangers in a *louage.*

A few kilometers outside Menzel, we pulled off the road and

we three men got out of the car to respect Raotha's modesty while she put on her borrowed clothes. Then we piled back in and continued the trip.

Dennis was our transportation expert. He was on these roads constantly. His focus was on bringing Raotha home with due speed and without complications. The police, he reported darkly, were swarming the roads. They did not need a "lost hooker" report to stop us for "security reasons." Dennis decided that we should get off the direct route south to Tunis at Mateur and head southwest on a secondary road, before picking up the main east-west highway into Tunis. By taking this sweeping detour, we would lose anyone who might follow us. He turned off the highway and took several back roads. We bounced along the hard dirt byways between rolling hills of esparso grass and sand, with no other traffic in sight.

"Anyone hungry?" Dennis asked.

Raotha said she was.

"I know a great little place a few kilometers from here. I don't know how I ended up there or why I went in, but I was glad I did. It has great *merguez* and the best *oja* I have ever tasted."

We soon came to the *restaurant populaire*. It was no more than a white stucco cube with a flat roof, standing by the road like a sentry post in the wilderness. But it was open. We had *oja*—scrambled eggs, tomatoes and a spicy red lamb sausage—with warm, baked bread.

"You are right, Dennis. This is the best *oja* I have ever tasted," Colombi declared. "It is a shame that Michelin and Fodor never list this place."

"Do you think tourists would come out here in the *bled* for this? It's good, but not that good," Dennis remarked.

"Dennis, you are a worldly and cultivated man, but you

underestimate how far a human being will go for spicy lamb sausage," Colombi said.

Raotha burst out laughing.

"Do you two know each other? You are like brothers."

"Please, I am already estranged from my family," Colombi said. "Do not add to my problems."

Raotha laughed so hard that she had to cover her mouth and then her face. But her laughter quickly led to a familiar place. She started to cry.

"Are you okay?" Dennis asked.

"I will stop talking, if you will stop crying," Colombi said.

"No, you must keep talking. I have not laughed in so long," she said. "It feels good, but I can't control my feelings."

The waiter and chef, two haggard men with dishcloths wrapped around their heads like kitchen *kefias,* stared at us as if we were strange life forms they had heard of and now saw for the first time. They did not view us with curiosity, but as challenges to the order in their minds.

Buoyed by food and laughter, Raotha seemed cheerful, and we all felt optimistic that things would turn out well. But when we piled in the car and resumed our meandering route to Tunis, digestion set in, followed by introspection. Raotha was despondent again.

"I wish we could do more to help," I said.

"No, please. You've done so much. I'm sorry. I know I should celebrate, but I can't," she said. "I am just so confused. When I was in that hell I never stopped believing I would be free again. But now—I don't know. What will happen to me? Is it possible to return after disappearing for months and resume my old life as if nothing happened? When people ask questions, what will I tell them? What will I tell my family?"

Dennis had been impervious to the emotional factor. But now Raotha's dilemma roused him as much as his machinations to elude the highway police.

"In your position, I would tell them you can't discuss where you were and what you were doing," he said. "Tell them you were working for your government overseas. Tell them your mission was a success and they can be proud. And they will be."

Dennis was at his best when he was talking fast and making deals, and Raotha's problem brought out the best in him. His cover for her was so heroic, and he delivered it with such conviction, that we believed it and were exhilarated by it.

But Dennis did not allow us to savor the illusion. He viewed our mission as an act of espionage posing tactical problems. He prepared us for the possibility that we would be stopped.

"We need to have a story and stick to it," he said. "The authorities might view us as rescuers, or kidnappers. We need a good reason to be on these roads on this holiday with this woman. Is she your *fiancé*, Rick? No. It might arouse suspicion or jealousy. What are you foreign men doing with a Tunisian woman?"

"It's simple," Raotha said in her English accent. "What if we're colleagues at the *lycée*? I am teaching you Arabic. It was once true, after all."

Dennis nodded as he turned it over in his mind.

"It's a lie that sounds almost true. Perfect. Let's go with it," he said.

Just as we agreed on our story, we heard a siren and saw the red light of an unmarked car reflected in the windshield. Dennis was prescient about *Sureté Nationale* stopping us.

"Look ahead, be quiet and let me handle it," he muttered between closed lips.

The *flic* tugged on his pants and swaggered toward us with a smug face. Four foreigners in a speeding vehicle exceeded his expectations.

He asked Dennis for his license and peered into the vehicle with a flashlight. Although there was ample sunlight, he wanted to try this cool technique he had seen in an American film. The presence of a woman in the backseat stirred his suspicions and he kept his light on Raotha.

Dennis improvised. "Sir, Raotha is our colleague. She had to work late and there was no bus or *louage* available in our town. So I offered to drive her to her family's home for *Id Aja*."

The policeman scrutinized us and was not appeased. He questioned Raotha in Arabic.

"*Sidi*, " she began in a deep, silky voice. "This man does not speak well and he may sound like a liar, but he is telling the truth. I have a job far from home. I was forced to work until the last minute. I missed my bus and there was no *louage*. I was so upset. My parents are elderly. My mother is not well and she hoped to see me. When I realized that I had no way of getting home, I cried by the road. These kind men saw me and stopped. They asked me if I was in trouble and if they could help. Now they have gone out of their way to take me home for the holiday and to make my poor parents happy. That is all they have done and if it is wrong, then what in this world is right?"

The burly patrolman stood transfixed and silent. He took off his hat and moved his arm across his face, pretending to remove the sweat from his forehead, when he was really wiping tears from his eyes.

"*W'allah!* At least there is some good in the world and why not on this blessed holiday?" he said. "I am also working, but with God's help, I should be home soon."

"*In sh'Allah!*" Raotha cried out.

"In sh'Allah!" he replied. By now Raotha had so charmed the policeman with her eloquence, the beauty of her voice and her warm spirit that he laughed and spoke volubly about his family. In the Tunisian dialect of musical intonations, clucking stops and throaty aspirates, the officer described in rhapsodic detail the *mechoui* that awaited him when his shift was over. He lost interest in his suspicions and checked his watch.

"Go safely and in peace." He tapped the car hood, tugged on his pale blue trousers and walked away. Raotha had succeeded in turning us from suspects into heroes for taking a poor, hardworking Tunisian girl home for the holiday.

"That was close," Dennis said as we drove away. "Nice save, Raotha."

"I told the truth. You *are* nice men and you are taking me home for the holiday," she said.

"At times the truth sounds as good as a lie," Colombi said. "It is a wonderful and rare thing. Not to be relied upon."

Without further incident, we arrived in her neighborhood in Carthage, an affluent Tunis suburb. Raotha asked us to stop at a corner, so that she could walk the rest of the way, compose herself and think of what to tell her parents.

She thanked us and kissed my cheek.

"Don't spend all of your time and money in places like that," she advised. "This time you were able to do good, but that was luck."

We watched her walk down her street. To reassure us—and herself—that all would be well, Raotha turned, waved her arm like a wand and flashed the brilliant smile I recalled from training camp, as if to say, "Remember me this way." She walked on; we drove off.

"I hope she'll be okay," I said.

"In sh'Allah," Colombi replied.

"She's better off than she was," Dennis rejoined. "Now we have a *mechoui* to go to."

21

PARTY ANIMALS

We were solemnly exhausted on our way back to Menzel. The successful mission should have been satisfying, but we doubted the happy ending. We freed Raotha, but did we save her? We kept our speculations to ourselves.

The car's speed and a fresh breeze through open windows revived us a bit. We tried to see what we had done as a day's work. Colombi looked forward to going home to Armelle, while Dennis and I anticipated the Halloween party. As Americans, fun was our birthright. Now we felt we *deserved* it. Each kilometer that brought us closer to the occasion and Cary's turkey *mechoui* pulled us out of the orbit of *Id Aja* and into the mayhem of Halloween.

At around eight we pulled up to the well diggers' house. Smoke rose from the patio grill and filled the room with a savory cloud. Cary squinted at the turkeys on the spit with perplexity. Apparently, the charcoal worked differently in this hemisphere.

Music pumped through the house and people were sprawled everywhere. Dr. Michel, in a safari jacket and a vintage French foreign legion cap, debated fate with Jann, the *I Ching* player from training camp, while Luigi, a gastrophysicist from Bologna, in parachute pants and soft slippers, argued with everyone against the consumption of meat.

Fargus and Livia walked in from the patio, covering their noses. When Fargus noticed me, he grinned and waved, while Livia held her hand over her eyes, shielding them from the flash bulbs of my astonishment.

Attending the party seemed like a mistake. I was in a grim mood. Besides, I already lived too much in the past and a Peace Corps reunion would only make it worse. We would dredge up the summer, which was still close enough to be confusing and painful. But now that I was here, I could not resist the tide of gossip and "catching up."

When Livia retired to the restroom, Jake, the well digger, stared intently at her butt, while Fargus said to me with pursed lips, "Don't look shocked. Miracles happen."

"I'm not shocked," I said. "I'm happy for you. So how did it happen?" I knew I was being tactless, but I was eager to hear how my best Peace Corps friend got together with his dream woman.

"You already know that Rodney went to Kuwait to make real money," Fargus recounted. "Livia thought Rodney was coming back, until he sent her a card from the Persian Gulf saying he wasn't. I guess it was soon after that when we met at a party. She fell in my lap. I still can't believe my luck."

Questioning another person's happiness is a sign of misery, so I stopped probing Fargus. In Tabarka, he had jerked off behind a rock when he saw Livia topless. Now he didn't need to.

"You deserve to be happy," I said.

"And by the way," Fargus warned. "Mamooni's desperate for a teacher in Metloui."

While we chatted in a corner of the living room, there was a commotion on the porch. Luigi, the vegetarian evangelist, was inveighing against the barbecue.

"You cannot eat the living meat," he cried as he pointed emphatically at the smoking grill. "You must love the living meat!"

"I'm just the opposite. I only love the meat when I can eat it. When's that bird gonna be cooked?" Jake asked. "I'm so hungry I'll eat Dennis's lemon peel cake."

"The bird has too much force to eat!" cried Luigi. "Every food has a force. The radish has force, the cauliflower, too. Broccoli *eeesss* a super power: stronger than the carrot. Even stringbeans have a force."

"Speaking of which, how's life, Stringbean?" Jann leered. "Heard from Tasha?"

"No, why would I?"

Jann picked up our abusive dialogue where we left it in training camp. Though his banter was irrelevant to my current state, his innuendoes still invaded my brain like hatching parasites. At times, I thought of Tasha and the look she gave me after Cerise arrived.

"Tasha sent me a card," he said. "She's looking for a job with the Peace Corps."

"I saw her in Tunis. She was walking arm in arm with someone," Livia said. "He was cute."

"A male nurse," Jann added. "She headed a training camp with 50 male nurses. Can you see it? Fifty men—and Tasha."

"She looked happy," Livia noted.

"There is a force in pumpkin and *e-e-s-s* only squash," Luigi scolded Cary, the well digger, as he carved the jack-o-lantern and spilled its guts on the deck.

"Murkey, you look sick," Fargus said.

"He had a thing for Tasha," Jann commented.

"You don't know that," I said. "You're just trying to embarrass me because I appear lonely and pathetic. I love Cerise."

"You've said that all along," Fargus said. "I don't see how you keep it going."

"She's your pen pal," Jann said.

"No she's not," I insisted. "She's the love of my life."

"I had a long-distance *amour*," Livia said. *"Ohhh please.* He dumped me and I didn't know it until three weeks later. It was creepy. For almost a month I thought I was loved when I wasn't. I wanted to wrap my lips around a gas-jet."

"Cerise loves me," I repeated. My skin, throat and eyes were burning from the smoke in the room. I gulped my wine.

"It's *très romantique*, but can you live on letters?" Livia asked.

I shrugged and tried to lose this discussion. I was too drained to justify my commitment to a long-distance, part-time lover. The moments Cerise and I shared were hard enough to revive in my mind, much less to convey to a skeptical listener.

The pumpkin's mouth and triangle eyes glowed yellow. Luigi implored Cary not to serve the roasted birds, but to bury them, while our American pitmaster in his American Revolution army jacket pierced the turkeys with a sword and drew pink juices.

Luigi had clearly stumbled into the wrong party.

"We want turkey!" shouted various guests.

Cary waved his gray Stetson at the smoke.

"You want it now? Eat it raw!"

He brought down his sword and plunged it into the turkey.

"Eat it raw!" roared the well diggers, in tribute to "Firesign Theater." There was a stampede to the porch, where Cary slashed the turkey into slabs of pink meat. The revelers shuffled in across the crowded room, faces over paper plates, hands stuffing hunks of undercooked fowl into their wine-dark mouths, chewing and spitting gristle in a chorus of *"Ummmmms."*

I wasn't hungry enough to trample anyone for undercooked turkey, so I waited for the first horde to be served. Watching the others enjoy their food and one another's company, I envied how well adjusted they seemed compared with my complicated unhappiness. Was I damaged because I clung to a romance more historical than real? If Tasha and I had become more involved, she might have been here now, instead of with another man. Of course, she might have found another man regardless. Would Tasha have lived with me in Menzel Bourguiba? Not likely. I took comfort from a bleak insight: no matter which woman I loved, my situation would have been the same. The inevitability of pain was its only consolation.

Candles flickered, swayed, jumped in and out of time, the visual equivalent to Tunisian music. They seemed to mimic the celebrants, reveling in a party of their own, in a parallel universe of light; leaning toward one another for intimate words, then darting away, they danced, coiled and languished along the walls.

My throat was parched. The smoke and warm, heavy air dampened my appetite. Usually deprived of the company of women, I was now surrounded by them. The possibility of sex rendered food irrelevant, but the ordeal at the bordello also rendered sex irrelevant. At least the women at the party were volunteers and free to engage in sex on their own terms.

Just then, a short, round man in a plaid flannel shirt walked in with two gorgeous Tunisian women at his sides. With cascades of torrential black hair down their backs and across their shoulder blades, these sequin-clad temptresses thrust sleek legs at right angles from their escort, cocking their buttocks into his hips. Their teasing winks blended irony and self-adulation.

The man in plaid was Dr. Olof, a veterinary geneticist heading a project to end world hunger by turning wild boars into domestic pigs. One of the most prolific libertines in the third world by the well diggers' account, Olof made two sex-runs per week to Tunis in a gold Mercedes, picking up call girls and transporting them to his experimental farm in Sejanon.

The well diggers knew Olof from projects they had in his area.

They welcomed him with handshakes and shoulder hugs and ushered him to a couch. Flanked by his two exquisite showgirls, Dr. Olof puffed on his pipe and expounded on the virtues of prostitution.

"It is the third world's most important resource, ya!" he declared. "These are healthy, young women in the peak of beauty and fitness. They can earn with their bodies in one year what a civil servant or factory worker cannot earn in a lifetime. Then, with these earnings, they can invest in businesses or the equities markets and lift up their lives, *ya*? They also raise their families' standard of living and their nation's underdeveloped economy."

"So they are prostitutes and patriots," I said.

Dr. Olof paused, pursed his lips and puffed his cheeks as he assessed the validity of my wisecrack. "Ya, you can say that."

"Hey, man, relax," Dennis whispered. "You're giving Olof bad vibes."

"Olof *is* a bad vibe," I snapped back. "We just rescued a woman from prostitution and he makes it sound like a dazzling career path."

"There's a difference." Dennis said. "Raotha didn't want to sell her body. These women do."

The mood of the party had grown quiet and morose. This might have been an outcome of digesting undercooked meat and a long day of transport and dissipation. But Olof's traveling 'ho show' also had a disquieting effect. Festive gatherings thrive in semi-darkness, in which analytical minds are guided more by a zeal for physical exploration than moral disclosure. In dim light, eyes play without probing; elliptical conversations do not come to a point, but drift along surfaces like a hand smoothing skin. Olof and his consorts changed that chemistry. They did not join the casual fun, but ironically commented on it, by translating the implicit lechery of the celebrants into blatant terms. In short, they made horny Peace Corps volunteers feel self-conscious.

Someone decided the party needed resuscitation and popped in a cassette. It was a hybrid of styles: the lyrical flavors of a Berber wedding band, with flutes, bagpipes, bells and *darbukas*, floating over a cool European dance track, textured by synthesizers and a choir of siren voices.

But the vibrant sound was too subtle to expel the clamor of Olof and his showgirls. The evening's momentum that surged on high spirits, food and drink now stalled in restless embarrassment. Olof and his beauties were an occupying force, aiming a searchlight on the party's intimacy.

I was butt-sore from sitting on the floor with my back to the wall. I reached behind me and realized that I was leaning on a *darbuka*, a clay drum with the skin held taut by ropes. Bored and unsociable, I played the *darbuka* lightly with my fingers, filling in the beats of the taped music.

Soon I heard another drum beat. Then another. A dozen *darbukas* along the walls that guests had been using as stools were now all being played.

The spontaneous drummers were liberating the party with a driving rhythm and a fierce tempo. Soon Livia and two English women rose to dance. I lost the beat, retrieved it and glanced nervously at the other drummers, whose eyes met mine, as if to say, "Be strong, we need you."

Energy surged through my body into my hands. I pounded the *darbuka* harder and faster. With eyes, hands and feet, the drummers kept the beat, exchanged cues, and held each other steady in mutual trust—a brotherhood of the drum. I fought back a tearful grin. It was a feeling less familiar than love, but equally intense, a sense of belonging.

The party was alive. As the Peace Corps women danced, Olof's Tunisian girls looked like cutouts. But they were performers, not spectators, so they got off the couch to twirl, writhe, and paw the air with their manicured fingers. Every woman in the room was on her feet and every man was banging a *darbuka* between his legs.

Finally, Olof joined in, flailing his arms like a drunk playing Zorba the Greek. At first, his escorts rubbed their backs against him as if he were a lamppost, but then pirouetted free, leaving him to clap his hands and force a laugh. He finally lost patience, laid his hands on the bare shoulders of his beauty queens and left.

Our drums tattooed a frenzied tempo. I was soaking in sweat. My fingers were blurs. My hands were moving so fast that they seemed to unhinge from the wrists and smack the drumskin by themselves. I lost the beat.

The dancers stopped, their heads slumped on their chests. The other drummers looked at me with tired regret, as though they knew that whatever we had done, we could not resume or repeat. The rebellion of the drums was over. We had won.

The first yawns of night dispersed the party. I was exhausted and had a raw throat. Georgia, a mature English woman passing through Menzel with her daughter, Rose, on their way to the desert, asked if they could crash with me for the night. I said yes and off we went.

22
I LOVE IT, WHAT IS IT?

Back at the house, one large bed sat in the middle of a large, cold, dark room, medieval-style. I slept in the bed, curled up under an unzipped sleeping bag, and my guests, an English mother and her teenage daughter, slept on mats nearby.

During the night, I heard a woman's heavy breathing, muffled yelps. I was shivering in my sleep and having unquiet dreams.

Tasha lay on the bed, whispering, "Now that you've kissed my knee do you want to kiss my feet?" Later she entered the room at Zardook, screaming at Cerise, "You can have him. He's not man enough for me. Nurse! Nurse!" In walked Jerry Lewis slapping himself on the cheek. Then there were dragons, toilet bowls, my mother crying into her hands, "Why did I send you to college? I should have sent you to technical school!"

Then came the strangest dream of all: something soft, warm and alive was close to me. A woman had crawled under the covers. I rolled over. It was no dream. It was Georgia, my guest.

"Oh merciful God!" I muttered. Was it possible that a woman lay next to me, with fragrant heat radiating from her soft skin, her bosom heaving against my chest? No, I was having an out-of-body dream like a shaman in a sweat lodge. My sexual hysteria had reached a crisis. I wanted a woman so badly that I hallucinated one. I could not resist this; the illness must run its course. I buried my head between her breasts, believing they were pillows. But no— they were breasts. This woman was real. I opened my eyes and saw my guest, Georgia, the English mother, lying next to me. She tugged at my sleeping bag and blanket and curled away from me.

Why was Georgia in my bed? Apparently to sleep, since she was snoring comfortably. But now I was fully awake.

This was all new. I had never experienced a bed invasion. What did it mean and how was I supposed to react? At first, I was in disbelief that anyone would enter a stranger's bed without asking him first. But Georgia may have felt that she needed no permission, that I would be glad to share my bed with her. It wasn't that simple. I was aroused and confused.

Although I knew it was not moral, legal, acceptable or

desirable to make love to a sleeping woman, I wondered if this was a form of seduction of which I was naïvely unaware.

Georgia pressed closer to me. While I pondered the ethics of this situation, instincts overpowered my conscience. Georgia radiated a sweet-scented warmth. With her eyes closed, she opened her arms and enveloped me in her heat and intoxicating scent.

"That's lovely," she whispered. Her voice was like an invisible hand, stroking me.

Was she telling me that she was in my bed for more than rest? I accepted her invitation and moved my hands over her soft skin, the curves of her ample body, her private parts, gorging my senses and restoring my memory of these sublime forms.

"Mmmm. That's too hot. Let it cool."

I paused. My aim was not to wake her, or to have sex with her while she slept. I struggled for gentlemanly restraint, to cohabit the bed with her, like two sovereign nations on one island— Hispaniola, for instance. Yet, we seemed manifestly destined to unite. The dueling agonies of aching loins and moral recrimination stoked my excitement. I resumed caressing her gently.

"Ummmmm," she mumbled in her sleep. "I'll have more of that."

This vague feedback was all the encouragement I needed. I explored her womanhood with tender and ardent caresses and touched the hot moisture between her legs.

"Easy over, please," she whispered.

Did she want us to be facing? I pulled gently on her shoulders. She resisted. I relaxed, kissed her shoulder, and eased her toward me again.

"Mmmmmm."

As her body turned, Georgia moved her hands over my chest

and down my torso. She grabbed my penis, squeezed it and rubbed it in her hand. "No, please!" I whispered as I tried to pry away her fingers. She squeezed my manhood, not like a sex organ, but like a cow's udder. I felt my urge surge. Would multiplication tables help? When I had last tried that technique, I regretted not taking harder math.

I sensed the warm flow of life about to erupt. I climbed on top of Georgia and slid my hand under her panties. But just as I reached climax, my arm touched another body. I realized that Georgia had moved close to me to make room in the bed for her teenage daughter, Rose, who now lay next to me as I lay on top of her mother. It was not incest. I had no word for it, but I rolled off of Georgia and out of my own bed, hitting the floor with a thump.

Georgia and Rose slept soundly while I lay on the straw mat, trying to determine if our brief physical contact could be classified as sex. I tried to reconstruct the event, but most of it was eclipsed by the frantic attempt to delay ejaculation, the failure of which was apparent in my shorts. By the time I crawled back into my bed, mother and daughter had filled the space I vacated and I could reclaim only a narrow strip along the edge.

That morning, I made a breakfast of omelets and mashed potatoes for Georgia and Rose. "Mmmmm. That's lovely," Georgia intoned as she devoured her food. When I offered a second helping of potatoes, she said, "Ummmmm, I'll have more of that." I closed my eyes. These phrases sounded disturbingly familiar.

The women left my house soon afterward. I anguished over the incompleteness of our encounter. I wanted more, but more of what? I missed Georgia and this baffled me. How could I have feelings for manual stimulation?

For lack of a tangible thing to love, I fell in love with longing.

Two weeks had passed since my last letter to Cerise. Could I write a dull report and pretend to her that my night with Georgia never happened?

For days, I was in an emotional funk and did not leave my house. Being out of sight protected me from more serious problems, like the possibility that Raotha's captors were looking for a man meeting my description. I did not even pick up my mail at the *lycée*, because I feared receiving a letter from Cerise.

I started to write to her. I reproached her for not writing more often and noted that the long interval between letters suggested that we were drifting apart. I alluded to my infidelity by observing that love was disappointing.

My hand stopped mid-sentence. Should I reveal my transgression? Cerise had often said she didn't care about my infidelity as long as she didn't know about it, but I wanted us to have an honest relationship. She had a right to know what I had done and to react to it, even if it resulted in our break up. Yet confessing seemed self-indulgent—I'd feel better, but would it help her?

I didn't know what to tell her. As I pounded my head against the table, I heard a pounding on the door.

It was Colombi, holding a paper bag.

"Ah, *mec*. There are you. You are safe. I have not seen you since our escapade, so I wanted to find out if you were okay. When you were not at the marketplace, I believed you were in hiding, as you should be."

"I'm not hiding. I'm depressed."

"*Alors*, this will cheer you up. I brought you *mekla!* Food! Specifically, Armelle's delectable *ratatouille*."

While I devoured Armelle's four-star Provençal eggplant stew, I told Colombi about Georgia, her bed invasion and our sexual encounter. It was my way of singing for my supper and the great poet enjoyed it.

"You are joking, no?" he laughed.

"No. I'm seriously miserable. I don't get it. How could I feel so much about so little?"

"Maybe she was a masseuse?"

"You're mocking me."

"No. I make a little joke. But it is ironic, no? On the day you saved a woman from commercial sex, you engaged in it yourself."

"Do you mean she was bartering for a warm bed?"

"And she struck a bargain for both of you."

It occurred to me that he was right and that I had misread all of the signs from the moment Georgia pressed against me.

"I'm such an idiot."

"Don't be so hard on yourself. You are young. Now you will know that when a woman invades your bed on a cold night, sex may not be her priority."

"But why do I care so much about this brief encounter?"

"You learned one of life's fantastic secrets. Sex is best when it is surprising. But *mec*, why was it so brief?"

"Her daughter was sleeping next to us."

"*Ça y'est,*" he smiled with vivid memories flitting across his eyes. "Of course, *c'est compliqué*. I once had a mother and daughter. But they were in different cities under different names. There was also the delicate situation with two cousins who were fond of cucumbers."

"I still don't know what we had."

"*Vive, l'ambiguité!* We do not know what it is, but we love it because *eeet's* hot."

My Corsican friend stood up to leave. "It is sunset, *mec*. I must get on my horse and go home. A hot *cassoulet* will be waiting there if Armelle forgives me for disturbing her sleep last night with my passionate fondling. *Alors, c'est l'angoisse, mec!*" Colombi shook my hand and rode away on his bicycle.

The poet's worldy perspective and refreshments improved my disposition and gave me pause to rethink my letter to Cerise.

It seemed cowardly and hurtful to divulge the handjob in writing, so I was vague in detail and strong in melancholy. Cerise was a gifted interpreter of innuendo. She not only read "between the lines" but horizontally, vertically and diagonally, as if a text were a word puzzle with embedded messages. I knew that my carefully worded ambiguity would motivate her inner sleuth. She would peel apart the veiled meaning of my letter and deduce what I had done.

23

SUMMONED

After stealing the property of the well-connected bordello, I expected the Menzel Bourguiba community to close in on me, repel and expel me. I believed I had made mortal enemies in every sector—with the French, the Tunisians, as well as the small business establishment.

But I was wrong. People seemed to open up to me for the first time. When I appeared at the *lycée* to collect my mail, *Madame* Zaza smiled and told me there were now enough students enrolled in the Bourguiba School to form two classes. She sounded genuinely happy about it. Elsewhere, people also seemed warmer to me. It was as if they knew I had done something of which they approved.

Meanwhile, I had been virtually invisible to Dr. Mamooni and the Peace Corps for so long that I mistakenly believed they forgot about me. To the contrary, presence is often more strongly marked by its absence. Even though I was rarely at home and moved between the well diggers' place and my own, a messenger from the *lycée* had no problem finding me. He was standing vigil at the door of my house, bearing three letters, two from Cerise and a telegram from Tunis.

The telegram was from Dozier at Peace Corps HQ.

Any communication from the Peace Corps office was bad news. When Irving P. Irving had warned me that he didn't want to hear from me again, he was not only being obnoxious, but stating a bureaucratic truth: "out of mind means out of trouble."

"MEETING ON THURSDAY, ELEVEN A.M. IMPORTANT"

My Adam's apple bounced at the word, "important." In the Peace Corps lexicon, "important" was disastrous. Had Dozier and Mamooni finally conferred and concluded that nothing was happening in Menzel? Did Irving P. Irving suspect I was "juking"— his term for "jerking off?"

To take a break from the suspense regarding my Peace Corps career, I glanced at the two aerograms from Cerise to determine which one I should read first. One was her response to my disillusioned love letter. It would be explosive and I needed to avoid it for now. But which one was it?

I checked the postmarks of the two aerograms, but they were postmarked on the same date. I played letter-roulette.

I toyed with one envelope, unable to bring myself to open it, before inserting my finger in the flap. I would soon rediscover that fear of the imagined is no match for the impact of the real.

Dear Rick,

I just received your depressed letter in response to mine and I'm depressed that my latest letter will probably depress you even more. But look on the bright side: maybe its contents will anger you enough to make you act.

Though I reached rock bottom yesterday, I feel better today so I may be able to cheer you up. When you speak of your disappointment in love I think I understand, though I can't be sure since you never come out and tell me. Let's switch roles and I'll tell you, "Relax, it's not so bad, really. It's inevitable."

It's not shocking that you may not love me anymore. You can come right out and say it. I'm more convinced than ever that love—pure, ethereal, abstract and detached from everyday life—does not exist.

What do exist are traditions, marriage, children, social and monetary interest, sex, (which is all in the mind, anyway), fear of loneliness and our need for something beautiful in our lives.

I don't need much money, solitude is an enemy I have fought to a draw, traditions are fun to challenge, so what's left? I love you; you make my life more beautiful somehow. Not so many people or things do.

I have to go and teach now—the same subject I taught last year and will teach the next. I spent the entire weekend miserably grading papers.

Despite all the wicked things I've said and done, I love you— whatever that means. Whatever this love is, I feel it for you alone.

> *Love,*
> *Cerise*

I had opened the good letter first and it had a familiar effect. After reading it, warmth and well being flowed through me and into the space around me. The cold, empty and disheveled room glowed with light, as my life filled with meaning.

"But I DO love you!" I swore at the letter and kissed it passionately, "I'll prove it again and maybe this time you'll be convinced!"

It was the love fix that fixed everything—until I ripped open the second letter.

Dear Rick,

Got your letter today. Indeed, I can imagine your disappointment at not getting any mail from me. I guess I'm a woman who writes when written to. If you forgive me, I'll forgive you.

I'm also one of those women who wake up one morning with an aching breast. She feels a strange lump. How long has it been there? No way of telling. For reassurance she goes to the doctor; she leaves his office with a prescription for X-rays in one hand, a reservation for the cancer ward in the other. She waits for the results while her boyfriend is in a flea-ridden brothel.

The tests came back. There was no clear indication of cancer, but the results were inconclusive. After I'm on penicillin for a month, the doctor will decide whether to operate or not. Besides, the pill is giving me various problems and I've had to take another drug, which is making me swell up. You'll have to make love to me day and night to help me forget the nightmare these quacks have put me through.

I had a few rancorous words with Jeanne a week or so ago. She came up one night to "comfort" me after my medical ordeal. She announced a surprise as she came in—some guy I once met at a party at her place. She had invited him to spend the night with me. She's so crazy and insensitive at times!

I have nothing more to say. I'm sick of the life I've been leading and it translates into a perverse letter. Please disregard it. Just view it as a report on my state of mind. I am very dissatisfied and have come to realize that this can't go on. It feels like I've been waiting my whole life—and for what?

I love you,
Cerise

Cerise could be dying and it was my fault. If I'd only been faithful, diligently writing letters, this might not have happened. My mother claimed that cancer came from aggravation and I had been aggravating Cerise for as long as I knew her.

I had to see her; I had no choice. This was the final test of love, to be there for her when she needed me most. I had come too far not to see her one last time before she died.

I was relieved now that I had not written to Cerise about my momentary indiscretion with Georgia, the memory of which I would have torn from my brain with all the bloody, connective tissue included, stomped on and burned. Telling Cerise with her defenses down about my night of wasted lust might have been enough to kill her.

24
ULTIMATUM

It was a cold winter day in Tunis when I appeared at the Peace Corps office. A raw wind cut my eyelids that already burned from an exhausting night, spent crashing at a friend's apartment. Other volunteers were camping out on the living room floor, so I curled up in the bathtub. After waking up stiff and bruised from scraps of fitful sleep on a porcelain mattress, I was on a highball of adrenaline, exhaustion and anxiety over my future and the chance that I would be swiftly removed from the same hemisphere as the woman I loved.

Dozier sat at his desk. His nose twitched as if it were bickering with his mustache. A huge map of Tunisia, tattooed with flags tacked in numerous locations, papered the wall behind him.

"Dr. Mamooni cancelled the Menzel program," Dozier said, petting his mustache as if to settle its nerves.

"Why?" I gulped.

"Because there *is* no program," Dozier said.

"Things take time. I'm still working on it."

"Not anymore," Dozier said. "You have two choices: teach English at the Phosphate Company in Metloui, or go home. "

"What about an extension in Menzel? I can work things out. It has possibilities."

"Menzel is cancelled," Dozier refrained in monotone, to indicate the firmness of his position. "It's Metloui or home."

"Mamooni made enemies with the *proviseur* in Menzel."

Dozier looked as impervious to this breaking news as he was to my prospects for a long, healthy life.

"I never had a chance. It wasn't my fault," I pleaded. "But trust me, it can be rectified."

"Cancellation precludes rectification," he formulated in a flat tone, as if quoting from a Peace Corps administrative handbook. "Your hopes and promises for Menzel are irrelevant. Metloui or home."

On the wall map behind Dozier's head, on which Tunisia was blown up to the size of a universe, Metloui appeared on the lower left hand corner, a black dot in a vast yellow field, far from other names. Colors on topographical maps were not solely decorative and they did not lie. The colors surrounding Metloui represented bare rock and emptiness. Metloui was an outpost in a bleak wilderness, a prison with walls of space, devoid of life, perhaps of sand. Metlaoui was the end of the line.

I had often resented Menzel Bourguiba as a drab and hostile burg, but now I could think of no better fate than to be allowed to remain there to extend, twist and tie the plot lines that I had started to spin. If Menzel was nowhere, at least it was near somewhere. Metloui was Pluto on earth.

"You can't do this to me! I've been set up."

My outburst roused Dozier from his bureaucratic implacability. He seemed amused by my desperation.

"Murkey, consider yourself lucky that I don't terminate you on the spot—or leave you in Menzel to die."

He noted my astonishment and a smile curled his lips.

"Do you think we don't know about your Menzel mischief? We heard something about a man meeting your description associated with a house of prostitution. Paying for it, Murkey? I wouldn't have pegged you for a john. At any rate, you're a wanted man, and not for the right reasons."

If there were a moment toward which all of a man's training and talents inclined him, this was Dozier's. Although he often seemed to have been born with his clothes on and doomed to perpetual seriousness, the gloomy discomfort that typically occupied his face was now replaced by managerial zeal. By inserting me in the Metloui job, Dozier solved a staffing need and avenged himself on the only man who ever beat him in *filfil*-eating.

"Can I think about it?" I asked.

He pursed his lips, pausing to prolong my anxiety. If I had been in a stronger position, I would have been indignant at the enjoyment he extracted from my pain. But his grip on my future was too tight for me to do more than hope for clemency.

"One hour," he said, glancing at his watch. Dozier had

evidently excelled in his management workshop on assigning dirty jobs, issuing impossible ultimata and talking in monosyllables.

"Starting *now*," he said, dropping his arm as if he were starting his own TV game show and I was the contestant, with one hour to answer the Tunisia Question: Metloui or termination.

Once the decision clock was running, the assistant director did not intend to watch me agonize; he had errands to run. Rather than sit in the office or get a hamburger at the Embassy, I tagged along with Dozier. I never asked the man who was putting my life in danger if I could hang with him. I clung to him like a battered fighter in a clinch, waiting for an opening to score points, to humanize myself in his mind. If I was going to Metloui, I wanted something in return.

The streets were cold and dreary, with swirling snow flurries as light as ash. This was not typical December weather. It felt more like Paris than Tunis. I thought of Cerise.

Dozier stopped by the only lab in Tunis to pick up results of his wife's tests. He opened the envelope and cautiously, nervously skimmed the paper.

"Geez!" he muttered. "My wife's pregnant."

Dozier stopped walking and stood in the street. He stared at his hands, replaced the lab report in the envelope and re-sealed it, so that his wife would believe she was the first to know. He glanced at me in bewilderment, as if he had forgotten who I was and wondered what I was doing there. When it came to him, he looked mortified.

"My wife's been moody, now I know why," he said, picking up his stride. He was not sharing a confidence, but thinking out loud, and he quickly changed the subject.

"So, Murkey, have you ever celebrated Christmas in the desert? It feels historically accurate."

By the time we returned to his office, Dozier's managerial arrogance was gone. The Peace Corps hero looked like a man tearing down an autographed poster of himself. Fatherhood meant a final break with his Peace Corps life. In Tunisia, he had been a successful teacher, beloved local athlete, model volunteer, and now an administrator. Soon he would look for a secure job and start a solid career. Sadness fell over his face like a worn curtain.

Dozier's gloom matched my own. We both faced uncertainty and had mature decisions to make. The balance between us had shifted. This was the opening I needed. As a burden he was eager to lose, I was in a position to negotiate.

My choice was hard and clear: go to a wilderness where no volunteer had ever been, or go home after six months. Dozier counted on me to take Metloui, because that would have been his choice. But if I opted to terminate, who would go to Metloui? No one—the Bourguiba School would lose a lucrative contract and the Peace Corps would lose face.

"I'll go to Metloui under one condition," I said brashly.

Dozier blinked.

"What is it?" he asked cautiously, stunned by my sudden brio.

"Before I report to the phosphate company, I want a week in France. Cerise is sick. I have to be with her."

Dozier pursed his lips and knitted his forehead in a full display of administrative gravitas, as he weighed the "pros" and "cons" of my proposal.

"I can live with that," he said.

Condemned to Metloui, I left the Peace Corps office with a win—one more chance to see the woman for whom I came all this way, the only one I ever loved, and to atone for my indiscretions.

When I told Colombi that I was leaving Menzel Bourguiba in a few days, he looked surprised and disappointed. For the first time since striking my deal with Dozier, I realized what I was giving up in Menzel Bourguiba. Despite my problems, I had made a life there.

"I'll miss you, Jean-Claude."

"You will have the desert," he said. "That is not a bad replacement."

"It won't be as much fun."

"You know what they say, *mec, "La vie est dure, pass moi le beurre."*

"Who are *they*?"

"Al right. I'm the one who says it!"

"So life is hard, pass the butter: what does it mean?"

"We can't change life, so let's enjoy it," the poet said.

It was a perfect segue to a dinner invitation. Since Jean-Claude was on good terms with Armelle for the time being, she roasted a chicken and we drained a few bottles of smooth *Thibar Rouge*. Colombi pointed out another benefit of leaving Menzel now: I would no longer need to worry about the bordello owners, *les jeunes hommes* and Pierre Planque, who all wanted to harm me. I would leave my friends and lose my enemies.

The next day I received a letter from Cerise.

Dear Love,

At long last in bed after a hard day's work. Your letter lies next to me. I am much better after a restful weekend in the country, although I've finally come to understand what those menstrual cramps other women talk about are like. I don't mind the experience so long as it doesn't become too frequent, i.e. more than once a month. I attribute this phenomenon to the "treatment," which, by the way, has given me gigantic boobs!

No need to tell you how much I look forward to the 24th. I will stay home and grade papers until the moment you arrive, at which time we will make haste for my parents' house for the Christmas ritual of over-eating. If you get to Paris early, take the 4:21 arriving at 7:02. I rationalize my laziness at not picking you up at the airport by saying I'd rather spend less time on the fucking road and more in the fucking bed.

It is certainly difficult to advise you on your current situation. If I were you, I'd go home, rather than stay in flea-bitten Tunisia, which is and has always been just an escape for you and a poor one at that. If they have Nina Ricci at the airport, will you pick it up for me? Don't burden yourself with copper pots and heavy blankets. Just bring one thing.

> *Cerise*

25
INTIMACY ISLAND

I had arrived in Bidonville four hours late in the middle of the night. It was a combination of Paris traffic and bad luck, a train missed by minutes and another not leaving for hours on a cold Christmas Eve. But these were excuses.

In truth, I was afraid of seeing Cerise, of her sickness, of this being our last time together. I didn't purposely miss the train, but when I arrived at the *Gare de l'Est* five minutes late, I ducked into a *brasserie* to kill time, to postpone a *tête-a-tête* with death for two hours. But death would not be put off.

The one other soul in the place was a heavy, disheveled man dining by himself on Christmas Eve. He looked like a traveling salesman, much neglected and ignored, and so alone and accustomed to silence that he did not even mumble to himself. He ordered a supper of lamb chops and mashed potatoes, but barely touched his food. Instead, he stared off dejectedly, smoked, hacked and wheezed, so violently at times that his face nearly flattened the mashed potatoes as a tide of rasping phlegm washed his throat.

I was transfixed by this man who coughed over his comfort food. Eating and smoking suggested a conflict between belonging and solitude. Food meant family; cigarettes, loneliness. But this man had lost the struggle and now felt only loss. He ordered a meal to resuscitate the happy memory of a home, but could not enjoy it. Cigarettes were his sole companions.

The comfort food cougher's loneliness was contagious. Overwhelmed by the possibility that his present could be my future, I fled the *brasserie* and huddled in the *Gare de l'Est* for an hour, wracked with guilt for putting off Cerise. I hoped that she would forgive me and wait.

Two hours later, Cerise stood before me in her apartment, thinner than ever, her eyes intense with dark circles. Suddenly, she walked toward me with her arms in a hoop, like a ballerina, as a thick cigarette smoked between her fingers. I had one question, the same one that "made" me late, but I could not ask it. Instead, I sought the answer in her eyes, but found in them only traces of wistful pain.

"How are you, my love? How nice of you to come!"

"Thanks for picking me up at the station," I cracked, relieved that she had given me a way to avoid my unbearable question. "It took me 40 minutes to walk here. Luckily I found the way."

"Imagine how late you would have been if you hadn't. You might never have arrived."

She kissed me and her mouth was as soft and warm as I remembered it. Then pulling me back by the shoulders, she looked me up and down like a responsible sister.

"Welcome back, darling. Can I get you an *apéritif?*"

The apartment exuded belonging. Nothing had changed in the 15 months since I had been here. The felt-green carpet resembled a miniature golf green and attracted white dust. The foldout couch recalled 180 nights of cold crossbars that hurt my back and ribs. To negate the impression that she had bad taste, Cerise always told her guests that the furniture came with the apartment. I dropped into the hard, orange chair.

These furnishings were emotional sponges; they sucked in and exuded memories. Suspended among them in mid-air like invisible mobiles were the misconceptions and longings, classified as "growing pains." Even when we fought and Cerise made me feel more like an invader than a lover, I had to become a man here, because she always forced me to take a stand.

The studio was small, yet it evoked so many indelible routines. Every morning she would open the French windows to let in the world and lean over the balcony rail to wave our sheets like flags over the parked cars under the lime trees.

"Here you are, darling."

She handed me a glass of *Pernod* and water—opaque and refreshing.

Cerise seemed more glamorous and mature than ever as she smiled down at me, her agate eyes glimmering under shadowed lids, her black hair streaked with red and parted to the side. A red pullover and tight blue jeans were molded to her slim body, playing the curve of her hips and breasts against the length and formality of her stance. She was a sexy teacher, an icon of teenage lust.

Her exotic allure reminded me of when I first saw her. She seemed to conjure that effect, so that whenever we met, I felt I was seeing her for the first time. Regardless how well I knew Cerise, I was always falling in love with her again.

Yet now she had another layer. A veil covered her. Was it because she encountered "death," or did I project onto her my dread of her diagnosis? I tried to elicit an answer without asking a question, but she smiled inscrutably, as if she knew I was probing her. I stared at her pants that were even with my face. Not knowing what to say, I grabbed hold of her and kissed her crotch.

"Oh, no!" she laughed. "You'll make me spill your drink."

"I can't help myself."

"That's why it took you so long to get here," she teased.

"It wasn't my fault. *Hari-Krishnas* held me up at the airport."

"Rick! Honestly, *Hari Krishnas!* Admit it, you were late to get revenge against me for not picking you up at the airport."

"No. I argued with them and lost track of time. I said I would be in paradise tonight and they didn't believe me."

She dismissed my irresponsible sabotage of her plans with a ringing laugh, but it turned into a violent cough that folded her body. I reached around and patted her gently on the back to ease her hacking. For a second, I recalled the comfort food cougher. I hated myself for the comparison, but could not avoid it.

"You're cold, darling. I hope you're not sick," she said.

"I'm all right. Just letting off tension."

"So you were dying to see me," she said, as she came up behind the chair, draped her arms languidly around my neck, tickled my ear with her tongue and blew a raspberry in my ear. "I don't believe you."

The touch of her fingers and her breath in my ear were cold and made me shudder. Suddenly, she bustled around the apartment, preparing to leave.

"I planned a wild embrace for this evening, but you've spoiled that with your *Hari Krishnas*. No time. We have to go to my parents, *tout suite*. We'll be late for the Pope's Midnight Mass."

"Maybe they'll play it on reruns," I suggested. She never cared about religion before. Was this preoccupation with Midnight Mass a sign of disintegrating health and fear of death? Her face was taut. She seemed to be hiding something, but she also read my mind.

"It's not what you think. I thought we'd indulge my parents."

On Christmas afternoon, Cerise and I hiked with her farm dogs across the countryside beyond the village. Mist covered the muddy fields of rich and rutted black earth, stubbled by stalks of threshed wheat. The air was cold and damp on our faces. The overcast sky intensified the deep hues of the trees, earth and stonewalls. Cerise's tight red sweater was the only bright thing for miles.

We stood in a clearing in the woods, where the dogs stopped to sniff the damp leaves. The cold mist clung to our skin. Her face was pink and felt fresh against my cheek. For a moment, I forgot that she was ill. Maybe she looked healthy to me because I wanted her. I held her close and she responded. I slipped my hands under the red sweater and felt her soft, sloping breasts, pulled the sweater up around her neck and sucked her hard nipples. Our jeans were wrapped around our knees. I held her soft buttocks as I entered her. The dogs barked impatiently to move on. Her body arched on mine as I staggered back on trembling legs.

We lay under the trees. She kissed my eyelids. Her cold lips condensed the tears in my eyes. I was crying for her, for me and for who knew what else? I was ashamed that I let my urges overwhelm me. Was I evil incarnate? I came here to make her feel better, not to exacerbate her illness. But there I was fucking a dying woman. When we returned to vertical and resumed our walk, I acted as if everything were normal. As we trudged through the woods, the gray sky was fading to black.

"Are you okay?" I asked without looking at her.

"Yes, yes, my love," she answered exultantly, squeezing my hand. "Much better than okay."

"I wasn't talking about sex. I meant you."

"Yes, of course, I'm okay."

Why did she tease me? It was like the time she thought she was pregnant and kept me in suspense for a month, while she drove across the U.S. But this was cancer, not a baby. When I couldn't bear to avoid the subject anymore, I held her close, looked in her eyes, and asked, "Do you have cancer?"

"No. I thought I told you. The tests were negative. Don't you read my letters?"

"You wrote that you had a ticket for the cancer ward, but you were vague about everything else."

"You're crazy, do you know that?" she laughed.

I was ecstatic and relieved. In a strange way, her good health made the trip a success. Now that the tragedy was cancelled, I could relax. But after this first response wore off, I was deflated. The mission was declassified to a vacation. It had no urgency or noble purpose anymore—just sex.

"My love, you look disappointed," Cerise remarked, "as if you were cheated of what you expected."

"I'm happy you're going to live, but for weeks I've been in hell believing you might die. It's a major adjustment."

She laughed until tears streamed down her face.

"I suppose that I should have been more explicit about the outcome," she conceded. "The doctor called me in. He was so grave that I expected the worst. My heart was in my mouth. When he said the tests were negative, I nearly jumped into his arms—I was so relieved, darling! And you know what? It's had a positive effect I know you'll approve of. Once and for all, I have decided that my hypochondria must stop. I've also decided to get a less obsessed

354

gynecologist, who doesn't enable it. Do you approve?"

"Yes," I answered, coaxing a smile, as I tried to formulate a picture in my mind of a happy ending.

"But more importantly, I will never again indulge in cancer scares. Isn't that good news?"

"It's a start," I said. "But for the record, I came to support you in your illness. Not that it matters."

"Duly noted, darling. It was very sweet of you and I love you for it. You are less self-centered and more caring than ever. Is it possible that you're maturing?"

"Let's not go too far."

Cerise stroked my cheek, hugged me and planted a trumpet of a kiss in the hollow of my ear. "Please be happy, my love. I'm sorry I've put you through all my maladies and hang-ups. I suppose these are my growing pains. At any rate, your trip was not in vain. I'll make sure of that."

To quickly fulfill that promise, she guided my hand under her red sweater of good Scottish wool and pressed it against her breast. She lifted her leg, coiling it around me like a vine, and pulled me down with her onto the black earth. With moist lips murmuring endearments I could barely hear, she crossed her arms and lifted her sweater. The bright aureoles and hard nipples sprang up like poppies in the mist. I peeled her pants down to her knees and she drew me inside her with a cry that trailed off to a long, low moan. I banished my fear of impending loss and let myself live in the blissful interlude, the bubble of the moment. I embraced the prospect of the next interlude and interludes beyond, a lifetime of sublime interludes.

As I lay on the ground, staring at the gray sky through a lattice of dense branches, Cerise stroked my chest and touched the chain and pendant Lauren had given me for protection. I forgot to remove it as I had done when she visited Tunisia. Now her fingers lingered on the chain, as if collecting data and asking a question before she verbalized it.

I closed my eyes and felt a pang of despair. This perfect crystalline moment would now be shattered due to my carelessness.

"What is this, my love?"

"It's a good luck amulet. A friend gave it to me before I went to training camp."

After a long pause, she asked, "What kind of friend?

"From college. I've known her a long time, from before I met you. We had classes together. Her father's the Ambassador to Tunisia, so she invited me for lunch and gave me this."

I glanced at Cerise to see if an ironic grin would be twisting her mouth. But her face was relaxed and her eyes were pensive and compassionate. Still, I took precautions.

"If it bothers you, I'll take it off," I said. "She's just a friend."

"No. I believe you. And God knows, you will need the luck."

That was all she said about it.

The ensuing week went just as smoothly, without even an unkind word. Struggle was no longer part of our interaction. After years of fighting and letter writing, we were on a duty-free island of intimacy, where we could love one another like amorous strangers. We spent days in bed, laughing, listening to music, drinking whiskey, smoking cigarettes and making love with only a sporadic car horn on the boulevard to link us to the world. To be with her in the blue light of a late afternoon, free of loneliness, complexity and fear, seemed not only the best way to live, but also a plausible one. I wanted to believe that we could always be this way, yet part of me agreed with Cerise that it was impossible, so I did not indulge the wish or mention it to her.

In the evenings Cerise and I strolled by the Bidonville Cathedral, a Gothic colossus, and stopped at a *fin de siècle* café with blood red walls, a brass bar and birdcages suspended like chandeliers. In the glow of the glass lamps, Cerise's face was like an icon. As we sipped our *apéritifs*, I felt I could be happy in Bidonville. *It's just a visit*, I reminded myself.

Our reunion was almost over. I was having a great time, but it was borrowed time. Each day was like a year and *it was only a visit*. Cerise did not know that these ten days were a loan from the Peace Corps to be repaid with five long months. My face was pressed against the moment, about to make it burst.

"We're making the biggest mistake of our lives if we break up again. After four years, we finally get along," I said.

"You know your staying here wouldn't work." She held my hand with a sad smile.

"Because you say it won't."

"That's not true. We're on our best behavior now, but after the vacation is over and work begins—what then? We'd get on each other's nerves and be at each other's throats. I'd rather never see you again than have us hate one another. Be brave, my love. One day we will be together."

"You mean *for* one day," I said sarcastically.

"No, for all of our lives," she replied. A tear formed in the corner of her eye and perched there, as if afraid to roll down her cheek.

At that moment, a man I had never met approached our table. He had long, greasy hair and wore a leather jacket.

"*Salut!*" he said.

"*Bonsoir*, Bertrand. How are you? Rick, this is my colleague, Bertrand. Bertrand, my boyfriend, Rick."

Bertrand nodded coolly.

"I wanted to thank you for dinner a few weeks ago," he said.

"Oh, it was nothing," Cerise replied.

"Well, I'll be going. Happy New Year." Bertrand said as he swaggered out.

"Who is *Bertrand*?" I asked.

"I told you, he's a colleague," she said in a low voice.

"He seemed like a good friend," I remarked.

"What are you implying? Really, Rick, we don't have much time. Don't waste it with your jealousy."

"Okay, I won't."

But I couldn't help myself. For the remainder of the holiday, Bertrand might as well have been in the apartment, watching us make love. Until his appearance, I was the leading man in Cerise's life. But Bertrand was also in her life. He stood for every man she spoke to, flirted with and cooked for. He interacted with her in ways that I had not done for two years.

This glitch in the visit tormented, but did not surprise me. By all rights, this holiday that might never have happened had already gone too well. It was due for a correction.

On our last night, Cerise dragged me to a dilapidated theater where we used to see old movies during my junior semester abroad. "An American in Paris" was showing, a classic I'd heard about, but had never seen. I was reluctant to see a film on our last night, but Cerise insisted. "You are an American in France, after all," she said.

I liked the music, but disliked the story because it made my life feel unoriginal; I had inadvertently followed a Hollywood template. When Leslie Caron brushed off Gene Kelly at the boutique where she worked, Cerise squeezed my hand. "Just like us," she whispered. When Gene Kelly barged in on her party at the café, Cerise kissed my cheek. "Do you remember how rude you were in the dining hall?" During Kelly's dance sequence at the end, Cerise whispered, "I loved it when you danced for me in your room."

Yet the film also showed how far Cerise and I had drifted from the script. The Kelly character, Jerry Mulligan, was unswerving in his art, ebullient in love and supremely confident. In the end, he gave Leslie Caron the rose and she accepted it, choosing him and an uncertain life over her rich, famous boyfriend. That feel-good ending worked for Cerise. She was happy when we left the theater, but I wasn't. We walked to her apartment in silence.

"What's wrong, my love?"

Cerise kissed my cheek and squeezed my arm as our heels crunched the gravel to produce a crisp cinematic sound effect.

"My life's a cheap copy of an old movie."

"Nonsense. Your life *is* original. You're *an American in Bidonville*."

"It still hurts," I said.

She burst into boisterous, musical laughter that cracked the silence of the night and seemed to make the streetlights quiver.

"It's part of the collective unconscious," she said. "Myths are like the air we breathe."

She was right. We were living a movie, which was why we stayed together but didn't *live* together. We didn't share a life; we shared a myth.

It was our last night. Time was a vise, hour by hour, each moment closing in, compacting happiness to extinction. On the first night, time was a banquet hall full of celebrating moments. Now minutes and seconds ran from us, scattered and disappeared, like frantic commuters with somewhere else to go. Every feeling had to be savored before it vanished. Each second meant too much.

It would have been easier if this were our first separation. Hope would have mollified the pain. But separation was now just another phase in our cycle and I didn't think I could go through it again. Since it was unbearable to think this was our last tryst, we agreed to meet that summer. But I couldn't stop dwelling on the time between.

In bed, we touched in slow motion, as if applying a compress to a burn. Even when we tried to sleep, we caressed one another to make sure we were still together. I woke up every ten minutes to glance at the clock and watched with dread the first light sneaking through the blinds. One of the happiest weeks of my life was ending—I knew I would never have it back, and doubted I would get another like it.

At 7 AM, the alarm rang and I embraced Cerise one more time, trying to put sex to sleep, to numb desire and make us so sore from love making that we would not miss it.

Miscalculation. Love is manna, not money. It can't be saved.

"Goodbye, my love. Goodbye," Cerise said at the station. "Try not to be sad."

She smiled tightly and held back her tears. After a tremulous hug and a long, plaintive stare, she walked away, turned again for a last glance, and entered the depths of the crowd.

Like a character in a fairy tale, I seemed to turn into animated luggage, moving from station to terminal to plane, feeling grateful for a headache because it precluded thinking. When I arrived in Tunis, the pungent lake odors penetrated my numbness and the anguish I had suppressed overpowered my resistance.

She had begged me to return to the States, not Tunisia. That's what she would have done, but I needed to see her and this was my only way. For ten days of love, I would now pay with several months of isolation in Metloui and Tunisia's southern desert.

BOOK 4
GAFSA MAN

1

DESERT AND OASIS

The wide-bodied Citroën barrelled across the plains of esparso and scrub, deep into the interior of Tunisia toward Metloui, the Peace Corps version of solitary confinement.

The car was plush and dark as a coffin. It demanded introspection, but I was as restless as the landscape was remote. My eyes were drawn to the bright, empty plain where a shepherd stood more lifelike than alive on the brown steppe, gazing at his scattered flock across a field of light.

There was little here for the eye to take in and build impressions upon—only kilometers of barren land. The warm sunshine was a rebel, defying winter, not illuminating the earth so much as exploding on the eye. It ricocheted off the hard ground, splashing dust into a dense medium through which I struggled to see.

Le sud was a harsh environment, yet 10,000 years ago, the Capsian civilization flourished here. If *Gafsa Man* could survive in the *bled,* why shouldn't I?

We were headed to Gafsa, the capital of the southwest province, my home base, and then 40 miles farther to Metloui, the phosphate capital in the wilderness, whose name triggered fear in every volunteer and Tunisian to whom I mentioned it.

Our driver stopped for gas at a filling station in *Sidi Bou Sidi,* another strip of hovels at the crossroads of two highways. The Berber attendant's calm, green eyes squinted in the pale light. When I asked him how far it was to Gafsa, he smiled with the tranquility of a pool no stone had entered and said, *"Merci."*

The pump jockey's calm, vacuous eyes were a psychological caveat about staring into empty spaces. His non sequitur was a verbal mirage. If people only appeared to agree on what words meant, familiar items became props and the words had as little value as the currency. My anxiety escalated to panic as I realized that language would not serve me here.

Chadli, the pugnacious driver, whose black eyes converged at the flat bridge of his nose, slapped his hands, snapping me out of my demented meditation, and corralled me into the car.

"What is Metloui like?" I asked Chadli. Since I had already visited Metloui to organize the program and was familiar with its muddy desolation, the driver must have thought I sounded like a restive child, less motivated by curiosity than by nerves. Did I forget what I had seen? No, I asked the question repeatedly to obliterate what I had seen, or to confirm that it was a mistake.

"You will like it," Chadli replied with malice of portent, glaring with his third eye—a scar that crossed the bridge of his mashed nose like a purple ravine. It was a trophy he prized more than the medals he won as Tunisian bantamweight champion. "Metloui is very nice. Everybody is very nice."

I had run out of reasons to be in Tunisia; what held me were my deal with Dozier and the arbitrary finish line of my tour of duty. Instinct argued that being anywhere for no good reason leads to trouble. My body was accounted for, but my mind was rebelliously absent. My attitude was not conducive to survival.

As we careered across the dry, rolling *sahel*, I vowed to avoid social traps, ignore loneliness and whatever hostility I encountered and to enjoy the beauty of Gafsa and the desert, its golden, wind-burnished fortresses and glittering minarets, bare, lavender mountains and crumbling mesas. I would do a good job, represent America fairly and to hell with the rest!

By observing the other passengers—two men in suits, a woman in a coat, another in a *safsari*—I sought visual clues about my destination. But they were preoccupied, their torsos bent over papers, and as *renfermé* as Parisians on the metro. *People are the same wherever you go* is a futile, though reassuring truth, since our behavior is so alike that we lack the friction to connect. I probed an opening with the other travelers, but they denied access.

I glanced out the window at the undulating landscape, whose vacant grandeur tempted the eye to imagine it to life. Suddenly the road made a winding ascent and plunged into an oasis, where clustered palms shaded the road, suggesting balmy tropics. A break in the trees revealed Gafsa. Rocks and houses, streets and *oueds* intersected and tumbled down steep hillsides of crumbling stone into the bottom of a desert bowl, a dry reef, shaped and painted by sun and wind.

We stopped at the *borj*, a two-story villa on the far end of town. The *borj* was a company hotel for Tunisian trainees and visitors. I would be living with Tunisians in my age group and finally have a Peace Corps experience Dozier would approve of.

"*Monsieur le professeur,* you live here," Chadli said, as he yanked my bags out of the trunk and dropped them on the road.

"*S'balkhir! Shnoa hawalek?*" Nouri, the young caretaker, wrested the bags from my hands to carry them into the villa. Flat-headed, with thick, rounded cheekbones, Nouri strode with sure balance and a simple purpose.

"*Monsieur* Rick. Here, here," Nouri insisted officiously. Propelled by a teenage mania to succeed, he handled my luggage and me decisively to show his bosses how good he was at his new job. He also wished to demonstrate that he followed orders. Since none had been given about my room, he dropped my bags in the hallway, while Chadli the driver coaxed me back into the company car for the last lap to Metloui.

2

THE TEACHER OF ANGLO-SAXON

Monsieur Kouki, the Executive Vice President of Development and Training—an innovative division at *la Compagnie des phosphates*—let me wait in his anteroom, where two secretaries giggled and spat *glibbits,* dried sunflower seeds, until the dead-eyed doorman ushered me in. Kouki stared at a paper on his desk as I waited in the doorway for his invitation to enter. After a minute, he raised his head like a camera on a tripod, blinked as if taking a photograph and rose with stiff formality to shake my hand.

"Our teacher of *Anglo-Saxon*, please be welcome!" he said in a booming voice without moving a facial muscle.

"*Anglo-Saxon?*" I muttered in surprise. Was this a joke? Or did *Monsieur* Kouki mean "English?" Should I correct his gaffe? I could not risk insulting him.

The Director of Development's torso was a boulder in a three-piece suit. His large head pivoted heavily on a thick neck. His smile seemed forced, not from politeness but asphyxiation. Kouki was formerly the head of production, a mining engineer who escaped one tight enclosure to be put in a tighter one.

"Dr. Mamooni must have explained to you that the company needs to be *au courant* with advances in the phosphate mining industry. Most technical journals in our field are published in the U.S. For this reason, we must learn Anglo-Saxon in order to read them. This, *Monsieur*, is why you are here."

There. He said it again: Anglo-Saxon. I had an infuriating thought. What if the phosphate company really wanted Anglo-Saxon, and Dozier knew about it all along and set me up to fail?

As Kouki made perfunctory remarks on my responsibilities, as

366

well as his hopes and dreams for a rise in the price of phosphates, I frantically went over my options to manage his expectation, which was strange but not impossible in this outpost of civilization. Fear overwhelmed logic. Old English was the only course I skipped in my major, believing it useless. Who could have predicted that Tunisian phosphate engineers would want *Beowulf*? The blade of irony entered and twisted. Should I admit that I knew no Anglo-Saxon, potentially terminating the program and myself? In a second I was forced to decide.

"So, *Monsieur*, do you have a lesson plan?"

"Sir, I don't think I can help you."

"What is this? You are giving up before you have begun?"

"I am not qualified because I don't speak or read a word of Anglo-Saxon. Middle English is all I can do."

"What is this, an example of English teacher humor?"

"No, sir. I am just being honest. You said you wanted me to teach Anglo-Saxon and I think it's a dead language."

"*Monsieur,* you misunderstand me. Anglo-Saxon is my way of saying 'English.' Your people refer to all Muslim people from North Africa and the Middle East as Arabs and our different languages as Arabic. This is an inaccurate simplification. I only wanted to show you the same courtesy."

"So your protest against being oversimplified is to oversimplify me. I see what you're getting at, sir. How can we learn who we really are if we hide behind ethnic labels, right?"

Kouki's face strongly suggested that he had no interest in finding out who I was. Tossing all English-speakers in one pile was his linguistic revenge, and he liked it. However, his glare suggested that his distaste for me was more than generic. In beige clogs, white jeans and brim-down sailor's cap, I may have seemed less than professional.

"We are making changes at *la Compagnie des phosphates.*" Kouki paused to regroup his thoughts for a last assault. "Teaching Anglo-Saxon is one. I will make every effort to assist you, but you must be patient. The Department of Human Development is under development, just like Tunisia. Heh, heh!"

Kouki guffawed at his political *double-entendre.* I laughed along. I was starved for humor and consumed what little I received. Laughter transformed Kouki's face. His boyish cheeks inflated like balloons with puerile joy, pressing his thick neck against his snowy collar. His open mouth revealed thick, white teeth. Seeing the personality of a five-year-old boy emerge from the director's dour face made me laugh even harder, but when I noticed Monsieur Kouki staring impatiently, I coughed myself to composure.

"The teacher of Anglo-Saxon has a sense of humor. He will need it," he said reproachfully.

At first, the director's tendency to speak of me and to me in third person singular struck me as an amusing quirk, reminiscent of exotic characters in old films; it prompted me to stand outside myself and savor the importance of my role. But now I found it disturbing. For the director, my identity and my job were interchangeable. He seemed to be objectifying me now to dispose of me later. Worse, he was talking to my face and behind my back at the same time.

"Sir, you can call me by second person singular," I said.

"So, *Monsieur*, do you have a special project to help us master your difficult language?"

"Sir, your insistence on calling my language Anglo-Saxon gives me an idea. You are right: English is complicated, but precisely because it is *not* Anglo-Saxon. English is made of many languages: German, Danish, French, Latin and bits of others. This explains why English is such a difficult language for spelling and pronunciation. Yet, despite these complications, English can be simple if you know certain tricks."

"Tricks?"

"Short cuts. Many English verbs have different meanings when you combine them with prepositions. The word *look* means 'pay attention,' '*shoof*' in Arabic. 'Look into' means 'investigate.' 'Look over' means 'review.' 'Look out' means 'be careful.' One verb with three prepositions creates three new verbs."

"Will this help us read phosphate mining journals and textbooks?" Kouki asked.

"It might," I said. "It can't hurt. But that's not the point. I am proposing nothing less than the power to communicate in English simply and effectively."

Kouki did not appear to appreciate the magic of verb idioms I offered him. But having his important title and position entitled him not to rely on his own judgment. Winded from uttering many weighty declarations, Kouki summoned his assistant, Mabrouk, to offer a second opinion on my proposal.

"Ten verbs and ten prepositions, we get 100 new words," Kouki said to Mabrouk, a large man with a shaved head who would be my handler. "Is it a good return on investment?"

Mabrouk puffed his cheeks and rolled his eyes discreetly.

"Hmm. Ten verbs, ten prepositions. That is 20 words. In return, we receive 100 words. That is a 500% return on our verbal investment. Yes, it is an excellent ROI."

Kouki brought his fingertips together at his mouth, forming a mystical triangle before his chin.

"Then go, *Monsieur le professor*. Teach and write this book. See to it, *Sidi* Mabrouk, that our professor has all he needs to write this...what do you call it?"

"A verb idiom guide."

"Then go and guide us."

3

TRAVELS WITH MABROUK

Mabrouk led me to his office in a trailer across the muddy compound. There I assumed he would tell me his vision for the program and make practical suggestions for how to implement them. Instead, he seemed more inclined to probe my life and character, inquiring about my studies, travels and sexual orientation. Since I reported to him, I took my role literally, by informing him about myself until his eyes indicated siesta time and his brain had presumably erased all that I had said.

"So you like girls?"

"Yes."

"Have you ever had relations with a girl?"

"Yes."

"With a Tunisian girl?"

"No, of course not."

"Why of course not?"

"I believe it is against the law."

"Hmmm. So you have respect for the law."

"Yes."

I wasn't sure why my new supervisor probed me. It occurred to me that he was scouting for weaknesses to use against me later, or indulging his curiosity about an alien life form. Yet his interview was impersonal and casual, to pass time rather than collect information. I seemed to amuse Sidi Mabrouk like a crossword puzzle. He was no doubt filling the hole in his brain that boredom—a spiritual hunger—corroded; or exercising a penchant for interrogation.

While Mabrouk analyzed me, I reciprocated. An attorney by training, Mabrouk had the bitter air of one who had reached the pinnacle of his manhood when he was 22 and had tumbled since. Corpulence can be a clown suit serious men wear to negotiate social acceptance, but Mabrouk was too proud to be silly on purpose. He was that rare amalgam—a grim, fat man.

Lacking prestige, Mabrouk perfected the role of a subversive gofer. Obsequious and evasive, industrious and phlegmatic, he disdained his superiors while he followed their orders. Mabrouk had fallen down the corporate ladder and I signified the distance of his fall. He regarded me with resignation, as if I were his affliction. For this reason, I tried to be less unbearable and cooperated with him as much as I could.

"We must first promote your classes. You must meet your students and assess their capabilities," Mabrouk said.

For days we trekked across the barren mountains in his blue *"Deux Chevaux"*—a toy-like four-cylinder car that consistently got stuck in the mud—and pitched the English program to engineers at the remote camps. All eligible personnel took the placement exam and committed to the class. Some, however, asked openly what others hinted at with their eyes: "You expect me to study English after a hard day's work without a monetary incentive?"

The engineers had job security and we could not compel them to enroll in the program, so Kouki made the Anglo-Saxon course an "optional requirement."

4

BLOOD ON THE BLACKBOARD

After tests, polls and interviews, the first class finally convened in the boardroom of "The Big *Borj*," an imposing brick *chateau* in the central compound. Engineers and executives, the brightest minds of Tunisia's most prestigious government-subsidized corporation, sat at the long table and repeated after me, "*I like couscous; he—he likes couscous; we—we like couscous...*"

Never were dreams of power and influence so diluted. With the opportunity to say anything, we were stuck with "Lesson One, Page One" of the Bourguiba School text. Kouki and the others exchanged bemused glances and answered in childish voices. I was ashamed, yet determined to overcome the ridiculous text. After all, I was supposed to be a teacher and a leader, even if I was by far the youngest person in the room. While I plowed through the lesson plan and guided the adult students through their sarcastic responses, I recalled my practice class in Ayn Draham, the excitement of the students and my nervous desire to simultaneously control and please them. How had I fallen from such an auspicious start into this parody? Adult education had seemed the easier career path, but it was deceptively difficult. No doubt, school was better suited to young people, even those who could not sit still, because they could be convinced that classroom learning was worthwhile.

Given my youth and the irrelevant curriculum, classroom discipline was soon tested. Kouki blurted out the answer to a question meant for another student. Instinctively I wanted to rebuke him for his rudeness, but I hesitated and merely stared at him, since he was my boss and this class was his idea. I asked more questions and Kouki answered them all. In many respects, he reminded me of myself when I was in primary school. I guessed that Kouki was either showing off, demonstrating his knowledge of basic English to set a standard for his colleagues, or establishing his authority. Whatever his motive, it seemed prudent to ignore his disruptive behavior and hope he would get bored with monopolizing the class.

But appeasement never works; it only gets you trampled. Within a quarter of an hour, Kouki was the only student participating. As soon as one of his peers opened his mouth, Kouki took the words right out of it. Did he realize he was killing his own brainchild?

For the Director of Education to disrupt a class that he established made no sense to me, so I tried to make sense of it, myself. It occurred to me that my boss's rudeness might be a test. He was deliberately acting out to judge whether I had the guts and maturity to assert my authority. If this interpretation were correct, it was my duty to reprimand the phosphate company's second-ranking executive. When I called on another student and Kouki shouted the answer, I admonished him to speak only when called upon. The Executive Vice-President looked stunned; he blushed and apologized. The adrenaline of doing justice—or committing insubordination—engorged my brain. I experienced the confusion of acting decisively in an unprecedented situation.

The only feedback Kouki gave me for my teaching performance was his abrupt departure ten minutes later. He timed it to simultaneously express outrage and save face.

The class was quieter and more congenial after Kouki's departure, but a palpable anxiety had crept into the room. The other mining executives had been humiliated by the Executive Vice-President's incivility, yet my manner of handling him troubled them more. They believed that I had told my boss to shut up, a taboo demanding retribution. They winced as if they expected something awful to happen to me and were shocked that I did not collapse or die before their eyes.

Their attitude perplexed me. Wasn't a teacher supposed to manage a class impartially? By reproaching the second-ranking

373

executive at the Phosphate Company, I showed that no one was above classroom decorum and that education was for everyone.

Yet for the mining executives, etiquette was an abstraction. If I had not censured Kouki, they would have viewed me as a lackey, kowtowing to power—in other words, as a typical employee. My credibility would have been diminished—not that it was high to begin with—but I would have made more sense as a human being.

Integrity is rarely defended with impunity. Kouki never attended another class. Many other executives, who had enrolled to curry favor with him, now ingratiated themselves even more by dropping out. The final class roster in Metloui dwindled to six. When I tried to recruit younger engineers, they laughed. English class? Was I crazy? Then, to annoy me, they asked how the English classes were going.

Kouki did not kill the program. Canceling the first initiative of his new department after just a few weeks would have made him look indecisive, capricious, and ridiculous. Instead, he cast *Anglo-Saxon* into the desert of his indifference to die of its own irrelevance.

My commute and routine became inconvenient. The driver assigned to pick me up often came late or forgot to pick me up. When I was in Metloui, there was nowhere for me to sit and work. I roamed from the reception area to Kouki's outer office, where the secretaries teased me with questions about my bachelor status, while they painted their nails, complained of headaches and spat *glibbits* into their palms.

However, in Moulares, the most remote and most productive of the mining camps, news of Kouki's classroom embarrassment had the reverse effect of turning me into a folk hero.

Before becoming the first Executive Vice President of Development and Training, Kouki had run the mining operation in

Moulares and worked closely with Ramzi Abdennour, a respected engineer and a cultured man, whose dapper personal uniform comprised a tweed jacket and a red sweater. When Kouki assumed his new role at the top management echelon, Abdennour believed he would succeed him as mining chief in Moulares, but he was passed over in favor of Kouki's cousin, Hassen Gobso, a man 20 years his junior with far less experience and skill. Abdennour blamed Kouki for this preterition and seized on the English program as an instrument of revenge.

While Kouki tried to let my class die in Metloui, Abdennour brought it to life in Moulares. My first Peace Corps teaching success since training camp resulted from corporate infighting and subversion—but I would take it anyway.

While the car to Metloui often failed to deliver me to classes and was usually unavailable to take me home, the Moulares car, under the auspices of Abdennour, was always prompt and convenient in both directions. The classes in Moulares were always well-attended and I was always fed a delicious meal afterward. Such were the spoils of a political pawn.

However, class dissension soon surfaced in Moulares. Ramzi Abdennour had a gift for languages. With his tweed sleeves crossed confidently over his sweatered chest, he always responded correctly to questions, and had limited patience for less able students, like his balding cousin, Mootez Chiboub, whose nervousness made him stutter and frequently answer incorrectly.

At first, Abennour limited himself to loud exhalations and whispered insults whenever his cousin attempted to participate, but he finally discharged a tirade against him. "Do you think you can learn English? You cannot speak Arabic!"

Since Moulares was my only haven and Monsieur Abdennour my only benefactor, I tried to defuse the conflict by defending

Mootez Chiboub, while acknowledging Abdennour's superior language skills. Each day, I pondered what new psychological contortion I would need to perform to keep order. I was not presiding over a class so much as a volatile family dispute.

However, class management in Moulares was easy compared with the hardship of getting there. The road was a bumpy, swerving ribbon of rock and dirt on a ridge between two steep cliffs. When the little car hit a dip, the doors rattled and my head smacked the roof. Ahmed, the driver, was a small, nervous man with darting eyes and a thin mustache. Built like a jockey, Ahmed drove the little *Deux-Chevaux* wagon as if it were a horse. He jerked the wheel as he maneuvered the hard winding road, making the tires skid. For 50 kilometers, there was nothing between us and the chasms on both sides of the road but two low rock piles and the skill of the driver. Returning to Gafsa, our headlights formed a bright tunnel in a black void. I closed my eyes and prayed, "Don't let me die in this forsaken place."

One afternoon toward sunset, I saw strange activity near the road. Two men walked through the canyon, carrying shotguns. A second later, they were gone. Farther down the road, a Bedouin wearing a white *bernous* and wielding a long staff drove a pack of hopping camels, whose ankles were tied in square rope formations. Such fine animals were reduced to oversized bunny rabbits.

"They train them or they no good," Ahmed said, his eyes darting with anxious intensity. When I tried to engage the young driver in conversation, he often cut it short with, *"Menarafsh."* But Ahmed's "I don't know," meant something different than when Ali, the woodworker in Ayn Draham, said it. Ahmed's translated to, "I don't know and I don't care."

5

THE OTHER AMERICANS

My mission had a secondary objective: to find the American couple in Gafsa and share the ounce of pot Fargus had provided for my journey. Those were his wishes when he cut a large pile into several smaller ones with his Turkish scimitar. Fargus had purchased the stash from American sailors he met in Bizerte. The sailors threw in the scimitar for free.

I'd never forget the day in Menzel when we filled the well diggers' house with fragrant smoke and everyone looked at me with pity in their red, glassy eyes.

"Rick," Fargus had confided in his most avuncular manner, "in honor of my late Uncle Ned, who died with a splif in his mouth, I'm giving you an extra ounce. Uncle Ned used ganja to reduce the pain of terminal cancer and he often said, 'Give the most to the one who needs it most.' Rick, you will definitely need it most."

I thanked Fargus, but accepted only one ounce.

"You'll need to share it with John and Paula," he warned.

"I'll share what I have, but it's not smart to carry two ounces. One I can hide in my tobacco pouch, but two are more difficult. Anyway, you're already being generous."

"So be it," Fargus had said. "I'll take the extra ounce."

Everyone mentioned an American couple, but no one said where they lived, or how to reach them. I reconnoitered Gafsa, seeking a Caucasian who knew their whereabouts.

In a desert, even a small town can feel like a metropolis. Gafsa was the provincial capital of *le sud*, but the south was the most sparsely populated province and Gafsa took little time to explore.

Downtown was arranged around a tree-lined square whose spacious design dwarfed its light pedestrian traffic. The formality of the public grounds and government buildings conveyed the French urban aesthetic, which glorified the state, but the desert also made a mockery of such grandiose architectural features as domes and columns.

There was also a farcical disconnect between the government and the governed. Like slack sentries guarding invisible treasures, *bernous*-wrapped *fellaheen* leaned on the wrought iron posts bordering the plaza. Across a vast, pot-holed avenue stood the central market, a dilapidated stable covered by a canvas roof. There I foraged for something edible, but found only Jordan's almonds, which were abundant, cheap and sold by the barrel.

When clouds rolled in, the sky was sullen, and the air cold and penetrating. Winter covered the land, bleeding color from the rocks, buildings and faces, making one forget that the African sun ever existed. In the desert, humans put up simple defenses against the atmosphere. At the *Café du Marché*, an alfresco colony of Formica tables, tattered old men huddled over cups of hot, sweet tea. These stragglers on a stationary march to death gripped their glass cups so tightly that their fingers seemed frozen to the steam.

A street vendor sold me a red *merguez*. The piquant lamb-dog tasted good; its fat and *harissa* heated my throat. Men in orange *bernouses* hunched against the cold wind dashed between the stone and mortar walls of the medina, to absorb the scant heat stored in them. I turned my eyes from a gust of dust, and noted a blond beard and floppy, leather hat.

"What the hell are these?" the stranger asked as he scrutinized the *merguez* on the smoking grill. "They look like candy coated hot dogs!" He laughed hoarsely at his observation and winked. "You must be American."

"Peace Corps," I said.

"Stephen Howe, world traveler," the man in the afghan parka

said, extending his thickly mittened hand. "Do you know John and Paula? They're Peace Corps, too."

"You know them?"

"I mentioned them, didn't I?" he laughed. "Come, I'll take you to them."

He cocked his leather hat with the flair of P.T.Barnum leading a mark to a three-legged chicken. We took my usual bus and got off in front of the *borj*. From there, we walked down my street along the *oued* and stopped at a blue-walled compound.

"There you are, you son-of-a-gun. We were wondering what happened to you," John said, pounding my back zestfully. He was round-faced with blue eyes and a scruffy, black beard, "Do you have the stuff?"

They knew about the medicinal aspect of my visit.

"I'll bring it later," I promised, glancing at Paula, who was pretty and reserved, and had lovely, olive skin.

John was particularly fond of grass. When the joint was spent down to a speck of a roach, he tweezed it between two matches and lit it, so that the roach and matches went up in one plume of smoke. This he snorted zestfully, making the smoke whistle up his greedy nostrils. When he was done, he opened his blood shot eyes and cried out, "Mama, that's good!"

Paula drifted quietly around the table, making sure something was in front of everyone—a piece of cake, a cup of tea. She did not comment, save for the occasional twitch of her gently sloping nose.

Stephen, the world traveler, entertained us with his adventures, but he was mainly preoccupied with his sexual habits. He held out his hand and looked at it with the kind of interest one would devote to a favorite instrument. "I love my hand. Do you know why? Because this is the hand I jerk off with," he said. "Masturbation is the key to my success. Don't get me wrong—I can use both hands. I'm *ambisextrous*. But this hand is the first of equals."

John listened to Stephen with interest, while Paula reacted with disgust. I wondered if the world traveler came into my life as a divine messenger, to tell me what I needed to do in the coming months.

The next day, I accompanied Stephen to the Algerian consulate to help him obtain a visa that he had been thus far denied, in part because he could not communicate with Algerians. I explained to the officials that Stephen had dreamed of seeing Algeria and had spent his life savings to make the trip, but now his money was running out in Tunisia while he waited for a visa.

The officer was moved by this gibberish and summoned the world traveler into his inner sanctum. I followed them in, but was quickly ushered out since the Algerians felt uneasy at equal numbers with Stephen and me.

That evening, the onanistic adventurer boarded a bus to the Algerian town of El Oued. As the bus pulled out, he waved his favored hand.

6

LONG DISTANCE LONGING

Mon Cheri,

Only when I returned to the apartment did I realize that you had gone and we had undergone another traumatic separation. It was unbearable. I miss you so much, to the point that this week has been strange. I missed two classes on Wednesday and didn't even try to get the notes. Then I daydreamed for the rest of the day, slept until noon on Thursday, overslept on Friday, went to school at ten instead of nine, felt nonchalant about it and left for my parents' place at three because I could not bear to be alone this weekend in my apartment. Since arriving at the farm, I have done little more than sleep. I feel more like a lover and a woman than a teacher and a student.

Now I am drinking a Manhattan at my desk and smoking the last of the Dunhills you brought me. I am supposed to be doing lesson plans, but have been painting my nails bright red instead. This is as far as I can go with my preparations. For the past week I have been busy trying to reconstruct the atmosphere of when you were here. Every night I have gone to sleep with your arm around my waist, have woken up in the middle of the night and turned around for you.

Agony!

Please, my darling, supply more details of your living conditions. At least in Menzel I had been there and could visualize your misery. If you can, write often—I need you. I love you more than ever.

I adored every minute you were with me. I am left with nothing left to say. You said it all in your latest letter. Why am I here? Why are you there? This is making me sad—and drunk.

Cerise

P.S. After the above, I had a good sobbing session. I feel better now and have managed to do some work. I have resolved to get more involved in things here. Otherwise how will I survive?

Red Eyed Cerise

•

The language of longing is more potent than lust, since it arouses what it cannot release. Cerise intended to convey her unfiltered emotion, so that I would feel her inside me, but without her body to ground them, her words exploded in my mind.

Intense love, rapidly withdrawn, causes agonizing need. Our recent tryst was a love-bender I was withdrawing from; I recalled it in excruciating detail.

Cerise's torrid phrases of long-distance desire flagellated me. From her naked words, I conjured her sensuous nudity. Her longing became as alluring in my memory as her parted legs—yet beyond consummation.

Rather than bringing us together, Cerise's emotional surges triggered disturbances in my brain and a frustration too intense for intimacy or nostalgia.

With each reading, I writhed in febrile excitement. I wanted to fuck the words, but the intercourse of language is *interpretation*.

Unable to move between her soft thighs, I pried apart her images and stroked her metaphors, but was unable to find a groove, establish contact, build to a climax, or achieve release.

How long could I function if I continued to live in two places, always missing something and pining for it?

7

BORJ BROTHERS

Lingering to pay a debt is captivity of a kind. In the lock-down of obligation, time becomes your most important relationship. Under existential arrest, you care less about people than about days, hours and minutes. People exist outside this relationship and you cease to care what they think.

Psychological confinement is internal, yet no walls protect the *prisoner* from judgment. Exposed and vulnerable, his discretion eroded by routine, he gambles with others' reactions. Tense and acutely sensitive, he feels threatened, is quick to take offense and defend against slight. Indifference makes him susceptible to pratfalls, traps and disasters.

At the *borj*, I was living with Tunisians for the first time. When I was in a good mood, I believed I might have a bona fide Peace Corps experience. But good moods were fleeting.

The Tunisian engineers at the *borj* were candid about their feelings toward me. They asked snidely about the English classes, called them "useless" and me a "parasite." In the evenings they camped in the living room, obliterating time by playing a three-card game, which they resolutely refused to teach. It was the same game Cerise and I saw men play in all-night *Ramadan* cafés. The players held their cards so tightly against their thumbs that they creased them down the middle before slapping them on the table, amid shouts and clattering teacups.

Since the *borj* lacked the facilities and staff to prepare meals, the lodgers dined at the Bayech, a hotel in the oasis. Sometimes my Tunisian housemates invited me to their table after the meal. I'd bring over a half bottle of wine to share with them and while we drank in camaraderie they revealed their prejudices, which I was meant to receive with equanimity, as a token of their trust.

"Why are you here?" Zoubeir, an ursine young man with a petulant face asked, squinting irascibly.

"Are you a spy?" Lakthar, the psychologist from the south asked.

"I'm here to teach English," I replied.

"Haha!" they laughed. "That's ridiculous. Nobody comes here for that."

"All right," I conceded to humor them, "I'm a CIA agent on a top-secret mission to uncover the true workings of the *borj* and—"

They leaned forward, the light of fulfilled expectations

glowing in their eyes. "And what?" Zoubeir asked impatiently.

"To steal Nouri's secret formula for tea."

Unfortunately, the engineers believed this story and harassed me for more details. Finally I confessed that I was no foreign agent, just a confused adventure-seeker trying to be in the same hemisphere with his French girlfriend.

They guffawed incredulously. But Zoubeir appraised my sincerity with his calculating squint and attacked me on another flank.

"If it's true what you say about the French girl, I wouldn't bother with her. She's probably out with some other guy right now as we speak."

"Cerise isn't like that," I protested.

When they heard her name, they jeered and hooted, "Cer-e-e-e-s-e!"

"Do you think you're the first one who ever had a French girlfriend?" Zoubeir asked. "I was engaged to one. Ah, she was beautiful! I loved her so much that I was her slave. We were going to be married, but she would not live in Tunisia. I hate her!"

"Cerise isn't *like* that," I insisted.

"If Cerise isn't like that, where is she? Eh, *Hooyeh*?"

The *borj* brothers hooted and slapped palms at the exposure of this wounding truth. My protests were countered by a louder and more cynical response, until I walked away. Yes, I was angry, but I was also humiliated because I believed they were right.

What I had with Cerise in Bidonville was like a small relationship film, performed in close-ups on a small set, sealed off from the world. The story was about what we said and did in a bed, on a street, in a restaurant. We worked out our complications in long, drawn-out sessions of tender lovemaking. The film ended on an ambiguous, yet hopeful note. Cerise and Rick kissed, said goodbye, still in love, with their futures in doubt.

Now the film was over. The lights went on and I was no longer in the movie or in the theatre, but blinking in daylight. With each passing moment, the magic faded and all I was left with was the post-movie argument with other filmgoers about the meaning and value of what I'd seen.

8

THE STAR OF THE FILM ANSWERS HER CRITICS

My Dear Love,

I want to make amends and shut that foul trap of your housemate. Your girlfriend in France still loves you.

Tell him that on days like today she gets up at 6:30, has breakfast, which always includes an orange for Vitamin C, makes her bed after a few seconds on the balcony, notes that the birds are singing for the first time, and thinks that it is warmer and spring will thankfully come sooner than expected.

Then she takes a bath. It is 7:10. She applies her make-up, does her hair, dresses, splashes on some perfume, chews a stick of gum and off she goes. It is 7:45.

From 8 until 1, she teaches classes, pleasant and nasty, has an apple at 10 for energy, shakes hands with the Spanish teacher, and compliments him on his tartan tie, then returns to class. At 12:15, she buys stamps and cigarettes across the street, drops her boyfriend's letter in the mailbox and heads home for lunch.

She tunes in to breaking news on the radio, reads her boyfriend's letter and sighs from missing him while catching the report about a boy who strangled on his scarf. At the folding table by the kitchen window, she has her usual slice of ham on a bed of lettuce drowned in her favorite salad dressing, a crust of bread, a slice of Camembert and a yogurt, while she prepares a lesson plan for an afternoon class. Then she washes the dishes, while the water boils for her instant coffee. It is 1:30.

After brushing her teeth, she adds a touch of lipstick and a dab of cologne to cheer her up, and returns to school from 2-5. At 4 PM, there will be a cigarette and a word with a colleague. At 5, she invites another colleague for a Coke at the student hangout down the street and she does all the talking, since this colleague never says a thing.

Home by 6, she prepares her work for the next day and gets sick of it by 7:30. So she goes upstairs to visit a friend who has just returned from a long weekend in Paris with her new boyfriend.

At 8, she returns to her place, prepares an omelet, canned spinach and more yogurt for dessert. She washes dishes, gets undressed and pulls out the bed, then reads Kubla Khan— but not for long, since she is dog-tired and dozes off.

She turns off the light at 10:30 with tender thoughts about her boyfriend and sleeps like a log till 6:30 the next morning, when the cycle repeats itself. She earns 1000 francs a week and deserves every sou.

Colleagues marvel at her energy and bright, unfailing smiles. "One orange in the morning is the secret," she tells them.

What do you think of this girl, my love? And where could she fit in a husband or kid in her life?

I look forward to your response.

Love,

Cerise

•

Dear Cerise,

What do I think of this girl? That she works hard, likes her job and her colleagues and feels at ease in her environment.

This girl likes to be by herself, enjoys life, including her solitude, and has no room for her boyfriend.

Could this girl fit me in her life, like furniture in a cramped studio? No.

If she wants us to be together, I want to be with her, but if she believes she can't fit me in, how can I change her mind?

When I was about to sign, I stared at the letter and tore it up.

9
BATTLES OF THE BORJ

Making friends at the *borj* seemed hard, if not impossible. These Tunisian men were not my peers. They were a few years older and already becoming established in their careers. They viewed me as a young and undeserving interloper.

If only I could show them that there was more to me than their stereotype of a spoiled American youth, I might break through their resistance.

One evening, their usual card game ended early and the *borj* brothers dispersed. A new engineer, more poised in his manner than the others and as much a stranger to them as I was, reacted to the sudden dispersal with a bemused laugh.

"And I had a breath mint," he said. "Ah, well, not much loss. I don't play cards. In fact, I don't understand people who do."

"Do you dislike cards, specifically, or games, in general?" I asked.

He pursed his mouth to consider his reply.

"No, it's cards I hate. I prefer games of skill—chess, for instance. I like that game very much. But it is hard to find a good opponent."

"Well then," I said, taking my cue, "I can't guarantee my quality as a competitor, but I have a magnetic portable chess set and I'd be glad to play you a game."

"*Très bien!*"

I retrieved the chess set from my suitcase. This was my first chance to use it.

My opponent had a haughty air. He wore a dark suit and had a thin mustache that trickled down to a goatee. He and I started to play casually, chatting between our moves. Our game felt more like a conversation than a competition; I paid less attention and lost my rook in a careless gambit.

At that point, he started talking about sex. He asked me if I had ever had sex with a man. I told him no. I wasn't gay.

"That's a technicality," he said. "Have you tried?"

"No."

"Then how do you know?"

"Educated guess," I said.

I sidestepped his questions as I struggled to regain the initiative from being one rook down. I finally maneuvered him into a position in which I could always put him in check; if he tried to escape, I would take his rook and checkmate him.

But as I applied pressure on the chessboard, he raised the sexual pressure.

"Aren't you curious? Don't you think it's an experience you should know about as a young writer?"

He had hit me in a vulnerable place. In principle, I was committed to gaining experience, without consciously drawing a line. But I sensed a trap.

"I don't need to have every experience."

"How do you know if you never tried it? Isn't that dishonest? Are you afraid?"

I told him fear had nothing to do with it. Then I realized that there was only one way to rebut his argument and stop his attempts to seduce me. I remembered a proverb attributed to Voltaire: "Once to the orgy, curiosity; twice, perversion."

I told him I had tried it and didn't like it.

He sensed that I was lying and asked for specifics.

"Why didn't you like it?"

"Oh, you know," I said vaguely. "It wasn't my thing."

Now my self-contained opponent was frustrated with my stalling tactics, in sex and chess. He studied the board as if he wanted to destroy it, his cheeks puffing with impatience.

Suddenly, his eyes widened. He tapped his finger on his lip. He appeared to have a game-winning insight. "Let me try this."

He moved his piece with a decisive thump, the chess version of saber rattling. He believed he was about to checkmate me.

If chess were based on physical posturing, I would have resigned. But I studied the board. I had been sure that my trap was inescapable. I was right. He tried to slip my repetitious trap and his defense collapsed. In three moves, I had his rook, his queen and checkmate. He threw up his hands. "I am too tired for this."

•

A few days later, when I returned from my class in Moulares, a frail and popular Egyptian singer was performing a concert televised from Cairo. The *borj* brothers were ecstatic. They bounced on the couches and chairs, sang along and whooped as the wan and handsome singer crooned in his tuxedo.

Cameras showed the trembling, wailing and flailing of Abdul-Alim's star-crossed worshippers, who could only watch and listen helplessly as their idol faded toward his death. After each instrumental coda, Hafez's clouded eyes beamed with dark serenity.

The doctor slapped his thighs in time to the music while the others tried to slide into his groove. He asked repeatedly if there was a drum in the house, but none of the Tunisians had this simple, inexpensive instrument. Finally, bored with smacking his thighs, the doctor stopped keeping a beat. The others slumped in tired dejection.

I had been ill for a week—sneezing, wheezing, snorting, trying to smell and taste with limited success—and wanted to go to bed. But my *borj* brothers were despondent and I had the means to raise their spirits. I adapted the immortal charge of John F. Kennedy, the Peace Corps creator, "Ask not what your *host* country can do for you; ask what you can do for your *host* country." A passage from a self-help book, *Give to Receive,* which I borrowed from the Peace Corps office library on Dozier's recommendation, also came to mind.

> *"When you ask the world to give to you, the world shrugs.*
> *When you ask the world what you can give, it hugs."*

To be a Peace Corps hero, all I had to do was reach out with a friendly drum. The *borj* brothers would have to see me as more than a parasite. I retrieved my *darbuka* and handed it to the doctor, who revived the party with a hot Berber beat.

In a small way, I was fulfilling my mission to help people in my host country enjoy more gratifying lives. I waited to be transported by the Peace Corps spirit. But after an hour of hearing the Phosphate Doctor doing his impersonation of Buddy Rich and Keith Moon, the pounding of the clay drum matched the throbbing in my head.

I returned to the living room to tell the *borj* brothers that I was ill and needed sleep. When I asked for the *darbuka,* they implored me to let them play on. Their sad-eyed supplications persuaded me that curtailing their fun would undo the good will my drum loan had fostered. I shuffled back to bed and tried to sleep amid the fierce pounding and yells from across the hallway, but a half hour later, I returned to the living room.

"Brothers, please give me my drum."

After my entreaty, the doctor, usually the most pleasant *borj* brother, beat the drumhead more intensely. He was the one Tunisian whose civility I had come to trust, but he scoffed at me, my illness and the Hippocratic Oath. Gradually, the others sensed my presence in the doorway, and stopped singing. The doctor played solo.

"Please, Doctor, I want my drum," I repeated.

"What will you do about it?" his eyes taunted me as he beat the *darbuka* more ferociously, like a shaman exorcising demons. With snapping hands, he smacked the skin as if he wished to puncture it.

I strode across the room and landed my fist on the *darbuka,* which swallowed the beat with a muffled grunt. The doctor's hands froze above the drum skin. His knees released their hold of the *darbuka.* I apologized for breaking up the party, repeated that I was sick and walked out.

10

SOCIAL PREDATOR

After the battle of the drum, the *borj* brothers weren't talking to me. In the evenings when I returned from classes, I went to my room across the hall from the den, where they congregated every night, conversing boisterously, playing cards and making obscene gestures at the TV set whenever a woman appeared on screen.

My alternative was to escape down the street to John's and Paula's. When I visited my American allies, I always brought a joint or two. It was not enough to elicit a warm welcome, but at least I would not be asked to leave.

One evening, I slipped my last joint in my pocket and took the muddy path to my American neighbors' villa. Would they remain my friends once it was smoked?

As I ducked my head under the low cross-beam lintel, I braced myself for John and Paula not being happy to see me. Paula moved restlessly, taking things out and putting them away. John sat at the table, with papers were stacked in front of him like an indigestible meal. All of this was familiar, yet something was amiss. For one, John's legs were not crossed at right angles in his laid-back manner. Yet more significantly, John and Paula were not wearing their usual matching dark turtleneck sweaters; instead, his neck was wrapped in a bandage up to his chin.

Despite his immobility, John's head pivoted my way. His eyes focused on my pockets to guess where the joint was. It was his usual greeting, a game he played with himself, since I would smoke with him whether he guessed right or wrong.

"What happened?" I asked.

"I fell off the bike," he said from the side of his mouth. "I was carrying the gas-bottle down the hill and hit a rut."

Paula swept around the stove with ferocious energy. She did not seem to be cleaning so much as exterminating dirt.

"I told you you'd get hurt. You should have carried it on foot," she snapped.

"And get a hernia? No way!" he shot back.

"So now look at you!" She waved her hand in disgust.

With most couples, I would have felt awkward and tense to be privy to a family quarrel, but this was more emotion than John and Paula routinely showed in my presence and it made me feel welcome.

However, within moments of my arrival, this visit lapsed into a familiar pattern: silence stifled the room, they glanced at me, I tried to chat, they waited for the joint and we lit up. I could have gone straight to the joint, but I didn't want to be just the cannabis deliveryman. This was my last joint and my last chance to become their friend. I had to penetrate their silence.

I tried starting a conversation, but each attempt fizzled like a damp match. In the isolating chill that invaded their walls and bones, personal warmth was as hard to come by as home heating.

I was socializing with two people who breathed, yet showed no vital social signs. I surmised that they played dead to defend themselves. Nevertheless, I felt rejected.

If this had been college, I wouldn't have wasted time with them, but they were the only potential friends I had in the vicinity, so I was determined to make them like me. I thought that they might be unsociable because my presence was amorphous—I was neither friend, nor stranger, nor colleague—so I resolved to establish a distinct role to put them at ease.

As I held off the sacrament of the weed, I recalled Edward R. Murrow's program, "Person to Person." I had once seen his interview of Bogart and Bacall. Murrow was so friendly and engaging that even his personal questions made Bogart smile. If John and Paula would not respond to me as a Peace Corps peer, they might prefer me as an interviewer.

I already knew their back-stories. She was a pretty star baton-twirler in college trying to please her religious bartender father, a violent, yet compassionate man. He was a handsome, fun loving, pot-smoking son of the Jersey Shore, with ideals and talents but no urgency to realize them.

John and Paula came to Tunisia with the Peace Corps "couples experiment," but since technically they weren't married, the Peace Corps did not view them as a couple. They were assigned to teach in Gafsa separately since none of the married couples wanted to live in such a remote location. Ironically, they were the last couple from the experiment that remained together in Tunisia.

John and Paula lived without compromise and bent the system to their will. Yet, they seemed depressed and defeated. Did they no longer love each other, or were they as empty as the gas bottle John carried on his bike?

I was a lonely outsider, the interviewer, probing for life below the surface. If they viewed me as a social predator, they were right. Their silence was protective, yet their code of looks, sighs and silences could not conceal them from me, the natural enemy of private people.

"So Paula, at college you were a star baton twirler. How did it feel to excite so many inebriated men?"

Paula stopped stacking doilies on a counter. Her hazel eyes became luminous.

"It was exciting. We always wore short skirts and no tights, no matter how cold it got. But I never felt it. Once after a game, someone told me my fingers were bent and blue. They were numb. I also couldn't feel my feet and nearly got frostbite. But I never felt more alive."

"When I worked in a pizza joint, I used to hang out in the freezer room to feel alive," John cracked.

"Shut up," Paula said.

"John, how did it feel to watch your girlfriend shake her butt for thousands of horny men?"

He shrugged. "I was proud of her. I went to a game for the first time my junior year. That's where I saw her. It was love at first sight. I would fantasize about seeing her naked."

"John! You're embarrassing me."

"Don't be. I've heard worse," I interjected. "So Paula, how did your dad react when he met the dope-smoking hippy who was having sex with his little girl?" I asked.

She looked stunned at first.

"Oh, no, this is it," I thought. "If she didn't already loathe you, she does now."

Then she started to talk.

"My father hated John. He's a tough guy from the old country. He has these ideas about how his little girl should be. Plus, he sees all kinds of depraved behavior in his bar and he wants to protect me. When he met John, I thought he'd kill him."

"Were you scared, John?"

"I should have been," he laughed, then winced because of his neck. "But I was like, hey, I learned from the ocean, man. I became like the water, you know, flowing and overcoming but not resisting."

"He was high the whole time!" Paula exclaimed.

"A good thing or I would have run out of that asylum."

"My family is not crazy," Paula protested.

I saw the craving in John's eyes. They were asking me, "Did you bring a joint?" I knew he could taste the reefer in my pocket, but I had one more question.

"How does it feel to be the last and only couple left from the historic couple's experiment?"

"You mean the only couple not to get divorced? We had an advantage. We were never married." John laughed and cried out in pain.

"What kind of a thing is that to say?" Paula fumed.

"That's interesting," I said brightly, to keep the conversation moving. "Is there anything to be learned from the fact that you were the only unmarried couple and you're the only one left?"

"Maybe we just had a stronger relationship. Or we just wanted to be here more," Paula said.

"Did you have more to prove because you weren't married?"

"I don't believe in proving things to other people," John said.

"Right. Not even me," Paula said.

"What's that supposed to mean?" John asked.

"Is it normal for a man not to touch his girlfriend?" Paula demanded.

"Is it normal for a woman not to invite her boyfriend to meet her parents at Christmas?" John countered.

"We're not married. I didn't want any fights," Paula replied.

"What do your parents think we're doing here?" John asked.

I was feeling nostalgic for the grim silence that had only minutes before characterized this visit. John was now too angry with Paula to beg me for grass and Paula had forgotten about it. But THC seemed to be what we all needed then, so I extracted the joint from my pocket.

"It's the last one," I said. "Smoke up and be happy."

After we smoked the last joint and John and Paula had no more use for me, it was my turn to wait for them to give or withhold their friendship. John's red marble eyes gazed at the corner of the ceiling and he had an epiphany.

"When I was a kid, we'd smoke at the beach. The beach was ours. The waves were ours. The whole damn ocean and the plankton were ours."

"Especially the plankton," I said.

When only a roach was in the tray, John performed his roach-finishing technique and drew the smoke into his nostrils.

He tried to fine-tune the radio dial, scanning the bands for the *BBC*. But the weak signal sounded like a teakettle. Paula swept the floor and beat the dust-pan against the oil-drum garbage can. Her resentful stare, the wheezing radio, John snorting through a stuffed nostril, all beckoned me to speak.

"What's the most important thing in your life?" I asked.

John scrunched his face.

"Truth," he said with the casual finality of someone stating his favorite soft drink.

"Truth," I stammered in disbelief. "That's a pretty big thing."

"The biggest," John said, staring into space.

"Do you think you'll find it?"

"I already did," John began, stroking his patchy black beard. "I was tripping my brains out in the *Ponte Vecchio* in Florence and suddenly there it was—the *Atomic Rooster*."

"*The Atomic Rooster*?"

"It's a bar where I used to hang out." John's eyes had a high-beam intensity to cast light on distant memories.

"So truth is *The Atomic Rooster*?"

John stroked his beard and smiled. "You had to be there."

Truth, The Atomic Rooster, John stroking his beard, Paula sweeping their floor. I laughed nervously—and didn't stop. John and Paula joined in without knowing why. They only became suspicious of me when I didn't stop.

"Why are you laughing so hard?" John asked.

"Yeah, what's so funny?" Paula demanded.

"It's not you," I said. "It's everything."

Apparently satisfied with this explanation, John nodded significantly and returned to marking the stack of papers on the Formica table.

"What's the most important thing in your life?" Paula asked.

"My girlfriend," I replied. "And my writing. What about you?"

"Love," she said. She looked at John for corroboration, but he was staring at the homework while chewing his lower lip.

"Love is the strongest thing there is— right, Honey?"

John grunted. "After truth."

"Love *is* truth. For me it is," she insisted.

"Isn't love scary?" I said. "It's all about need."

"What's wrong with need?" Paula asked. "It's the most natural thing in the world."

"Do you mean that?" I asked. "Most people are afraid of need. Think about the word, 'needy.' Nobody wants to be that."

"We don't feel that way," Paula insisted softly.

She and John huddled over their tea and glanced at me as if I were an intruder. For ten minutes they said nothing. Is this what Cerise feared would happen to us if we lived together? Maybe it was better to just see someone on holidays.

"Rick, please take this the right way," Paula said suddenly. "We'd appreciate it if you wouldn't come by for a while. We're going through stuff and we need time by ourselves."

I had feared being used and thrown aside when I needed friendship. Now that it was happening, I tried to fully absorb the sensation so that I would remember it, but I was too numb.

"It's disappointing. I hoped I could drop by," I said.

"We're sorry. Please understand."

As I passed under the low doorframe, Paula said, "You can come over in an emergency."

"Great, I'll be sure to come by if I'm dead."

"And we'll let you know if we hear of a party," John said.

11
A TOP SECRET MISSION

I sat in the lobby of Metloui's big *borj*, between a morning and afternoon class, working on my book of American 2-word verb idioms and trying to figure out how to discreetly consume the caviar I had removed from the company refrigerator, when Mabrouk lumbered through the doors, looking exasperated. My face flushed and I looked down, but he did not judge my manner as suspect. He may have believed that I was finally showing him due respect.

"*Professeur*, please follow me," Mabrouk said querulously.

We crossed the gravel courtyard to his office. I assumed that now Mabrouk would convey his hopes and dreams and expectations, or ask how often I masturbated each day to get a better handle on *Anglo-Saxon* culture.

In the confines of his office, Mabrouk studied me with narrowed eyes and a tilted head. He must have assumed that this prosecutor's pose would give him the best view of my soul. After a minute, he broke the silence.

"How do you behave when you are alone with a woman?"

"That depends on the woman. And on our relationship."

He pursed his lips, cocked his head back and scrutinized me with an incredulous grin, unwilling to accept that I was being truthful.

"We have a proverb," he said. "When a man and a woman are

in a room alone, the devil is the third party."

"I've heard it, but what does it mean?" I asked.

"*Il est très simple.* When a man and woman are alone together, they cannot avoid the unavoidable." Mabrouk paused, waiting for me to show that I understood his innuendo. When I didn't, he spoke literally; "A man is weak, a slave of his senses and his desires. A woman is weak and foolish. When they are alone together, they must behave like animals."

I could feel a test prompt coming. Momentarily, I would be expected to discuss my moral conduct. Mabrouk fixed me in his canny gaze.

"Have you ever been alone in a room with a woman when you did not behave like animals?" he asked.

"Of course," I replied. "In fact, I've been in bed with women when the unavoidable was avoided."

His eyes and his mouth widened. Even the pores of his skin seemed to dilate with astonishment. Tilting back in his chair to assume a safe distance from my perversity, Mabrouk broke the balance his bulk struck with gravity. He and his chair disappeared behind the desk amid the sound of bones rapping hard objects and his irrepressible curses. *"Merde! Merde! Merde!"*

Mabrouk was wedged between his desk and the back wall and could not lift himself. I gave him a hand. When he was upright, he brushed himself off, though there was no dust on him.

"How was this possible?" he resumed.

"Not every woman who let me sleep in her bed wanted me to make love to her," I explained. "She might have shared her bed out of kindness because it was more comfortable than the floor."

Mabrouk shook his head in amazement. "You Americans are in another world."

"Monsieur, why are you asking me these questions?"

Mabrouk blinked abstractedly, as if this were a key question to which he had misplaced the answer. He knitted his forehead, as he strained to recall the matter, then studied me with pensive petulance, before a thin smile twisted his lips.

"*Jeune homme,* at certain critical moments, the right man comes along who can change history. I believe this is such a moment and you are such a man."

"I am? It is?"

"*Professeur,* you are on the threshold of a watershed event. The women's classes have been authorized to take place."

"*Hamdulleh!*" I said.

"Yes, your enthusiasm is understandable. But inadvisable."

He leaned across his desk and his head floated toward me like a slow-moving asteroid.

"Young man, this is unprecedented. You are in a very serious situation. All Metloui will be watching. Fear and anger are everywhere."

"About an English class?" I asked mockingly.

"It is highly controversial. You may be in grave danger."

His persistent grimace crashed into my bravado and shattered it into fragments of fear.

"Do you want me to teach the women or not?"

His furtive smile returned.

"There is no turning back. But be careful. Your conduct must be conservative. Do you have any idea what I am talking about?"

If I had been honest, I would have admitted I had no clue, but I nodded emphatically that I understood.

"There are rules. But you may be the man for the job, if what you said about doing nothing when you were in a bed with a woman was more than a perverse fiction to impress, or *depress* me. Self-restraint may save your life."

I believed that Mabrouk was grossly exaggerating and that his imagination had run amok in fields of boredom and paranoia. Yet, his relentless glare and the beads of perspiration gathering on his shaved head suggested that he was in earnest.

"You must not walk too closely to any woman, or ask any one too many questions. You must maintain a public voice and never use a familiar tone. You must not smile or laugh with the women, nor make conspicuous eye contact. You must avoid individual conversations. This is a major opportunity, but we must go slowly. *Shweah b'shweah*. Do you know what that means?"

"Little by little," I said.

"Yes, that is what the words mean. Now you must act on them."

It was obvious now that Mabrouk had probed my sexual background in order to vet me for this unique opportunity. He wanted to be sure that I had the right stuff to teach nubile women, in other words, that I had the traits of a eunuch. I made a note to provide no further details of my stunning sexual self-restraint.

<h2 style="text-align:center">12</h2>

<h2 style="text-align:center">MAN IN HAREM</h2>

The first *Anglo-Saxon* course for women of Metloui started that Monday. Ten students were seated and waiting in the boardroom. Only one had a *safsari*. The others wore French skirts, blouses and sweaters, their fashionable coiffures streaked red or blonde. I expected the women to be in white cloaks so it would be safe to look at them, but they looked contemporary and sophisticated. I had to mentally draw *safsaris* over them.

My students helped me to ignore their femininity by staring intently at the blackboard easel. They appeared determined to prove that they were serious about their education, and that this was no diversion from their bleak, monotonous days.

"Hello," I began.

"Hello," they replied in one warm, mellifluous chorus, with enough of an accent to make it charming.

To break the tension, I asked their names. I started with the student in the *safsari*, who stared at me but did not reply. When I softly repeated the question, she glanced nervously askance. I hoped she wouldn't burst into tears, and was going to move on to another student, when she finally said her name. The next woman I called on smiled shyly, with warm, quizzical eyes. But she quickly regained her self-consciousness and glimpsed with embarrassment at the other women.

The third student I addressed, a glamorous and more mature woman, with red hair and green almond eyes, stated her name and asked me mine.

In my nervousness I had not written it on the board.

I asked her how long she had been living in Metloui.

"Too long," she retorted. The other women laughed.

"Is that how all of you feel about Metloui?"

They giggled.

"Oh, no!" another student called out. "I love it here."

They laughed harder.

"Why do you feel this way about Metloui?"

The woman with the red hair asked, "You have eyes, don't you? Ask them!"

Women's laughter filled the conference room, doubtless for the first time, and it sounded like strange and beautiful music. I could not believe it; I was having a conversation with Tunisian women. It was one of those milestones when a voiceover in my head said, "You're actually doing this!" It was more astounding because these women sounded smart, their eyes were alive with understanding and they had sharp wit. Why was I surprised? They were normal people; it was the culture that had made them appear mysterious and remote.

I asked my students if they had gone to the university. All but one raised their hands. I asked one pretty woman with black-rimmed glasses what she had studied.

"English and archaeology," she replied. "Two useful subjects. Actually, this would be a wonderful place for archaeology if I could go out in the field."

"How long have you been here?" the lady with the red hair asked me. Her name was Nabila.

"Two months."

"You must feel that it's too long. You're a young man. What is there for you here?"

I did not reply.

"What's wrong?" she asked. "Why won't you answer?"

I stood impassively to maintain a professional distance, but felt stupid doing this. How could I tell her and the others that Mabrouk had ordered me not to speak directly to individual students? But since it was absurd to teach a language class without interaction, I broke a rule and answered her.

"My reasons for coming here are too complicated. If I tell you my story, I'll be the only one practicing English."

"We don't mind," another student chimed in.

"So, Professor," Nabila cut in with ironic emphasis. "Where do you come from?"

"Washington, D.C."

"What did you study?"

"English."

She peppered me with questions. I answered her and asked

questions of my own. It was a natural demonstration of conversational English. However, our casual exchange of personal information swiftly evolved into a private conversation. When we paused, I looked around. The other women were stunned. I felt embarrassed, as if I'd been eavesdropped upon.

Nabila smiled. "Why are you red, *Professeur*? We're just talking."

I struggled for a discreet way to say I felt naked, when I noticed the clock.

"It's time to go," I said with relief. No one reacted, but in a moment, the students emerged from a collective trance, gathered themselves and left the room.

Mabrouk had warned that teaching this class was dangerous, and I understood now what he meant. Regardless of how many women were in the room, when I spoke with one of them, for that instant we were alone. Pedagogical distance was an illusion. The women became personal and drew me in. That made it interesting for them—and precarious for me.

Two days later, fewer students attended the second class. The shy, reticent women at the margins were gone. Only the better and more extroverted students had returned and now they had more time and freedom to practice conversation. But I already knew that classroom discussions among a few participants could become personal. Their content might be repeated out of context, distorted and turned against me.

Mindful of Mabrouk's caveats, I did what I could to run the class in a conventional manner, with textbooks and drills. But the returning students were too advanced and too highly motivated to be satisfied with drills. No matter how I tried to put the text and drills between us, I could not prevent genuine dialogue from breaking through.

"What are you doing here?" Nabila asked. I tried explaining in Peace Corps jargon, but my reasons sounded transparent.

"I'm here to do this."

"To teach us English? Your government is generous," one woman quipped.

The primary mission of the Peace Corps was clearly not to teach wealthy engineers' wives to speak English. The New Frontier ideals and I had gone awry. Yet my students and I understood each other. They believed I was a fraud, but no more bogus than they were. We tacitly acknowledged that we were in that room to escape boredom, broaden our knowledge of the world and make contact with someone different from ourselves.

One woman studied me intensely.

"I think you are here because you are perplexed about your future. Or your past. You are running away."

She spoke swiftly in a soft tone as if thinking aloud, then covered her mouth. "My God. What am I saying?"

"It's all right," I laughed nervously, "I don't mind being a character in your story."

"Doesn't your family worry about you?" a woman asked.

"Or maybe you ran away from a woman, from an unhappy love," another woman added.

Her classmates nodded. They liked this story.

"No," I confessed. "I ran toward one."

Their attention, and my alternating desire to reward and deflect it, stimulated and exhausted me. Their minds wrapped me in their interest. While I tried turning the conversation to their lives and opinions, they deftly eluded this tactic. Answering their queries seemed more apt than silence. If I gratified their collective curiosity, they might attend the class until there was nothing left about me to be curious about. By then the program would be successful and I'd be gone.

More importantly, as long as the women focused on me, I could not ask them about themselves and their husbands could not suspect me of showing inordinate interest in their wives. Yet, this tactic could backfire, as well. The husbands might become jealous of me, not for occupying their beds, but their spouses' minds.

By the third session, only five students remained. The conversations were now so casual and relaxed that the six of us seemed to be chatting over lunch and drinks at Le Café de France in downtown Tunis. We were drawing too close. I had to turn our intimate tutorial back into a class.

Halfway through the Friday session, I announced that writing would be added to the curriculum. I asked the students to compose short essays describing themselves or something important in their lives. This seemed a safer way for them to communicate privately and at length; it was also my way of enriching the course by helping these adult students develop a desirable skill.

Even so, when they received the assignment, they bristled with anxiety and confusion. This was a typical response. They were under pressure to perform and writing about themselves in English must have seemed overwhelming. I urged them to view this as a letter to a stranger, and to write it in a casual style, as if they were speaking.

This advice did not seem to help. The women stared with perplexity at the blank sheets, as if trying to read the invisible. They felt safe asking questions, yet writing was a risk. It was hard for them to reveal themselves. They viewed the self as a dangerous place to dwell in or to visit. I saw in their faces the hardship they endured, conceded that the assignment was a blunder, and was about to retract it, when they started to write. As their hands moved across paper, their heads were down and their faces close to the table, as if they were shining a light on a dark path, or concealing a subversive act.

When the women finished, each folded her paper and brought it to me. Some looked away. Nabila put her writing in my hand and smiled with a raised eyebrow. "I hope this is what you want, *Professeur*."

"I'm sure it's fine," I replied.

"*Bon soir, Professeur*."

13
BOUDOIRS OF THE MIND

I brought the essays home with keen interest. I knew I was entering a place where I had never been—inside the protected space of Tunisian women's minds. As soon as I arrived at the *borj*, I closed the door of my room and started to read.

"I cannot write what I think. I am unsure if I do think. Oh, yes, I can name what I will do each day when I wake up. And I know how to answer questions so I must know how to think. But who I am and what I believe, these are not things I can easily discuss. I am not sure I know my own mind, as something separate that belongs to me.

I guess that must tell you something about me."

I glanced at the top of the page to see who had written this, so I would know to whom I should address my comments. The student had omitted her name. I flipped through the other papers. They were all unsigned! It was like being in a dark room hearing soft, intimate whispers.

"I'm sorry. I don't know what to write. I feel I cannot share

this with someone I do not know. I cannot share this even with my husband and family.

I tried. I cannot do this. Please don't make me do this again!

I went to the next one.

"What is important about me is what is important for everyone else. Like many people, I do what seems right at the moment. When I was young, I went to school. I studied hard because everyone said it was the best thing to make a good future. Then I went to the university so I would enter a profession and have a good job. Then I married because this was the best thing to do. Now I live in a nice house, I have a French car and a good life, with good friends and a husband. I go to Tunis a few times a month. Now I am taking English. And you, Professeur, what is important to you? Have you decided?"

There was one left.

"You know me. I can feel it. You have met me before. I am the woman you have yearned for and the one who has broken your heart. I have a body you wish for even without knowing what it looks like. You make love to me in your mind, though, frankly, I am in many ways an ordinary woman, who loves to gossip and to shop, to eat and sleep. You love me and crave me, because you believe my love is special, that my embrace would make you more of a man. Why do you feel this way? Why do we always meet like this?

This is one question you should ask yourself. I'm sure I don't have the answer. Bonne chance!"

Again, I was tortured by psychological arousal unrelieved by physical release. But this was a different sensation than the frustrated longing Cerise's transmissions often evoked. Reading the last essay, I felt that the author was in the bedroom with me, removing her clothes after a social evening and bantering with me in a mocking, yet provocative way, all with the intention of generating sexual passion. But where was she and who was she?

I knew that what I was doing was taboo. The stealth with which I reviewed these short pieces confirmed it. Yet, I was doing nothing more or less than any teacher would do in an American English class.

The papers, which were no longer than a page, amazed me. These female students had invited me into places in their minds that probably few people knew about. Although I did not know the authors' identities, I marked their first assignments with encouraging comments in the margins, and keenly anticipated the next class. I felt that I could finally make a difference in Tunisia, if only with this small cadre of smart, educated women.

14
SCHOOL SCANDAL

The following Monday, I went to the boardroom for my fourth class, expecting the students to be eagerly waiting for their essays to be returned to them with my comments.

The room was vacant. I shrugged off my initial disappointment. It was early. The novelty had faded. At the class starting time, I remained alone, speculating about why the students were late. Some, I surmised, might have dropped out. Others were ill. Or they were testing me. I practiced nonchalance. A half hour passed and still no one appeared. Had the room been

changed without telling me? I tried to be blasé even though I felt is
if ten women had stood me up. I heard footsteps. Mabrouk walked
in.

"The women's class has been canceled," he reported.

I asked why.

He looked at me with regret. It was not clear whether he was
responding to the cancellation, my role in it, or my inability to
understand why it took place.

"There were problems."

"What problems?"

"Reports," he said. When I asked for specifics, he replied, "I
warned that there were risks, that you should be careful. *Shweah
b'shweah,* we agreed. I explained that when a man and woman are
in a room, the devil is present. You didn't listen."

"But there were ten women! Nothing improper took place."

"That's not the information I have."

"What did I do?"

"Having women write love notes to you. Was that smart?"

"They weren't love notes."

"Do you have them?"

His hand was outstretched. I thought about the writing
samples, in particular the last one. It was not a love letter, but it
was intimate, even erotic. They were all personal—and
incriminating. It would be inferred that I prompted them.

"I left them in Gafsa," I lied. "I was angry at myself. I thought
the students would be disappointed."

He regarded me with disbelief and grudging respect, as a
slippery veteran who saw potential in a protégé.

"Sir, there was nothing wrong with those essays. They were
short. I asked the students to write about something important to
them. I did not tell them what to write."

"You wanted to know them better. This is worse than I suspected."

"It's not what you think. I wasn't prying into their lives. I asked them to write about a subject they knew well."

"To learn their secrets. This is not a teacher's role. It is unseemly for an English class."

"But writing assignments are an important part of education in the United States. I'm American. This is how we teach English."

"And this, *jeune homme*, is how Tunisians respond to your American methods."

I was distraught. Without meaning to, I lost a class and was at the center of a scandal. No one mentioned it in my other classes, but the engineers seemed to know what happened. They looked at me and spoke to me differently, as if I were a deviant. Some of their wives might have been in the class, but it was useless to ask my male students what they knew; to raise the topic and state the facts would only stir the controversy.

At the *borj,* news of the women's class also took hold. I could hear the young engineers jabbering in falsetto, in what little English they knew. "Oh, *Professeur*, how much do I love you? Let me count...One, two, three."

It was not the ridicule of Elizabeth Barrett Browning's verse that bothered me. I could even abide their misrepresentation of my teaching methods and their mockery of the students' essays. What hurt most was their implication that I had sought the response they now derided.

Yes, I was foraging for love, like a jackal, exuding hunger in my prowling eyes. I had become addicted again during my passion binge with Cerise, and now I was that depraved social pariah—a love junkie in withdrawal.

15
CERISE SHAKEN

Dearest Love,

Please forgive my silence. I have had a rough week. In one of my senior classes, I led a spirited discussion that turned to sex. It all seemed like harmless fun. Anyway, it was useless to suppress it, since students need to let loose at times. They have been good all term and I have always felt that they respected my openness.

At any rate, the next day, I walked into the classroom to find scrawled on the blackboard: "Mlle. Sevigny, Commie Whore." It was like a kick in the gut. I trembled. It took all I had to fight back tears and not bolt from the room. The students were quiet. Some smiled. They were probably expecting me to break down.

I took a deep breath, smiled, joked about the handwriting and erased the board. Then I went on—unsteadily—with the lesson. But this small victory did not make me feel better. I had no one to talk to and even if I did, it wouldn't have helped since no one else has this problem. I blamed myself for being too lenient. Yet I felt that my students were like friends. I went home and broke down. I could not stop crying. It was impossible to get any work done. I admit that I lost faith.

How could I teach this class again? They must have lost respect for me and my nonchalant reaction would inspire them to new feats. To make matters worse, I did not know who wrote the message.

The next day after class, a shy girl gave me a note and left. It was an apology. She had been shocked by the mention of sex, but on reflection, realized that it was not my fault. Later, she came by my apartment with roses.

My God! What a reversal! My faith was restored. But I felt for a day as if I died. I wondered how I could earn my living if I gave up teaching. At my age!

Yesterday I went to Odille Grognon's new apartment, where she has moved in with her two children. She seemed composed, served delicious sandwiches and spoke optimistically about her future. She does not seem to miss Gaspard. To the contrary, she seems more radiant than I've ever seen her. She has no intention of going back to him. In a way, her leaving him was the first sound emotional reaction she has had since discovering her husband's sexual addiction. But how will she make ends meet with two small children on her small salary?

Marie is playing a vicious game with Odille. She tells her how much nicer she is since leaving Gaspard. She seems to take fiendish delight in making him suffer. While she plays the go-between, she tells Gaspard that his wife hated his lovemaking. What has gotten into her?

When I returned late, who was outside the building to greet me but poor Gaspard! He looks like he never sleeps. Marie claims he wakes up drunk and I believe her. He insisted on coming up and pumped me for information about Odille—how she lives, what she said. He is pathetic. He believes she will return to him and refuses to face reality.

People are breaking up around me. Others are miserable together. I wonder what would happen if we married. Do you think I could tolerate your infidelities and flirtations? Would we succeed in making each other unhappy?

All the same, I love you and all my thoughts are with you. Yet it goes to waste. We will have to make up for all of these wasted moments. At least I think so. Please take care of yourself.

Tenderly,

Cerise

16

TRAPPED

More than a month had passed and I was in a cage of solitude. I wore many masks—spoiled American brat, has-been pot courier, social interloper, teaching eunuch and educational whoremaster. I played so many roles that I was forgetting who I was.

To regain a sense of myself, I visited volunteers who lived in Beja and Kasserine, small towns in the *bled,* north of Gafsa. I slept on floors, listened to rock and swapped stories. It was vintage Peace Corps, but my peers had adjusted to their lives, so telling them about mine made me feel worse about my failure to adapt.

Being away for a few days a week, I thought, would cool the *borj* social temperature down to normal—mutual indifference—but the reverse happened. Every Monday morning when I returned, the atmosphere in the *borj* was more hostile; antipathy for me apparently fed on my absence. Trying to escape the situation only made it harder to deal with, so I stayed put on weekends.

When I returned from teaching one evening, Ali handed me a folded slip of paper. *"Professeur*, an American woman came to see you. She left this."

It was a note from Paula:

"Party Saturday. The Beauchamps. See you there!"

John and Paula were good to their word. They would not share their home, but were generous with their social life.

A French *coopérant* couple, living in a large villa down the road, was showing slides of their trip to Pakistan and Afghanistan. I felt confident about attending this *soirée,* because I had experience now in French slideshow parties, and knew what to expect and how to behave.

The Beauchamps' home was spacious and luxuriously decorated, with sumptuous carpets and massive wood furniture. They even had a fireplace. I marveled at how people could live so well in Gafsa and wondered how different my life would be if I were a French *coopérant*, making double a French salary at 1/3 the cost of living.

The slide show was more socially conscious than the norm: instead of beach scenes, the Beauchamps focused on people hanging out of bus windows, riding on bus roofs, and hitching to the backs of buses.

But the slides were a sideshow. The hostess was the toast of the party. Marianne Beauchamp was a sensual woman with a mop of curly red hair and a tattoo on her arm. She liked me and we lived close by, so I read her gracious attention as an invitation to see her privately.

Marianne never suggested that I come to her. She and her husband seemed to be on good terms. And while wooing wives when their husbands were at work violated my code, I rationalized that it was part of my education, like apartment hunting and grocery shopping, as well as a hallowed tradition, epitomized by rogue priests, traveling salesmen and crafty students. It required style and guile; in short, it was a life experience I should have.

Before 2 PM, when afternoon classes started in Tunisian schools, I skulked down the stony road and checked the Beauchamps' driveway for a parked car. If their wagon was gone, her husband had probably left for work. On my first try, the car was by the villa; he apparently had the afternoon off, so I aborted the visit. On the second try, the car was gone, but I lost my nerve and turned back. On the third try, after much self-reproach, I watched Mr. Beauchamp's car pull out, waited five minutes, and descended on the house.

When Marianne opened the door, she was surprised to see me. I needed to explain who I was and how I knew her. When I told her that I was stopping by to hang out and listen to music, which I could not do at the *borj*, she invited me in.

We chatted, but our small talk shrank to short statements and throat clearing. Marianne sat on an overstuffed chair across the room, with one curvaceous leg slung over the arm. She asked which record I wanted to hear. I asked for *Santana*, thinking *Black Magic Woman* would put her in the right mood.

Two minutes into the song, I wasn't sure if it was taking effect. Marianne returned to her chair and held her head in her hand and put her finger over her lip, as if she were struggling to recall where she put her colander.

I wished I had bought that book on body language at the airport newsstand in Rome so that I could decode her signals. Did a leg slung over a chair arm mean she wanted me? Did the hand bracing the side of her face indicate a toothache? Did her serious stare beckon me to leave—or make a move?

I approached the situation like a chess game, but I was one of the pieces and had to move myself. How could I go from sitting with my hands poised on the knobs of the chair arms to a standing position, then cross 12 feet between me and the sensuous treasure of her curled body? It seemed as complex as a lunar landing. Each step required logic and motivation. To start, I needed a pretext for standing up.

Stretching was a subtle, but suggestive way to show her my body, but it posed a logistical challenge. From standing, how would I cross the room in a natural way? Tripping and stumbling were options, yet doing this for 12 feet seemed unmotivated, unattractively clumsy or symptomatic of a neuro-motor disease.

Then I remembered the oldest line in the book.

I asked Marianne if she liked to dance. She said, "Yes." Did she want to dance right now? No, she had to hang the laundry to dry. Did she mind if I danced?

"Not at all," she said.

My plan was working. I stood up and started to dance with sinuous sensuality, intending to hypnotize and eroticize her, as I had seen peacocks do to peahens on a National Geographic TV special. Marianne watched me with what I believed to be a spark of interest in her eyes, until she abruptly stood up and vacated the room, leaving me to dance with myself to *"Oye come va!"*

I didn't know how to react, so I danced until the song was over. This delay gave me time to plot my next gambit. It occurred to me that if the laundry was interesting to Marianne, I should probably get involved in it. For one, a rooftop of clotheslines with hanging sheets would add suspense to the seduction. More importantly, I had read somewhere that women found nothing more appealing in a man than when he showed interest in what they were doing.

"Marianne, where are you?" I called out.

"On the roof."

I climbed a stairway through a trap door and crawled onto the flat roof, where Marianne was pinning connubial sheets and her spouse's bikini briefs to a clothesline. It was a cold, harsh place to be. A raw wind kicked up, but I inhaled deeply and gazed at the horizon of dust, sage and rocks as I had seen actors do in films when they tried to signify a meaningful moment.

"What a great view!" I declared.

"You must be joking," Marianne replied dryly. But I noticed a smile trembling on her lips and a chuckle she covered with a cough. "I'm winning her over despite herself," I thought.

"Well, it's interesting for me. When do I get a chance to hang laundry on a roof?"

"Yes, it's quite an experience!" she cracked. I was so pathetic that she couldn't help but like me, or so I hoped.

Marianne moved behind a row of linen. I watched her skin-tight silhouette walk, bend, turn, stretch with arms raised and breasts lifted as she pinned laundry to the line behind the opaque, flapping screen. She seemed to be doing a seductive shadow dance for my benefit.

We walked together, divided by a curtain of sheets and underwear. I confided to her my dreams, hopes and expectations. At some point during my oration I lost track of Marianne. I looked up and her shadow was no longer behind the sheets.

"Marianne, where are you?" I asked.

I realized that I was alone on the roof. I pulled on the door but it was locked. Now, without the anticipation of Marianne's embrace to make me hot, I realized how cold it was on that sunless day in the desert and I shivered violently. Any beast with a survival instinct lay under a rock or by a fire, but I wasn't that smart.

I heard a car engine and the crunch of tires on gravel, then silence and the click of a car door. I crouched by the storm drain and saw Marianne's husband emerge from his car. I was trapped! I never even kissed Marianne's full lips or copped a feel of her breasts. Yet, there I was, caught not in the couple's bed, but with their bedsheets. This was so unfair. But my situation went beyond considerations of fairness.

How would I explain to *Monsieur* Beauchamp why I was on his roof? Should I say I was doing his and Marianne's laundry to repay them for their slide show of Pakistan? Even an egomaniac would find that hard to believe. The smarter move was to flee unseen. I wondered what Colombi would do. He would look for a rope to rappel down the side of the house. I had no rope, *alors*—but plenty of sheets! I tied three of them end-to-end and fastened one to a hook that appeared to have no other design purpose than to abet my escape.

I stared over the edge until my jaw ached from cold and my tears froze. I dropped the sheets and let myself down. Between the two floors of the house, a knot slipped and I freefell to the ground. When I scrambled to my feet, Marianne's husband glanced out the window and saw me. I didn't know what else to do, so I waved like a friendly neighbor, walked away and did not look back. I would let Marianne explain the sheets dangling from the roof.

17

COMMUNICATION TABOO

Having failed as a love-in-the-afternoon backdoor man, I spent my days working on the dictionary of two-part verb idioms that would be my legacy to the phosphate company. I sipped the strong, thick tea that Nouri, the young caretaker, brewed for me, while I translated and wrote synonyms for "Look out, look into, look over..."

During quiet afternoons, I had the *borj* to myself. When I took breaks, Tlili, the head caretaker, recounted growing up in Gafsa. Tlili was a small, wiry man with a thin, expressive face and large eyes. He was highly animated. His huge smile had an array of inflections. It conveyed light mirth, mordant irony and black humor, and gave variety to his words, which were few in number and delivered in a deep, sonorous voice. Tlili was honest and compassionate. Of all the Tunisians I met in Gafsa, he was the only one who seemed to like me.

One evening, Nouri sprang toward me in the hallway as soon as I came in. He seemed to have been waiting for a while and needed to see me in secret, out of sight of the Tunisian engineers.

"*Professeur*," he said, "I have something for you. *T-fath'l.*"

He handed me a small, red envelope. I went into my room and opened it. It contained a red card with a delicate ink drawing of a man holding a languid woman in his arms. The inscription read, "I want to know you better."

Inside the card was a printed message:

I was thinking of you. I had to leave your class, Professeur. I was afraid. I am sorry. I am writing because I wanted you to know that I miss you and your class. You are a very interesting person, I think. And very funny, too. I think you are a fine teacher, or you will be. It must be lonely for you. I am sad for you, but I don't want you to be sad. I know it makes no sense. Please don't be sad, Professeur. May I call you by your name? Yes. Rick. This is how I will remember you.

Your friend

Under the message appeared the start of a signature, one plume rising to a curve before abruptly ending. The sender had almost revealed her identity before losing her nerve. There was an imprint along the bottom of the card, with the name and address of a posh card shop in Tunis.

But there was more. I noticed in the envelope a thick square of paper folded many times. Unfolded, it read in French.

"There are two tragic thoughts in life. One belongs to youth: 'This time will never be again.' The second perception comes with age. 'I must one day die.' I believe that if we can hear the first voice, we will never fear the second. What do you think, Rick?"

For days, I was acutely agitated.

I had tried to assemble the pieces of my existence into a whole, to achieve balance, clarity, *realism*, when this card split my life again into two irreconcilable realms—the world I yearned for, where intense feelings and bold acts ruled and desire and romance were the norm; and the one I occupied, where not much occurred but the struggle to survive.

The romance and mystery of the card and note mocked my attempt to live realistically. It intimated a dimension of life beyond my everyday experience that I imagined but could not reach. Without it, I knew I was wasting time by failing to be fully alive.

Then, one Friday afternoon, after returning from the Gafsa market, I found a small envelope on the bed. Its placement aroused my libido and suspicion. It suggested that Tlili and Nouri guessed its contents and knew about this embryonic development in my private life.

"My dear. I know this is crazy. But the idea that I will never see you again is unbearable. I am suffocating. It is no accident that we met. It is fate. I believe that everything that happens, everyone we meet, is for a reason. We have important things to say to one another. I felt this when I was in your class.

Please, meet me. Friday night, 8 o'clock, at the old fortress. Don't disappoint me. This moment will never be again."

From the *borj*, I gazed at the old fortress. It was a solitary colossus in the middle of the desert, like a brown sugar cube on a dusty plate. To get there, I would need to cross the dry *oeud* and a mile of empty plain.

Why had my secret pen pal picked this exposed, yet isolated spot to tryst? When I once asked the *borj* brothers what the forlorn citadel was used for, they said with straight faces that it was a whorehouse and laughed at my astonishment—but they never retracted the answer. They may have expected me to take them seriously and visit it.

The note was postmarked Wednesday. The writer must have known that I would receive it at the last moment and have just enough time to react. At 7:00, I set out on the road to town. When pedestrians passed, I stared at the dusty road with exaggerated interest, to avoid eye contact and look inconspicuous. Instead, I attracted attention by appearing disoriented. One passerby asked if I had lost something.

"No, no," I muttered. "Only my mind."

Another man offered assistance. This time, I thought I should not say that I lost my mind, or he might take me literally and call the police. I told the helpful citizen that I was studying rocks. These rocks were very interesting...Yes, prehistoric...Gafsa was interesting, no?

The good man stared at the same spot I was perusing but did not see what I pretended to see. He nodded, wished me a good evening and hurried on his way.

At twilight, after several furtive glances to be sure no interlopers or rescuers were nearby, I descended into the dry rift, climbed up the other side and strode across the open plain. When I was in junior high school, I often went out secretly at night, believing that darkness hid my mischief from view. Here I knew that no manner of locomotion—crouching, skulking or hurrying on all fours—concealed my mission. The fortress was the most visible, least obstructed, landmark in the vicinity. I might go there unseen only because the archaic structure had an aura of taboo, from which most people turned their eyes. I swaggered toward it, feeling naked but oblivious.

When I reached the forsaken citadel I found that there was a dry moat, eight feet deep running along two sides. I walked up to the great wooden doors and imagined how 50 years before, these doors had opened and French foreign legionnaires on foot and horseback stormed out to battle truculent Bedouins. I tried opening the doors but they were immovable.

I walked around the fortress. *My Lady of the Cards* was not to be seen. Maybe she was hiding until she received a sign of my presence. I searched the ground for a clue that she was there—an amulet or handkerchief, even a tissue would have sufficed. I wanted to call out her name, but she never gave me one.

Anxieties multiplied. I sorted through the typical reasons for a cancelled assignation: it was a joke; she stood me up; a last-second obligation or crisis prevented her from coming. Perhaps at that moment, her jealous husband was interrogating her—or worse.

After exhausting every reason for her not to be there, I wondered if I had misread the time or come to the wrong fortress. In college I once waited all night for a date at the wrong party. Was this a Tunisian sequel to that fruitless night? On the other hand, how many old forts were there in Gafsa? If more than one existed, Gafsa had more bastions per capita than anywhere in the world, though the chamber of commerce would probably avoid this claim in its tourism materials.

Out of the silence, I suddenly heard footsteps. For a second, I was joyful and relieved that I had not come to this forsaken place in vain. But I was divided between caution and anticipation: should I walk toward the footsteps or hide for a better look? I moved toward the voices, keeping close to the fortress wall.

The footsteps were closer now, heavy and crunching. Unless my amorous correspondent was a large woman, these footsteps belonged to a man. I noticed a tubular light and heard men's voices. In a moment, the light was in my eyes.

"*Shoof!* What are you doing there?"

I protected my eyes from the light and thought quickly.

"I am looking for bones," I replied irritably to cover the quaver in my voice. "Prehistoric bones. I am a Peace Corps anthropologist. My project is to find remains of *Gafsa Man.*"

"But it's dark. How can you see a thing?"

"Uh, yes, of course. Phosphorescence. Rocks glow in the dark," I paused. "See?" I held up a rock for a few seconds, before quickly tossing it. "Of course, they can only be seen at night."

The men sounded like police. Why were they here? Did the passersby who tried to help me on the road watch me trek into the barren flat and report my odd behavior to the authorities?

"You must go now. No one can come here after dark."

"Please, sir, this is important."

"It must wait. Now go!"

I walked up the side of the ravine and approached the men. Close up, they did not look like police. They wore street clothes and were unshaven.

"Were you stealing?" one man asked.

"Or visiting the bordello?" his sidekick interjected.

"I'll bet that's what he was doing," the first man replied.

"No, I was studying rocks," I insisted.

"So you like rocks," said the first.

He lunged and gave me a push. I tumbled back into the dry moat. The men chortled and shouted profanities in Arabic. Aided by a flashlight, they threw stones at me. One hit my shoulder, another my leg. Other stones skittered and smacked the dirt around my feet. I had to get out of the pit or they could kill me by one of the oldest means of execution.

I raced to the other end of the ravine, filled my hands with stones, and scrambled up the side of the gulch, crouching to make a small target. With their flashlights trained on me, my assailants pelted me at close range. When I reached the crest of the embankment, I sprang from my crouch, brought back my arm like a pitcher and heaved one handful of stones as hard as I could.

The assailants shouted and recoiled from the counterattack, pausing their fire. I bolted. They pursued. When a sharp rock hit me in the back and I felt them close behind, I pivoted, planted my feet and hurled the stones in my other hand. By throwing several rocks at once, I improved my odds of hitting the targets.

My second pitch stopped their pursuit. I heard them cry out in pain. The rearguard action gave me enough time and space to retreat into the darkness. I sprinted to the other side of the fortress and across the desert plain toward the *oeud*.

My escape looked certain until I heard a loud engine. Two white stripes of light covered the ground in front of me. My attackers had driven to the fort and were pursuing me on wheels. The bright circles of their high beams put a target on my back.

I turned my head. Their wreck was 50 feet away. It sounded tired and abused, and its tires skidded in the dust, but it was faster than I was. They had not stoned me to death, so they meant to run me over.

I ran faster, but my pursuers closed ground. As I turned, the car was just behind me. I dove sideways and rolled out of its path. The car went straight, spewing smoke and spitting up dirt, its brakes screeching as the driver tried to change direction and finish me off.

A man on foot could not outrun a man on wheels but he could outmaneuver him. I ran now in zigzags and erratic circles. The car followed my crooked trail, but when the driver accelerated, he could not handle the sharp curves I made. The car skidded and spun out of control. By the time my pursuer adjusted to this maneuver and picked up speed, I had reached the *oeud* and was out of danger.

18

FALSELY DIAGNOSED AND ACCUSED

The cuts and contusions I received were minor, but my consternation over what had taken place lingered. Was my pen pal a real woman exposed, detained and replaced at our tryst by her male relatives? Did I randomly stumble on Tunisian thugs at their rendezvous point, or did anonymous enemies conspire to lure me to the citadel with bogus love notes in order to kill me? If it was a set up, who was behind it: Kouki, the husbands, sons and brothers of my women students—or someone else?

For a time, I was obsessed with finding the truth about this incident. But a crime that almost happened, perpetrated by almost anyone, was beyond investigation and prosecution, so I decided not to pursue it.

Escape from the routine and my deepening malaise came out of medical necessity: bronchitis and black, itching dots on my groin. I took the slow bus to Tunis that Friday to see the Peace Corps doctor on Saturday, but when I arrived, I was told she would not see patients until Tuesday. I lingered in Tunis until then, coughing, scratching and dashing around the capital in sunglasses and a *kefia,* a towel wrapped around my head Bedouin style. It was my way of saying, "The desert made me do it."

The doctor was a prim English woman with no patience for nonsense. She asked me to pull down my pants as she snapped on plastic gloves, slipped a mask over her mouth and nose, and goggles on her eyes. I tried to match her clinical approach with nonchalance. I told myself that as a doctor, she must have seen millions of male genitalia.

Yet, I could not expel from memory the last woman who inspected my testicles in an official capacity. Mrs. Slocum, the county nurse, determined whether a seventh grade boy was mature enough to play sports. When she fingered my testes, I had an erection. Mrs. Slocum slapped my face to indicate she didn't share my feelings.

Lifting my scrotum now with sheathed fingers, the English doctor peered at the black dots with stiff formality.

"Blackheads," she declared.

With my pants and shorts roped pathetically around my knees and my gonads shriveled in her cold hands, my shame became indignation.

"I haven't had blackheads on my face for five years and you're telling me they're on my crotch! I want a second opinion."

She shrugged. "I don't know what else to call them."

"Crabs, lice, fleas, a mysterious sexual disease. Call it anything, but not blackheads!" I exclaimed.

The prim physician was nonplussed. It made no difference to her whether the dots were lice or zits. In her view, the latter was a less serious diagnosis. She did not perceive dignity in disease, or that a sick man could bear his illness but not its belittlement.

The doctor took a second look and agreed that crabs made more sense. She prescribed the *Kwell* cream in my first aid kit.

I returned to Gafsa the next day by company car but that afternoon and evening and for the rest of the week my drivers did not come by the *borj* to take me to my scheduled classes. I questioned this hiatus, but since I had no phone access to Metloui I waited in the *borj* and completed my burgeoning dictionary of two-part verb idioms.

The next Monday, the driver showed up grinning with a note from Mabrouk. The note requested my immediate presence in Metloui. All signs pointed to catastrophe as Mabrouk handed me a certified letter from the Peace Corps office in Tunis. It was from Irving P. Irving.

Dr. Mamooni informed me that the phosphate company has reported you absent for five school days. He has therefore requested that I recall you from your job. Additionally, I think it's time we talked about a number of issues that bear directly on your future with the Peace Corps. I want to talk to you about your unsatisfactory performance in Metloui as well as your previous experience in Menzel Bourguiba, your history with this office, as well as the general attitude you've exhibited since coming here.

As you'll certainly not be returning to Metloui, I advise that you bring your personal belongings with you. I expect to see you in my office as soon after you receive this letter as possible.

    Irving P. Irving

Now I understood why there had been no driver or classes the previous week. Mabrouk pretended not to know that I was in Tunis on a medical matter through Tuesday and purposely did not send a driver for the remainder of the week, so that I would appear to be negligent. Mabrouk smirked at my shocked reaction to the letter. He seemed completely satisfied.

"This is wrong. I've been in Gafsa since Wednesday. I took the company car. I have witnesses," I said.

"Your name wasn't on the list," Mabrouk replied.

"It must have been on a list, or the driver wouldn't have let me in the car. It's company policy."

I described every person on that trip, including the driver with the red *chechia*. Mabrouk summoned him. The driver identified me as a passenger that day. Mabrouk asked him why my name wasn't on the list. The driver insisted it was. Mabrouk realized that he had consulted the wrong list. After pounding his fist and vituperating against corporate incompetence, Mabrouk phoned the Peace Corps and put me on the line with Irving P. Irving.

"Murkey, the games are over," Irving barked. "Pack your bags. I want you here in 48 hours."

"There's been a misunderstanding," I told the Peace Corps Director and passed the receiver to Mabrouk, who explained the situation to Irving in French, then returned the phone to me so that I could translate into English what he said. When the situation became clear, Irving did not apologize.

"I want you in my office Thursday at four!"

"Am I reinstated?"

"We'll discuss it."

"Sir, you blamed me without getting the facts and without hearing my side. With all due respect, you made a mistake!"

"I said we'd discuss it. Four sharp, Thursday."

19

THE HOT SEAT

Irving P. Irving sat stiffly at his desk reading a document when I appeared at his office. He glared at me, returned to his reading and signed a paper with exaggerated finality before barking my name and nodding for me to sit. He put his finger over his mouth, as if going over his lines for the last time before he launched into his remarks.

"First it was a fag tank-top. Now I hear that you're wearing

430

French jeans and an Arab headdress. Are you completely insane, Murkey?"

For this meeting, I was conservatively dressed in a work-shirt and loose-fitting denims, in order not to arouse Irving P. Irving's "inner terminator." But I had worn the Arab *kefia* into Tunis on a few occasions, as a fashion statement. He must have received reports about it and now I had to answer for it.

"Sir, I know I've been criticized for taking cross-cultural exercises to an extreme," I said. "But it's also true that turbans and French jeans are more acceptable to Tunisian tastes than American work shirts and baggy pants. I've gone beyond cross-cultural for its own sake. Now I know *what* my hosts do and *why* they do it. I wear a turban because in the desert, the winds can be strong and you need protection from the dust and sand. The *kefia* is also a good way to keep your head warm."

The Director studied me without moving a facial muscle. "So you didn't do enough dress up as a child and now you're doing it on Uncle Sam's dime."

I considered my response carefully.

"You may be right, sir, that certain childhood circumstances predisposed me to wear native clothes, but Tunisian culture and the desert appeal to me. I hope there's nothing wrong with that."

The Director exhaled heavily through the nose.

"Murkey, your conduct has been less than appropriate. Your effort has been subpar." Irving coughed into his fist and tilted his head to view me with one stern eye.

"There have been serious allegations," he said.

"Sir?" I had believed when I entered his office that I was secure from termination because of the company car mix-up, but now the director had fresh allegations against me and since I was unaware of having committed new infractions, I was concerned.

"You were seen stealing pillows from the storage bin..."

"Pillows?" I stammered. "This must be another mistake."

Irving set his laser gaze on me.

"Sadok's been with the P.C. for 31 years. He's a reliable watchman and he says he saw a man fitting your description steal two pillows from the storage bin. A Peace Corps audit has confirmed the loss of two pillows. You did it, didn't you?"

Irving coaxed my confession, not with righteous wrath, but with the quiet confidence of a man who holds a swatter over an injured fly. I had borrowed a pillow from the Peace Corps office during my recent medical weekend, because I slept in a bathtub for two nights, only to replace it when I found better accommodations. The watchman's account had another flaw. Two pillows were reported missing though I borrowed one. The thief remained at large, but Irving would not believe it. If he kept an inventory of cheap pillows in the office basement, he surely meant to terminate me regardless of how trivial the charge.

"Sir, what was the date of Sadok's report?"

Irving fidgeted with his notes. "February 23."

I remembered that day. It was entered in my notebook and emblazoned in my brain.

It was a Saturday night. I was dining alone at the *Bayech*, doing my best to finish a bottle of good Tunisian wine, when a party of three French couples invited me to their table. I joined them with my half-bottle, a gesture they appreciated.

Wine was poured. Spirits soared. When the restaurant closed at 11, *Monsieur* Yves Renaud, a French engineer with a gray goatee, and his stunning wife, Chantal, invited the party to their villa in the fashionable French quarter in the heights above Gafsa. While Renaud entertained us with tales of his mistreatment at the hands of his Tunisian colleagues, Chantal circulated among us, serving cognac and cakes. While playing the attentive hostess, she did not miss an opportunity to bend over with her *derrière* in my direction. And what splendid gluteals they were, perfect spheres snugly contained in her designer jeans. When *Madame* Renaud was not flagellating my manhood with her posterior, she served *hors d'oeuvres* with a deep, graceful bow that displayed her pendulous breasts under a white sweater.

All of the above brought deep color to my face, of which her husband never suspected the cause. I disguised it by nodding eagerly at every point he made, while barely understanding a word he said. Yet, I imagined that other guests fixated on the squirming rodent trapped in my pants.

Eventually, *Madame* Renaud ceased to bewitch my twitching member. Yet I was addicted to her titillation and could not resist stealing glances at her, hoping for fresh helpings. When they didn't come, it didn't matter—I saw traces of her skin and inhaled her scent for hours of cocktease aftershock.

When Engineer Renaud drove me to the *borj*, I tried memorizing the street names and the number and direction of turns, in order to wend my way back to his home in daylight and have a private audience with his wife.

The next afternoon, I hiked into a neighborhood above downtown Gafsa, attempting like a lost pet to track the scent back to *Madame* Renaud. As I crisscrossed the quiet, affluent enclave of French villas to reconstruct the route to her house, I passed several Tunisian *fellaheen* on the street. They walked so slowly that it seemed that they would not arrive anywhere, no matter how close they came. It disturbed me that on the surface, I seemed no different from these idle men. I told myself I had a purpose, but the search for *Madame* Renaud's El Dorado buttocks did not rank as a world-class expedition.

I gave up my quest and headed home, lamenting my pitiful behavior and wondering why *Madame* Renaud led me on so cruelly. I reflected that her provocative movements comprised an intimate dance she performed for me. She displayed her body as barter–by arousing me, she aroused herself. Meanwhile, she made me hate my virility and turned my desire into a joke.

As I contemplated the meaning of my encounter with Chantal Renaud, Irving P. Irving, a proficient reader of distress in the human face, having caused more than his share, interpreted my troubled countenance as a sign of guilt in the pillow caper. It was true, I contemplated pillows, but not the foam-filled kind. Yet, like a hungry omnivore, the Peace Corps Director could not resist feasting on my weakness and distraction. With hunched shoulders, he leaned in and attacked.

"You took the pillows, right, Murkey?" he asked in a hypnotic tone, staring into my eyes with the hint of a paternal smile.

My trance broke as he trespassed upon it.

"Sir, I could not have stolen those pillows if I wanted to."

"*And why not?*" he asked. His jaw clenched, his eyes narrowed tightly. "Murkey, this had better be good. You've already wasted more of my time than I can justify."

"But you called me in, sir—"

His fist gaveled the desk.

"Shut up! See this?"

He drew his thumb and forefinger together.

"What am I looking at, sir?"

"The distance between my thumb and finger."

"I can't see it, sir. Can you try another angle?"

"You don't see the distance, because there isn't any! That's what separates you from termination. Now take responsibility for the pillows and I might consider keeping you on. No promises. No guarantees. But there's a chance."

I swallowed hard at my options: incriminate myself and stay in Tunisia; profess my innocence and risk deportation. I was innocent. I had to tell Irving why.

"Sir, I couldn't steal those pillows because I couldn't be in two places at the same time. The evening of the 24th, something was stolen." I bowed my head. "But it wasn't a pillow. It was my dignity—*again*! That evening I was in Gafsa, being teased by a woman who was an expert in the art. And it wasn't the first time. Since coming to Tunisia, I've been teased repeatedly."

Irving thought he had pushed me to breaking point, when a suspect's defenses crack and he sees his prosecutor as a redeemer for whose acceptance he will confess to anything.

"Get a hold of yourself!" The Director urged gently. "What is it? Come clean. You'll feel better."

I told him about my evening with Chantal Renaud and her penchant for bending and doing the tail-shaking mating dance. I glanced at Irving to gauge his response. He looked at me with anger and dissatisfaction.

I had to do better. I told Irving my own *201 Tunisian Nights*, tales of sexual failure and ineptitude. I described Marianne Beauchamp on the roof, the mugging at the fortress, Georgia invading my bed, and Dorothy. *Dorothy*? Yes, even Dorothy, a seductive sophomore my freshman year, popped into the monologue. Once, while I rushed to complete a paper, Dorothy came to my room, naked under a fur coat, and draped her sexy body all over my typewriter. Halfway through the anecdote about Dorothy, I realized that I borrowed it from Fargus.

As I filibustered about years of excitement and abuse, Irving's gaping mouth and bulging eyes signified that he was in my power. He resented wasting his time, but could not resist. Like car wrecks and naked people, few objects are as compelling as a tortured sex life. When I stopped, Irving looked drained. His voice emerged from across the desk. "Want a Coke?"

He handed me an old-fashioned bottle from a crate in the corner. Parched from my *tour de farce*, I cocked back the bottle in a vintage American pose and guzzled the soft drink with a lusty thirst. After pulling the bottle from my lips, I made the universal sound effect of refreshment, "Ahhhhhhh" and slumped in my chair.

Irving framed his face with the right angle of his fingers, like a psychiatrist. He anticipated a pay-off to my story—how years of sexual frustration led me to steal cheap pillows for the purpose of sexually penetrating them.

"So, what do you think, sir?"

"*I think!*" Irving growled indignantly. "I *think*, Murkey, that's the most pathetic life story I've ever heard."

"Thank you, sir, I mean, for putting it at the top."

"It's nothing to be proud of," he snarled. "Murkey, when you first came into this office I had you pegged as the usual self-centered, immature loser we occasionally attract. But I was clearly wrong. You're much less than that."

"Thank you, sir."

"—You're a sick, selfish, perverted sociopath. And I have one question for you. How do you live with yourself?"

"I practice a lot."

If Irving based his case for terminating me on circumstantial evidence, the main circumstance being my personality, I had to remind him of due process.

"Sir, if you need to confirm my whereabouts on the 24th, I can give you my witnesses—Yves and Chantal Renaud."

"That won't be necessary," he replied, as he closed his eyes and massaged his temples. "I see no reason to terminate you. You can serve until the end of the year."

"That's great! Thank you, sir!" I sprang from the chair and raised my arms in a victory sign, then reached to shake the director's hand. Irving ordered me to sit until he finished.

"At the end of the year we'll review your record and decide if you can continue for a second one. Dr. Mamooni won't rehire you. We would need to find another position for you in a high school."

"Sir, don't go through any trouble on my account. I'm not sure I want to stay another year."

Irving P. Irving was stunned. He expected me to grovel for another chance, to learn the myriad ways I could become a model Peace Corps volunteer, how many droopy-crotched pants I needed to wear, how many Tunisian boys I should be seen walking with.

The joy of not being terminated was soon replaced by the anticipation of several more months in Tunisia. I recognized that I had gained a draw, not a victory.

20

FRENCH GIRLS & SPANISH FLY

With an hour to kill before the last car to Gafsa, I basked on the terrace of Le Café de France, across from the towering, blue ice-cube known as the Hotel d'Afrique and admired a group of exquisite French girls in white blouses, dark sweaters and tight jeans as they chatted and burst into peals of laughter.

There were only five or six years between us but I felt much older, as if I knew more than they did and was ruined by what I knew. These teenagers reminded me of a Maxim LeForestier song, in which a man stares out his window at the same time every afternoon and watches a girl walking home from school. In each verse, he describes her in a different situation and with a new physical detail. By the end of the song, the singer admits that he has fallen in love with an entire girls' school.

In high school, I had classmates who dated older men, but now that I was an older man, going out with high school girls seemed degenerate. At any rate, I didn't want to date them; I just wanted their *joie de vivre*.

The French girls must have changed my mood by osmosis, because I returned to Gafsa buoyant and excited. Gafsa was no longer a prison, but a prize, fought for and won. Every moment would be a gift, reclaimed from premature termination. The pastel city sprawled among desert hills and an oasis of lush palms, dappled by sunlight, now seemed a place of spectacular beauty.

Even the *borj* felt like home. "*Labess, Professeur!*" Nouri yelled as he poured a cup of thick, sweet tea and put it on the table. Tlili nodded significantly with his toothy, Jolly Roger smile. Everyone apparently knew about my ordeal and sensed my victory. It amazed me that the same old shit could seem so fresh and new.

Living here for another few months would be easy, I thought, even fun. I went to my room and found a letter on the bed. I knew it was from Cerise. How great life was being to me. All of my needs were cared for. I lay down and opened the letter.

•

My Dear Love,

How are you? I was alarmed to read about your pubic lice. Isn't that a disease contracted from prostitutes? How can you be so careless and stupid and so frank about it? Do you think your sordid habits and their impact on your health endear you to me?

Anyway, I love you. If you tell me you were infected by

infested bed sheets, I believe you, since the standards of cleanliness in Tunisia must be extremely low and your status equally low, so that no one washes your linens. You have a knack for being mistreated; have you considered why?

Since my last letter, things have been quiet, but busy. After believing my world caved in, I am grateful for the grind of teaching, studying and taking classes at the Faculté des Lettres on Wednesdays. I learned my lesson. I am now circumspect about what I say and how I say it to hormone-besotted teenagers.

This reminds me of an idea I had on my way home. To what extent are our thoughts, feelings, actions, desires and personalities just the words we give for chemicals flowing through us? What are these precious faces and bodies we slave over but vessels, arbitrarily formed, that contain our chemistry?

Whooo! Reading Emerson has had a strange effect on me, the opposite of what he would have intended! Yet I am being transcendental in a way, n'est-ce pas?

I went out with colleagues for a movie and pizza last Friday. It was such fun, talking and laughing, engaging in the very sort of BS that college students love and at which you excel. I wished you were here, but you were scratching your pubic hair in Tunisia.

One day we will laugh. That is some consolation. And please, if you insist on reveling in a decadent life, take precautions.

Love,

Cerise

What a nice letter, I thought. It was upbeat, cheerful and accepting, even whimsical. But behind the first letter was a second one, on folded notepaper.

Dear Raoul,

Thank you for your note. Yes, I had a very good time as well. To be honest, I feel a little awkward. I don't like to be in that position. What happened last week should not have happened. Of course, it was unplanned and I don't hold you responsible. It's no more your fault than mine. Let's blame it on the Sangria. Don't worry. It's all right. Of course, we can talk in the teacher's lounge. Don't be silly. We're adults, after all.

Affectionately, your colleague,

Cerise

•

Blame *what* on the Sangria, I wondered. *What* position didn't she like to be in? Was this the Spanish teacher referenced in previous letters, who praised her smile, laughed with her at 10 AM and had a Coke with her at 5?

When had Cerise shown an interest in Spanish—the tongue or any other body part? Just when I thought I knew her and felt secure about one aspect of my life, along came Raoul.

My letter and his note must have come at the same time. In responding to both, she sent them out together.

This was not our usual airmail quarrel, in which she wrote a hurtful thing and I responded emotionally. Here I saw the workings of her mind and reconstructed a betrayal.

Intimacy was supposed to be our special place that no one else knew about or visited, but this note suggested that Cerise shared herself with others and that our pristine wilderness was an old neighborhood in her expanding world.

Repeatedly I asked myself why she had an affair. Was she matching my pubic lice with Spanish fly?

I ambled around Gafsa to ponder these mysteries, divert

energy from my jealousy and induce exhaustion. It didn't work.

Finally, I had an insight. Cerise planted the note to make me jealous. She only needed to imply that she had sex with a Spanish teacher to achieve this effect.

Raoul was no Spanish fly, but a red herring.

I re-read her letter to test my theory and paid close attention to Cerise's unlikely insight that humans were body casts full of chemicals. Such an idea fell into her category of BS—abstract, speculative notions with no practical value.

The only reason for Cerise to formulate such a theory was that she had violated her character in a way that her usual thinking could not excuse or explain; hence, she resorted to chemistry.

Her excited phrasing suggested how happy this concept made her. Yet something was amiss. Cerise could read minds like musical scores and play them like a virtuoso. Her genius was not theory but human chemistry, itself. This was not her idea.

"We are chemistry!" Raoul must have whispered in her ear as he kissed her neck and put his hand between her legs. *"Non, non! Arrête, Non, je vous prie,"* Cerise moaned as she made her neck accessible to his hungry lips. She pulled his head back by the hairs, arousing him like a *toreador d'amour.* "We are chemistry!" Raoul growled. *"Mais oui!"* Cerise cried. "Fill my beaker!" Afterward she showered and believed the beaker was clean and ready for the next experiment. *Mais oui!*

Cerise's affair had mushroomed in my mind from an inebriated violation of trust into a conspiracy with a propaganda machine to sanitize the deed. The "chemical theory" exonerated her by making sex seem abstract and impersonal. It gave me more to think about than two sweaty bodies in libidinous embrace. How could I be jealous of molecules?

But I was. And it was particularly painful that Cerise believed

I was naïve enough to think that when she and Raoul had intercourse, only chemicals were involved.

Still, even the whip hand of jealousy gets tired. I decided that Cerise's letter was no low blow to our relationship, but an ambiguous scenario about which I could only speculate. I suspected my suspicions and devised alternative interpretations to preserve our unity. Maybe the chemicals Cerise referred to were alcoholic spirits. They drank too much Sangria and kissed before saying good night. Or they tried to have sex and couldn't. Or did it once and badly.

For once, I did not write Cerise immediately, but let my anger cool before responding.

21

THE MAGIC TRICK

Dear Cerise,

Today I had a close call. The Peace Corps Director wanted to dismiss me but I didn't give him a good enough reason. I can stay at least until the end of the term, when I hope to see you again.

It felt great to get back to Gafsa. It seems strange, but nothing gives a thing more value than almost losing it. I am also closer to you here than I would be in the States.

I know you never wanted me to come here. You think I've wasted a year. You also think I chase women and cavort with prostitutes, though candidly, I wouldn't know where to find one.

The truth is that I came to this arid and isolated place to prove myself worthy of you. You laugh. But wait.

Nothing defines character more than loneliness in a hostile place. I have to be self-reliant. I am also clearer than ever about what I want.

442

Your chemical theory of human personality surprised me. We've switched roles. You used to mock me for claiming that sex was an urge like eating, sleeping or shitting. I thought simplifying sex would convince women to go to bed with me, but this approach rarely worked because minds work ironically. Generalizing something emphasizes its individuality and trivializing it makes it larger.

Now you're simplifying behavior with a universal truth. Yes, chemicals can affect our thoughts and actions, but what about free will?

It's an intriguing theory, so in your next letter, please include a picture of a molecule, so I can see you in your naked splendor.

Rick

PS. I found this note with the last letter. You must have misplaced it.

I sent my letter with Raoul's note and waited. A week later, I received Cerise's response. It was a letter, not an aerogram, and I was hesitant to open the onionskin envelope. It seemed to come with an indelible stamped warning: "Hazardous contents."

Dear Rick,

I was glad to learn that you escaped your latest scrape unscathed. You have had many close calls and are developing a talent for them. But remember that getting in and out of trouble is a dangerous game. I only hope your luck doesn't run out. Yes, you need luck to be a rogue. Don't be deceived that you can rely on your nerve and gift of gab forever.

It also struck me that your year in a hostile foreign country has taught you at least one thing: diplomacy. You know how to avoid saying what you mean while saying it anyway.

For instance, do you really think I don't know that you read the note to Raoul and drew jealous conclusions from it?

But I give you credit. You are too shrewd to openly criticize me for infidelity, given your own indiscretions. You know that you have no right to judge my morality. Yet despite your tact, every word you write is full of hypocritical judgments.

I had to laugh at your request for a picture of my molecules. You seem shocked at my musings. After all, you are the self-proclaimed thinker of this couple, so why should I expect you to give me credit for an original idea?

Your big ego is dangerous—to you.

Your claim that you came to Tunisia to be worthy of me, as if your dismal situation were a trial by ordeal, is the pièce de résistance. Are you sane?

Face it, Rick: you went to Tunisia not to be with me, but because you didn't know what else to do. You are lost. It's sad that such a good education gave you no sense of purpose or direction. I wish I could help, but I can't.

Thank you for sending my parents the dates. Of course, they came in a filthy parcel and civilized people don't eat dates in warm weather. Still, the thought was appreciated.

Love, (Yes, believe it or not)

Cerise

Inside that letter was a smaller one, like the one to Raoul. Cerise was clever in matching form with content, and at bringing a theme to its conclusion.

PS. I want to believe that discretion prevented you from asking me about the note to Raoul. But something tells me it was probably just a lack of guts. Unfortunately, you are still so dependent on me, or should I say, on the commitment you believe I have for you, that you cannot bring yourself to question it.

However, I will give you the benefit of the doubt and relieve your probable misery. It is not what you think. Raoul is a colleague and, yes, I am fond of him. He has character, a sense of humor about himself and genuine feeling for other people. He is cheerful, optimistic and uncomplaining. It is remarkable.

Raoul has been strengthened by the obstacles he must overcome. He is bound to a wheelchair, but this does not reduce his stature.

A few weeks ago we all went to a movie and had pizza at the place we used to go. Afterward, I pushed his wheelchair and he held my hand and kissed it. This was the reason for his remorse.

So smile and sleep well tonight. Your Cerise is still faithful to you.

Cerise claimed that she wanted to relieve my misery, but her letter had the opposite effect. After reading it, I stretched out and stared at the ceiling, where a centipede was entering a long crack, or leaving it.

When a thing is communicated, whether true or false, its expression alone can give it life. Words are magic: they make ideas and imaginary things seem real and reduce what seemed real to nothing.

I didn't need to read this letter twice. I couldn't. It hit me with full impact. It said that everything I had done was wrong and that all of my intentions were false.

Like a brilliant illusion, her last letter and addendum turned my jealousy, which seemed justified moments before, into a ludicrous mistake. How much lower could I go than to suspect her and a paraplegic high school teacher? Even her fidelity made me sick. But my humiliation, like my desire, had no outlet.

I looked up to locate the centipede. When it was on the ceiling, I watched the long arthropod with detached curiosity, as if it were an exotic creature I never expected to encounter in real life. But now that it was on the wall behind my bed, I couldn't bear to be alone with it. I had to kill it. I scanned the room for a reliable weapon—no tissue or towel, but a hard object to produce blunt impact. I picked up the *darbuka,* lined it up over the centipede and smashed the drumskin against the wall. Then I wiped away the stain with the many hash marks that once were legs.

I wondered if Cerise had sent me her note to Raoul by mistake. She must have known how I would react and meant to turn my jealousy against me. The letter was a set up. This year in Tunisia was also a set up, only I did it to myself.

22

DESERT STAR

It was March and the sun shone again with heat as well as light. Abruptly, summer had supplanted winter. It was July in April and the desert was transformed. Shafts of pale light shattered on the stony earth in blasts of color. The pallid sand, cold rock and withered grasses yielded to brilliant hues of life, as if by alchemy.

Men wrapped in *bernouses* at the *Café du Marché* let sunbeams fall on their haggard faces. Spring turned the long palm fronds of the oasis into a lattice of green jungle swords. Tourists appeared on a warm, lazy Friday with cameras and smiles of amazement, then disappeared after lunch. Where did they go? Somewhere more genuine, deeper in the desert, closer to the sun.

Spring break was coming soon, but the sun had come sooner. There was nothing this weekend to keep me in Gafsa. I felt a familiar longing to start a new phase in my life, engage my senses, love and be loved, discover and be discovered, and to encounter something miraculous and new.

I caught the "Desert Local" as it pulled out. The bus was headed to all points south to the Sahara. It was packed with safsaried women carrying plastic baskets. Radios blasted "*Ahhyaah Halahala*" with weeping electric violins. I rode the backseat, bouncing high on the bumpy roads.

This was the *Chott* country. The light was a translucent screen, blinding and colorless, reflecting the glimmer of salt and sand. Three hundred million years before, this basin, broken by irregular red cliffs and chasms, was undersea, and it retained timeless tokens of the ocean. Amid salt crystals, cacti and scrub resembled desiccated seaweed, and a profusion of plush yellow, red and purple flowers on spiky stalks oscillated like coral in the shimmering heat, cutting the eyes with their glinting thorns.

I got off at Tozeur and booked a room at the Hotel Mamoon, a converted goat stable that came highly recommended in *The Tunisia Volunteer Guidebook* for its authentic vibes and hospitality. My room was a hovel with a bed and a sink on a cement floor and a Turkish toilet in the corner reeking of cat piss. But I didn't come to this desert oasis town to sit in a room. I quickly ventured forth.

In downtown Tozeur, rivulets of green slime oozed in the gulleys down the tilted stone streets that twisted like tense fingers between the ancient walls. Under the relentless sun and amid the sand gold parapets, Tozeur was slow and silent. Even business in the marketplace was transacted in whispers. I had come to Tozeur for escape, but the sun, the tall, dense walls and the sparse, yet constant foot traffic of taciturn inhabitants produced a sense of confinement and isolation.

447

I went to the Hotel Sahara to sit in the lounge, drink *Celtias* and look for something to happen. A Tunisian cop and a smiling soccer jock were slapping arms and talking loudly. Even in the desert, athletes were privileged, but what privileges were possible—a lifetime supply of dates, a camel with two humps?

A woman with sharply cut bangs of metallic-looking red hair moved across the room seductively in high-heeled slippers. Her tight, short dress revealed the curvaceous contours of her torso and her sleek, shapely legs. She sported a clipboard as she strutted around the room bending over to talk with people ensconced in the plush low couches.

It was Sunday and an unusual number of Europeans were at the bar. Could this be the long-awaited group of German nudists the bartender said he "expected any day now?"

A strong whiff of musky perfume overpowered me as a woman's face dropped into my unfocused gaze. The hennaed red bangs across her forehead were fringed awnings above dazzling blue eyes. The woman with the clipboard tilted her face and flashed a warm, yet inscrutable smile.

"Combien est-ce que vous mesurez, Monsieur?" she asked.

"How big am I?" I muttered. Why was she asking me this? Was it the latest, most provocative come-on of my life?

"Several inches," I replied coyly.

Her searching blue eyes demanded more precision than this. Was she a "size freak?" Should I stick with the truth or exaggerate? It occurred to me that she might not understand *inches*; I needed to convert to centimeters.

"Seventeen centimeters," I admitted. "Well, give or take a few millimeters."

Cleopatra-with-the-Clipboard burst into a throaty laughter.

"No, no, no," she replied, clucking her tongue as if to correct a child. "You're surely bigger than that."

"What's funny?" I asked, petulantly defending my manhood from her ridicule.

I found myself in another cruel encounter. Was this a cinematic nymphomaniac sent to torment me? Did she wear X-ray glasses and have an insatiable appetite, always wanting more, more, and more? What good were facts and numbers to her? Hyperbole was the order of the day.

"All right, if you insist," I bit my lip. "Eighteen, nineteen, twenty centimeters tops, depending on where you measure from."

Cleopatra stared at me in stupefaction; then in a burst of insight, she discerned the root of our confusion. The perfect smile returned to her face. She cocked her head and laughed.

"I want to know how tall you are, not the size of your sex organ. We are doing a science fiction film and we need men who measure one meter, ninety. That's six foot, one?"

"I'm six-four," I replied. My face burned in the bemusement of her blue eyes. This captivating woman—or I should more accurately describe her as ordinary, since all women were captivating to me in my wretched state—had *in three minutes* routed my defenses, learned the size of my gonads and the humiliating possibility that I measured them.

"Parfait!" She clapped her hands as if she had discovered an extraordinary talent. She wrote down my name and asked when I was available. I explained that I couldn't start until Spring break in two weeks. She squinted and said, *"D'accord!"*

I was delirious with dreams. For two weeks, I was convinced of divine intervention in my trivial existence. It seemed miraculous, yet inevitable, that Hollywood had discovered me in a desert oasis, 8,000 miles east of Sunset Boulevard. Destiny travels any distance. Did no less an expert than Jamal, the training camp

449

director and prominent sports educator, call me a "star?" Even here in North Africa talent scouts were kicking the sand for unique talent. My opportunity was as boundless as space: Who knew where this break would lead? Now I was up for space invader, and one day I would be promoted to ship commander and from there to space villain and even space monster. I would co-star with Godzilla and hobnob with King Kong.

Stardom is the most potent and addictive over-the-counter substance our civilization purveys, and I was a major abuser. Isolated and lonely, teaching first grade English to men twice my age, I had no defense against Hollywood mythology.

Midweek, I received a letter from Dozier. It started with a lyric from Dozier's favorite philosopher, Ringo Starr:

"They say they're gonna put me in the movies,
Make a monkey out of me.
They say I'm gonna make it to the big time
And all I have to do is act naturally."

Rick,

While I was in Nefta, preparing for the language conference, I was also approached to play a "space invader" in "Gone with the Galaxy." I turned it down as I expect you will, since it specifically violates Rule #43-59-14-S49 of the Peace Corps handbook, which bars volunteers from outside employment.

Looking forward to seeing you at the language conference.
Bill Dozier

23
BELIEVING THE DREAM

Just like that, my lucky break lay broken like a plate; dreams heaped on it now spilled over my brain. I was busted, but what hurt worse was that Dozier, my all-American taskmaster, had been offered the same part. I visualized Cleopatra-with-the-Clipboard asking him the same questions and gushing over his size. I fumed over this betrayal of my destiny. So much of my exhilaration had been derived from the notion, now cruelly exposed, that I was "discovered," no, *born* to play a space invader, because of a special quality I brought to the role—height and charisma, for lack of three better words.

I wasn't going to let Dozier or Rule #43-59-14-S49 abort my big chance. But now that he suspected my vacation plan, it had to become a clandestine operation. The Tunisian South would be swarming with Peace Corps volunteers. If I were recognized in Tozeur, particularly in a space costume, Dozier would have me discharged.

Whether such a discharge would be "honorable" or "dishonorable" was irrelevant to me. I was determined to endure a year, a deadline now two months away. To this extent, I was committed to the Peace Corps and sticking with it was a matter of integrity, though *what* I was sticking with was ambiguous. Dozier believed that integrity was about upholding every rule. For me, integrity meant perceiving and committing to one's destiny. I would do all I could to fulfill mine.

24
QUEL DRAG!

As the bus rattled and banged over the hard road, my

anticipation made me sick. The dawdling slowness of developing world public transport tortured me and taunted my ambition. Each sibilant brake fart made my mind and body race. The difference between my internal speed and the vehicle's creeping was so great that I felt I would explode. I wanted to commandeer the bus, floor the accelerator, make no further stops and turn all of the *fellaheen* into hostages of my celluloid dream.

Since the opportunity had come out of nowhere, could it not be snatched away with equal caprice? I had a premonition that I was late, that destiny waited impatiently, tapping its foot and shaking its head at my tardiness for the most important event of my life. Suddenly the two weeks that passed so rapidly seemed long enough for events to have passed me by. It was only a two-hour drive to Tozeur, but each minute was a bulb burning out in my name on the marquee.

During the slow, jerky ride I did not lose myself in the scenery, but found comfort in it. It raced with me, reflecting and absorbing my anticipation. The sun baked and painted the land. Einstein and Broglie were both wrong: in Tunisia light was a wave, a particle—*and* a stroke. The desert was no passive tableau, but a spectacle of plants and animals with open mouths and lavish pigments exuding appetite. Did so many living things blow in on a fertilizing wind like a circus dashing over sand? Their patterns pulsated and glowed like organic flashing signs of a natural Las Vegas. They gambled all of their resources to propagate, seeking permanence in the interlude between cold death and deadly heat.

I sauntered down Avenue Bourguiba in Tozeur, clinging to the shadows of shop awnings among the hanging displays of dates, unglazed pots and embroidered blouses. The streets were redolent of braying donkey piss; children tossed dry camel dung at each other in the local variation of "dodge ball" while their uncles and grandfathers ambled in white and gray *jebbas.* Easter tourists groped the merchandise and inhaled the exotic fragrances of Tozeur, which would have disgusted them in their hometowns. I finally located a dark spot, the Cafe des Dattes, wedged between a camel stable and a souvenir shop, and sat with my back to the door to devise a plan to avoid notice by other Peace Corps volunteers.

My outfit was meticulously coordinated to have an impact on the movie people. The cream-colored polyester suit with a permanent crease in the pants screamed leisure and had an amphibious sheen, suggesting fully clothed leaps into swimming pools. The collarless shirt was a blue and yellow print of mango-eating monkeys, purchased in Tozeur and imported by caravan from Mali. The rhomboid sunglasses made me hard to recognize— *as human*—and harder to forget. A red fez cap crowned the disguise, which would throw everyone off my true identity—except anyone who knew me.

That was the problem. I had dressed to get noticed by Hollywood insiders once I was among them—at shoots, at meals, or at the hotel bar soaking up their stories after a long day on the set. But if I wore these duds on Tozeur's pungent streets, Peace Corps people like Dozier, lurking in town on their way to the Arabic workshop, might observe me. This get-up was the flip side of incognito. It was a sign that read: "Renegade Peace Corps volunteer wasting taxpayer money to launch movie career."

Anyway, my Peace Corps peers had already seen my polyester suit at the Peace Corps initiation event. To avoid their detection, I needed a disguise.

A group of women walked by in their black *safsaris* and plastic sandals. I wondered why *safsaris* here were black instead of white; were the women in mourning, or was it a tribal shibboleth?

Black was a more attractive color for *safsaris* than white. And

453

these had a more stylish design. They billowed less and made the women seem thinner and shapelier. It was probably my imagination. Any deviation from the norm in the concealment of women was bound to arouse my interest. As I pondered the reasons for black *safsaris*, an idea came to me: I could only disguise myself effectively by covering myself completely. I would wear a *safsari* to and from the hotel.

I entered a tourist shop and found the biggest *safsari* in stock. They were out of black so I settled for white. It extended to my calves, but billowed well. I stuck two fringes in my mouth to cover all of my face except my eyes.

"*B'kadesh?*" I asked the proprietor. He stared at me in consternation, which helped me haggle down the price.

"Would you like me to wrap it, *Sidi*?"

"No, absolutely not. I'll wear it out, of course," I replied impatiently, as if my motive for donning a woman's covering were obvious. I draped the *safsari* over my head and my Hollywood threads, bolted the store and strutted through Tozeur, believing my identity safe.

With renewed determination I strode to the hotel, a palace just beyond the town center.

Suddenly I heard my name.

"Murkey?"

I was stunned by the recognition, but instinctively raced ahead to escape it.

"Murkey!" The voice was louder, more insistent now and a little breathless as if the speaker struggled to keep up. I wanted to run to escape my name as it reverberated down the narrow serpentine alleys, off the sunbaked walls, and disrupted the silent siesta of the desert town. But if I ran, I expected the voice to chase me like an excitable dog barking more repetitions of my name. I stopped and turned toward the speaker.

"Murkey, what are you doing?"

It was Fargus.

"Halalala," I ranted in Tunisian-style gibberish. *"Je suis pauvre veuve.* Poor widow. *Qu'est-ce que tu m'en veux?* Please, *laisse-moi tranquille* or I call police."

"Murkey, what's with you? Do you have sunstroke? Have they finally driven you insane?"

Each utterance of my name increased my panic. I looked both ways to see if anyone else was close by. Gripping the *safsari* between my teeth, I growled at Fargus.

"Keep it down. Nobody's supposed to know I'm here."

"You're not going to the language conference?"

"No."

"That sucks. I hoped there'd be somebody to laugh with."

"Where's Livia? Aren't you laughing with her?"

"Not really. She's pregnant."

"Congratulations."

"For what? It's not mine. I couldn't make that commitment, so she dumped me and found a Swedish tourist who did. She's with him now. Story of my life."

"That's rough. But I can't talk now."

"Yeah. I figured. What are you doing in a *safsari?* A *kefia* wasn't bad enough?"

"I'm on a mission."

"Impersonating a freakishly tall Tunisian woman?"

"That's it," I replied. "Don't blow my cover."

But if Fargus saw through my disguise, I had to fix it.

"How did you recognize me?"

He pointed at my feet.

"Who else wears clogs?"

I stooped to lengthen the *safsari* and hide my clogs under it.

"Look, if we continue to talk out in the open, the Peace Corps will know I'm here or the police will lock us both up as an American man talking with a Tunisian woman."

"You're right," Fargus said. "Talking with you isn't worth jail time. We'll catch up later."

I swore Fargus to secrecy. He shrugged, which meant more to him than a handshake.

"*Bislema, labess, hamdulleh!*" Fargus said, flashing a peace sign when we parted. "That's all the Arabic I know, which is why I'm going to the language conference."

The Sahara Palace lobby was in an uproar. Tozeur's stage mothers paraded their children, attired in home-stitched garments, by a scowling crew. Cleopatra-with-the-Clipboard was not around. I asked a production assistant if they were shooting the storm troopers soon. He shot me a look of bilious perplexity, prompting me to pull off my sheet. But my transformation did not faze him.

"Nothing's shooting until we find a goddamn *remorque*," he snapped.

I wasn't late, but ridiculously early. The production of *Gone with the Galaxy* had stalled for lack of a low-bed trailer to haul equipment in the desert. For three days, I skulked in my white *safsari* down the gold stone and green piss streets of Tozeur to the Sahara Palace, where the production was headquartered, and waited for my call. When a *remorque* was located in Kasserine, everyone rejoiced. How a grocer obtained a flatbed and whether he knew its uses or predicted its value were unknown, but it made him rich. I viewed his improbable success as a harbinger that my perseverance would pay off.

My hopes were quickly disabused. The storm troopers were

now low-priority. The children's scenes came first. I sat in the hotel lounge, feeling like a useless fool who had made a huge mistake. Cleopatra was still not to be found. She was probably in Jerba, where the principals were filming. Was it my fate, I wondered, to be presented with amazing opportunities that dissolved when I seized them?

I cloaked myself in my sheet and went outside the hotel for air. Cleopatra suddenly appeared, as if to restore my faith. She was studying her clipboard when I approached.

"Combien est-ce-que vous mesurez?" I said to remind her of the first words she had said to me, as if they had a mnemonic power or sentimental value. Glancing up from her work, she covered her mouth to suppress a scream.

"Combien est-ce-que vous mésurez?" I repeated more emphatically. I shed the *safsari* to reveal my cream-colored polyester suit and the monkeys-and-mangos shirt. Cleopatra's eyes still showed no recognition. "I'm the space invader, remember?"

She had not, until that moment. Reassured that I was no phantom dispatched to kill her, she nonchalantly informed me that the schedule had changed. "But come back," she said breathlessly, "One of these days we'll use you." She issued her standard, sympathetic smile, took an economical gasp of breath to punctuate the conversation and strutted off as her round bottom wiggled goodbye.

"Wait, wait, wait!" I thought disgustedly. Only two weeks after being discovered, I was a has-been. It had to be a record of some kind. As the crew corralled children, I grew more despondent. My big break had turned into a mirage, another disposable role, like Peace Corps teacher. I believed I was a star, but I was an extra in disguise.

25
SALT FLAT SPLAT

I walked without caring where I went. I wanted to get lost, to leave my life behind and return with a new one. How much more lost could I be than I was? I cut through the oasis, among the palms and came to the salt flats, with their miles and miles of silver emptiness before me. I continued to walk. If I went far enough away, I hoped to forget where I came from. Out in the Chott there was nothing to stop me or to wait for, none of my mother's irrelevant advice, or Cerise's empty promises and mordant reproaches. In the Chott el Jerid, there was no Cleopatra to tell me to come back and no Dozier to warn me away.

My clogs crunched the salt. In my cream-colored polyester suit I was the star. There were no cameras. It was an image no one would ever see, but I strutted, jumped, and danced soft shoe like Fred Astaire. Some passing scorpions were watching. The desert was empty, but all mine.

The Chott was a hundred miles wide. I headed into the salt flats, driven by anger and restless energy, without thought of time or destination. My clogged feet were sore and blistered. I was thirsty and my knees ached. I turned around, confident of seeing my starting line at the edge of town—but Tozeur had disappeared. I looked ahead. Nothing was there. Without a watch, I had no idea how long I'd been walking. In every direction, salt powder glittered like crushed glass. I tried not to panic.

"Just turn and walk back," I told myself.

"But which way is around?" myself asked.

"You walked in a straight line." I spoke firmly, trying to suppress the rising terror that I was lost.

"But maybe you didn't walk in a straight line."

"Dammit all!"

For lack of anything better to guide me and fueled by anger at my helplessness and stupidity, I marched off in what I took to be the right direction, westward toward the setting sun.

My mouth was dry and burning. Sardines from the *salade Tunisienne* were curing inside it. I licked the perspiration off my arm and kept walking, but the town did not reappear. There were no dunes to obstruct my vision, to give me hope of what might be beyond them. For miles in every direction lay a carpet of white salt powder reflecting dimly, tears without water.

"Why did I come here?" I berated myself. I could not remember the impulse that drove me into the desert. Even in this desperate moment, when fatigue and thirst threatened to stop me for good, I posed impossible questions. Coming to Tozeur had all seemed right, fame seemed close, yet if I dropped, the vultures would find me before anyone thought to look.

I burst into giddy laughter. I told myself I had not walked far; I had gone in a straight line; there was no need to worry. The salt floor in the distance bobbed before my eyes like a sea at sunset, shimmering with refreshment. It tempted me to dive in. Surely it was water. I played a game with myself: I'd hold off on water, walk as long as possible, get to town and swim later.

But my resolve weakened. "Why are you waiting?" I asked myself. "Dive in, enjoy the water. Your entire life, you deny yourself, *holding back* from what you want to do."

I fought with myself, but could not resist the sparkling promise of refreshment. I ran toward the liquid vision and leapt in.

Salt scraped my face and burned my eyes. I howled. The jolt to my head roused me from my hallucination. I pounded the ground with my fists. I bled under my polyester suit, my face was cut and my body was weak. In my exhaustion, I had one thought: "If you get out of this, don't ever wait again, or do what you don't want to do. You're not an extra. Now get up and get out of here."

I walked and walked, covered with salt, stalking the sun as it lowered in the western sky. The sunset provided a respite from the heat, but foreboded darkness and night predators. Would I survive the night sleeping among scorpions and sidewinders?

It was dusk. In the distance, I saw people move apart from each other, then stop, as in a piece of modern dance. I pinched myself. No more *Fata Morganas* like the swimming pool, I warned myself and continued to walk, with my eyes fixed on the band of violet horizon light.

The apparitions reappeared. They waved their arms, ran, stopped and turned in strange patterns. They looked so real that I wanted to run toward them. But the last bit of common sense I had warned that a long run for nothing would waste what little energy I had left. The moving figures appeared larger now. They seemed to be only 100 feet away. Suddenly a disk hovered in the sky. I ignored it as a hallucination and lumbered forward.

The sky suddenly darkened, a black line spun toward me. Before I could flinch or duck, it smacked me in the mouth.

"What happened? Who are you?"

The phantoms from my mirage stared down at me—one woman and two men. They spoke with English accents. I had interrupted their Frisbee game.

26
SIGNS AND COSIGNS

I could have died in the desert. My awareness of this changed my attitude toward life and what I was doing with it. I took my survival as a sign of salvation, but it told me nothing more than this. My life was spared—but for what purpose? Was it a warning to leave this dangerous place, or an assurance that no matter how impulsive I was, Tunisia would never let me die?

I had told Irving I would not stay in Tunisia for two years, but I wasn't sure now. I had been unable to connect with my hosts, establish roots, or maintain friendships, but I classified these setbacks under "false start" and "bad luck." The right assignment might have a different result. I wanted not just to survive, but also to succeed, to surpass myself and be aligned with a higher cause. I sought transcendence.

Would another year be a painful repetition, a waste of time, and a risk of life—or redemption? Each day I looked for signs in my environment to stay or go.

It was not a good time to look for anything. From twelve to three the bright, colorless light divided the eye from its objects. Regardless how short the exposure, when I came indoors I needed to lie down in a dark room to restore my vision.

But I didn't need eyes for the signs I was looking for. During a siesta I felt a bump on my arm, a hard mound on my bicep. When had it come? How did it grow to golf ball size without my seeing it? What should I do about it?

At the company, it was business as usual—two students here, five there, repeating, "Why don't you know my name?" and other standards. Mabrouk, my dour supervisor, had failed to oust me in "the company car affair." He avenged himself by editing my book of verb idioms with typical spleen, his fountain pen scratching and slashing the paper like a stiletto ripping my work.

It was my job to persuade Kouki's secretarial pool of two to type the final version. One winced and touched her forehead with her index finger, indicating migraine and fatigue, while her colleague blew on her freshly painted nails.

"Are you married, *Profes-s-s-eur*?" they asked, exchanging conspiratorial glances and smiling at me.

"What does that have to do with anything?" I inquired.

One rolled her eyes. The other giggled.

My single status was apparently a joke to my hosts. Meanwhile, a nonstop mirage of sex floated in front of me. My sexual hunger was so acute that even the maid, Marwah, a very mature woman with ample hips and a gold tooth, aroused me. And she knew it. She had a habit of barging into my room in the morning and making suggestive sucking and clucking noises while I was half-awake. She always found dirt by my bed, so that she could sweep it up and bend over to thrust her buttocks near my head. When I got up to use the bathroom, she blocked the door, forcing me to walk sideways to avoid brushing against her.

The days grew beards. I was tired of the murmuring din, the saturnine, turbaned faces and the slow-motion spectacle of people performing trifling tasks with weary inefficiency. A bus stalled for 15 minutes: road repairs lay ahead. Six men leaned on shovels and watched a seventh man smooth gravel.

These were signs to leave Gafsa, but not Tunisia, and I decided to liquidate my worldly goods in order to start fresh and be transformed.

I sent my possessions to Cerise to signify our bond. I packed two boxes of personal effects—books, underwear, a dozen long red hot peppers wrapped in a blanket, representing my passionate self—and carried them in a taxi to the post office.

The driver, who moonlighted as a marriage broker, viewed me as a young bachelor and offered to arrange a marriage: two sisters. "Veils on or off?" I inquired, recalling the story of Ali of Ayn Draham, whose female carving had disappeared from my room.

I left the post office and rambled along the serpentine streets and blue alleys of the medina, shielding my eyes from the two-o'clock sun. There were footsteps behind me. I turned. A Coke bottle smashed on a wall a few feet away; those who launched it darted around a crooked corner, leaving no trail but laughter. I walked on, repeating to myself that everything was fine, nothing could hurt me, these were not assaults, but signs of transcendence.

27

POISON PEN PAL

My Perhaps No Longer Love,

Back from home after a week of good work in the country, I was disappointed to find only bills in my mailbox. What kept you from writing from Tozeur?

I'm sick of this pen pal affair that makes me depend on letters. I made a resolution to change, but I know that I won't keep it. I'll think, "Mailbox," on my way home, like Pavlov's literate dog.

True, it's not your fault we're not together. Still, I've felt for a long time that you've been hiding something from me since Menzel: your feelings, no doubt. Those letters and many other things I've pretended not to notice. I have only one more month before I can relax; so if you want to make a clean break, do it now!

I want the truth from you very soon. This is perhaps my last letter. Rick, if I'm an A-1 bitch, you're a first class bastard. I wish I could vomit a torrent of abuses; I could if I looked at the photograph of you eating pizza.

Cerise

P.S. I am convinced you were glad I didn't come to Gafsa for the holiday and you went to Tozeur for fear I would come at the last minute! Do you think you can fool me? Let's be done with it.

She had enclosed a photograph of us taken years back. It showed a lanky, teenage boy in baggy pants and shirt, his arm draped around a woman whose narrowed eyes pierced the lens. He resembled a shy stork, smiling remotely as if waking from a nap.

I wanted to slap the face of this distant acquaintance, to warn him to be prepared to wake up one day in a bug-infested bed in a room redolent of sardines and invaded by a predatory maid.

"Stop dreaming!" I yelled at the picture. But that dreamer got me here. Time passed, dreams faded. I put the photo back in the envelope with the neatly folded letter.

28

TREASON ON CHANNEL 3

Every afternoon at the *borj*, Tlili and Nouri watched a treason trial on TV. Two young men were accused of trying to assassinate the prime minister, an obscure man who, after years in Bourguiba's shadow, became his successor. Across Tunisia, radios and televisions blared the trial of two Libyans who looked stunned and mystified by the spectacle of Tunisian justice that fated them to die in such a public way.

Tlili waved his hand at the set, his face contorted in a grin. "Another lover's quarrel," he said, winking and laughing his deep, dark laugh. This was, he explained, how Tunisia broke off her engagement with Libya. Quadaffi had wished the neighboring nations to merge for years and he wooed Tunisia like a rich suitor courting an impoverished beauty.

But Tunisia was always the tease, breaking the engagement.

Finally, Quadaffi lost patience. According to reports, 60,000 Tunisian workers in Libya had their money confiscated, and were terrorized, expelled and forced to walk home through the desert. In retaliation, the Libyan *souk*, a settlement of tents and canvas tabernacles near the Gafsa medina that sold such coveted foreign goods as Palestinian scarves, German radios, and monkey-mango shirts from Mali, was plundered.

"Tunisia and Libya will never marry," Tlili said, his eyes gleaming at the idea of nations having intimate relations. "Libya loves guns. Tunisia loves wine, beer and *tourisme*. As you Americans say, 'Make love, not war!'" He laughed.

The trial of the bewildered conspirators with pencil-thin moustaches concluded. As they were sentenced, the camera took a close-up. One man had a wall-eye and looked familiar.

"It's Ali!" I blurted out, jabbing my finger at the screen. Had the woodcarver of Ayn Draham tried to assassinate the prime minister with his slingshot?

"You know him?" Tlili asked. He put his finger to his lips to urge discretion.

"He was my friend. Ali's his name."

"Please, *Professeur*. You don't want to leave Tunisia in a box."

"But he's not a Libyan. *He's a Tunisian.*"

Tlili looked at me critically, then smiled and slapped my arm, like a friend sharing a good joke.

"Yes, this is Tunisian justice. *Très intéressant, n'est-ce pas?*"

To comfort me, Tlili explained that many people, including national heroes, were convicted of treason and sentenced to death, but few were executed. Ali would probably be allowed to flee Tunisia. I pointed out that Ali was not a prominent figure, but a poor woodworker living with his mother; could he also expect clemency? The sagacious caretaker grimaced under the weight of legal speculation.

"In that case, maybe they kill him. It's easier. *Menarafsh!*"

Ali's condemnation made me sick with paranoia. I believed I was in danger. The disappearance of the gentle woodworker's gift now seemed an omen of his doom. How many portents of my demise did I fail to recognize? Treachery and hatred at the *borj*, in Gafsa and all over Tunisia threatened to engulf me. In town, I was surrounded by baleful stares and sharp silences.

It was not my imagination. Even after living in Gafsa for six months, Nouri did not walk in town alone. As an out-of-towner from Kasserine, a town only 120 kilometers away, he feared beatings and arrest in Gafsa.

29

TEA AND CELIBACY

One afternoon when I returned to the *borj* with sardines and a baguette, Nouri accosted me with news.

"*Professeur!* Mademoiselle Paula came!"

As he handed me a folded note, Nouri's expression was radiant with hope. He took a fraternal interest in my social life and interpreted Paula's visit as an auspicious event. His enthusiasm was contagious. I could not resist reading the note.

"WHERE HAVE YOU BEEN?" was printed across the notebook paper. Was her memory so short?

"*Mademoiselle* Paula likes you, *Professeur*?" Nouri asked as he studied my face.

"*Mademoiselle* Paula is married," I said.

"Married?" he asked dumbfounded. It made no sense to him that a woman brought a note to one man while she was wed to another. But after mulling it, he solved the problem and grinned.

466

"You are lucky, *Professeur. Rod belek.* Be careful."

Such was my fragile emotional state that the naïve insights of the assistant concierge convinced me of Paula's interest. I had forsworn friendship with the American couple and vowed never to return to their house. But this note could be a sign that my luck in Tunisia was changing. Paula had seemed cold and hostile, but Nouri might be right about her liking me. I analyzed the lettering and ink flow; they revealed nothing, which aroused me more.

Paula was alone pouring tea when I entered the kitchen. Her thick, dark hair was roped back in a braid. Her face had a rich, golden hue.

"I bring the gift of sardines and a baguette," I said.

"We don't eat sardines," she replied.

"In that case, I'll save them for a late night snack," I countered as I awkwardly thrust the baguette in her direction like a baked erection. I suddenly realized how it looked and apologized.

Fortunately, Paula missed the unintended sexual symbolism and grabbed the lusty loaf.

"We'll have it with orange marmalade and butter," she said.

While she cut the bread into a basket, her hazel eyes glowed.

"Did you hear? They blew up the high school," she said. "But only the cafeteria kitchen was damaged, so we still have to work."

"Is that why you sent me a note?" I asked.

Paula's curved eyebrows rose in surprise, and I felt ashamed for showing impatience and threatening our *détente.*

"Not just that. I met my family in Greece during the Spring break. We got along for once. My father doesn't think I'm a whore for living with John."

"Congratulations," I said.

A familiar silence joined us in the room.

As Paula spread butter and jam on her slice of bread, my eyes detected her bosom rising and falling under her flannel shirt. I had to say something to draw her attention from my eyes to my mouth. "So, who blew up the high school?"

"Some seniors who were expelled for staging a hunger strike to protest the food."

"They might as well protest the weather," I said. "There's no good cafeteria food in the world."

I sounded like Fargus in Ayn Draham when we argued about the training camp food. I couldn't believe I had become so cynical. Nonetheless, these students would pay a high price for defending their taste buds. Any chance they had to lead productive lives was over. Tunisia was a liberal country that spent 50% of its budget on education, but dissent was not tolerated.

Paula stared into her tea, then directly into my eyes.

"We had to get away—from here and from each other," she said. "I know how it sounds. We still love one another, it's just that after two years of being together day and night—"

Her eyes dropped a few degrees. "We promised never to hurt one another."

Paula shot to her feet and arranged pots in the sink. In the ensuing silence, I contemplated the Formica tabletop, its easy-to-clean design and surface, and played with my bread. This visit had the look and feel of my last one. The familiarity of these awkward moments put me at ease.

Suddenly Paula turned to me, her eyes intense with a question to which she demanded a response. I held the bread in front of my mouth like a muzzle, unable to eat or drop it.

"Is it normal for two people to sleep together without making love?" she asked.

My excitement was frustrated and intensified by confusing signals. Although she raised a provocative topic, Paula stood across the kitchen with her arms unseductively crossed. Her eyes were not of the bedroom, but of the library variety; she did not seek romance, but reassurance. As the guy next door, an average adult applying contemporary standards, I was presumably an expert in sexual norms, according to a Supreme Court ruling on pornography. Paula wanted to know the norm so that she could feel normal. Her eyes exhorted me to a simple "Yes" or "No" response. Either way I'd lose.

"I guess it's normal."

Did I pass the test? I naïvely hoped that I put the issue to rest. If Paula and John were celibate, my response validated their relationship, while confirming that I was not a sleaze exploiting their situation.

Paula's face contorted in incredulous outrage.

"FOR SIX MONTHS?" Her cat's eyes darted between their almond-shaped corners like pacing tigers attempting to leap from their sockets.

"You didn't specify the time interval."

I blinked like a cartoon mainframe computer, as I attempted to swiftly calculate the situation based on a statistical formula for normal sexual abstinence.

"I guess six months is not normal," I conceded.

Apparently, this too was the wrong answer, because Paula responded with a long, disgusted look and went, *"Hmmph."* After sweeping the floor violently, she faced me with a hand on her cocked hip, "What if they love each other? You know, sex isn't everything, Rick."

"I hope you're right," I said. "Because in my case it's non-existent."

"You have a lot to learn," she fumed.

"Obviously," I rejoined, as I continued to play noble punching bag for her internal conflicts.

"You probably never had a decent relationship, so how would you know what goes into one?"

"You're right. I'm a bad relationship counselor," I admitted.

She continued to sweep pugnaciously while I waited for the next aftershock of her disdain. She stood before me, tanned, alluring and direct, her body language announcing, "This is who I am!" Did she seek another response?

Paula was now embraceably close. I squirmed in the chair. I was having an out-of-body in-body experience that controlled my limbs and made my torso tremble. My arms twitched and sprang forward.

The door swung open. John's ruddy face appeared. My arms were suspended like tree branches between Paula and me. To remove them from midair, I slapped my cheeks and covered my ears with my hands.

"Hey, stranger," John cheered, embracing me. "Going to the Peace Corps party? Everybody will be there. Everybody. Say—" He turned to Paula. "Guess what? Tasha's going to be there."

"That's great," Paula said with less enthusiasm.

"Tasha's in Tunisia?" I asked. "I wonder what she's doing."

"You can ask her," John boomed, as though I were standing across Gafsa. "You two are pretty tight, aren't you?"

He said this with a gossipy tone and mirthful eyes, as if the story of our relationship interruptus had entered Peace Corps lore. Regardless how dismal people's lives were, they turned to mine for amusement. John had no sex with Paula for six months, yet he viewed me as a dork whose misery was worse. It was apparently my most attractive social trait.

"I knew her," I said evasively.

"I thought so," he grinned.

30

TALKING DIRTY

When I returned to the *borj*, an envelope was on the bed.

"Where were you? Why weren't you here to read me?" It chastened me.

Months earlier, that envelope meant, "love." Now it was like an explosive that I did not have the specialized skills to open without having it detonate in my brain. But I couldn't tear it up without reading it. What if she wrote something nice? What if she changed her mind about me and about us? How would she respond after receiving my package with all of my worldly goods?

My Perhaps On Again Love,

Your letter came this morning. I was walking home, thinking "mailbox." When I saw the letter, I was annoyed because I wanted to sulk and now I couldn't. How could I? You are my first and only love, but a bastard all the same. How could you forget to write?

While I write to you, I'm thinking of going downstairs and inviting a passerby to sleep with me in the car—just a casual thing; I'm sure you wouldn't mind. Salaud! How do you like that?

Go to hell with your dried peppers! Civilized people don't eat them unless they want to die of heartburn!

I would have liked more details about the people you met on your vacation, but you wrote that letter, as one would do a chore, to get it out of the way. Why don't you go to Timbuktu and when you return I will have screwed you out of my mind? There is a mental illness called "optimism." Many Skid Row derelicts suffer from it.

I was thrilled to learn that the students in Gafsa blew up the high school. Wish our kids had the guts to do it; but first they would have to realize what is being done to them, which most of them do not. For instance, I am one of the few teachers who do not treat Humanities students like imbeciles because of their math deficiencies.

That's all for now.

Cerise

PS. Your parcels just arrived. One contained puzzling dried peppers so dirty that they must have been dragged across a camel path. What do you expect me to do with them? They were wrapped in a nice, equally filthy blanket.

The other package contained such junk that I could not believe it. Why did you send your underwear? Do you think it turns me on to wear men's briefs? Or is this your notion of being close? And why did you send hangers? Did you think we have a shortage here?

Now for news you won't like. I'll be out of town for the month of June, proctoring exams in Trouville. Of course, I look forward to seeing you, but I also planned to spend time in Scotland.

Hope your bump is not serious. You should get it treated while you have insurance.

I know that you are trying to decide what to do next year, to stay in Tunisia or leave. I also know that you are stubborn and want to complete your tour of duty, regardless of how it affects you. Tenacity is a virtue, but not at the expense of your sanity. Staying there would in my view be a terrible mistake and a waste of your energy and talents, but you don't need me to tell you what to do. You must choose. For all I know, you may have benefited from your time in Tunisia. I know I haven't.

Cerise

31

ANTICIPATION

I counted the days until the Peace Corps reunion party in Mahdia, a fishing village near Bourguiba's birthplace, where Tasha had taught for two years.

A reunion would force me to view my tour of duty objectively in terms of other volunteers. If others found meaning and happiness here, I might learn what I missed and transcend personal experience for a broader truth.

I was also eager to see Tasha. When I imagined alternative Peace Corps scenarios, they often began with her, a persevering volunteer who succeeded. My year might have been different if something *had* happened between us. I remembered her in the dunes at sunset, her arms stretched to the moon, as she cried out, "Isn't it beautiful?" If we were to meet again, she might inspire me to stay another year.

Yet, despite Tasha's frequent appearance in my thoughts, I was perplexed when people asked me about her activities and whereabouts. They seemed to continue our story in their minds, whereas I had not seen her since the previous summer and had no idea what she was doing. Maybe this was why people were intrigued. Just as we approached our climax, we were interrupted.

My English course at the *La Compagnie des phosphates* was an educational carcass, each session a case study in futility. The only self-respecting thing to do was to end classes. It was not a success, but it was the end of a job, not my Peace Corps tour.

My students, the smiling masochists who remained, said I was a rebel, but rebellion did not impel me to end the term. I was tired of empty gestures. Life was to be lived, not waited for, enjoyed, not endured. It should not be an anxious drift from moment to hour, from day to decade, until someone, somewhere said it should stop, like the fates sheering off one's cloth.

Meanwhile, the bump on my arm was egg-size. I played a guessing game about it. Too hard to pinch, yet painless, was it a cyst burrowed by a parasite hibernating in my flesh, or a tumor? For a month, this alien life form was a sign of transformation, though it could also be a badge signifying that I learned nothing.

Learned nothing, achieved nothing, changed not a bit? I couldn't accept this. I wasn't ready to leave. My story wasn't done. It had no climax or conclusion. I didn't even qualify as the hero, since I had achieved no goals, obtained no enlightenment, overcome no adversity.

I had to transcend these failures and be transformed.

32

MAID OF DISHONOR

Friday morning I got up early, withdrew money for the trip and returned to the *borj* to shower and pack.

Marwah was in my room, dusting and sweeping, as she gurgled a private song with *"Yayayayaya"* as the refrain. I watched her cautiously as she sluggishly proceeded with her routine, bending in front of me, filling my eyes with her ample backside. I had recently dreamed that Marwah danced around my bed, moaning, "You want me...Take me..."

My jaw tightened as the gold-toothed grandmother made me hard. It was a humiliating sign of my sex deprivation. With canny sloth she bent and swept until I couldn't stand it.

"Shokran," I told her. "Now can you leave?"

She smiled at my arousal. A young man could shelter no secrets from a grandmother, who had seen three generations of male genitals. She strutted out swinging her backside like a soft pendulum, as if to say, "It's a matter of time."

I stripped and left the clothes and Lauren's silver chain on the bed while I showered. When I returned to the room and put on my pants, I reached in my pocket—the money was gone. I looked for the pendant. It had disappeared, as well.

I was enraged over the lost money, but frantic about the pendant. It was supposed to protect me. Now something terrible was bound to happen. For starters, I would miss the reunion party. If I didn't withdraw more money from the bank before Friday closing at 1 PM, I would be unable to buy a bus ticket for Mahdia. But if I ran out now, without reporting the theft, I would have no chance of recovering the pendant.

Three people were in the house: Tlili, Nouri and Marwah. I went to Tlili the caretaker and told him about the money and Lauren's lucky chain and pendant. He grimaced, his dark eyes glowing with immediate comprehension.

"You lose money on your bed, in your room, when the door is closed? This is not logical, unless somebody stole it," he deduced.

He called Nouri, the assistant concierge. As the youngest in the house and so poor that he could not go out, Nouri was a natural scapegoat, but he was also an unlikely suspect; he never entered my room. Tlili asked Nouri if he took the money and the necklace. The assistant replied calmly with tears of indignation that he stole nothing, as if the thought of it were painful.

Tlili summoned Marwah, who was humming "*Yayaya*."

"*Le le le*," she burst into tears when Tlili confronted her.

"You were the only one in the professor's room!" Tlili insisted, "What else could happen to the money on his bed which you made this morning?"

She shrugged. "*Menarafsh*."

The incorruptible caretaker stared at me more sadly than any man ever had and sighed.

"*Professeur,* this is serious. We must do something. I have seen too much in my life. I worked at my uncle's snack-stand for 15 years. Everyday, 12 hours a day. So one day my uncle tells me, *'Go, Tlili, I don't need you anymore!'* My cousin gets the business and Tlili finds a new way to feed his family. In the War of Independence, I fought in those mountains. It was cold and I had no *bernous.* We ate only *filfil.* Then we won the war and Ben Youssef was sentenced to death. *Professeur*, I saw many bad things and I could do nothing. Now you lose 15 *dinars* in my house: I must do something."

He gave me a long, hard look.

"We must go to the police," he said solemnly.

"But we have no proof," I said. "I didn't see her take it."

There was a glint of warning in his eyes.

"The money and the chain were there. Now they are gone. *Yes?*" Tlili reproved me. "Then they were stolen and we must report it to the police."

The uncompromising caretaker slid his spindly arms into his jacket and gave instructions to Nouri, while Marwah gathered her *safsari* and handbag. Now that I set the process in motion, I knew that reporting the loss to Tlili was a mistake that the police would only make worse. But it was too late to recant. In Tlili's idealistic mind, even a small crime was a major violation and when a thing was said, it was real until proven false. If I dismissed the loss, he might suspect that I lied. I needed to see my grievance through to its conclusion, not to obtain justice or recuperate my loss, but to keep the friendship of a good man.

After Marwah wound the sheet around herself, we set out for the police station at an absurdly casual pace, considering the grave purpose of our procession. Various women, their plastic baskets heaped high with groceries, greeted Marwah as they passed. With each step, my strength drained away from me, producing a weightless sensation as heady as freedom and as nauseating as fear. I knew I was acting imprudently because I was the accuser, yet I felt as though I were going to my execution.

It was 11 AM and the desk officer's khaki shirt was dark around the armpits.

"This lady stole from you?"

"Yes."

He wheeled around in his chair. A vague curiosity twisted his mouth as he typed out my statement. Marwah unwrapped her *safsari* and wailed her tale of painful shame, as an honest woman, now defamed. I had been nice to her, so why did I lie about her now?

The other *flics* in the room all listened to Marwah's story. They smiled and suppressed their laughter. Someone guffawed when she said that I had been nice to her.

"So you are making a formal accusation?" the desk officer asked incredulously.

"I have no proof," I admitted. The rancorous eyes of the *gendarmes* were on me. The headlines in their brains read: "Rich, young American accuses poor Tunisian granny of theft."

Hatred filled the room like humidity and clung to my neck; I would be lucky if they did not arrest me for stealing my own money and silver chain. I had to present my side.

"Officer, I don't want to be here. The money is not important. But the silver chain was a gift—from a friend. She gave it to me and made me promise never to lose it. I don't know if I will ever see my friend again and this is all I have left."

A few policemen nodded and murmured.

"Yes, well, of course, you are upset. I am sorry you lost your gift. Perhaps you will get it back. *In sh'Allah!*"

"*In sh'Allah!*" the others repeated.

No one expected me to recover my cash and keepsake, but the process lumbered on. The officer filled out the form and obtained signatures—mine, his, the supervising officer's. Marwah had swiped the money and the chain, but they would never charge her. There was no proof and even if there were, she would still go free.

An hour passed; the ordeal was over. Marwah skulked away, trembling. Naïvely, I asked Tlili what would happen to her.

"*In sh'Allah,*" he said.

I bolted for the bank before it closed.

When I returned to my room, I noticed something shimmering on the floor in the shadow of the bed frame. It was Lauren's chain. I kissed it and put it around my neck. It was a good sign.

33
REUNION DISUNION

Whoever said, "Seek and ye shall find" did not attend the Peace Corps party in Mahdia.

The *boum* was in a lazy fishing village. Only two guests were present when I arrived, a married couple that had served in Tunisia ten years before and returned to recapture their good times. They sat together on the porch with a view of the fishing docks and attempted to excavate from hours of jet lag the ruins of vibrant memories.

I asked how they were enjoying their trip.

"It's all changed," he sighed wistfully. "But not how I wanted it to."

"So many tourists," the woman lamented with rolling eyes. "Tourists ruin a country." With sudden animation, her fingers curled together like French fries. "They impose their values and expectations, rather than embracing the host culture."

"Most volunteers teach English," I replied. "Isn't that an imposition on the host culture?"

"The best places become resorts," the woman insisted. "Their charm and uniqueness are lost. Tourism turned the culture into a sideshow. The people once smiled and shook your hand. Now they look to the next customer."

"They're like us!" the man exclaimed.

"Tourism brings jobs and raises the standard of living. Isn't that our mission?" I asked.

"Yes, but not to change their culture," the man opined with aching regret. "We wanted them to progress within their own."

"You can't control change, but if we're not here for change, why are we here?" I asked.

They stared blankly at the riddle.

•

The reuniting volunteers spilled into the house throughout the evening with no reference to time or place, mission or ideal. We were released from a confinement of solitude.

Each arrival brought wine or beer. Local Tunisian children circulated among the revelers, hawking soft drinks out of metal buckets of ice as they did on summer beaches. *"Coka! Fanta! Gini!"* they cried out as if in tribute to our glorious past.

As the party surged, I was anxious about the camaraderie that surrounded, yet excluded me, which I sought but others already shared.

479

If I received a report card for my year in Tunisia, it was my dejection in the middle of the revelry. We were not strangers as we had been in Philadelphia, with nametags on our chests and apprehensive faces. A year ago, we had the potential to be close. Now we were strangers by choice.

I anticipated Tasha's appearance with dread, glancing so often at the door that it was like a tic. Tasha was a masked enigma, for whom no quantity of cool could prepare me. I should have worn sunglasses, since I lacked the confidence to look at her directly. My life was in disarray. I was worried about my health and my future, ashamed of how my assignments turned out and guilty about the betrayed look on Tasha's face when Cerise joined me in Ayn Draham.

These reflections were interrupted by a hubbub in the room. Excitement welcomed a new arrival.

Livia flowed through the crowd in a long, peasant dress that eddied around her legs. She stroked her pregnant abdomen in circles, as if to say, "Look at us." She beamed at the other women volunteers, as they engulfed her in their hugs of congratulations.

Unlike the previous summer, Fargus was no longer gazing at Livia. He had a new girlfriend who lived in Tunis and worked for Dr. Mamooni. They were on the patio. Depending on one's interpretation, Fargus looked mellow or depressed, his default expressions. We exchanged greetings and made small talk. His new girlfriend said she had to pee. They kissed soulfully and she went indoors. I congratulated Fargus. He looked perplexed.

"It took you no time to get over Livia," I said.

He shrugged.

"We broke up in the winter. Livia's amazing but demanding. I won't lie: it hurt when she dumped me, but the damage was temporary."

"Your resilience is amazing."

"Not really. I've just been there before. That's one good thing about pain, Murkey. You get through it, you get used it and you get over it." He slapped my back. "You need a beer."

•

We left the party and took a turn around the town, dangling bottles of *Celtia* by the necks as we stumbled along the dormant streets with early rising fishermen. Down at the dock, we leaned on the jetty rail and gazed at the dark water.

"Shouldn't you take care of that?" he pointed at the tennis ball on my arm.

I shrugged. "It's like another muscle."

"Can I sign it?" he cracked.

We returned to the villa, which swarmed with celebrants.

A knuckle tapped my tumor.

"Hey, Metloui Man!" It was Jann. "How are phosphates?"

"*I Ching*," I countered. "What's in the future?"

"I don't *I Ching* anymore. I'm between beliefs." Jann grinned smugly, his slitty blue marble eyes gleaming in the dark. He had grown a goatee to cover his sharp chin.

"The future is an illusion," he said, "but Irving is history. He's looking for a job. Like me!" He clapped his hands. Even Irving P. Irving became sympathetic when Jann talked about him.

"And get this," Jan continued. "Dozier and his wife split up."

A year ago, Jann separated from his wife, but now he seemed happy, or he was pretending to be joyful to exacerbate my misery.

"Will he stay on?" I asked.

"Dozier's Joe Peace Corps. But one day he has to go home."

Jann's acerbic remark about Dozier was supposed to unite us

in malicious laughter, but it forced me to face my own problem.

Eventually, I'd be going home. I had believed that escape was possible, but gravity was a horizontal force that pulled me back.

What was waiting for me?

A mother who expected me to be gone for years? Who liked me best when she saw me least? A maintenance job? Of course, Cerise might visit. She liked the United States.

Jann's eyes twinkled with benevolent brotherhood. He seemed certain of my woes in Metloui, but I refused to feed his appetite for my failure. I glanced around.

"Seen Tasha?" Jann asked, as he stroked his beard mischievously. "You didn't know? She's working in Tunis."

He always suspected my feelings for Tasha, but his warnings in training camp were irrelevant now. I looked for the bathroom to get away from him.

"Don't you say hello?"

I turned to meet her voice and splashed beer on my shirt.

"Hello."

"Are you avoiding me?"

"I wouldn't be standing here if I were."

Tasha laughed. Her long, luxuriant brown hair with the middle part had been cut shoulder length and the sides flipped forward, prim and businesslike. The mole on her cheek was still like a jewel embedded in her skin, and her teeth gleamed in the dark.

"So how are you doing?" she asked.

I laughed.

"That bad."

She scrutinized the bump on my arm with clinical fascination.

"You should have it checked out," she said.

"Thanks. So how about you?"

She pursed her shapely lips, calculating the response.

"I hear you're in Tunisia," I said impatiently. "What are you doing?"

"A little of everything," she said, averted her eyes to check out the party. "Mostly learning. I'm Interim Assistant Director."

"Last summer you swore you were done with the Peace Corps."

She grimaced at the reminder of a personal dilemma.

"You don't sound happy that I'm back," she said.

"No, it's great to see you," I blurted out. My face was burning because I had given myself away so easily. "It's been a long year—but last summer was a high point." It was a relief to speak honestly to her; I even liked it. "Dunes, sunsets, chicken fights, pistachio ice cream—I didn't realize how special those days were."

"They were good times," she agreed, still only half-looking at me as she took in the scene around us.

A man inserted his compact body next to her. He was blond, fair and even-featured. "Can we go to the beach?" he asked, as though transcribing my thoughts. "Remember, you promised we could play midnight Frisbee."

Tasha laughed. She introduced her friend, a Swiss engineer working in Tunis. They did not kiss or embrace. She apparently had no interest in making me jealous. Still, I felt an unbearable anguish that had been building for days. If Tasha kissed this man, my hopes and illusions would be obliterated. She didn't, yet her decorum only increased my uncertainty.

"I wanted to tell you how sorry, I mean, how badly I felt at how the summer camp ended," I said.

"You did nothing wrong. You were happy," she replied.

"Yes," I paused. "But you and I had a great friendship."

She stared at me curiously as if waiting for a statement to

which she could respond, but I couldn't state my mind more explicitly. Fortunately, she guessed it.

"Murkey, don't apologize. I enjoyed being with you. We were friends. That's the sad part of the Peace Corps. We're always saying goodbye."

"Thanks," I said like a man going through a pack of damp matches. "I haven't been a model volunteer."

"Someone said you weren't staying two years," she remarked.

"I'm not sure," I admitted.

"Do you have a job for next year?" she asked.

"No."

"You need one if you're going to stay," she said.

"Who decides that?"

"We'd have to look at what you've done and what's available."

"Would it be a problem?" I asked. Here was what I had hoped for—to meet Tasha and have her show me the way.

"I don't know," she said. "We'd have to sit down and evaluate it. I think you could have done better. But you pulled Menzel and Metloui, the worst assignments, so you're off the hook a little. Even so, you might have paid more attention to work and less to whatever it is you do. But that's not your style."

"It could be," I replied.

"Really? I don't think so. Well, it's good seeing you."

Tasha nodded, smiled and moved on to other volunteers. I felt pardoned for every sin, yet condemned. Tasha wouldn't play my spurned lover, reproachful sister, mentor, muse, or role model. She didn't even want to be my boss.

I leaned against the wall late into the night. I felt that I had received the final sign that my life was changing, but I could not be alone with it. The party was cold and exhausted, in the dregs of celebration. Couples slow-danced, leaning on each other, half-asleep in inebriated tenderness, holding on to the moment that was already gone. Their private lives lingered in a public space with no other place to go.

In the darkness, Tasha stared my way from across the room, as she had done when Dozier showed us how to teach English without words. Her glowing eyes formed the question: *Why didn't you take a chance on me?* She did not look away when our eyes met, nor did she beckon me. I had to go to her now or I knew I would regret it. I walked across the room toward the corner where she was sitting.

No one was there. I glanced toward another dark corner, where Jann flicked his forefinger and smiled.

34

DEAD OCTOPUS

When I returned to Gafsa, it was raining for the first time since winter.

Tlili met me at the door, his eyes sad and pleading.

"I told them not to do it, believe me, I told them not to do it."

In a pile in the foyer, behind the dining table, were all my worldly possessions covered with ink.

I picked up a blue-smeared clog, as if it were a wounded child and demanded to be taken to Metloui. Thunder cracked and rain poured from the sky as if the heavens were returning the desert to the ocean. I barged into Mabrouk's office. He was looking out the window at the rain, mesmerized by it.

"Look what you've done to my clog," I said, my voice filled with indignation and grief.

"The classes ended, *Monsieur*," Mabrouk replied blandly. "We wished to make the room available to other guests and we assumed you would no longer be needing it."

In a calm, trancelike voice, Mabrouk made it all sound reasonable, as he stared out the window.

"The American government is going to hear about this," I threatened. My former supervisor smiled wearily.

"That your shoe has ink on it? Buy another pair of shoes."

"But what If I can't find another pair like it? What then?"

Mabrouk kneaded his eyebrows impassively. "I cannot advise you on that. I'm not in the shoe business. Is that all, *Monsieur*? I am very busy."

"What's going to happen to me here? Where will I stay and how will I get out of here?"

"Arrangements will be made," he said.

When I left Mabrouk's office, I walked around Metloui in the driving rain, holding out my clog like a cup to show everyone the injustice. But no one seemed to see the injustice, only a grown man holding up a wooden shoe.

Two French engineers, who mistook my grief for performance art and believed I was being funny rather than compulsive, offered me a lift to Gafsa. We were forced to stop several times as the rain intensified and the road submerged in vast lakes and spontaneous streams. Finally traffic stopped. In the downpour, all of those dips and bends that made a jolting ride in the hard dust and sunshine had become the beds and banks of turgid rivers. We made our way on foot down the side of a chasm and crossed the swift-flowing *oued* on stones strewn by the flash-flood into a fortuitous path. On the far escarpment an emergency bus waited to take us to Gafsa. Amid all of the bureaucratic delay I had encountered in Tunisia, the timely appearance of that bus seemed providential.

There was no place for me at the *borj*. I stayed with John and Paula for a few nights while I waited for the company car to take me to Tunis.

When the end is near and the deadline is days away, you exist at the intersection between yesterday and tomorrow, as if your life were shipped ahead. The present is preparation—but for what? Caution and calculation are inadequate for the unknown. Transition may yield a premature freedom, like thoughts of spring in a winter thaw. The mind, drugged by hope, floats in a frontier of speculation while the body is tethered to the present.

Between now and then, nothing belongs to you but your baggage and the past if you can remember and make sense of it. John and Paula finally seemed to like me during those few days when I moped around their little house. No doubt it was because I was like them, quiet and perplexed as I lay on their couch, replaying my year in Tunisia, trying to do two things at once: find the mistakes I made and the hidden moments of revelation to help transcend them. Yet the more I pursued a truth about the people and the place, the more elusive it was. I sought something definitive: a moment, a connection, *anything* to give shape to my time here.

John knew what I was thinking. The night before I left, he brought from the market a large, slimy octopus and announced that we would feast to my new beginnings.

"How can we eat that slimy thing?" I asked.

"Let me show you," he said.

We went outside to the wall of the compound. He held the tentacles of the cephalopod with a towel and smacked its body against the stone wall, leaving strands of mucous to glisten and dry on the rough surface.

"Here, you try," he said. I swung the octopus a few times. It felt good.

"That's how we turn octopus to *pulpo* for our pasta sauce,"

John laughed. We each took turns swinging the octopus. "It's just beating a dead cephalopod, but it's fun, right?"

When the octopus and our hands were clean, John shook mine.

"The secret of life I learned at *The Atomic Rooster* is that there is no secret," he said. "Making sense of random experience is a path to madness."

That night we ate delicious linguine with *pulpo* in a hot Tunisian tomato sauce. The next day I was in a *louage* to Tunis.

35
BISLEMA, HABIBI I

"You're just the one I want to see," the nurse said when I appeared at the Peace Corps office. I was seasoned enough by then to react instinctively when anyone wanted to see me, by running as fast as I could in the opposite direction. But I was surrounded by my luggage and needed to store it.

"You're scheduled for a check-up on June 17. Is that okay?"

The nurse wasn't asking but telling me. I calculated that the 17th was a month away. Until then I could travel around Tunisia and see the parts I'd missed. Then I remembered Cerise's letter. She said she would be gone for the last two weeks of June. If I left a week earlier, I could meet her in Bidonville before her travels and discuss our future.

"Can you move it up to June 10th?" I asked.

The nurse scowled. It seemed smart to be less demanding.

"Okay, I'm on for the 17th!" I conceded as I lifted my bags with a burst of strength and turned to leave the office. But the nurse wasn't done with me. My deference mollified her. "You can have any date you want, dear. Just clear it upstairs."

"No, it's all right," I assured her.

But protest was as futile as compromise. The nurse's wish to accommodate me was inexorable. She escorted me to the second floor.

"Tasha Theodore will have to sign off on it. She's the Acting Associate Director."

The officious nurse escorted me into an office I last visited when Dozier was its occupant. "This volunteer wants to change his checkup date," she announced.

Tasha Theodore sat at her new desk with her head down and her arms splayed, as if praying to disappear. She might have learned the pose from Dozier, or maybe it came with the job.

At first I was nervous, but in Tasha's mind, I had apparently gone from forgiven to forgotten. She glanced at the nurse and me, as if she had never seen us before and wished not to see us again. She signed the form without reading it and blinked to signal our dismissal.

But her voice stopped me on my way out. "Wait, Rick. Shouldn't you be in Metloui?"

"The program's over."

"So why are you here?"

"I'm waiting for termination day," I said impatiently.

Instead of blinking, her eyes flashed.

"The Peace Corps isn't a bus station. You can't wait around. You're terminated."

"Schedule his physical for today," she told the nurse.

Tasha called on Dozier. In his final days in Tunisia, he was her mentor.

"Bill, Murkey's project is over. I think it's a bad idea for him to linger. Do you agree?"

Dozier signaled agreement with a head nod and a grunt.

"You have two days, Rick, Your ticket will be ready the afternoon before you leave. It will be valid for 72 hours. If you're not in Washington by then the ticket will be invalid and you'll have to pay your way back."

"Tasha," I pleaded softly. "Why are you doing this?"

"This is termination. It's not personal. You have to change planes in Paris or Rome."

"Paris would be better."

"Let me see."

She studied the wall map and a manual on her desk. "Rome is the closest city with a direct flight to the U.S."

"I don't know Italian. I know no one in Rome."

She stared at me blankly. "You'll be at the airport. Your foreign language proficiency won't be a factor. Rome is closer, so you'll stop over in Rome."

"Tasha," I pleaded hoarsely, holding back tears.

"Yes?" she asked, bewildered by my lingering.

"Shouldn't my arm be looked at before I leave?"

I stroked the bump to demonstrate its abnormality. "Do you want a closer look?"

"I can see it from here," she replied abruptly, glancing at my arm as she picked up the phone. Tasha had a brief conversation and hung up. I believed the mysterious mass had saved me.

"The doctor wouldn't be able to get X-rays on your arm until late next week, so you can have it checked in Washington."

I swallowed again.

"Tasha, why are you being such a—?"

"—*Bitch*?" she asked evenly. "That's the word you're looking for. Maybe I am, or maybe I'm just doing my job. I warned you at training camp that rules aren't convenient. You're not working, so you're terminated."

She stared at me resolutely to indicate that the conversation was as terminated as I was.

I bowed my head and was halfway out the door when she called me. I hoped she had changed her mind.

"Murkey, take care. I'm glad we met," she said.

Regret and confusion overcame me.

"Really? Thanks. Under different circum—"

"Under different circumstances we wouldn't have met."

36
BISLEMA, HABIBI II

Even a nomad has roots, if only memories scattered over time. I had lived all over Tunisia, but leaving it was more complicated than I expected.

For 48 hours I handled exit business, collecting my effects, closing my accounts and exchanging currency. On the last point I had a problem. I had accumulated 200 dinars with typical Peace Corps frugality. Volunteers were supposed to save for vacations and spend the money in Tunisia to support the economy. I had meant to travel and splurge for a month before termination, but now that my time was curtailed, I had too many dinars to legally exchange. If I didn't convert surplus dinars to western currency on the black market, most of my savings would be worthless.

How stupid it seemed in retrospect that I had reported Marwah for stealing 15 *dinars* when I could have given her 100—at least she could have used them.

However, it wasn't too late to give most of it away. I could make amends for my useless year by handing out *dinars* in the streets to beggars and impecunious passers-by in one last magnanimous Peace Corps act. At first, I tried passing bills to pedestrians as I walked, but I learned that most people did not accept objects from moving strangers. Then I distributed dinars in a stationary position on a busy corner. This worked too well. Pedestrians felt at ease with me, as if I were a lamppost or a kiosk. When they looked at my handouts, they surrounded me and clamored for more. I had to flee the mob I incited.

On my last night, I sat in Le Café de France, tired and despondent amid the noise and frivolity, when I felt a tap on my shoulder. I turned and there was Raotha, the teacher we had rescued from the Menzel Bordello. She was strikingly beautiful and glamorous. Her large, almond eyes were limned by dark curves of mascara.

"Is that you, my hero?" she said. "Why do you look so sad and lonely?"

"My assignment is over. I'm leaving Tunisia tomorrow and I won't be going anywhere else because I have 150 worthless dinars."

"I'm sad you are leaving," she said. "After all you have done and seen, this should not be your last memory. Let me help."

We went to the medina, where she knew someone who knew someone who exchanged currencies. It was a sultry night. The air was thick with incense and cooking smoke. Raotha had an internal compass for these crooked backstreets that narrowed at every turn. In apparent dead-ends she saw passageways and noticed the fissures and doorways that accessed a world that was dense and complex—and invisible to western eyes. We came to a door that gave way to a stone stairway leading to another. Here we stopped. Raotha knocked. The door opened. A man with a shock of massive curls leaned against the door. He had a churlish manner and was visibly perturbed by our appearance.

He didn't want to be bothered with an *Americani,* but Raotha prevailed on him. I handed her the envelope of cash to give to him. He slammed the door. "Don't worry," Raotha said. "I know him. He has bad manners but he will change your money."

After a few minutes, he did not return. She knocked on the door. There was no answer. Then she pounded on the door. My nervousness escalated to panic. I asked her if the money was gone. She said we were not leaving until I had francs in my pocket.

"I'll call the police on you, you petty, stupid thief!" Raotha cried out. The door opened and the man with the curly hair emerged with a large and unfriendly colleague.

"What do you want?"

"We gave you dinars. Now we want our francs."

"Are you crazy? You didn't give me any money."

"Yes we did."

"Are you calling me a liar?"

"I don't call names. Just give us back the money we gave to you."

"So you're calling me a thief."

"I will if you don't give it back. This young man needs it. He's leaving tomorrow."

"It's good for him that he's leaving. But he may leave sooner—from this world. I could kill you now and no one would know where to look for you."

My abrupt departure, inconvenient stopover, premature return to the dreary suburb and economy from which I fled and the loss of all my savings were devastating setbacks, but seemed trivial compared to the threat of that moment.

"Raotha," I whispered, "Maybe—"

She kicked my leg and hissed, "*Tais-toi.*"

"Here, you need money for your trip?" the moneychanger jeered, as he tossed a 50-*millime* piece, a copper coin that clanked on the street.

Mr. Curly laughed hard at my predicament, which was now worse than when we came. He enjoyed the fear and despair on my face so much that he left himself vulnerable. Raotha kicked him in the groin. As his bodyguard lunged for her, I tackled him and he staggered backward, slamming his head against a wall. Then Raotha and I swarmed on Mr. Curly. The moneychanger flailed his arms, punched wildly and gouged us with his fingers to fend us off. As he made it to his feet, I threw my shoulder into him waist-high and drove him into a wall of trash between two buildings. Mr. Curly tried to lift himself out of the heap, but sank deeper into it as we pelted him with garbage. To keep him down, I jumped on top of him and hit him repeatedly with an empty can. While he spat blood and panted, Raotha found a wad of French bills in his pocket, counted it quickly—1,500 francs for me and 100 for her— and tossed the rest on his spent body.

We ran the winding streets to avoid capture, heard whistles and sirens of police giving chase, while my wooden clogs clopped and echoed on the paving stones. Eventually, we found *Bab Souika,* the Times Square of Tunis, where we mingled among the men leaving theaters and milling among cafés, before escaping the Arab quarter into the grid of the French city.

Only when we had slowed to an amble on the wide, bustling Boulevard Bourguiba were Raotha and I able to speak.

"Thank you. You saved me."

"This is not the best last impression of Tunisia," Raotha replied. "But you have your francs and your freedom—and you know I am always your friend. Let this be your enduring memory."

"How did you learn to fight?" I asked.

"I was always an athletic girl. I knew how to defend myself. But when I was held in Menzel, I was lost. Sometimes in your life, there are things you cannot fight. Nothing in your experience prepares you for them. When they happen, you need a miracle—or a friend. When you walked into my room at that *house*," she paused and closed her eyes, "you were both. *Shokran* and *bislema*, Rick. Please don't forget me. I will always remember you."

She touched my shoulder, kissed me on the lips and smiled. I experienced a moment of intense pleasure, surprise and confusion. The full taboo of what she had done overwhelmed me. Yet before I could react, she turned, flashed one last smile and walked off, merging with the crowd. In seconds, I lost sight of her in the diffuse lights and enveloping darkness.

•

The next morning, after retrieving my final mail delivery from the Peace Corps office, I sat on the terrace of Le Café du Belvédère and read Cerise's letter while partaking of my last *lait au poule*— the best breakfast drink ever—a banana milkshake with an egg yolk blended in.

My Dear Love,

The letter you sent from Mahdia arrived today whereas the one on the 15th came two days ago. (???)

My poor love, you sound so mixed up, you destroy me. Why do you refuse to admit how depressed you are, to be open about it, instead of pretending to enjoy the chaos and confusion?

I don't believe in your war with the company, the Peace Corps and the system: they are battles with yourself.

Do you want a balance sheet? In my view, what has come out of Tunisia is a wreck. Yes, you are very sick and I would have been too if I had spent a year like you have done. You have been contaminated and have succeeded in contaminating me, as well. For months now, your letters have depressed me. Do you realize how far we have drifted apart?

It's true that I love what you are, but I don't like the way you're wasting it. I feel that for a whole year you've been living like a cabbage! If you don't start making yourself happy very soon I will lose faith in you completely.

I have already lost faith in us.

I, too, am dying to see you, but it's you I want to hold in my arms, not the product of a screwed up year in Tunisia.

Please don't misinterpret my words again. If you misread my letter and thought I was with other guys, it was because you sensed that you had been setting yourself up for it. You know that I view your refusal to look at the future rationally as a proof of your lack of genuine attachment to me.

Still, what I want to say is that I love you very much.

Tenderly,

Cerise

It was a fine morning. The elephants in the zoo nearby rumbled behind the drooping palms as I inhaled the scent of jasmine and sipped my *lait au poule*. After folding her letter, I wrote a febrile response, as I had done many times before.

You claim that everything I've done to be close to you has pulled us apart. If you're right, it's a fitting end to a baffling year. If I sabotaged our relationship while trying to perpetuate it, I have the self-awareness of the mosquito squatting on my arm.

I swatted the bloodsucker. The elephants trumpeted—either

applauding my aim, or deriding my letter writing. I had no time to post this response and no forwarding address, so I tore it up.

There was nothing left for me to do in Tunisia. My ink-splashed clogs were now black, the typewriter that perforated paper was oiled, my dinars were francs and a plane ticket was in my pocket.

I savored the moment and acknowledged gratefully that such times were rare and unrepeatable. When would I feel so free again, with so much to anticipate and so much unknown?

I reread the letter from Cerise, kissed the round handwriting and inhaled the perfume from her hand. The elephants screeched. They knew what a fool I was. I wiped the croissant crumbs from my shirt, lifted my bags and started to walk. The load was heavy, yet I felt lighter than I had for a while.

"I take it back, Cerise. You are an experience!" I called out to no one in particular.

BOOK 5
ROME, IN RUINS

I took a room in a hotel across from the Maggiore and flung myself into the eye-enthralling Roman cityscape, where sightseeing meant a walk around the block. Rome was not built in a day, but I had to experience it in less than three, since the Peace Corps plane ticket expired in 72 hours. I paced grand boulevards and curving, curbless streets with exaggerated purpose, looking side to side, up and down, like a ravenous predator, Sisyphus on furlough from hell.

The next morning, I went to the airline office to reserve a seat on a flight for the next day, presumably my last, but both flights were booked. I was frantic. I hated to leave, but not as much as being stranded and broke. I pleaded with the clerk that I had a 72-hour ticket and if he did not find me a seat, I would end up homeless in Rome. He told me not to worry, that I could reserve a seat for the day after, or even later. I believed he was being kind or careless to stretch the limits of my ticket, but I accepted the oversight and returned the next day to book another flight. That went so smoothly that I returned the following day to cancel and reschedule a second time. Again, there was no problem.

It became a habit. I stopped by the ticket office each day for two weeks to postpone my flight. It was like a strange dream—my last day in the Eternal City repeated eternally. But I was unsure if this was Roman hospitality or a bureaucratic oversight, so I could not enjoy my extended stay. I dreaded that once the airline discovered their error, my ticket would be cancelled and I would waste away. I did not dare to ask the clerk to clarify the situation, until my anxiety became so intense that I broke down.

"Why is the airline letting me extend my ticket? Am I missing something—or are you?"

He smiled.

"*Signore,* there must be a misunderstanding."

"Misunderstanding? That's what I was afraid of."

"You have an open ticket. It is valid for a year."

"A year? How is this possible?"

"Let me show you." He pointed to a place on the back of the ticket. "You see? If this ticket had an expiration date, this box would have been checked and a date would have been written on this line. But you see it's blank."

"You're right!" I told him. "Thank you."

"*Prego, signore*. But you do not need to thank me. I am only reporting the facts."

I was so happy about this windfall that I nearly flew out of the airline office. But I soon returned to earth. While sipping an espresso at a *caffè*, I indulged my bad habit of analyzing everything. Did the Peace Corps travel office overlook the 3-day limit on my ticket, or was this Tasha's parting gift? It must have been Tasha. How wonderful she was! She gave me a year in Rome—if I lived a year. (The mysterious bump on my arm had grown so large that one passerby called it, "the eighth hill of Rome.")

Regardless, I had to make the most of this unexpected boon. An open ticket was the sign I needed to truly live. If I was dying, what better place to be than in the Eternal City? I owed myself the rapture and the pizza it provided before mortality claimed me.

I wandered without itinerary, delighted by the magnificence and *significance* of Rome. There were gorgeous, inspiring sights in Tunisia, even in the barren mountains around Metloui, but they were often surreal and surprising, and I did not know how to interpret them. In Rome, I knew where I was at all times, even if I didn't know what I was doing there. I was a foreigner, but everything felt familiar, so that without knowing the language, I understood what things meant. Every Westerner is at home in

Rome—in a mythic sense. Rome is to our minds what the ruins are to Rome: a relic, a source, a witness and survivor of time.

Besides, Rome was a slacker's paradise, where good food, lively streets and a warm sun favored idleness. People strolled casually, without apparent destination, yet not in a vagrant way. They were taking in the wonder of everyday life as if it were their sacred duty. They were not busy, nor did they strive to be. In their minds, living in Rome was their principal occupation and the Roman lifestyle was their job description.

I wanted to lead a Roman life and it seemed attainable. I drifted in the languid current of Rome, playing the tourist. I circulated silently among the Piazza Navonna, Palazzo Farnese and the Villa Borghese, climbed the Spanish Steps, ambled in the Trastevere, and stood before the Trevi Fountain—framing each site and each moment, absorbing the urban circus to make it eternal in my mind. But what was my subject, my story? I was like an animated figure slapped against a glorious backdrop. After a week of monuments, I knew what my Roman escapade was missing.

I settled in the Albergo Paradiso, an inexpensive, lively hotel near the Campo di Fiori. On torrid afternoons before going out, I took cold showers, the only kind available, in a water closet down the hall. Through a small window, I saw an elderly woman on a nearby roof as she tended her garden: a luxuriant plot of palms, coleus, roses, orchids and eucalyptus. She moved in and out of her penthouse shack, with the dome of St. Peter's in the haze behind her and watered her plants with doting domesticity. She stepped gracefully among them in a silent dance, as if extracting rhythms and melodies from the traffic seven stories below. My neighbor had transformed her ramshackle roof yard into a sky island—not grand, but intricate and deeply felt, a feat of devotion and individual genius. This roof oasis encouraged me. It suggested that even within the context of two thousand years of Roman architecture, one might create a private world of beauty out of dull concrete, without fantasy or pretense.

At seven one evening, I walked by the Piazza Argentina, an alfresco depot, where buses careered, rumbled and stopped around a sunken ruin and stray cats darted among Roman columns. People with bags on shoulders, parcels on strings and groceries in nets boarded and exited the buses—pushing, strutting and squirming with beads of sweat on their foreheads and upper lips, exhaustion and determination etched on their intense faces. This was life. It wasn't beautiful, but these people were part of it. Their faces betrayed essential yearnings—for rest, food, home, comfort, friends and family, or the immediate need to get out of their sticky clothes. I longed to be like them, but I was removed from normal routine and haunted Rome instead of living in it. What I needed was not a series of locations, but a scene.

An Italian election campaign was taking place, the 15th in 12 years. I tried to immerse myself in the issues, parties, ideologies and the competition for power. But Italian politics bewildered me. In Venice, I went to a Communist rally at the Piazza San Marco; I never before saw so many chic women in one place. Back in Rome, the Radical Party staged a "pro-choice" demonstration. The denim-clad candidate, Panatta, a bandanna swathed around his flowing white hair, addressed the crowd from a cart flanked by three pregnant "virgins" in white, plunging gowns. In the middle of the rally, with "We Can Spend the Night Together" blaring through loudspeakers, Panatta brandished a large knife and slashed the gowns of the three "virgins" across their waists to extract three pillows. It was unclear whether the candidate was representing the horrors of illegal abortions or the rise in c-section deliveries. Regardless, his crowd gasped and cheered as baroque gargoyles in the splendid Piazza Navonna fountains drooled into marble basins.

The Italian political scene was a rollicking carnival, but I knew I was viewing the human side of Italy as an outsider. If I belonged here at all, it was in a community of expatriates like myself. I had met a former volunteer in a Tunisian dance club. She was teaching English in Rome and told me to call her if I was ever in town. I phoned her and we met for coffee. She burst into the *caffè* in Trastevere like a romantic movie character in large-framed glasses, a mass of curly hair and a green silk blouse. We chatted at a window table and I relaxed and became more casual. I asked if she lived alone.

"It's none of your business," she snapped and stood up abruptly to leave. When I profusely apologized, she regained her composure and we continued to talk.

She shared little of her personal life, but offered to help me find work. She said there might be openings at her school, which specialized in teaching English to Russian refugees. According to a rumor, a new cohort of *emigrés* was soon arriving from Vienna and the school might need more staff. I visited her at the school and interviewed with the director, Clay, a kind and rumpled sophisticate in his '60s, who exuded the breezy nonchalance of one who had no use for value judgments, his own or anyone else's.

After asking cursory questions about my teaching experience, Clay shifted the conversation to his own long and tortuous story. It was late morning, so he invited me to go downstairs and join him for coffee. He showed me around the Trastevere neighborhood where the school was located and recounted the major moments of his life. He said he had been a diplomat with the American Embassy in Paris before his nervous breakdown. Now he moved comfortably around Rome in a high decibel Hawaiian shirt and flip-flops. During our "interview" he stopped several times for yogurts and *frulattis*, fruit smoothies, to "keep up his strength."

"World War II was the best time in my life," Clay said. "Everyone was united for a greater cause."

Clay agreed to give me a chance to prove myself in a demonstration class. I returned to my hotel and prepared a lesson plan, as I had done in Ayn Draham. The next morning I performed my lesson. The 15 minutes went swiftly, which boded well, and the students were attentive.

Afterward, Clay gave me a brief review. "You're good. You have presence. You're tall." He promised to contact me when an opening arose, but the Russians stayed longer in Vienna than expected and their classes were postponed.

Although I was hemorrhaging my travel funds and desperately needed income, missing the teaching opportunity did not disappoint me. ESL was a continuation of the Peace Corps and I needed a break. I sought new experiences and a new crowd.

The Albergo Paradiso was an excellent place to meet people. I became acquainted with a young, blond opera diva at the *caffè* downstairs. When I mentioned that I was an aspiring writer, she told me her ex-boyfriend had also been a writer and she burned his notebook. She was often with a young actor friend, who had roles in several films at the *Cinecittà*, Rome's Hollywood. He and the diva appeared together at clubs and events so that paparazzi would photograph their fictitious romance.

At the Paradiso, I also met an American architecture student who had paid his way to Rome by driving a New York cab for 30 straight days and nights; a German woman who called American suburbs a "mass lobotomy"; a sad Brazilian economist who was plagued by nightmares of inflation; and an unemployed Danish baroness, whose research required that she visit museums that were rarely open.

One rainy afternoon I found myself in the main floor reading room with the Danish baroness. She was an anthropologist in her late 30s and her expression oscillated between anxiety and resignation. I remembered my friend, Colombi, and adapted his classic rejoinder for her: *"C'est l'angoisse, Baroness."* When I said it, she smiled. She asked me to teach her the phrase, which I did, and we became friends.

Her name was Karen. When she lost her job, the Danish government gave her a stipend to pursue her doctoral work, an abstruse study on cultural literacy. Baroness Karen had very little, but like other residents of the Albergo Paradiso, she had a high tolerance for poverty. She seemed to need someone in her life more than the other guests, so I determined to know her better.

Baroness Karen lived on the same floor as the 90-year-old sisters who owned the Paradiso. On the same evening that I made her laugh in the study, I sneaked up to her room and knocked quietly on the door while the hallway floor creaked under my feet. The owners must have heard me because they opened their door; at the sound of their turning doorknob, I bolted up the stairs.

The next afternoon I paid the baroness another visit. She opened the door and asked me in as if she expected me, which added intrigue to the clandestine visit. The baroness wore red and white striped pajamas. Sardines were cooking on a hot plate and a small dog was barking. The intimacy of the small room, the large bed, the woman in striped pajamas and the pungent aroma of sardines combined to overpower my good manners. I impulsively reached under Baroness Karen's pajama top and pulled her on to the bed. I had not had a woman for months and was ravenous for sex, but I never anticipated how beautiful she was. Simply touching her was intoxicating. Her body was all warmth and curves. I moved my hand over her soft skin and between her legs, mounted her and held her shapely buttocks. We made swift and passionate love. For the first time in memory, I felt calm and free.

The next day, Baroness Karen asked me to accompany her to Peruggia, where she had studied Italian. At first I was ambivalent and ashamed. I liked her but did not want to be her boyfriend or her male escort. It was an overcast day in Umbria and the low mountains were hidden in the mist and clouds.

When we arrived in Peruggia, she dropped me off in the town center and disappeared. I walked around Peruggia, ate hotdogs and sauerkraut in the main square and waited for the baroness to return. A few hours later we drove back to Rome.

I was in a sullen mood, but could not blame it on Baroness Karen. She believed she was being kind to give me a free, no-strings ride to a place I had never been. She never volunteered as a tour guide. Besides, she respected my autonomy and never made me feel I owed her for our intimacy. I liked her for that but I was still depressed.

The baroness broke our silence.

"You're quiet," she noted. "What's wrong?"

"I appreciate your driving me to Peruggia," I said. "But I didn't know anyone. It was pretty lonely."

"I'm sorry I left you alone. I had to speak to my old professor," she said. "I need his help to extend my grant."

"Why did you bring me along?" I asked resentfully.

"I thought you'd want to see Peruggia. It's a beautiful city."

"You're right. And the hot dogs weren't bad, either."

Our silence returned. Finally she spoke.

"I am often lonely," she said. "I am sorry I made you feel that way."

"It's all right," I said, but I doubted that she was sorry.

Baroness Karen and I did not see each other afterward, except

once in passing. She was excited that she had located a museum in
Ostia with normal opening hours. She left Rome for a week and we
lost touch. By then I realized that the trip to Peruggia was her way
of closing our relationship, which was like a 3-day package tour—
flirtation, intimacy and a brush-off.

But the Danish baroness's absence only simplified my next
romantic diversion. Rome was a peerless setting for romance, and
the blonde diva, Madalena, was made to play the leading lady. She
had lovely skin and hair and a nonchalance that suggested she did
not bother to enhance them. Madalena was neither tall nor short,
neither thin nor plump. I could not single out any of her features.
She was a rare woman who came in one piece, contained in an
aura that obscured the individual parts, like Glinda in *The Wizard
of Oz*. We often spoke at the *trattoria* downstairs where we had
our meals. I wanted to be alone with her, but she was always with
her androgynous actor friend.

A language instructor at Clay's school invited me to a party at
her apartment. I asked Madalena to go with me, but she had plans
to see her actor friend in a dress rehearsal of *Dangerous Liaisons*.
She added that I was welcome to come along.

Two bus trips later we were the only spectators in a cavernous
theater, where a cast of 40 costumed actors onstage took turns
chattering in Italian. Of course, I understood nothing. The first act
was an hour long—and it was a five-act play. I asked Madalena if
we could leave and go to my party, but she was loyal to her friend.
She said slipping away now would be impolite and the cast would
be discouraged if they played to a vacant theater.

In desperation, I plotted our escape. After the third act, I
winced and trembled.

"*Stai bene, caro?*" Madalena asked.

"No. It's my arm!" I poked my tumor and grimaced.

"What is it? It's so big."

"I don't know but it hurts and I can't focus on this great play."

"*Caro*, how can your arm prevent you from watching a play? It is far from your eyes and ears."

Apparently I needed a more elaborate ailment to convince the diva to leave.

"Madalena, you may not have heard because they kept it quiet, but there was a war in North Africa. It was a small, intimate, war, but unfortunately, a bomb exploded. I had a concussion. Now I'm dizzy, I see double, and my head pounds like a drum. I also have this bump on my arm."

This story, though implausible, ingeniously linked a headache, serious but invisible, with a visible and painless bump. Madelena was moved.

"*Poverino!*" she cried and touched my forehead. "Of course we can leave."

I finally found a way into the diva's heart as a phony war casualty. But once we had left the drafty theater for the warm summer twilight, my symptoms improved. She saw through my machination and resented me for it. When we returned to our hotel our date ended.

Meanwhile my arm bump grew. People stared at my tumor and me with alarm and pity. They offered unsolicited advice and dire prognoses. But a doctor was out of my price range. I tried to ignore this strange addition to my body, but I could not deny that beneath the sensations and anxieties that played along the surface of my mind, changes were going on inside me unrelated to my surroundings—and these changes, though mysterious and unidentified, were more real than my external existence. As I moved through the lush and lustrous environment of Rome, I withdrew from it. Each day I felt lighter, less involved, as if I were becoming numb. Was I dying or was my surface peeling away so that something could replace it?

On the Spanish Steps, at around 2 PM one afternoon, I met Agrippina, a barefoot foot-washer. For five thousand lire, she washed men's feet as she knelt before them in her low-cut peasant's blouse. The water in her bucket never changed.

"Why don't you try to be an actress?" I asked her in a nearby *caffè*.

"I AM an actress!" she protested, "I touch their feet, don't I? I make them think their feet are clean when they've been in the filthy water, eh? What more do you want?"

"It doesn't matter what I want. Is that all you want?"

"I like my job. I'm outdoors. It's healthy. I meet many people, wash many feet. And I make contacts." She pulled a card from inside her blouse. It was damp and faded, the business card of a movie producer.

Agrippina's attitude inspired me. Her job seemed menial and repulsive, yet it was full of meaning and purpose for her. She had found a task that met her needs, made her useful to others and connected her with life. I saw that what I needed more than anything else was a job, and I resolved to get one, regardless of how small, temporary, or part-time, just to play a useful part in the world.

Rome accommodated me. I found a job waiting on tables in a small restaurant I frequented, La Botte de Frascati, owned by a genial man named Alberto. Alberto did the seating and the talking and his wife did the cooking. The usual entrée took about an hour to serve. Many customers left unfed before their meals arrived. Apparently, even unhurried Romans did not have time to eat at La Botte de Frascati. After a week, Alberto fired me. He claimed that two spoons were stolen because I was chatting with customers.

After losing the waiting job, I returned to the English school, but the promised Russian cohort had not yet arrived, so there were no openings. I inquired at other schools, but it was the start of summer and all positions were taken. I sought private tutoring assignments, but Americans were not presumed to know the language well enough to tutor it. If only I could make the right connection.

For weeks I wandered Rome and Italy, changing hotels and moving bags between the train station and the airport, preparing for a departure I was unready to make. I circulated from *caffè* to *trattoria* to *tavola calda* to *pizza rustica*, consuming as much food and life as I could squander, while my funds dwindled. Yet despite all of the travel, hotels, events, sights and people, I was always agitated.

The novelty of visiting Rome was getting lost in the struggle to live there. I was in a tourist rut, making fast contacts on the surface, but without a job and a permanent place to live, I had nothing to build a life on. I was supposed to learn from my travels, but I avoided what was most important to me. The boulder on my arm mocked me when I stared at it. Staying in Italy felt like procrastination and I hated myself for it—yet if I faced the important questions my adventure would be finished.

That's when I met Henri. I had found the best thin-crusted pizza yet at a *trattoria* near the Maggiore. When I returned that evening for an encore pie, Henri was at the next table, a slight, neatly dressed man with a groomed, gray beard.

"*Ça va, mon ami?*" he asked.

"I can't say. I may be dying—but I'm not sure. The only belief I had I may have lost. The only woman I loved I seldom think about. I want to stay in Rome, but I think I'll be forced to leave. Does that sound all right to you?"

He nodded sympathetically.

"La vie est dure. Passe moi le beurre," he said, pausing to judge my reaction, which was perplexed enough to make him laugh. "It's my favorite proverb. It's famous, I think, but I'm not sure where I heard or read it. It would not surprise me if I made it up."

"Thank you for that," I replied sarcastically. *"Life is hard, pass the butter."* This man's adage had all of the facile profundity of an herbal tea bag. Then I realized I had heard that phrase before.

"Monsieur, have you heard of Jean-Claude Colombi?" I asked.

"J.C. Colombi? Of course I have heard of him. He is one of my favorite poets. And you are right. I must have stolen that line from him. I believe it is from his poem, *My Principal Meal Is Life.* It's extraordinary. Do you know it?"

"No, but it sounds like something Jean-Claude would write," I replied. "At any rate, I'll ask you what I often asked Colombi: what does it mean?"

"My friend, you think too much and miss the simple meaning of things. It means what it says. We live and we die and we question where we came from and where we are going. We suffer pain and anxiety and so many problems and annoyances that we cannot even imagine their number or complexity. Yet despite all of the debris flying around in my brain, I have a piece of bread in one hand and a butter knife in the other and I must bring them together. Does it make sense now?"

"Yes, in a ridiculously simple way."

"Yes, well, you seem intelligent and will learn even before you reach my age that life is ridiculously simple. By the way, I am Henri Mouffetard. And you, *jeune homme,* what shall I call you?"

Henri was a dental technician. It was an exhausting occupation by his account, but a vital one for the many toothless people in the world. Yet if his everyday life was routine, his vacations were exciting and vigorous. He would have gone to Sardinia, he said, to dive for coral, but he had already done that once this year. A souvenir of that holiday dangled from a gold chain around his neck—an impressive spiral of the finest salmon-hued coral.

"My job," he said, "is highly stressful. There are many details. And I admit that at times it is so tedious that I want to drill a hole in my cranium. But I also derive great satisfaction from my work. I am a craftsman. At times I feel the exhilaration of the artist. I am like Stradivarius and my teeth are sublime instruments of mastication. Of course, I realize that the dentures I make are not violins. A Stradivarius will be played for centuries; no one will be using my teeth for so long. *Mais alors,* listen to me go on and on. *Che cozzo dico*! What crap I am speaking!"

After the meal we ambled around the city before calling it a night. Henri described his affinity for Rome.

"I come here whenever I can. My family, you see, was Italian. But then my ancestors had political problems. You know, the usual. Specifically, one was beheaded, another was disemboweled and another was boiled in oil. So, the others decided to immigrate to Switzerland."

We stopped in a bar and he bought us two whiskeys.

"My salary never goes far enough, but I'm satisfied. Life is good," Henri said as he raised the glass of whiskey and poured its contents down his throat in one gulp.

"So, Rick, I don't know you, but you seem to find yourself in a complicated and confusing position. You have lost your love, your faith and your job, and all you have left is an impressive bump on your arm. Do you see the beauty in this? No? That bump contains all of your questions—and answers. It is like a crystal ball. Perhaps you should rub it and a message will appear. Or you can take the more conventional approach and have a doctor look at it."

Henri glanced at his watch.

"And now, Rick, I must return to my hotel and get a good night's sleep because tomorrow I have extremely important business to transact. *Bonne nuit, à bientot.*"

The next morning I went down to breakfast at my usual *caffè* around the block. Henri was seated at a table reading a paper. The news headline was familiar—"French Newlyweds Assailed by Young Gang at the Colosseum"—but Henri had his own headline.

"After our drink, I went to Via Nazionale and found the fattest prostitute I could find," he related. "She was big and soft, with really limitless quantities of flesh in a thin, silk dress." His eyes wandered off as he ruminated the last explicit detail of the encounter. "Her underarms were deliciously damp."

Slight and abstemious in appearance, Henri looked like the last man to seek out a fat, damp prostitute.

"Of course, it was most enjoyable," he admitted as he savored the memory. Perceiving my bafflement, he patted my arm. "When I want a woman, I look for a fat one. Then I know I am getting the most for my money."

He laughed.

"Ah, you must think I am a shallow individual, and in some ways you would be right. Like the ocean, I have my shallow banks, sandbars, if you will. But if I have given you the impression that I came to Rome only to seek out voluptuous prostitutes, eat delicious pizza and drink Chianti, you are only partly correct. In fact, I have come here on business. Well, not precisely business. A man can only be deadly serious 90% of the time or he will certainly have a breakdown. In the other 10% he must have a hobby. And so I have mine. A good hobby gives a man diversion and depth. Mine has brought me to Rome."

Henri explained.

"I have told you that I am a dental technician, but I never explained how I came to this occupation. I am not from a long line of prosthodontists. My father, in fact, was a produce wholesaler. But one day when I was a small boy, my parents took me to a museum and this outing determined my destiny. It was an exhibition on the history of dentistry. There I saw the most beautiful object I had ever seen, a set of dentures made of gold and ivory. There were other works of beauty, as well: dentures made of silver plates and teeth of porcelain, animal horn, horse and donkey teeth and rubber gums. But most of all, I was mesmerized by the Waterloo teeth embedded in animal bone. These were not merely false teeth, but works of art and history. They created a picture of heroism and romance in my young mind. Have you heard of Waterloo teeth? No? They were made of teeth plucked from the mouths of dead soldiers on Napoleonic battlefields, then embedded in hippopotamus jaws. As a child, I was terrified of death. But when I saw that these brave men had not died in vain, that they gave their lives for the Emperor but gave their teeth to eternity, from that moment, I no longer feared death.

"That afternoon, on the tram ride home, I pledged my life to dental technology and to all things prosthodontic. You see, I did not become a dental technician to make a living, or because I took an aptitude test that pointed to prosthodontics as the only occupation suitable for my talents and temperament. No, it was my calling, and it consumed all of my time and effort. I became a student of dentures, a denture historian, and finally, one of the foremost denture collectors in the world.

"Now I am on the threshold of one of the greatest attainments of my life. Tomorrow I will meet a man who may sell to me an

516

Etruscan denture of gold thread and human and animal teeth, dating from 500 BC. Mind you, I have Phoenician teeth from the ruins of Carthage and a jeweled set of choppers from the Mayan ruins of Chiapas, but this will complete my collection."

Henri paused to spoon the espresso and sugar syrup from the bottom of his cup into his mouth. I did not know how to react to his unexpected epic. In five minutes I had learned more about the history of dentures than I ever imagined to exist, yet I did not know how to value this information or what to think of my new friend, Henri. Was he a monomaniacal genius or simply maniacal. In either case, I was too worldly and too lonely to judge him.

"But that is tomorrow," Henri resumed. "Today I will meet an old friend, a married woman living in the suburbs. And what will you be doing?"

"Looking for work," I said.

We wished each other well and set off on our respective paths.

In the late afternoon I stood at the Trevi Fountain, tossing coins like a moron because legend said it would guarantee that I was coming back. I felt a tap on the shoulder and turned. There was Henri's smirking face.

"So, my friend, we meet again. How did it go?"

I frowned.

"I'm being shut out by the new Europe; they think the only thing Americans can do is spend money. And I'm underqualified for that."

He laughed. "Don't be depressed. I'm afraid my day didn't turn out well, either. My married lady friend was *pas gentille* to say the least, on the verge of a nervous breakdown to be precise. Of course, she has her reasons. Her husband is unemployed, her child is sick. She never wins the lottery. Ahhh, *'la vie est compliquée.'*"

"So what can be done?" I snapped, angry not at him, but at the truth.

"We can get a drink."

"A drink doesn't solve anything."

"It relieves thirst," he laughed. "My young friend, life requires patience, as well as the capacity to find comfort in conspicuous consumption and foolish pleasures. For instance, look at my pants. I was unhappy, so I bought them today."

He stepped back for a second with his arms wide apart to demonstrate his new pants. They were bright, turquoise chinos with a sharp crease and a silky, synthetic sheen that glowed in the waning daylight.

"They'd be perfect for nighttime golf," I said. "I can't believe you came to Rome to buy them."

Henri chuckled and smiled beatifically. "I have a talent for going a long way for strange things."

He insisted on a *trattoria* with wood-paneled walls and a moose head over a fake hearth, where greasy smoke wafted from the kitchen. After four courses and a bottle of wine, Henri raised his glass to proclaim another gourmandizing proverb. "Eat well and send the rest to hell."

"But I'm stuffed and drunk and I'm still not happy. I don't believe your aphorism," I scoffed.

"You are still young. But you will learn to accept life's limitations as surely the inevitability of death," Henri replied calmly. He raised his glass again, as if it were an isometric exercise, and held it in midair for several seconds, because he had forgotten his proverb. "*Zut alors!* Drink, laugh and forget!"

Over espressos, Henri became solemn.

"I believe I told you how serious I am about my hobbies," Henri paused. "So, Rick, what are your plans tomorrow?"

"I may have a job as a footwasher's assistant—you know, learn the business from the ground up. I also have a lead on a job teaching English to hotel bathroom attendants. And if neither of those work out, I heard that certain travel agencies use English speaking guides."

Henri stroked his goatee.

"All intriguing career paths. But what would you say if I offered you a temporary assignment? I am prepared to pay you 20,000 lire for the day if you join me on this business meeting."

"I'll do it," I said.

"Very good, *allons-y*. Or as we say in Rome, '*Andiamo!*'"

The next morning we met at the *caffè* around the corner. Henri wore a suit and tie. In my tee shirt, I felt underdressed.

"*Ne t'en fais pas, mon ami!*" he said. "Don't be concerned. You are there as my muscle!"

"Have you looked at me?" I asked. "In the Peace Corps they called me '*Haricot vert*,' or 'Stringbean.'"

"That's fine. Nothing frightens well-fed people as much as someone who is hungry. They think you will eat them. And please by all means gnash your teeth. The people I am meeting are almost as infatuated with dentures as I am. They become rattled when they hear real teeth crunching. You will be a great help."

We drove to EUR, the pristine business center Mussolini built for the 1942 World's Fair, which was preempted by the carnage of World War II. EUR embodied the solemn geometry of a de Chirico painting and gave the surreal impression of being too big to tear down and too cold to occupy. We passed the Colosseo Quadrata, a massive honeycomb with arches on every side, and the semicircular, columned arcade of the Palazzo dell'INA, before crossing a footbridge and descending a stairway to a lake. There we waited for Henri's contact and the coveted Etruscan teeth.

For ten minutes Henri paced and repeatedly checked his

watch. "*Merde!* Giovanni is one Italian who is never late. Now he is like the others."

A moment later, a squat man in a dark suit, holding a gym bag, crossed the footbridge and approached us with a steady gait.

"*Ciao*, Henri," he said.

"*Ciao*, Giovanni."

Giovanni glanced at me suspiciously. "Who is this? The tooth fairy?"

That riled me. I gnashed my teeth on cue, but Giovanni did not appear intimidated.

"He is a friend who shares my interest in teeth," Henri replied.

I grinned to show my full set.

"So you have what I came for?" Henri demanded.

"Yes. Do you have the cash? Giovanni countered.

Henri extracted an envelope from his jacket pocket. Giovanni flipped through the fat packet and slipped it into his jacket. He handed the gym bag to Henri, who extracted a wooden box, which he unclasped. Ensconced in the crimson velvet lining of the box was a ring of gold, resembling a bracelet. Several animal teeth were wedged on one side.

"*Quel putain de dentier!*" Henri intoned as he tapped a yellowed tooth. "How exquisite! *Voyez.* Real hippo!"

"The Etruscans knew how to live," Giovanni remarked. "They did not let having no teeth stop them from eating."

Henri slipped on a white glove and delicately removed the gold and toothsome artifact from the box with a pair of tweezers. He held the 2,600-year-old denture to the light to admire his new treasure and assess its authenticity.

"*E allora!* So now you own it," Giovanni said. "*Grazie a Regolini Galassi.*"

"Say no more. I must not know the details," Henri snapped.

"*Ovviamente* no!" Giovanni replied. "So you have what you want. Your collection is complete. Was it worth all the years and money you spent? Eh, what do I care as long as I'm paid!"

"This denture was made in 650 BC. When I look at it, I travel not kilometers, but millennia. *Capiche?*" Henri said. "I can see my ancestors masticate. What price can I put on that?"

"Your ancestors cannot masticate," Giovanni jeered. "Their teeth were taken from their tombs."

"*Basta!*" Henri cupped his ears. "*Avanti!*"

He carefully replaced the denture in the box, the box in the bag and slung the bag over his shoulder.

"*Ciao!*" Giovanni called after us.

We headed up the winding stairway and crossed the bridge. Two men approached us from the other end. These men did not seem to be on a stroll to enjoy the scenery. They walked toward us with predatory stares.

"What are you doing here?" they asked.

"We are tourists," Henri replied. "Move aside."

"What do you have there? You stole our grandfather's teeth for a glass of wine? What kind of men are you?" the thugs taunted us.

As the toughs stood in our way, we could only walk toward them or run back toward the area by the lake, where we would be trapped.

"*Mon ami,*" Henri whispered. "Hit the tall one and I will handle the short one. Then we run."

From a cowering stance, Henri and I charged the two men and took them by surprise. I gave my target a sharp kick below the belt and swung hard at his face, causing him to fall back, while Henri made short work of his adversary. We ran to the car Henri had parked a few blocks away and sped away, as a bottle shattered against the hood. I was shaken but Henri was exhilarated. The acquisition of his priceless Etruscan teeth was a great personal coup, yet he also reveled in the complications that came with it.

Henri turned to me as we drove on the highway back to Rome.

"So, *mon vieux*. You have now had an experience. Buying and selling, stealing and fighting. Welcome to the world."

"Won't they come after you?"

"I don't worry about them. I must be careful about the government and insurance companies. When I am in Switzerland they will not look for me. We Swiss have a reputation for honesty."

Despite his bravado, Henri changed his hotel and wore a disguise. He had his hair shaved, and wore wrap-around sunglasses and a Hawaiian shirt. For the next few days he and I visited the beach at Ostia, the Villa Borghese and the Colosseum. At each place we stopped, we ate and drank while Henri held forth like my older brother about life's necessities.

"A man should always have a profession, something he can do to survive." He paused and frowned. "My work is serious and difficult. Dentures must fit. They must be beautiful and lifelike. There is always a customer to please and of course they're a pain in my ass. They mourn for their teeth so they blame the dentures and naturally, they blame me. Then there's the boss—*Ach!* It's sad. It's ridiculous. It's life. But I have my pastimes and I love being alive."

"Do you love anyone?"

Henri pondered my question and the half-eaten *saltimbocca* on his plate, which the question precluded him from slicing.

"No, love is missing in my life but frankly I don't feel deprived of it. It is a sad admission of a sad fact, my young friend, that as a consequence of a long, selfish life spent pursuing my own pleasures, I don't feel the need for love."

We were both quiet after Henri's confession and he resumed

slicing his meat.

"At any rate, whether you love or not, you must find something you like to do that you do well to sustain you when you are between loves, religions, or whatever it is you are between." Henri paused to consider something. "You know, it is astounding how much of our lives is spent *between.* Maybe we have everything reversed: the beginnings and the ends are not as important as what lies between them."

If what Henri said was right, and being in limbo was the norm, then I was okay.

"I always wanted to be a writer," I said. "Now I don't know."

"You have not written anything recently?"

"One miserable love poem to a diva I met at the hotel. And many letters."

"*Malheureusement,* you cannot do much with letters. After all, they are in other peoples' hands. Yet the fact that you wrote so many suggests that you have talent, dedication—and practice. More than that, you have a gift, the universal experience of being young and lost. *En effect*, your future is bright, but you must write. Do it now when you are young. Make it a habit. Do not delay."

"So, there's hope for me?"

He laughed and patted me on the back.

"I see it on your face; the happiness my suggestion brings to you is the surest sign."

Henri left Rome that night. I accompanied him to the station and saw his train pull out. In the manner of a true friend, he had given me courage, though I barely knew him. I could leave Rome now and face my destiny: death and love did not matter now, so long as I knew what I wanted to do in life.

As days passed, Henri's positive influence waned. My doubts and conflicts returned and intensified. Rome was part of the problem. My life was in flux: friends appeared and vanished as in a magic act. This was the Roman lifestyle, improvisational and spontaneous, alternating waves of bonding and separation, all in a day.

When I ran low on money and had to leave the Albergo Paradiso, Clay, the Director of the English school, let me crash at his apartment in Montesacro, a hilly outlying neighborhood, where he lived with a burly, young laborer. They spent hours watching boisterous Italian TV game shows in a disheveled bed. The apartment was a mess and smelled like a locker room, which induced me to stay away until I needed to crash.

I knew my time was running out unless my luck changed. For the past few weeks I had become friendly with three women I served at Alberto's restaurant weeks before—Letitsia, Graziella and Nadia. I called them "The 3 Fates." While they waited for Alberto's wife to prepare their orders, we had long conversations, which led to my firing and our friendship.

Letitsia, a half-Ethiopian stewardess, was pregnant by her married boyfriend, a pilot for Alitalia. Graziella was a junior travel agent, young and bitter, whose fiancé of nine years left her after she supported him through medical school. One afternoon when business was slow, Graziella said she was fed up. We left her office and drove to the beach in Ostia. Whenever a plane soared overhead, Letitsia thought of her pilot boyfriend, waved and cried out the make of the airplane, "Boeing 747! McDo-o-o-nell Douglass *Bellissimo!*"—before breaking down in sobs.

Nadia, an elegant Egyptian-born woman with the large, dark eyes of a soothsayer, was Graziella's boss at the travel agency. After a day of wandering around Rome, seeking any opportunity to hold me there, I stopped by their office before closing time. Graziella and Letitsia were usually around. Nadia ordered ice coffees and entertained us with word play and funny impressions.

While Graziella often treated me coldly, her fiancé's treachery having made her mistrust men, Nadia was gracious and attentive. Charming and worldly, she possessed such a fine understanding of life that the wisdom of millennia seemed to flow through her mind. Having such deep insight into human behavior might have made most people cynical and stale, but Nadia's old soul and vast experience rendered all things familiar and amusing to her. No doubt, what drew me most to Nadia was her grasp of reality. She was confident and stable, which I was not, and had mastered the riddles of money and survival, which still beleaguered and bewildered me. I had no idea if her security was real or for show, but I sensed that she had answers to questions I had not thought of asking. Despite my desperate penury, or because of it, I asked her to go out with me.

Nadia picked me up one muggy Saturday afternoon and said we couldn't stay out for long, or return to her flat, since her sister was sick. Instead, we drove around Rome for two crazy hours, weaving in and out of traffic on curbless streets, nearly hitting pedestrians and walls. Nadia laughed while I tried to talk seriously. I pleaded with her to stop the car.

"Why can't we just go somewhere for a coffee?"

"I'm late. I have to take care of my sister."

She wanted to spend time with me but could not justify it, so she drove us in circles.

"What do you really want?" she asked.

"To stay in Rome. To see the world."

"So do it."

"But I have no money and no job. And I have to know what this is on my arm—and if I am going to live or die."

The brakes screeched. The car stopped. She smiled at me

frankly.

"That's your answer. You know what to do. And now I'm late for my sister. Go home, Rick."

She left me out in the middle of a high-rise suburban housing project where sheets were draped like white flags from terrace railings. I stood transfixed by the cluster of skyscraper monstrosities that seemed ready to collapse on me. The light brick buildings resembled the one my mother lived in. The life I had tried to escape was reclaiming me.

Nadia had not been playing a practical joke on me. With her encyclopedic insight, she had prepared me for home.

I walked back to Rome, found the airline ticket office and made a reservation I meant to keep. Afterwards, I drifted through the city and found myself alone in the Colosseum. I swaggered into the arena like a gladiator and waved at the ghostly multitudes hanging in the arches of the massive walls.

I showed thumbs up, thumbs down and then gave them the finger before lunging, swinging my broadsword and tossing an invisible net over a prostrate foe. Applause and jeers from the spectral arches filled my ears. I bowed to the apparitions, but rather than spur me on to more ludicrous invention, they made me see that my pantomime was a childish caper in a magnificent site. I was in a ruin, but the ruin was in better shape.

What kind of gladiator was I? A tired one. I sat on the dusty Colosseum floor with my arms around my knees. I had squandered a year of my life and left incomplete the story I began. I came all this way to be with a woman to whom I no longer wrote and had nothing to build my life on because I had apparently been living a lie. Worst of all, none of it made sense.

I was snared in my own net, food for whatever voracious

beasts the ghosts of carnal Romans cared to spring on me.

"Run me through, vicious adversary. Eat me, hungry lions. Bite my tumor!" I shouted.

"What a come-on."

Her voice and shadow fell on me. Lauren Ardsley stood behind him in a *pareo* of black linen, tied at her shoulders like a Roman toga.

"If you lie there long enough, you'll be devoured by wild animals, but not the beautiful feline kind. Rats will eat you."

She nodded gravely and I snapped to a seated position, as if going through *rigor mortis* and coming to life at the same time.

"Rick Murkey, what *are* you doing here?" Lauren laughed. "It's my afternoon off. I'm scouting locations for a story when I find a man lying in the Colosseum. I'm about to call for help when I hear him deliver speeches in English. I thought it could be only one person—and there you are."

"And there *you* are. What are you doing here?"

"I'm on assignment covering Italian winter fashions. Shouldn't you be in Tunisia?"

"Not anymore. Now I'm supposed to be in Rome. And tomorrow I'm supposed to go home."

"So why are you praying for a gruesome death?"

"Despair. What else?"

"I'm disappointed in you."

"We're off to a good start. I'm disappointed in myself."

"Do you have the necklace?"

I reached under my shirt and pulled out the silver tealeaf medallion she had given me.

Lauren rolled her eyes and every muscle in her face broke into a warm, brilliant smile. "I'm starving. Let's eat," she said. I dusted myself off and we walked back to the center of Rome.

She had been all over the planet, reporting on events and doing celebrity features. She even interviewed a prime minister. Just when I thought I could feel no worse about the year I had, Lauren brought me to new depths.

Still, I was glad to see her and insisted on introducing her to my prize discovery, the best *pizza rustica* in Rome. I knew Lauren would never even look for such a place on her own, but she humored me with her enthusiasm. The pizza was baked in a brick oven in a small room at the end of a dark catacomb behind a massive door on a winding alley near the Pantheon. The oven coals emitted a blue and orange glow.

We ate pizza squares piled with mushrooms and onions in the twilight of the Pantheon rotunda, where gods and heroes were honored and the perpetual dusk made you feel you were in the Elysian Fields with such immortal shades as Achilles, Helen of Troy and other pagan greats.

"Why are you in despair?" she asked.

"My adventure's over," I said.

"You'll have others."

"No, this was it. I screwed it up and now I'm doomed to a typical life."

She smiled and wiped the corners of her mouth with a tissue.

"Well?" I asked impatiently, hoping she would disagree with me.

"You'll never have a typical life," she said. "Because you're not typical. Everyone has experiences. It's what we make of them that makes our lives interesting."

Lauren chewed thoughtfully. In her long, elegant hands, the sloppy *pizza rustica* looked like a *brioche* deluxe. I admired her for elevating all that she did, but I also wanted to laugh. She brought her lips slowly toward the square, as if she were kissing it good night and snared a morsel with her front teeth to protect her perfect lip-gloss. Lauren encountered ordinary things without truly experiencing them.

"You've come a long way," she said, "even if you don't know where you are."

"I know where I am. I'm nowhere."

"You're seeing it the wrong way. Things didn't turn out how you planned, but that could be the best thing that ever happened to you."

In college I would have argued with this statement. In fact, such arguments led to our break up. But Lauren arrived with impeccable timing, if not to extend my adventure, then to share my final night. Tired and depressed, I nodded, chewed and stared across the dusky rotunda, accepting that she solved problems like she ate pizza—with no mess.

"Even if your year was a disaster and a waste of time, you survived," she concluded. "You're free. You can do something else." Lauren's nonchalant optimism was meant to cheer me up. Instead, she made anxious. She challenged my sense of reality, which was all I still believed in. She could make me see failure as success and make poverty seem rich. I needed to present her with a problem for which she could find no easy solution.

"I wanted to return as a hero," I said. "But I'm more of a casualty."

"We're all heroes," she replied. "It's Democracy 101."

"I missed that class," I said.

"You were there. You didn't take notes."

She brought me to a club where a Cyclops eye in a peephole inspected us before Lauren whispered a password and the door opened. She was a celebrity there, so I shared her with her many friends. The dancing was more aerobic than intimate, for clusters, not couples. When Lauren and I hit the floor, others joined in to form a happy swarm.

It was my last night in Rome, but as hard as I tried to live in the moment, I spent most of my time peering beyond the strobes into the darkness, as if I were already gone. This was different from a loner's detachment, which is often just a frustrated desire to belong—I was truly shutting down, one switch at a time. I stared *through* the scene of slinky dresses, sleek legs and writhing torsos with neither excitement nor regret, transforming it into a composition of colorful dust. My present was already on loan from the future.

Early the next morning I left Rome. As the bus slalomed down the quiet, empty roads from Montesacro to the Stazione Termini, I was overwhelmed by the sadness of losing something forever.

Reflecting on two months in Rome, and the previous ten months in Tunisia, I traced a continuous, yet not inevitable, descent to this finale. At any point, my past year might have taken a different turn, but which person, place or event would have made the difference? —I couldn't say. When one came to mind, another followed and I dismissed them both.

"So much potential gone to waste."

The dirge-like words of Cerise vibrated in my ears. Another wave of dejection washed over me. My life overseas had potential, but now that it was ending, what could have happened, never would.

Rome looked lovely, serene and impervious to my departure. Despite the transient uncertainty and loneliness I had experienced here, I knew I would miss it. I had spent two months in Rome by mistake, yet would probably never return by plan.

The bus was empty and so was the wet, black pavement of the

Via Nomentano. The driver whistled a tune while the conductor, a distinguished man with a gray, up-curling mustache, and an impeccably pressed suit, stood in his booth near the back, perusing his paper in a learned manner like a misplaced professor.

Since I was alone with the conductor in the back of the bus, I imagined his biography. I speculated that he was once a promising literature student at the University of Rome who dreamed of writing screenplays and becoming his generation's Fellini. He graduated with honors, but was too poor to live, much less to hang out with film people. After living at home with his parents for two years, he succumbed to pressure, passed the bus conductor exam, moved into his own apartment and dated a woman who admired his dreams and talent and put up with his working class failure. They married and raised a family in the low-incoming housing project where Nadia dropped me off yesterday.

"*Pecato,*" I punctuated the bitter bio. "So much potential gone to waste."

Was Cerise right? Would I have the same fate as the underachieving conductor, passing my days in a random job drawn out of the hat of circumstance?

As the bus traversed the residential neighborhoods and entered the commercial district, the imminence of permanent departure forced itself into my consciousness, tearing me from the moment. If I had one more day, everything might become clear, but probably not. Drifting among hotels, scenery and situations would only lead to more confusion.

Maybe it was not so bad to be a distinguished bus conductor. Although he was irrelevant to millions of commuters who encountered but barely noticed him, he read his paper with dignity and discernment, and perhaps wrote witty couplets on ticket stubs. It was doubtful that anyone asked him an intelligent question. To the contrary, the public probably treated him like an imbecile, even while he conjured complex thoughts in the studio of his mind. Yet if his life lacked stimulation and status, at least it was grounded.

"People get what they want," Tasha once said in Ayn Draham. I still didn't agree with her.

I stood in front of the Stazione Termini for one last look at this gritty sliver of Rome with its glistening, washed pavement—the Eternal City's gesture to make each day a new beginning. This last impression was nondescript, yet its unexpected beauty triggered a dismal reflection. My adventure ended here; the experience of exotic places would be no more.

On the train to Fiumicino, I stared at the margin of weeds by the tracks and considered my future as an antidote to regret. I squeezed the bump on my arm. Its diagnosis was something to anticipate and gave meaning to my departure.

Of one thing I was sure. If I lived, I would write. I recalled Henri's advice. *"If you finally write a novel, my friend, choose realistic characters with everyday struggles in normal circumstances. Excess conceals the truth."*

My goal was to be truthful. Yet, how could I be realistic? My first year of adulthood was a fiasco of squandered opportunities, aborted escapades, lost love and botched sex that wrecked my confidence.

I might have to invent an extraordinary tale, full of heroism, exotic locales, passionate romance and every missed possibility and bungled opportunity imagined to the fullest degree.

Realism or fantasy? I had some hard choices to make. The train stopped at the airport. *"Shweah b'shweah,"* I muttered as I hoisted my bags and typewriter and stumbled toward the terminal

APPENDIX

GLOSSARY OF TERMS

Allah y berek	"God bless you!"
Aslema	"Hello."
Barakala o fik	"God bless you!" "Thank you!"
Bara na'ik	"Go f**k yourself!"
Behi yessir	Very good, very nice.
Bernous	Man's woolen winter cape
B'kadesh	"How much is it?" "What does it cost?"
Cawa Cahaley	Coffee with milk
Chechia	Fez cap
Djin	Spirit, demon
Fellah, fellaheen	Worker(s), peasant(s)
Filfil	Hot pepper, source of harissa
Fitna	Struggle, challenge, male sexual hysteria
Hamdulleh	"Thank God!"
Hanoot	Store
Hobzeh	Bread
Hoot	Fish
Hooyah	Brother, buddy
Insh'Allah	"God willing " or "It's in God's hands."
K'bir	Large
Kefia	Turban fashioned from a scarf
Kif-kif	Same, equal
Labess	"How are you?" "Are you okay?"
Leh	No
Meklah	Food, meal
Menarafsh	"I don't know."
M'nin	Where
Natte	Woven straw mat
Noshrub	I drink
Otini flous	"Give me money!"
Rod Berek	Be careful!
Safsari	Woman's cloak or shroud
S'balkhir	"Good morning."
Shnoa	"What is it?"
Shnoa ha welik	"How are you?"
Shokran	"Thank you."
Shoof	"Look!"
Shweah	A little
Shweah b'shweah	Little by little
Sidi	Sir
Souk	Market
T'bib	Doctor
T'fathl	"Here!"
Tisbalakhir	"Good night."
Wullah	"I swear!" Or "By God!"
Zoobi	Male sex organ

Made in the USA
Middletown, DE
28 September 2015